INTO THE FIRE

INTO THE FIRE

CONJURAGIC SERIES, BOOK THREE

LEANN M. RETTELL

ISBN-13: 978-1729627709

ISBN-10:1729627706

Copyright © 2018 by Leann Rettell

Cover Design by James Christopher Hill

All rights reserved.

No part of this book may be reproduced in any form or by any electronic or mechanical means, including information storage and retrieval systems, without written permission from the author, except for the use of brief quotations in a book review.

1
STREGA

"Master, you called for me?"

"Ahh. Strega, you're better?" Master bent over his desk scribbling at various papers, not bothering to look at her.

"Yes, I'm improving." Strega rubbed her back where the rocks crashed upon her as she ran from the collapsing buildings. *Damn that girl.*

"Have you been able to transform again?" Master raised one eyebrow, appearing nonchalant, but Strega knew better than to underestimate him.

"Yes, Master." She wouldn't disappoint him again. The last punishment had been brutal. Not that she deserved any less for allowing the girl to escape.

He swiveled around in the chair, gliding to his feet with a natural grace she'd never be able to replicate. "Show me."

Her nose wrinkled for a fraction of a second. This was really going to hurt. Her human form quivered, preparing for the transformation. Her scream morphed into a wailing screech interlaced with cracking of bones and rearranging sinew. Moments later, a tiny black tailless cat perched on its haunches staring up at the blond man.

He flashed an award-winning smile that didn't reach his eyes. "Excellent." He gestured, and the cat expanded as if inflated, bones snapping, fingers pushing past the claws. Nausea passed through her from the pain. Hate aided the pain. If she ever saw that girl again, she'd end her.

"Come." He didn't wait to see if she followed. There was no question of that. With his hands together as if in prayer, he strolled the length of the Pyre on bare feet. He flung his dark blue robes outward to keep them from acquiring ash as he perched upon his make-shift throne. Beads of sweat poured down her back. She disliked being so deep within the volcano. She disliked being here. Her earliest memories were of this place. The endless, insufferable heat, dim light, and pain. Her mind, body, and spirit had been broken and remodeled in this hell hole. She clasped her hand behind her back, waiting, careful not to displease him.

"Now, my pet, tell me what happened."

"Master, the girl isn't a Nip. She's like nothing I've ever seen. She drew power from all cores, merged them into one, and that's what destroyed the Unity Statue."

Master's lips pulled into a thin line. His interlaced fingers paled under the angry grip. Anger pulsated off him in waves. "You mean no one helped her? She destroyed the Unity Statue all by herself?"

Strega gulped as the sweat morphed into cold chills of fear. She wouldn't be the first of his experiments to be lost in one of his rages. "Yes, Master." Bending at the waist, she stared at his dirty toes, holding her breath, not knowing if she'd be dead in a few seconds.

Master breathed in and out, slow, monotonous, as he wrestled with an idea in his mind.

"There's something else, Master." Strega braced herself for what she must tell him. He would be even angrier because she'd let them escape, but if he found out from another, her punishment would be much worse.

"What is it, Strega?" His tone hinted at boredom, but this ruse didn't fool her. He paid attention to every word, every gesture or eye movement. Her Master missed nothing.

"She wasn't just with the human, her Defender, and the traitor Protector."

"Oh."

"She was also with one of the Geminates who escaped you long ago," she said, her words whispered.

His anger erupted without warning or mercy. His water whip slammed upon her scarred back in wave after wave of stinging agony. A single scream echoed off the walls. She bit down on her tongue hard, bringing blood, and balled her hands into tight fists, knuckles white. He wouldn't tolerate her screams. Her years with him had taught her that much. She reigned in any sound, refusing to let the wail leave her lips. The Nip magic inside her struggled to break free, to take his magic, pull it within herself, to claim it as her own, but that would mean death. His mercy alone allowed her to live. Blow after blow landed, striking her back, legs, and buttocks. *One more*, she told herself, and waited her punishment to end. *Just one more. One more.*

The water whip fell to the ground in a puddle, mingling with the constant, warm, thick droplets of blood from her newest wounds. Angry fingers dug into the soft flesh under her arm, yanking her upright, dragging her back to his office. Master jabbed a finger at the pictures of the Geminates who'd escaped him so long ago. "Which one?"

Her finger hovered over the picture of the younger version of the blond woman she saw with Ora Stone the day the world changed.

Master released her. He spun away from her, leaned over his desk, long white fingers tapping on the blacked wood. He laughed. "Of course."

Strega stumbled backward, pulling on all her strength to remain standing.

Master faced her, blue eyes reflecting neither warmth nor depth. "Gather all your brothers and sisters. I'll not stop until she's mine."

"The Geminate, Master?"

"No. The girl."

"Yes, Master." Strega bowed, the pain in her back caught in the back of her throat, but she held it back, tasting blood.

When she straightened, Master pointed a finger in her face. She hadn't even heard him approach. "She'll come to me unharmed. If you touch her, I will kill you. Slowly. Understood?"

Her chin lowered to the floor. "Yes, Master."

"Strega, my pet, you will get your revenge. It'll be so much sweeter than her blood on your hands."

What could he possibly mean?

"How's the boy?" Master tilted his head to the side.

She hid her confusion about the change in conversation. "Healing. But his questioning is growing more intense."

"Excellent. Excellent. I believe it's time for you to go on a little rescue mission and make a new…friend."

A shadow entered the office, interrupting them. Master smiled. "Corporal Bizard, how good to see you. This is Strega, one of my most trusted partners."

The young Tempest dipped his head but said nothing. His glare told her all she needed to know about Master's new ally. He might be here, but his hatred of Nips oozed from his very pores. He would abide her presence, but only because the Master allowed it. He hated her on sight. "I'm not a corporal anymore. Remember?" He didn't bother hiding the bitter tone from the statement. The stench of resentment wafted off him, something she'd never have been able to pick up if she hadn't spent years in animal form.

She flicked a glance to see what Master would do about the Tempest's disrespectful attitude. The corners of his mouth turned upward a fraction, but none of it reached his eyes. He'd get his revenge for the insult, but not now. Master was calculating in all things.

"An injustice was done to you, young Jabez. An injustice I will help you right, which is why you are here." Master put one arm around Jabez and the other around her, caressing the new lacerations in her skin. "Now, let me tell you both what we're going to do."

2

ORA

The faces of the Naiad High Council stared downward from the middle of the Eye in the Haven. The banging and crackling of broken wood and glass halted the moment the Council appeared above with the latest announcement from Conjuragic. Those in charge of cleanup stood frozen with all eyes turned skyward. Like me, the Gayden worried our small victory overtaking the Haven would be short lived, but Sabrina assured me we couldn't be seen. The Naiad prisoners had been secured back on the island. We should be entering the next phase of our plan, but my mind went blank as horror flowed through my blood.

Damien's words bounced around my brain like a wayward pin ball, taking several long moments to penetrate my awareness. He knew the identity of Master, the man behind the creation of Geminates, like my mother, witches with two cores of magic, and the kidnapper of Gayden. Because of this man, I'd been born and was the reason for the war.

Out of nowhere, he'd solved the mystery we'd been trying to figure out for so long. I asked, "What? How?"

At the same time, Mom paled, eyes roaming the faces of the Council and their advisors.

"Which one is he?" Sabrina asked.

Benjamin's chin tilted upward at the screen. I followed his gaze. Of all the luck! Master couldn't be a member of the High Council. It wasn't fair.

It would make everything harder. If so, were they all in on it? Damien pointed above. "That one is Master."

"Which one?" Sabrina had tucked her long blond braid into her blue Protector's leathers so it couldn't be used against her in battle. Her beautiful face contorted in concentration. She shifted into a defensive position, ready for anything. The leather hugged her body, revealing curves in all the right places. Her beauty added to her deadliness. Despite all that, she was one of the kindest and most thoughtful people I'd ever met.

"The blond man," Damien said as his gray eyes unfocused. Alarm raced through me at his expression. He'd been brainwashed since childhood. No one needed him to turn sides.

"They're Naiad. They're all blond. That doesn't help." I grabbed his thickly muscled and scarred arm to break his trance.

Damien shook his head, as if clearing bad thoughts, and focused on me. Devil, his alternative personality while he was under Master's influence, flashed in his eyes then disappeared. I didn't like that. Not one bit. "He's standing to the left of the man sitting in the chair."

Talon and Cilla Souse, the High Councilmen of Naiad were the only two sitting. I hoped that meant they weren't involved.

Sabrina supplied the name. "That's Mathesar Enochs. Naiad's advisor and the favorite to be the next High Councilor for Naiad House. This isn't good."

Mom, already fair skinned, paled further with a touch of green. She swayed on her feet as if she might faint. The carotid artery pulsated fast on the side of her neck. The steady cadence echoed in my head like a drum. *Boom. Boom. Boom.* I grabbed her by the hand and led her away to a chair. She slumped in the chair, leaning forward to place head in her curled arms. I couldn't help it, I collapsed into the chair beside her. We'd just found out that John was alive and now the identity of Master. Both revelations within the space of a few minutes was more than I could handle.

John, my sweet, wonderful fiancé, who I thought had been killed by Strega, a shape shifting she-devil, during our escape from Conjuragic had not, in fact, died. He'd been under an enchantment that left him in a state like death. Guilt ate away at me. I'd left him behind. Left him to the magicians. Alone.

If that wasn't bad enough, I saw him kiss the bitch, but whether that'd been real or a nightmare, I couldn't say. I balled my hands into tight fists by my sides. If John been standing here right now, I'd slap him.

I raised my head and touched Mom's arm. "Mom."

She peeked above the rim of her arm but said nothing. Her losing it made me hold my tongue. Nothing had ever shaken my mother's resolve. It wasn't the time to disclose the information about John and Strega. Instead I asked, "Are you okay?"

What a stupid question. How could she be okay? How could she be after seeing the man who held her prisoner until she escaped while pregnant with me? Her magics prickled on her skin, something I'd never seen before, a mist of sparkling energies of blue and purple, clashing with one another. I shot a worried glance at Sabrina. She shrugged as confused as I was.

Mom took a deep breath, and the sparkling faded into nothing. She raised her head from her arms. "I'll be fine. I knew I'd see him sometime. Just not so soon." The color already returned to her cheeks. She shuddered as if something cold brushed her skin or as if someone stepped on her grave. Such an odd saying I'd heard somewhere. I clasped her hand, hoping it was enough, not liking my gruesome thoughts.

Sabrina coughed behind me trying to get my attention. I shifted in the seat to face her. "How bad is it?" I asked.

Her eyebrow's lifted. "How bad is what?"

"That Master is an advisor to the High Council."

Sabrina waved a hand as if in dismissal. "What difference does it make? We're going to have to challenge the High Council as it is. At least now we know who he is, and he can't take us unaware. That he's an advisor changes nothing."

"You're right." The emotional revelations of the day had clouded my judgment. *Will have to work on that. Can't let those things get in the way.* I'd have to figure out soon what to do about John. Why was he with Strega? Had he betrayed us? Betrayed me and went over to Master? Or had something happened? Something I knew nothing about? Aryiana's words worried me the most. *I'm sorry, child, the boy you knew is dead.* But he wasn't dead, so what did the seer mean by that? Had she envisioned something wrong?

Sabrina tapped her foot. "Okay. This is no time to go all weepy and weak. We still have a job to do. We have the Haven, but our secret isn't going to last for long. The war has begun."

The blond-haired man strapped in the chair bellowed at the top of his lungs at three Gayden guards who stood watch. The profanities were…interesting. When he spied us, his curses quieted. His eyes narrowed in surprise as he stared at Sabrina. One word left his lips, a mix of surprise and accusation. "You!"

Sabrina stopped in front of the man, put one hand on her hip, and cocked her head to the side. "Hi, Dad."

What? I looked from the man to Sabrina and back again. I didn't see it before, but now the line of the jaw, the shape of the nose, and the piercing stare jumped out at me. I knew Sabrina had family here. In fact, I met her sister and nieces briefly before coming to the holding cells, but I never would've imagined her family as prisoners.

Sabrina's dad stared in shock, then as he looked between her and me, his eyes gave way to an accusing glare. "You're helping her?"

Sabrina gave the tiniest of nods.

"Traitor! You should be ashamed. I raised you better than that. What's wrong with you? You're a Protector of Conjuragic, and you…you… betrayed your kind to help a bunch of Nips! You helped them invade our home? You're not my daughter." He said all this very fast, growling the last line.

Sabrina rolled her eyes and shook her head with a sigh. "Nice to see you too, Dad. Glad to see your understanding and willingness to listen hasn't changed."

His expression dissolved into the epitome of disgust. "Now you listen here."

"Enough!" I said, surprising myself as well as Sabrina and her dad. He faltered under my gaze which surprised me. The guards stood still as stone, loosely holding semi-automatic weapons in their hands, pointing them at Sabrina's dad. At times like these the reality of my life really hit home, and I felt as if I was living someone else's life. How could I, an eighteen-year-old girl, fight alongside an army of humans who have the power to steal magic, holding people prisoner with military-grade weapons. I not only had magic, I could use all those fancy weapons. Not that I could remember any of their names. I didn't really care if it was a M380 or an M&M, I needed to know how to load and shoot. My trainers hated that about me.

The guards met my gaze as I bobbed my head toward the door. "I think we've got this. You all may go. Check on the other security officers. Most of them are probably coming to by now."

Healer Roos and Charlie's sleeping spells worked perfectly during the invasion, despite feeling like bringing water balloons to a knife fight. Once hit by the pouch, a spray of sleeping potion released in an aerosolized cloud. Whoever inhaled the mist fell into a comatose state. Much easier to deal with a sleeping enemy than a conscious fighting one. But the spell didn't last forever. We'd gathered up the security officers for questioning, so imagine my surprise when Sabrina led me to the holding cells to question the head of security, and it happened to be her dad.

"You know you might've mentioned this...predicament before we got here," I said with a sideways stare at Sabrina. She shrugged as if to say, "It's no big deal."

I cleared my throat, "Hello, Mr. Sun."

"Robert," he interrupted me.

I nodded in concession, surprised he would let me use his first name. "Robert. My name is Ora Stone and I am—"

His nose curled. "A Nip."

My anger rose to the surface in a flash. Being accused of being a stealer of magic had become old. Besides, Gayden joined forces with me so their existence wouldn't be questioned or threatened anymore. Not that winning a war would end the prejudice, but at least it would be a start. Resisting the urge to display my unique ability to wield magic from all four cores, I took a breath and said, "Nip is a racial slur. They call themselves Gayden. I'd appreciate it if you'd not call them that again. To answer the stunned look on your face, no, I'm not a Gayden, but I'm not human either."

Confusion flicked in his expression. "What are you?"

Sabrina rolled her eyes. Couldn't the man shut up? I wondered if someone knew a muting spell. "What I am is none of your concern at the moment. What is your concern is that we have taken your home. The Haven is under our control and will remain that way. We have no intention of harming anyone unless our hand is forced."

"Your little secret won't stay that way forever. Sooner or later, the Council will hear of this."

"This is where you come in. We've already removed the majority of the non-essential Naiads so they should be safe."

"Moved them where?" he asked, as if he were interrogating me instead of the other way around. I debated on whether or not to answer him, but decided, in the end, if we could win him to our side, things would go a lot smoother.

"Across the Veil." Anticipating his reaction, I held up a hand halting his next question. "The Veil is still sealed, but I can manipulate it, and don't ask me how. Back to the matter at hand. You're right about the Council. Ask yourself this, if it were you, and an army of Gayden was threating to take over your world, what would you do to the Haven?"

My words hung in the air between us. Like a venomous snake, they slithered into his ear and my meaning finally hit him. The blood drained from his face, leaving him pale and a little green. "They're going to destroy it."

I nodded once, letting everything sink in. "Which is why we need you. We need your help to make sure our little secret doesn't get out until we're ready so we can save your home."

His head hung low, knowing we'd backed him into a corner. He said nothing for a long time. "Okay. What do you need me to do?"

~

My head pounded after leaving Robert Sun. He had to be the most stubborn, egotistical, prejudiced man I'd ever met. Sabrina laughed when I told her. "Yup, that's my dad." She tried to hide it, but I caught the sadness in her eyes.

We reached the Eye, and I opened my mouth to tell Sabrina we should go check on Arameus, when something caught my attention.

Simeon appeared as if from nowhere and held a bouquet of flowers. An actual bouquet of flowers! If I had to guess at the things I'd see in the middle of an invasion, flowers wouldn't even be in the top one hundred.

Sabrina shared my thoughts. "What're you doing?"

When he knelt to the floor at her, feet I knew. I backed away, trying my best to disappear from this very private moment.

"Sabrina, when you disappeared, and I thought you were gone forever, my world ended. I thought of the times I wanted to ask you out. To tell you how I thought about you every day. How I worried every time you went out on a call, and now that your back, I don't want to lose you again. I love you Sabrina Sun, and would you do me the very great honor of being my wife?"

3

ORA

Two weeks planning a wedding and doing recon missions flew by. I'd never be able to explain how Sabrina pulled together all the plans of the wedding while keeping our presence a secret.

The day of Sabrina's wedding arrived with all the fanfare one would expect at a fancy event. The activity and excitement of one of the main siphuncles, or hallway of the Haven, overwhelmed me, as most things did these days. Volunteers roamed up and down the siphuncle carrying champagne glasses, flowers, and plates and plates of food. I had to hide, for a little while. The noise of the volunteers became louder but less intense with my eyes closed. They gave off such pleasant sounds of happiness and it held the promise of good things to come, but no matter how much I tried, I couldn't join in the celebration.

A clearing of a throat ended the escape, and with a sigh I returned to the real world. Mom leaned against the doorway to Sabrina's quarters and motioned for me to come inside. With a nod, she disappeared behind Sabrina's private door into her camerae, what the Naiads named the pod like structures that made up the different living quarters. The overwhelming joy rose even higher in here, but with a wide fake smile, I joined the others.

Mom rubbed my arm, knowing how I felt, and offered her unspoken support, as always. Her deep green eyes emanated the same encouragement shining underneath.

She'd pulled her blond hair into a tight French twist with fine tendrils of hair framing her still beautiful middle-aged face. Less than a year ago, she'd appeared twice her age. She'd broken the aging spell she'd placed upon herself to get her power back and to save me, but the shocking difference in her appearance still sometimes took me by surprise.

For the longest time, she'd pretended to be my grandmother. I thought a lot of things back then—like I was human, magic was in fairy tales, and I'd live a long and happy life with John.

Mathesar Enochs, aka Master, aka Bastard of the Century, had heard of a prophecy of power and took it upon himself to make it a reality. He'd faked the deaths of prisoners scheduled for execution and forced them to breed, mixing the magical bloodlines, and created Geminates, magicians with two cores of magic like my mom. Another had been my father, Philo Stone. After my parents discovered my mom was pregnant, they escaped, but my father died in the attempt. He'd never made it out of the Veil. My mother crossed the Veil and had me, a witch with the ability to control all four cores of magic, unlike any witch in history. Go me.

Mom put her hand at the small of my back, guiding me into the bathroom where the bridesmaid's dress waited for me. The door closed behind me with a soft clink. Alone at last. Slipping out of the purple leather Protector's outfit, I grasped the thin dress with spaghetti straps and pulled it off the hanger. I crinkled my nose at the horrid gray dress with its sequins from head to toe, making the hideous thing weigh a ton, maybe two.

I eased it over my head, and the dress fell with a *thunk*, pulled at my shoulders, and landed with a weird tinkling sound. Reluctantly turning, I studied myself in the mirror. My fingertips ran down the dress smooth as silk and slid over the sequins like oil. A large scowl covered my heart-shaped pale face, making me look like a stranger even to myself. The vibrant red hair I'd inherited from my dad hung down my back to my waist in a tight braid. Annoyed amber eyes stared back at me. I didn't have to pretend to be happy in here.

The dress reminded me of shiny fish scales ending above my knee with a sheer material hanging the rest of the way to my ankles. Gray shiny stiletto heels waited to be worn to finish the outfit. It wouldn't have surprised me if the shoes would've looked like some sort of fish tail. At least I might not fall in a fish tail. If I didn't break an ankle by the end of this wedding, I'd consider the day a success. Regardless, the ensemble made the bridesmaids look like want-to-be mermaids. I rolled my eyes and made fish faces at myself. I laughed, a hollow sound.

"O, did you fall in?" Charlie called from outside the door. My shoulders fell in defeat as I slipped on the heels. Standing, I turned, hoping not to fall, and opened the door.

Charlie's mouth dropped open. "O.M.G. You look aweeeeesome!" Her honey brown hair had been swept onto the top of her head, dangling curls kissing her right cheek. Her green eyes sparkled with excitement, and deep red lipstick highlighted her pouting lips.

Smile. Come on, smile. Smile. It didn't reach my eyes, but I managed it. "Thanks. So do you." I hated lying to my best friend, but how could anyone be beautiful in a dress that made you look like a fish?

Charlie didn't seem to share my opinion, because at my words, her smile grew wider, if that was even possible. "Thank you. Can you believe we get to be in a magical wedding?"

"Yeah." My awkwardness increased at my attempt at small talk, and a wedding was the last place I wanted to be. I was happy for Sabrina, but what a strange time to get married. As if on cue, Sabrina knocked and entered the room. Her blond hair flowed free from her customary braid and curled down her back with a flowered headpiece wrapped around her head like a halo. Her baby blue eyes sparkled with happiness. I groaned inwardly. The beautiful witch had proven me wrong yet again. I thought no one could look beautiful in a dress with fish scales, but Sabrina's white sequined dress glimmered like a thousand diamonds. Then again, Sabrina could put on a pillowcase and look like a supermodel.

Charlie squealed in excitement and ran over to Sabrina, clamoring on and on about how beautiful she was and how this day was going to be perfect and what a great couple Sabrina and Simeon made. *Blah. Blah. Blah.* I really was in a mood.

My best friend, once so shy, now radiated beauty and confidence. Whether that change was getting involved with my former Defender Arameus or obtaining Tempest magic, I couldn't say. Not that I could blame her. I wished I could shine with the inner strength she'd found, but she didn't bear the weight of my insane predicament with John. Charlie avoided the subject, and Mom tried to ask me why I refused to speak of him, but I didn't know what to tell them.

"Ora, doesn't she look beautiful?" Charlie asked, interrupting my thoughts.

"She does. Sabrina, you look beautiful in anything, but you look extraordinary today." I smiled, genuinely this time.

Charlie joined me at my side, clasping my arm. "Oh Ora, isn't this so wonderful? I wonder who will be next, Arameus and I, or you and John? As soon as we rescue him."

"Yeah, I wonder…" My words trailed off. Sabrina shot me a questioning look.

"Ora, can I talk to you for a minute? In private." Sabrina already had her hand on the doorknob.

"Yeah, sure." We excused ourselves and left Sabrina's camerae, walking down the corridor at a snail's pace. Our heels clicked upon the mother of pearl floor of the underwater city. The place pulsated as if alive mingling with the sounds of people running around getting everything ready for the wedding. The delicious smells of exotic underwater flowers and the baking of sweet cakes and pies filled the halls. Despite myself, my mouth watered, and my stomach gave a little growl. But I knew as soon as someone put food in front of me, my appetite would vanish.

Sabrina wore a contented smile upon her face, instead of the usual scowl. Her father, Robert, still wouldn't speak to her and refused to give her away today, yet he would be attending the wedding. I've wondered if he refused because she betrayed her kind by helping the Gayden or because of her marriage to a non-Naiad.

"I know you think I'm crazy," Sabrina began, not meeting my eyes.

I didn't want to hurt her feelings, but part of me did think she was crazy, getting married in the middle of a war.

"No, I…" I stammered, not knowing how to answer.

"If I were you, I'd think I was crazy too. Pausing the battle plans for almost two weeks just to plan a quick and dirty wedding, but after thinking I'd lost Simeon after the escape, I couldn't lose this opportunity, and if we win this war, then hopefully our marriage will be allowed. Children or not."

"If we lose?" The question left me before I realized its implications.

Her expression turned reflective. "If we lose, then we'll all be executed, so this might be my only chance at happiness."

My guilt rose to the surface like an angry beast. *I'm the reason for this war.* If I hadn't lost my amulet. My magic wouldn't have been freed, and she'd never have had to cross the Veil to arrest me. If she or anyone else dies, the blame would lie at my feet. How selfish could I get? She should get married.

"It doesn't matter what I or anyone else thinks. You deserve every happiness." I didn't add "while you can." She already knew her days could be numbered. "I'm sorry. Ever since we came here through the Bridge I've been so distant. War is harder than I imagined."

Sabrina smiled, and her eyes twinkled with mischief. "Speaking of being distant, I'm not the only one who has noticed you are less than quiet when John is mentioned and have been avoiding Damien."

I debated on whether or not to keep quiet and gazed upward at the crystal ceiling and concentrated on the colorful fish swimming above. I loved the way their colors changed as the light from the Haven grazed their bodies. A mermaid swam past. This one had green hair and skin with webbed fingers. Unlike in the cartoons, she didn't wear a bra, making me blush as she swam along the edge of the Haven.

"I guess I have to tell someone. At least you can be somewhat impartial."

Sabrina said nothing, waiting, as I gathered my thoughts. Should've known she'd use her interrogation skills on me.

"Before I understood I could open the Veil and create the Bridge, I traveled through it in my dreams. In one of those, I saw John. He was with a woman named Strega. He looked happy." I paused, gathering the courage to say it out loud. "They kissed." The great weight had finally been lifted.

Sabrina's brows narrowed. "Strega?"

"The cat woman who we thought killed him," I said, unable to make eye contact. "Damien said she's Mathesar's personal Gayden."

"But that was a dream." She shrugged her shoulders, trying to reason with me.

"I may have been dreaming, but I really traveled in my dreams, and Aryiana told me the boy I knew was dead. If he is alive, then he isn't the same. Not anymore." My heart pounded with my confession but also relief that I could finally tell someone. How was I supposed to confess this to Charlie? She was John's sister and happy that he was still alive. How could I be the one who killed him all over again, but in a different way?

"Aryiana? The Ember woman you trained with?" Sabrina asked.

I nodded. "The Ember and the seer."

Understanding filled her face, and she squeezed my arm, offering her condolences.

Crash. The sound tore through the wall, ricocheting off the walls. The tickle of crystal shattering mingled with startled screams nearby. My body jumped back into battle action as had been trained into me. Time slowed down. My body moved by instinct into a defensive position. Arms held at the ready, magic below my fingertips. Feet spread, light on my toes. Ready to jump into action in a heartbeat. The sequins on the dress flittered around my legs, like small bells. *Ding. Ding. Ding.* Down the hall, Naiads picked up shards of glass from the floor, shoving the broken pieces into an empty carton off to the side. A spreading puddle of champagne shimmered against the Haven floor.

I relaxed my stance and saw Sabrina in a similar position, and we shared an uneasy smile. A titter of laughter threatened deep in my throat. "Glad I'm not the only jumpy one."

"We should get back," she said, as we retraced our steps, heels clicking. "What about Damien?" Sabrina asked, trying to sound casual. "I see the way you two avoid looking at each other. Simeon and I used to act that way." She smiled thinking of her soon-to-be husband.

Considering what to say, I reached behind me, pulling my long braid forward and removed the tie at the bottom. Using my fingers to brush out any tangles, I sent my power into the air, pulling out the molecules of water, soaked my hair and twisted the strands, curling them and pulled the water from it, now dry. My new curls bounced around my face and back.

"Impressive." Sabrina nodded with a smile. "I couldn't have done it better myself."

A warm flush caressed my cheeks. Coming from a Naiad, that was quite a compliment. "Thanks."

How embarrassing and, quite frankly, ridiculous, talking about boys when we should be concentrating on winning the war. "Damien..." I sighed. "I'm so confused. I mean, on one hand, I was engaged to John and in love with him. Really in love with him, not just teenager stuff. But then I thought he died, and I started this whole revenge thing." The craziness of it all gave me a headache. "Anyway, then I met Damien, who has this sweet side underneath those big muscles, and the whole brainwashed thing. It kind of snuck up on me, and the way he can use his power to mix with mine. It's so—intimate." My flush grew a deeper shade of red. I could die, talking about this. "But the whole time I've known him, we've been on the run, having to constantly look behind our backs. It's, ya know, I don't know if I would like him under normal circumstances or if he would like me."

Sabrina scoffed. "Ora, you're a witch, working with an army of

Gayden against the High Council of Conjuragic, and trying to find the traitor, Mathesar. Your life is *never* going to be normal."

Titters of laughter rose up in me. I wasn't sure if that made me feel better or worse. I craved a normal life. I should be finishing up my first year at college, getting ready to come home for the summer, maybe get a summer job. I wanted to become a doctor, get married, and have a family, eventually.

My life had never been normal, not really. Mom and I had been on the run until I'd turned eight, avoiding the Quads and Master's Hunters. Not that I remember much of that time since she'd given me the amulet blocking my magic, but sometimes bits and pieces came back. After the spell, life had been pretty normal. I went to school, did my homework, and hung out with Charlie, but even with my magic hidden, everyone else in our small town of Raleigh, West Virginia, stayed away. I guessed they could sense our differences, wolves amongst the sheep. I hoped moving away and going to college would've changed that, but that didn't happen, and now, Sabrina was right. I could never lead a normal human life.

Sabrina, sensing my dark thoughts, touched my shoulder. "That came out wrong. I meant, things are the way they are. Don't question it or wonder how you'd feel if circumstances were different, because they're not. If you care for him, then you should tell him. You never know when you'll lose the opportunity."

I considered her words and lifted my hand, letting my fingers trail over the cool sleekness of the walls, shining like pearls. The magic radiating within the home of the Naiads filled and strengthened my own power. I didn't understand before the connection of the homelands to each of the magical houses, but I did now. It also explained why I felt stronger within the confines of the Great Hall during my trial. The city flowed with the power of the Unity Statue, all four cores, the only thing that matched my own power.

Sabrina bumped me, shoulder to shoulder, a very girly move, and surprising for her. "He is handsome enough, but you know I'm not a fan."

Memories of her lying helpless on the forest floor on the brink of death after Damien stole her magic flashed into my mind, and I understood.

"You know his mind was poisoned. He did as he'd been brainwashed to do. I can't imagine his life after Mathesar kidnapped him at four-years old, but he came around." I didn't know how I'd feel if the tables were turned and I was the one who almost died at his hands.

Sabrina's stopped mid-step. *Crap. I hope I didn't piss her off.*

Her eyes flitted left and right as her thoughts whirled through her mind. "That's it!" She stared at me as if expecting a reaction out of me, but I must have missed something. She rolled her eyes when I didn't get it. "His mind was poisoned."

My hands went out from my sides into the air, palms up as if holding an invisible platter, still not getting her. "Yeah, I know."

"No. Not Damien. John! His mind was poisoned, brainwashed. That's why he kissed her, and if Damien can be brought back, why not John?"

Something stirred within me, dare I call it hope? Or something else? Like hope but tainted with something darker. I wanted it to be true that he didn't betray me so easily. The thought of seeing John and Strega together sent a feeling of uneasiness to my stomach, like a sickness I couldn't shake, but would he forgive me for having feelings for Damien since I thought he'd died? Would I be able to get the image out of my mind of them kissing? If he'd been brainwashed, would that change the way I feel? Or did I want…someone else instead.

"There you are! Come on the ceremony is about to start!" Charlie appeared from around the corner, thankfully stopping our conversation and quieting the little voice in my head.

I pushed my feelings to the back of my mind and smiled for Sabrina. "Come on. Let's go get you married."

4

ORA

The Eye of the Haven sparkled with decorations from top to bottom. The chairs from the nearby shops had been rearranged to form two rows and a center aisle. Trying to give both Sabrina and Simeon traditional Naiad and Tempest weddings, the remaining Naiads and Gayden worked together to decorate. Seeing the two groups cooperate brought a smile to my lips and hopeful this revolution would work.

They used their powers to manipulate water to create a descending curtain at the end of the aisle that Sabrina and Simeon would stand in front of during the ceremony. The curtain shimmered from reflected candlelight around the Eye. Mom called it breathtaking. Naiad blue and Tempest purple interlaced in delicate silks covering the chairs. The blue and purple theme continued to be showcased in exotic flowers. The Tempest's snow drifted from the ceiling in lazy waves. The diamond-like flakes weren't cold, and no one bothered to explain how that miracle worked. I couldn't have imagined a more romantic wedding.

The biggest risk we had with this wedding was getting Simeon's family here. Not wanting to get married without them there, he traveled with a group of Gayden in disguise to his homeland in the Meadow. There he secretly got his parents and brothers to return with him to the Haven. Once they found out Gayden had taken over the Haven, there had been a moment of panic, but eventually they settled down and listened to reason.

Luckily for us, since my attack on the city, travel between the homelands and to the major metropolis of Conjuragic had trickled to a minimum. The city itself had become unstable with the buildings cracked and on shaky foundations. The High Council went into hiding, and no one knew exactly where they were although the High Councilors of each house did address their homelands regularly, so they couldn't be far.

The state of Conjuragic meant most people never left their homelands. Considering more than half of the population of the Haven was now in the human realm, under lock and key, that was good for us. It would've been hard trying to explain hundreds of people missing work.

I didn't like the idea of sitting here and doing nothing or being frivolous and planning a wedding, but we had to keep living. Otherwise, what was the point of all this? Plus, the Gayden and remaining Naiads left in the Haven enjoyed the distraction. The wedding plans had come together quickly. The local shops supplied the dresses that Charlie and I wore. Sabrina wore her mother's wedding dress, so she had to get it out of storage. Simeon, his brothers, and Arameus wore simple Tempest formal robes. What an odd coincidence that all of the men in the wedding party were Tempests. With their red hair, green eyes, and pale freckly skin, they looked quite handsome in the black robes with the accents of Tempest purple around the collar and sleeves. Underneath the robes, they wore simple black slacks. I didn't know why, but I felt better knowing the men did not walk around with just robes on and nothing underneath.

Sabrina's sister, Massie, also wore in the same gray dress that Charlie and I had. I took an immediate liking to Massie. She had blond hair like Sabrina with blue eyes, but other than that, they were total opposites. Where Sabrina was subdued and cautious, Massie was light-hearted and bubbly, but not annoying. As soon as I met her, she put her arms around me and thanked me for keeping her sister safe. Sabrina, in fact, had kept us safe, not the other way around. When I said as much, she laughed good-naturedly and said, "I should've known. My sister, always the Protector. Even when we were kids."

Since Sabrina's dad refused to give her away, Arameus volunteered for the job. The wedding ceremony itself, except for a few of the vows, was very much like a human wedding. When I remarked on the extraordinary coincidence, Sabrina explained witches came up with the ceremony of marriage when they combined the magic of the two people who wanted to spend the rest of their lives together. This had happened a very long time ago when humans and witches lived together, so humans took up the practice of joining together even without magic.

A few Naiad had chosen to stay and help, making Sabrina's side of the pews sparse. Some, like Sabrina's dad, were security team forced to help, but some others came to our side willingly and agreed to help. What she lacked in Naiad guests, the Gayden more than made up for it. They filled the rest of the seats on her side and most of Simeon's side as well. I felt bad that Simeon had so few people from Tempest to witness his wedding. Only his parents sat in the front row to see their son married. But when I said something to him, he smiled, and said, "The most important people in my life are already here."

I hadn't known Simeon long, but I immediately understood why Sabrina loved him. He reminded me of my mother, supportive, but he allowed Sabrina to be herself. Immediately you could tell he would sacrifice anything and everything for her, but wouldn't get in her way, and he would be content to be the wind beneath her wings, to be cliché, and let her fly. I couldn't have been happier for her and not jealous. Really, I wasn't.

I snuck a glance at Damien, who wore dress robes for the occasion. Someone had trimmed his brown hair short on the sides but left it longer on the top. The image of him rubbing his scruffy chin across my jaw and neck sent shivers through me. My face burned. As if he read my mind, he focused his piercing blue-green eyes on mine. My breath caught in my throat, and I felt his power searching for mine. As if in answer, my magic rose to the surface, tingling beneath my skin. My lips parted as the thumping in my chest increased. The air charged between us, across the room from each other. Out of my peripheral vision, his lips curled upward in an arrogant smile as if he knew exactly what was happening to me. I broke the spell and looked at his full lips, seeing his own pulse beating fast on the side of his neck. I wasn't the only one affected.

Horns blasted. At the same moment, the band keyed up playing a cheerful melody and the wedding party moved to get into position. I shook my head, clearing away the last of—well, whatever that was—and moved to my designated place in the back. I didn't risk looking at Damien again.

Several Gayden and two Naiads made up the band. They positioned themselves off to the side and played orchestra music for background noise. They finished one song then led into the one that signaled time for the actual ceremony to start. Simeon appeared from a shop on the left, and his two brothers trailed him. They walked down the center of the aisle to stand in front. That was Charlie's signal to go. When she'd made it half-way down the aisle, I stepped forward, quivering and hoping I didn't fall with these stupid heels, as the music faded, replaced by the pounding of my own heart. Why should I be nervous? It wasn't as if I was the one getting married. The people watched me with vague interest. I made it to the front and took my place beside Charlie. She held a bouquet of flowers and smiled from ear to ear. I turned in time to see Massie finish her slow procession to the front. Next came Sabrina's nieces, Emilee and Kayla, in white dresses similar to Sabrina's. The cute six-year-old twins dropped purple rose petals and blue forget-me-nots on the ground leading up the aisle.

The music changed, and Arameus met Sabrina at the end of the aisle. I thought she was stunning before, but that was nothing to how she looked now. She looked timeless. The candlelight reflected off her dress making her glow like an angel. Arameus hooked his arm around hers, and they turned, facing the crowd. Everyone stood as Sabrina walked down the aisle. She didn't look a bit nervous. Arameus had a small limp where he'd been injured during the invasion, but overall, he'd healed from his injuries. Finch, with his high degree of sophistication, hollered, "Get 'em girl!" as Sabrina passed him.

My mom and I shared a look, and I couldn't help but laugh. Even Finch couldn't spoil the day for Sabrina. She reached Simeon, and Arameus linked his arm through hers. He maneuvered around them, taking the place as the officiator. Sabrina's dad sat in the front row, his arms crossed, scowling, but didn't say a word. Tears glimmered in his eyes.

The ceremony continued much as I'd seen in the past on TV. Growing up with your mother and no other family didn't allow for invitations to weddings. It wasn't until the end that things looked differently than on TV. They exchanged vows, repeating Arameus, promising to love and honor each other before exchanging simple gold bands. When it came time to merge their magic, the magicians in the crowd tensed. For the first time, Sabrina's hand shook, showing her nerves. They placed their left hands together, interlocked their fingers, and raised their arms. A low hum reached my ears as their power merged and released into the air above them into a swirling cloud of water and air, looking very much like a rolling thunder cloud. Tears filled Sabrina's eyes, and I wasn't sure what it meant. Everyone stood staring at the cloud as if expecting something. I made a small motion with my hand to get Arameus's attention. He looked my way with brows furrowed.

I mouthed the words, "You may now kiss the bride."

Understanding flooded his gaze, and he repeated my words, drawing Sabrina and Simeon back into the moment, and each other. They leaned in and their lips touched. Sabrina's shoulders relaxed. At the same moment, the storm cloud stabilized and changed before my eyes into a flowing arch of a rainbow. I wasn't sure if it was because of the kiss or the rainbow, but the people in the crowd let out roars of cheers and clapped. I assumed if their magic didn't mix, then they couldn't be married. I decided then and there *not* to ask.

The kiss ended, and the new couple turned, facing the crowd. The orchestra music reached my ears and Arameus said, "Ladies and Gentleman, Witches, Wizards, and Gayden, it is my great honor to introduce Mr. and Mrs. Simeon and Sabrina Weston."

The Eye transformed yet again from the wedding ceremony to the reception in thirty minutes with guests working in tandem. The tables lined the periphery of the Eye, and the wedding party took their seats in front of the waterfall. A great banquet of food served buffet style sat to the left. Fountains of champagne flew through the air in the shapes of fish spitting champagne into glasses. I loved that little Naiad touch. The dance floor dominated the center of the room. The orchestra transformed as well because they changed clothes and jammed to rock music after the wedding. Loud music filled the air while the champagne flowed, relaxing the guests and transforming them into a sea of dancing bodies. Even I smiled in spite of myself and my sadness and distraction melted away.

Sabrina and Simeon couldn't have looked like a happier couple when they danced their first dance. The expression on Sabrina's dad's face changed from scrutiny into happiness at some point from the wedding to the reception. He even went to the band and asked for them to announce a father-daughter dance. I don't know what he said during their dance, but tears shimmered in Sabrina's eyes. At the end of the dance, she hugged her father, and he kissed her lightly on the cheek. He even shook Simeon's hands. Things were coming together.

The delicious food permeated the chronic nausea that had plagued me since finding out about John. Mounds and mounds of fish and lobster as well as various kinds of poultry weighed down the buffet tables. Not to be outdone, the sides had been placed in-between the main dishes. Potatoes prepared a thousand ways, butternut squash, asparagus baked with oil and garlic, beans and rice, hush puppies, and some strange vegetables that I'd never seen were piled high on silver platters.

I could live at the dessert table. I'd never tasted anything so smooth and sweet. I heard the word decadent used more than once. Mini chocolate cakes melted in your mouth with a rush of cream at the end, almost like drinking a sip of milk. Cookies and donuts and mousse spread over every surface.

Sabrina and Simeon didn't cut the cake or share champagne like the traditional wedding practice I'd seen on TV. I couldn't see how Sabrina would allow anyone, even Simeon, to smash cake in her face.

I danced mainly in big groups with Sabrina, Charlie, Finch, and even Mom. We laughed as we stepped around the dance floor. During the slow dances, I wondered back to my table and sipped on champagne. Those were the only times when I got sad, watching Sabrina and Simeon, Charlie and Arameus. Finch even asked my mom to dance. The reception guests dwindled as people excused themselves. It had to be close to evening. We had to be done to the last few dances of the night. Another slow song began, and I made my way off the dance floor. Someone tapped my shoulder. Damien blushed beside me, looking, well quite frankly, hot in his dress robes. That lopsided grin of his warmed my heart, and he said, "I figured I should ask you to dance before it's too late."

I slid my hand into his. "I'd love to." *God could I be more corny?*

He pulled me into his arms, and I placed my left arm over his shoulder and he held my right hand in his as we swayed back and forth to the romantic song. Guilt interlaced every look between us and each place we touched. Why couldn't I just be happy dancing with Damien instead of worrying about John? The two of us danced liked teenagers. We had absolutely no moves other than to sway back and forth. Clearly, neither one of us had a single dance lesson in our entire lives. I always thought when I went to a wedding, I'd be on the dance floor moving like a professional like they always did in movies and books. It seems that life is much less glamorous. The thought made me laugh.

"What is it?"

I told him, and he laughed. "I'm pretty sure that magic and this war we're fighting would be in a book or a movie somewhere."

"Right."

We didn't speak for a few minutes, lost in our own thoughts. I looked into his eyes and said, "You know, so much of the time I look around and can't believe what I'm doing."

"For what it's worth, I'm glad you are, because otherwise, we wouldn't have met."

I opened my mouth to tell him I was glad I met him too when the hair on my arms stood on end. The voices in the crowd changed. The mood of the room went from being light-hearted, relaxed, and sleepy to high-pitched, on edge, and nervous. I scanned the crowd for the commotion. I caught sight of Finch talking with Sabrina, Simeon, and Arameus, his expression grave, and he threw his arms about agitated. Wade had been placed as head of security during the wedding. He jogged over, and I spotted Jeremiah pushing through the crowds toward me, his face the picture of panic. Whispers spread throughout the crowd, and people began to fidget and scampered to their chairs like frightened mice. Jeremiah reached me at a trot. I knew something was terribly wrong even before he said, "The Quads are coming."

My blood ran cold and the knot in the pit of my stomach squeezed. "How many?"

"All of them."

5
ORA

The people in the crowd transformed from easy-going wedding guests to the trained army in a few moments. I shared a one significant, "oh crap" look with Finch before he shouted, "We're under attack! Teams, at your stations. Now!"

The confusion vanished in an instant. People snapped to attention and moved with deliberation. The men sprinted to the edge of the room. They stripped out of their dressed robes to the Protector's leathers underneath. I dashed to a nearby shop along with the rest of the women. Glad that Wade suggested we keep our gear ready. Without any thought to modesty, I pulled the heavy dress over my head, flung it to the ground, and kicked off the heels. Using magic, the Protector's outfit slid over my legs and around my waist, tying the straps together while boots slipped on my feet, all, in one fast fluid move. Magic rippled at my hair, pulling at the curls and forcing them into a braid. I shoved a comm in my ear and wrapped a tie at the end of the braid, sliding it down inside my suit. The whole thing took less than three minutes.

Back in the Eye, most people were already in position. The civilian wedding guests hid in the back of various shops. I prayed it would be enough to protect them. Finch passed me a pistol. I chambered a round, clicked off the safety, and held the weapon at the ready pointed at the ceiling.

The Quads were coming. Thousands of them floated down the deep blue sea right above the Eye. They weren't planning on coming in the entrance at the ends like we had. They were going to break through and drown us out.

Sabrina's voice fired from the comm in my ear. "Aquatics team, when the Eye breaks, your job is to keep that water out of here. Understood?"

No, that's what they expected us to do. I touched my ear and said, "No! Aquatics team, stand down. Aerial team, your job is to put bubbles around everyone's head so we can breathe. Sabrina, do you remember what Fox said?"

"Don't use hands," Sabrina answered.

"Yes, but the Quads will. Their hands will be slower in the water."

Sabrina interrupted through the comm, "They'll be easier to see, and we can out think them."

"Exactly!"

"Excellent!" Sabrina said. "Aerial team, you got it?"

Arameus said, "We got it!"

I couldn't see him, but I didn't have time to look. Above the Eye, thousands of magicians floated downward. A ball of magical energy surrounded them. It zoomed toward us at lightning speed like a missile. It got closer and closer until finally—*Boom!*

The ceiling exploded into a thousand pieces. I braced myself as the sea erupted into the Eye. The sound rang out like a bomb, deafening. Time slowed down. The water poured in like a waterfall, and we had seconds to brace ourselves. The water hit me like a giant fist. It slammed me to the ground. Bodies floundered all around me. A moment of panic flooded me like the water. If the comms weren't waterproof, we would be deaf to each other.

I tried to stand against the pressure of the water, but the force of it held me down. The water swarmed around me, blinding me, blocking all other senses. I knew everyone else had to be the same. We were sitting ducks. Something had to be done. I could send my power out and push the water back, but it would take all my concentration, and last time I had the Naiads here to help me.

I knew what I had to do. I sent my power up and pulled the sea water farther into the Eye. Instead of a waterfall, one solid mass filled the space. At the same time, the remaining air retreated upward and out in a great bubble. Within seconds, I'd filled the Eye with water. My magic zapped to life. It shoved the water away from my head forming a bubble. I sucked in a delicious breath of air. I holstered the useless pistol after reattaching the safety. Every movement became a great effort in the water. I touched my hand to my ear and shouted, "Aerial team, now! Now!"

The first of the Quads made it inside. A few still descended, but most breached the barrier. Spells cast down upon us. But there was nothing we could do until we could breathe. Helping the aerial team, my magic scampered away from me, pushing air bubbles around those near me. Each time, their shoulders shook with relief as they drew in their first breath. The aerial team took over. The Gayden had been trained well. Those who had magic cast their own spells at the Quads. The others would soon enough. The Quads continued to descend. Every so often, one would go limp and then start shaking, their power captured by a Gayden.

In my ear, someone said, "I've captured an Ember. What can I do with Ember magic underwater?"

"Water boils." I winced not counting on my words echoing inside the bubble.

Everything slowed down as if the battle played out in slow motion. All the magicians had made it inside the Haven. The Gayden kicked off the bottom, swimming upward. The spells rippled through the water. Each time someone was hit, the bodies floated backward amidst a sea of red. Except for the sound of my panting and grunts, the battle raged in silence. It wasn't right. There should be loud explosions, screams, or something. It was like watching a movie on mute.

A ball of magic laced air whizzed past my head at an alarming speed. It broke the surreal moment, and the world sped back up. I released the hold on my magic, letting it zoom away from me. The Sight closed in. The world transformed into swirling particles. My power focused on the nearest body and froze the water around him. To another, I ripped the air out of his lungs through his chest in a gush of blood. I moved on to the next before I could let reality sink in. The magic jumped from person to person as bodies went limp. Some frozen, some in pools of blood, others unconscious. One after another, again and again, but there were always more. Voices on my comm screamed commands and others begged for help. None of it made sense. The world became nothing but chaos.

Our training to move in tactical positions fell by the wayside. At this point, it was kill or be killed. I'd never felt more alive, but something had to give.

Unconscious or dead, Gayden and magicians' bodies floated in the Eye. I couldn't attack without provocation. The next body could be friend or foe, but hesitating could mean death.

No matter how many went down, it felt like a hundred more took their place. Gayden fell too. Bodies floated around me, this one a Gayden, her chest gone. The water, once clear and blue, was now stained red and murky. The perfect water to attract sharks.

The distraction was all it took. One second I fought, the next an ice shard hurtled toward me. It struck the side of my head inches from my temple. Blood poured from the wound, stinging from the pain. My head swam. Weightless, I drifted through the murky water. Blood filled the bubble around my head, still miraculously in place. Nausea gripped my stomach. Darkness pulled at me, but a buzzing in my ear kept trying to get my attention. My vision cleared as I fought to stay awake. The battle still raged on, but a quick glance revealed we were losing. Sabrina's voice on my comm, "Ora! Ora! Where are you?"

I touched my ear, rolling to avoid a ball of boiling water. "I'm here."

Sabrina called, "We're done. We have to retreat. You have to open the Bridge."

Trying to get my bearings, I swam and weaved around spells. Pure power shot out of me, taking out two more Quad members. "Everyone get to Section A. Get the Sphere team in front. Pull the floors up. Barricade us. Then I'll open the Bridge. Get as many as you can out."

"What about the wedding guests?" Jeremiah buzzed in my ear.

Crap! I'd totally forgotten about them.

"I'll get them," someone said. It might've been Wade.

Inside, the magic took over. It shoved the water behind me, jetting me like a bullet toward the entrance. The Gayden fell back, and the Quads pushed forward, not letting up. The Sphere team worked together, and the beautiful mother-of-pearl floors splintered apart. When the wall rose high enough, the Bridge inched open, pushing the water aside. I pushed people inside yelling, "Go! Go! Go!"

Body after body disappeared into the black hole with sparkling rainbow light at the edges. The barricaded wall was shattering into pieces. A shard ripped through a woman as she lifted a leg to step into the Bridge. One moment she'd place a foot into the Bridge, the next she floated in the bloody water, cut in half, the upper and lower parts of her body drifting in opposite directions. I stared for a second, paralyzed, before pushing her body away, like a piece of trash, fighting nausea, and ushered the next in line out.

Tiny fragments of the wall remained. "Sphere team. Get through the Bridge. I'm closing it in one minute."

Charlie appeared at my side. The bubble around her made her hazy. She screamed at me through the comm. "You can't close it. Arameus is still out there."

The remainder of our wall exploded. More of the Gayden flew backward, bleeding, either unconscious or dead. I didn't know which, but I couldn't do anything to help them now. The Quads closed in. It was now or never. My power jumped out of me, shoving the water back away from the Bridge so I could move faster. On solid ground, the air bubble disappeared, and I dragged a screaming Charlie from the Eye.

She clawed at my arms. Her feet tried to kick me. "You can't leave. Arameus is out there. Arameus is out there."

I shouted to those remaining, "Get out! Get out now!"

Charlie fought me. She called me every name, spat in my face, and even gathered the wind around us in an attempt to use her Tempest power to stop me. My magic knocked hers away, and the fight seeped out of her. I stepped into the Bridge, dragging her with me, and sealed the Bridge as soon as a member of the Quads breached my bigger bubble. I locked eyes with Corporal Bizard before the Eye vanished.

6

ORA

The Veil sealed. For the first time ever, inside the Bridge I had no idea where to go, and I'd shoved people inside not holding onto one another. Pure blackness surrounded me, interrupted by thousands of screams. Had I inadvertently trapped the surviving army in the Veil? Then someone bumped into me. My shoulders relaxed. At least now I knew they could move around without me, and they weren't stuck in-between worlds. Adrenaline still rushed through my veins. Now without the battle, my hands quivered and the fast-paced breathing favored a panic attack. Jiminy's buttery cinnamon smell surrounded me, easing away the tension. I pushed forward, grabbing the arm of the first person I found, and said, "We have to go. Grab onto whoever you can. Keep moving."

"Okay," the person answered.

My message reverberated away from me in a series of fading whispers. Without waiting, I pulled the person and walked, flying by the seat of my pants, one foot in front of the other, with no clue where to go or what to do. Jiminy whispered, *Where would you like to go?*

"Somewhere safe."

This way.

I sensed more than felt Jiminy in front of me. Blindly, I followed him, pulling the arm along behind me, one foot in front of the other, while my hand held a stranger's. I tried to drown out the sobs and screams of pain.

There was nothing I could do for them or those we'd left behind. Hundreds, maybe even thousands, had died today and the guilt surrounded me like a thick wool blanket on a summer's day, suffocating and uncomfortable, making me miserable.

I touched my free hand to my ear and said, "Team leaders report." My voice sounded dead even to my own ears.

Static answered me. Perhaps the comms didn't work inside the Bridge. I held onto that belief, not daring to let the thought that all of the leaders had perished. I felt as if we walked forever, but finally Jiminy stopped moving. It never occurred to me before now to wonder what Jiminy was. Was he something like Lailie, an oxygenian, but trapped in the Veil? I didn't know, and I didn't have the heart to ask right now. He said, *Through here.*

My heart rate sped, either from fear or exhaustion, as soul-crushing fatigue crashed upon me. The Bridge resisted opening. I searched for the power, deep inside, hiding and wallowing in guilt as well. Like encouraging a scared puppy from underneath the bed, my magic rose, timid, and eased the Bridge open. It was slow, almost as if trying to create a whole in tar. No lightening of the darkness to allow me to peek on the other side. Could our days of traveling be at an end?

I stepped out, letting go of the person's hand behind me, making sure more danger wasn't on the other side. Jiminy led us to a forest with old, old trees hundreds of feet high. Their trunks so large it would take three grown men holding hands to wrap their arms around them. The forest breathed with life, which sounded of small animals scurrying, tweeting of birds, but nothing else. No sounds of people at all. I looked up at the sky, and it glowed with a purple-pinkish glow of either dawn or twilight, I couldn't tell. Sabrina's wedding had taken place in the evening, so I assumed twilight, but with the way time moves in the Bridge, I couldn't be sure. I guess we'd find out soon enough when the sky would either grow lighter or darker.

Advancing on tip-toes, I made my way to the edge of the forest, but I found no signs of human life. Returning to the Bridge, I reached inside, found a hand, and pulled. A Gayden I didn't recognize emerged with a rifle hanging loosely on his arms, still dripping water.

The rest of the army exited in a controlled fashion. How they didn't fall to the ground in their exhaustion I couldn't say, not that I would've blame them. I tried to do a mental count, but I couldn't handle it. We were so many fewer than before. Sabrina didn't have time to change out of her

Into the Fire

beautiful white sequined dress. The once-exquisite gown hung in tatters, soaking wet, and covered in blood. Her haunted face held the most desperate and sad expression I'd ever seen. Simeon stood by her side and held her hand. Her sister huddled nearby, holding her nieces to her legs, neither having any obvious wounds, thank God. When Mom exited, she ran to me, throwing her arms around me in a desperate embrace, and I returned it, thankful that she had made it through alive. The tension I wasn't aware of holding eased out a fraction as I continued to look for my friends. Damien emerged with a shard of mother-of-pearl sticking out of his leg, glistening with blood that ran in a steady stream down his leg. His face had gone paler than pale, and his eyelids drifted open and closed as if he would pass out soon. Sweat or sea water glistened on his forehead. Two men carried him past me as his head lulled and bobbed. He didn't even recognize me when the men carried him to the Healers. Jeremiah's expression wavered between exhaustion and shock. A look I'd wager mirrored my own. He had no obvious injuries either. He patted me on the back as he walked by. Charlie sat on a nearby patch of the forest floor, staring into the distance, looking as if she had no idea how she'd gotten here.

When the last of stepped out, I limped to her side. "Charlie, I..."

She whipped her head in my direction, scrambling from the ground. She rushed at me, fists flying, while she screamed, "You left him behind! You left him behind! You left him like you left John! How could you? How could you?"

Her attack took me by surprise, but it shouldn't have. I knew I'd left Arameus, but I could've either left him or risked all of us dying. Still, it wasn't fair for her to throw John in my face. I knew the dark place she had been forced into. I faced her, allowing her to land her blows, not lifting a hand. Several Gayden pulled her off of me, dragging her away, while she screamed as if her soul were being ripped apart. This pain I couldn't touch. Just like no one could reach me through mine after we'd thought John died, but the person I held accountable had remained in Conjuragic, while Charlie blamed me. Plus, Arameus could still be alive. There was hope.

Somehow, I figured karma would be cruel. I'd had no hope John had survived and lo-and-behold he was, but now Charlie had hope and it'd be our luck he'd die.

Arameus's face swam before my eyes. My eyes filled with tears as the drama of what happened flooded me. Images of Arameus when he walked into my cell like an angel, carrying me to the infirmary. Him in court defending my case while joking with me in his office during breaks. How he showed up to warn Mom and I when the Quads discovered I hadn't died during my execution. When he helped train the Gayden and as he fell in love with Charlie, and now he was gone.

I almost lost it. I wanted to throw myself on the ground sobbing, but I couldn't. I had to lead. I didn't know where we were, whether we'd made it back to the human realm or were still in Conjuragic. Our injuries and damages would have to be assessed. We had to regroup, either setup camp or move again. We would need supplies to take care of the wounded. Healers would need to be gathered. We would need to eat and drink and go to the bathroom. All these things didn't stop. All these things would have to go on. Or we'd already lost the war, and those who had already died would be for nothing.

Gathering some unknown inner strength, I went in search of Sabrina and Mom. Sabrina's head rested on Simeon's shoulders in a light embrace. Her back straightened at my approach. She pulled away from her new husband, her face set, ready for whatever came next. Somehow, she and I had become a team, reading each other without speaking. We'd have to grieve later because, for now, we had things to do.

"We need to gather the leaders."

Sabrina stood, hand gripping the shreds of her wedding gown. "I'll get on it. Then we need to figure out our next move."

"Exactly."

Sabrina adjusted the comm in her ear, pressed the button, and her voice echoed in my ear, "Team leaders, gather your troops. Do an assessment, separate the wounded, and make a note of your supplies. Medic team, gather together as quickly as possible then separate into equal groups to each of the teams. We need everyone to be at their best."

I spoke into my comm, "I don't want to lose anyone else today. Team leaders, we meet in five near where we entered the forest."

With our commands, our troops we're on the move. They stood from the forest floor, straightened from leaning on trees, or pulled themselves together. They needed us. They needed someone to tell them what to do. *I wish someone would tell me what to do.*

While I waited for the leaders, I surveyed our current location. In several small sections, spaced randomly through the forest, groups of small mushrooms grew. My gaze swept past them, but movement caught my attention. Little tufts of a smoky substance puffed from their centers giving off a weird *Alice in Wonderland* vibe. I pointed them out to Sabrina through the comm, and her reply gave me the chills.

I made my way over to Damien. Had we really been dancing together such a short while ago? A Healer had fixed the cut in his leg, the skin still raw and tender. "You okay?"

He nodded. "I'll be fine. How're you?" He reached out and swept back a stray lock of hair that escaped from my braid and tucked it behind my ear.

"Physically, I'm fine." He grabbed my hand and squeezed as his magic wrapped around me, not pulling but seeking to comfort. "Thanks," I said. "I should get back."

As I moved to stand, Damien reached behind my head, pulling me toward him, and brought his lips to mine. Fatigue and the recent trauma held the passion our kisses usually brought, but this kiss brought comfort and an unspoken promise that he'd always be there. I gave him a quick kiss of my own before heading back to the leaders.

It took a little longer than five minutes but who was left of the leaders gathered. My heart sank when an ashen-faced Wade said, "Finch is missing."

Arameus and Finch gone. Damien hobbled toward Jeremiah and tapped him on the back. Sabrina hugged the young Gayden before making her way toward us.

Mom stood in Protector's pants and boots with a sopping wet t-shirt. She hadn't gotten enough time to get fully changed. Charlie wasn't there. Healer Roos had spelled her with a sleeping bag. She'd been moved and dozed underneath a nearby tree. She would have to sleep it off, thankfully. I couldn't face her again, not so soon. The loss of Arameus was too new and raw like Damien's leg.

Wade, Sabrina, Healer Roos, and I were all that remained of the original team leaders. Damien took over for Finch and Jeremiah for Arameus. "What've we got?" I asked.

The heavy silence pressed around me as if no one wanted to speak.

Sabrina swallowed. "We have sustained heavy losses. A little more than a third of our army is gone. Another quarter or so are injured. The Healers are working as fast as they can, but some of them need real medical attention. They'll need time to heal and more powerful spells than we have here."

Wade pointed off to the left. "I've had some scouts go out. We're still in

Conjuragic, in one of the outer forests of the Willow near the Shadow Forest."

I nodded, processing the information. It was worse than I'd feared. A third of the army missing or dead, another quarter injured. How many of the Quads had we taken out? "Does anyone know we're here?"

Wade shook his head. At least we had that going for us.

"What should we do?" I asked, feeling a pressure building behind my eyes.

Mom answered, "I think we need to go back to the island. Just for a little while. We can renew our supplies, heal our wounded, and get some reinforcements." She emphasized the last. A large group of Gayden had stayed behind to guard the Naiad prisoners. We could strip those down to a skeleton crew, but that would increase the risk of the prisoners escaping.

Sabrina's voice broke in one quick sob. Everyone was on edge, but this wasn't like her. Had I missed something?

Sabrina had a hand to her nose, as if holding back a sneeze. I recognized an internal struggle to compose herself. After a few deep breaths, she succeeded, then looked at the group, "Our prisoners are mainly Naiads. The Haven has been destroyed. We might be able to convince some of them to join our cause. Take revenge for the Haven. Even at the end, my dad sacrificed himself for the Haven. If I can tell them what he did, then I think they'll follow us."

Before I could think, the words left my lips. "What happened to your dad?"

Sabrina looked away, unable to answer. Her husband spoke for her. "When you called for us to flood the Haven, he protested. But Sabrina reminded him that as long as we were successful, we could push the water back out. It could be fixed. He gathered the remaining Naiad security team, and he fought with us during the attack. He fought bravely, but when a Tempest was sneaking up on Sabrina and she didn't see him, he broke from his formation rushing to her side. He took out the Tempest, but it was too late. Behind his back, a Sphere attacked. A piece of seaweed went through him, sticking out of his chest. I got the Sphere, but," his voice cracked, "the damage was too much. As he lay in Sabrina's arms dying, he said, 'Tell our people. Tell them what happened here today. Tell them and they will follow you. *You*. Avenge our home.'"

Sabrina's face wilted, her loss barely contained, etched in every line of her face, nose and eyes blotching, as if her pain couldn't be held inside her body. It bled out of her and infected the rest of us, like a virus, my own eyes burning and a hand clutched over my heart. "I promised him," she murmured, more to herself than anyone in particular, "I promised and then he...he..." She flung herself into Simeon's arms, burying her face in his shoulder. His arms enveloped around her like a veil.

He finished, "He was gone seconds later."

Sabrina peaked from Simeon's shoulder, eyelashes damp with blotchy cheeks, and she told me, "He said he was proud of me."

My heart ached for her. It took everything I had not to hug her or even turn and throw myself in my mom's arms so she could protect me, make me feel safe like she did when I was a child, but no hugs would bring back the dead, and no amount of comfort could change our reality.

I bowed my head. "We will not forget his sacrifice. We will avenge your home."

Giving her a moment, I stepped back and watched the somber army. Soft whispers escaped people's lips, broken by the wails of those being healed, or dying, I wasn't sure which. We would have to go back to the island, and fast.

The sun dipped closer toward the horizon. Night would fall soon. The forest shadows lengthened, and the scurrying of animals transformed into slithering sounds. The peaceful forest transformed into something ominous. It was probably my imagination and paranoia, but with each second, the unease grew. We had to move. I dismissed the leaders to organize their individual groups and aid the injured.

As soon as we were ready, I opened the Bridge, which slid into existence like the hundreds of times before. Placing Wade in front, I had them leave in small groups, retreating back to the human realm. The weight of defeat rested heavy on all of us, but we hadn't been destroyed. We could still fight. This was one battle in the war. It wasn't over yet.

7

PERDITA

Walking through the Bridge was as difficult as walking through waist-high water. Every movement, every thought even, took tremendous effort. Perdita hated it, despite its necessity. They also had to hold on to someone next to them or risk getting lost. Directions disappeared here. There was no up or down or left or right. Yet somehow, they could travel in it, but Perdita suspected they traveled not with how they moved, but with thought. It defied all rational logic and instead remained clearly bound by the magic of the enchantments that created it. Ora's magic had been able to control it, but she should never forget that even though she'd collared it, the Bridge remained a wild beast. Each time they entered the Bridge, she feared it'd be their last. She never knew when or if Ora would lose control. Perdita's first experience going to the Veil had been during her escape when pregnant with Ora. It didn't surprise anyone, least of all her, that she feared the Bridge because Ora's father died inside it. Back then, they knew nothing about having to open it using two cores of magic, for which she already possessed, but also it took something more. Some odd mixture of self will and magic. Otherwise, when you stepped through the Veil, you risked more than death. You could lose your soul in it. That's what happened to her husband, Philo, and each time she traveled through the Bridge, she felt his presence. A nasty trick of her subconscious, no doubt, but in some ways, it comforted her, but mainly, it gave her the creeps. It felt as if his ghost watched her.

Another problem they'd discovered while traveling through the Bridge was the time abnormalities. Everything about it made no sense. Sometimes you could go a few miles and it took what felt like forever, but other times, they could travel great distances, and they arrived in a matter of minutes. She guessed it happened because it has something to do with whoever led the group and the power of their concentration. Perdita never had to lead the group, but Ora explained it to her. She said that she had to concentrate, listening for a familiar sound or see a familiar place inside her mind, almost like a premonition, and then she had to walk toward it. The degree of her concentration and the strength of her connection to the desired location changed the time it took to get there.

Wade must have been able to find his home almost instantly because in no time they stepped back on the sandy shores of Gayden Island. Time also did weird things when you traveled through the Bridge. When they left, it had just turned dark, but here the sun shined bright in the middle of the day. The transition from the pitch blackness of the Bridge, where no light penetrated, into the bright sunlight of the Bahamas stung her eyes. Squeezing them shut, she used the back of her hand to wipe away the watering of her eyes.

As soon as the army appeared at the edge of the beach, security soldiers swarmed them, demanding to know what happened. Strangled whispers spread through the crowd merging with sounds of the waves crashing on the beach. Perdita knew how hard it would be for the Gayden to come home and admit defeat. They needed to recuperate both mentally and physically and come up with a new plan.

Once the last person exited, Ora turned and closed the Bridge. Perdita couldn't help but notice that the circle of rainbow surrounding the pitch blackness inched closed, like a gate that had rusted, instead of smooth like it had been before. That sight left her uneasy. Fortunately, no one else but Perdita noticed.

Almost without thought, the leaders gathered on the edge of the beach near the dunes. Sabrina said, "We need to talk to the Elders."

"That was my first thought." Wade curled his hands into fists, looking as if he'd aged ten years in the last few hours.

Each of them touched their comms and sent messages to the Gayden. Some would transport the wounded to the hospital while the rest would gather what supplies they could, restock, and report.

The dismal mood of the army tore at Perdita's already fraying nerves. Everyone's shoulders slumped and each movement was sluggish with sadness in their eyes. Even her daughter had lost something great. Strength no longer shimmered in her eyes. Back in the forest, Ora'd been close to tears, but she'd pulled herself together, and in that moment, Perdita realized her little girl had grown up. She was no longer a child, but a woman and a leader. Ora carried the weight of their losses on her shoulders, and no matter what anyone said, she wouldn't share that burden, as if Ora felt she should be punished for simply being born, and that destroyed Perdita's heart.

Perdita had suffered a great deal during her childhood. How could she not have? Raised as a slave, her mother taken away from her, and always under the threat of harm or death. But through that, she met Philo, her husband, and found love and happiness, even in the worst of circumstances, and from their love, they'd made Ora. Their daughter was her greatest blessing. Ora had always been a sensitive and smart child. Part of it, she knew, stemmed from the rejection from humanity, who could sense the power within her, but most of it was Ora's personality. Ora had always been the first to help someone who needed it and blamed herself when things went wrong. She was passionate about school and loyal to a fault. Perdita couldn't have been prouder of who Ora had grown up to be, and she knew that Philo would feel the same if he still lived.

As always in moments like this, when he crossed her mind, she wondered how different things would be if he'd lived. How many times had she wished he could be there to see their little girl as she grew up. Each time they would go to the park and Ora would beg, "Push me, Mommy. Push me." Perdita would smile as she pushed her sweet little girl with her pigtails flying behind her, as Ora giggled. Squeals of, "Higher, Mommy! Higher!" hid the sadness that her father wasn't there. On the rare occasions when they went on vacation, she would watch Ora splashing in the pool or running around on the beach chasing the seagulls and she would wonder what it would have been like if Philo had survived their escape.

Perdita's one regret, if you could even call it that, about Ora was the position it put her in. Each time Ora used her powers and grew stronger, it made Perdita so proud, but they had to keep it locked away to protect her because other people would try to control that power or feel like she shouldn't have it. Those same people felt the same about Geminates. Instead of fighting back, Perdita had hid, proving how much stronger Ora had grown up to be, and now Ora had to fight simply to be allowed to live.

No one else noticed Perdita had lost a lot of weight in the last few months. Her stomach twisted in knots each night because Ora could die at any moment. Her baby, her daughter, could be taken from her, and there was nothing she could do to save her. She would stay close, but every time she thought about Ora getting hurt or dying, she would break down in tears and have to excuse herself. Her baby was in danger all the time.

The tears threatened to return, but she didn't want anyone to see her cry, most of all Ora. The leaders who remained made their slow, somber walk to the Town Hall to give report to the Elders. As they approached the Defense Tower, one guard met them at the door. As soon as they reached him, this a new man bombarded them with questions. Wade waved the man away and asked for the Elders. This man spoke with a Jamaican accent. He had thick corn rolls hanging down to his mid-back and wore a white wife-beater and black slacks. He sat his rifle on the porch propped up against the door and picked up his walkie-talkie. He pressed a button on the side and relayed the message. A few moments later, static rang from the walkie-talkie and another said, "The Elders already know. They're on their way."

Mr. Corn Roll motioned them inside, picked up his rifle, and followed behind them. Perdita accompanied the group into the main meeting room. An old church had been renovated and turned into the Town Hall. They left the aisle seats intact. At the front, where the altar should've been, sat rows of chairs for the Elders to address the town. Near the front, Perdita sat at the end of the second row, her back and legs aching. Her T-shirt clung to her, still soaked with sea water from the Haven. The drying salt itched, making the shirt stiff and cold. Goosebumps lined her arms as the A/C kicked on with a hum. No one else sat, but then again, besides Wade, the rest were younger. They didn't feel the aches and pains as much as she did. She envied them that.

No one spoke while they waited. Damien favored his injured leg and, as always, kept a half an eye on Ora, his expression longing. Perdita couldn't say when Damien had fallen head over heels in love with Ora, but neither one of them knew it. Every time Ora looked at Damien, she would smile with the slightest movement of her mouth, and other times ones that would light up her face. Ora used to smile all the time, but these days, only being around Damien would bring that smile, but then something would flash in her eyes, and the smile would fade. Perdita had no doubt thoughts of John caused the smile to falter. After Ora found out that John was alive, she didn't react like Perdita thought she would, and it had to be more than having feelings for Damien. Ora hadn't told anyone, as far as she knew, but something happened and not knowing did nothing to help the constant ache in her stomach.

Sabrina and Simeon held hands while Jeremiah laid his head on Sabrina's shoulder. The two of them had become as close as brother and sister. Perdita marveled at how they had become a family, even in these hard times. It eased her mind to know that if something ever happened to her Ora wouldn't be alone.

A door to the left side of the altar opened, and the Elders took their seats, looking grim. No one in particular was in charge, but Winslow and Aggie usually did the talking.

Right on cue, Winslow, the oldest of the Elders, with wisps of white hair and eyebrows that went halfway up his forehead, shook his head and said, "We've heard some serious rumors. We hope they aren't true." His raspy voice gritted as if he had spent the last thirty years smoking. He, like most of the Gayden, had dark skin that contrasted nicely with his silver hair. He had the largest set of eyebrows Perdita had ever seen. The stress must have finally got to her because at the sight of those eyebrows, she burst into a fit of laughter and everyone stared at her as if she had gone crazy. Which made the situation that much funnier.

Someone, she guessed Sabrina, flung ice cold water in her face. That ended her giggling. She wiped the excess off her eyes and said, "Thanks, I needed that."

A stern-looking Aggie said, "Right, if you're done with delirious laughter, can you please tell us what's going on?"

Ora took a step forward. "We'd taken the Haven, and while we were getting everything into position, we also had Sabrina's wedding. During the reception, we got reports that the Quads were coming. It was our fault. We were unprepared. Distracted."

"No, it was my fault. We shouldn't have had the wedding." Sabrina looked at Simeon as she spoke, a longing in her expression, conflicted with her guilt.

Wade shook his head, his face ashen. "No, you should always declare your love when you have the chance."

Winslow scoffed. "Regardless of what should or should not have been done, what happened afterward?"

"They ambushed us. We had moments to get ready before they arrived. They flooded the Haven, and the battle raged under water. Both sides sustained heavy losses, but we had to retreat. We left behind a lot of our side because they could not get to the rendezvous point. That leaves about a third of us missing, wounded, or dead." Ora held her head high, ready to take their reprimands.

Aggie asked, "You retreated here?"

"No. Initially we retreated to a forest outside the Willow, the Sphere's homeland. We needed to figure out what to do, and we decided the best course was to come back here and reassess the situation in a friendly zone before we make our next move."

Perdita would give anything if Ora hadn't been forced into this life.

Steve, the youngest and most disagreeable of the Elders, jabbed a finger as he spoke. "You made one right move. You came back home, where are you all should have never left to begin with. I told you all this was a bad idea. Now we are in an active war with Conjuragic and the Council, and there's nothing we can do about it. I'd say we send an ambassador to Conjuragic through this Bridge of hers, hand her over, and request a truce and a renewal of our original treaty."

Winslow leaned back, swatting one hand in Steve's direction. "We *all* know you were against this from the start, but we're in it now, and besides, the girl you want to turn over is the one who would have to get you there in the first place. I highly doubt she's going to hand herself over."

Aggie nodded while rolling her eyes. "Besides, she's done so much to help us. We would never betray her like that."

Perdita noted murmurs of agreement passing down the line of the Elders.

Aggie crossed her hands. "If we showed up there now with our tales tucked between our legs, we'd be slaughtered. They'd see us as weak and attempt to end us. The war has to be fought. We've sat back idly for too long. They've kidnapped Gayden children, or this Master person has. Besides, they tried Ora as a Gayden, and we weren't notified, as per our agreement in the treaty. They violated it first. The treaty is over. We are at war."

"I agree. The question is what do we do now? Obviously, your original idea of having Haven is a home base is out of question now. What's your plan?" Winslow gestured with one hand to the group.

Ora looked to the up and to the left. "The retreat got me thinking. I have control of the Bridge. It seems like we've underutilized its importance. I think now we have to strike back and strike back hard and fast. What I suggest is to separate into teams like we did before. We should open the Bridge at several points, but this time we attack using strategic areas. We get in, do as much damage as we can, and get out. The people of Conjuragic are already afraid. That much we found out during our time in the Haven. The city is basically at a standstill with most of the buildings in the process of being rebuilt. People are hiding out in their homelands. We can use that fear. We can increase it until they're too afraid to even blink."

"To what end?" Wade asked.

"In hopes that the High Council will offer *us* a peace treaty, and in response, we can ask for Master to be turned over to us. We discovered he is one of the High Council's main advisors. His name is Mathesar and a Naiad. In addition, we'll make them reinforce your original terms, and I suggest making it public to all of Conjuragic."

"What about our hostages?"

Sabrina stepped forward. "We have the majority of the Naiads. We can negotiate an exchange of the POWs. It seems very unlikely they'd kill the remaining hostages, but instead take them to the Nook."

Ora cocked her head to the side, her unmistakable move of figuring something out. Her body pivoted, and she looked right at Perdita. "You broke into the Nook undetected during my imprisonment. I never asked you how you did it."

All eyes turned to Perdita.

Sabrina raised one eyebrow. "You broke into the Nook?"

Perdita stood and joined the group feeling inappropriate for sitting while everyone stared at her. "Yes, I did. I wasn't able to rescue her, and I had Lailie the oxygenian's help, but I got in and out of the Nook undetected."

"How?" Steve asked.

Perdita could almost feel her mother's arms around her as she remembered the last night with her. The insufferable heat never wavered inside that volcanic mountain, but Perdita didn't mind when her mother held her close. It was dark with a single candle light illuminating the cave walls, her mother's face half hidden in shadow. Her mother's voice echoed through her memory. "My mother was a prisoner at the Nook. She was supposed to have been executed, but Master…"

"Mathesar," Ora interrupted.

Perdita blinked at her daughter.

"His name is Mathesar. He isn't anyone's Master here. Not anymore. Not ever again, and soon he won't be anyone's master. If it's the last thing I do."

Perdita cleared her throat. "Okay. Mathesar would steal prisoners who were supposed to be executed. He experimented on them and forced them to make Geminates."

Steve made a rolling motion with his hand. "We know this already!"

Perdita bit her tongue. "Yes, but my mother told me about a secret passage out of the Nook. Mathesar used that passage to sneak prisoners out. My mother remembered the location and told me. I used that same passageway to enter the Nook. I wouldn't have gotten far if I hadn't met Lailie. She helped me reach Ora's cell, but I couldn't get her out."

"How did you remain hidden?" Sabrina palms faced the ceiling.

"Partly Lailie scouting ahead and telling me which way to go, but the invisibility spell helped."

"Invisibility spell?" Almost everyone in the room said at the same time.

With a shrug, Perdita said, "Yeah. Invisibility spell." All faces wore identical looks of amazement.

Wade turned to face her. "You mean you knew how to make yourself invisible and in all this time you've never mentioned it? Never thought having an invisible army would come in handy?"

Actually, this hadn't occurred to her. "Why are you asking me? I can't be the only one who knows about invisibility spells."

"I'm from Conjuragic, a Protector, and I've never even heard of an invisibility spell except in theory. How did you learn of a spell of invisibility?"

This was news to Perdita. "Oh! I would've said something if I'd thought about it, but I hadn't realized no one else could do it. After Philo and I escaped from Mast—Mathesar, we'd planned to meet up with a seer in the human realm. My husband didn't make it, but I did. Her name is Aryiana. I stayed with her until Ora was born. She taught me a little magic, but we had to be careful to not let the Quads detect my magic at her place. When I set out with Ora at a few weeks old, she gave me a few spell books. I found the spell in one of those books."

"Where is the book now?" Aggie asked.

"At the Haven in my bag."

Everyone let out a collective sigh.

"Lost to the Severn Sea." Simeon shrugged.

"A lot of good that does us." Damien ran a hand through his dusty blond hair.

"I had years and years with that book. I'd study it at night. That spell was one of my favorites, because if a Quad ever came, I planned on using it to help Ora escape. I kept a small vial of it which I used when I tried to break into the Nook, but I also memorized it."

Winslow tapped a finger on the side of his chair. "Finally, some good news."

Mr. Corn Roll's walkie-talkie buzzed with static followed by a voice. "Pardon me, Elders. There's someone else here. One of those Healers. She says she has information about the wounded."

Winslow nodded his head and Mr. Corn Roll picked up the walking-talkie, pushed a button with a beep, and said, "Let her in."

Seconds later, Healer Roos stepped through one of the large double wooden doors. She faced the front, head held high, and walked up the aisle without a hint of hesitation. Despite being a short woman with long black hair graying in places, olive skin with a few fine wrinkles, and the dark brown eyes of the Spheres, she had years of experience, confidence in spades, and fierce passion. When she reached the front she bowed, a habit prominent in Conjuragic. "Excuse me for interrupting."

Aggie nodded. "Not at all. How bad is it?"

Her expression turned even more serious, lips set in a thin line. "We have separated the wounded into groups. Critical, minor, and those in between. We're extremely short on Healers so your human doctors are doing what they can. I cannot stay long as I have to get back and help. The worst are in surgery where I have instructed those Gayden with Sphere magic to help mend the tissues, but there simply aren't enough of us. We're doing the best we can, but there will be many who do not make it. Once the critical are taken care of we'll move on to the rest. The minor injuries are being tended to by your doctors. Those should be fine without Healer treatment."

"How long before the soldiers are back in action?" Sabrina asked.

"It all depends. I couldn't say. Those somewhat injured, I'd say a few days to a week. The minor ones later today or tomorrow."

"Thank you. Do what you can," Winslow said.

Healer Roos nodded. She pointed to Damien. "Stop by the hospital and get some blood."

"Yes, ma'am."

Her finger moved to Ora. "Get that cut fixed."

Ora dabbed at the cut above her eye.

Roos dipped her head to the Elders then spun on her heel.

Ora called out before the Healer stepped through the door, "Roos."

The Healer stopped, half in and out of the door. "Yes?"

"Don't waste time or resources on those who aren't likely to survive. We need numbers. The focus should be on those who aren't critical, but more than minor injuries. We need them operational."

A look passed across Roos's face; Perdita couldn't tell if it was respect or something different, but she nodded. "Yes, sir." Perdita recognized the conoctation of military leaders in Conjuragic despite their gender.

The door closed. Ora squeezed her eyes closed, fine tears clinging to her lashes. No one said anything to contradict Ora's orders. Perdita didn't envy her daughter, but out of everyone present, Ora would say what needed to be said. In war, hard decisions had to be made. Decisions on who lives and who dies, and no one else said it.

"Back to this invisibility spell." Aggie cleared her throat. "How easily can you teach it?"

The question bore some thinking about. The complex potion required certain ingredients that had to be harvested at the precise time of the year or hour in the day, but since Ora had learned from Fox how to manipulate the growth of plants, harvesting it shouldn't be an issue. The first time Perdita made the potion, it had taken half a year in order to gather all the ingredients. The potion itself took roughly two days of simmering, but she wasn't sure if it could be boiled in large patches to accommodate a whole army. In order to activate the spell, the caster had to drink the potion while chanting a spell to ignite it. If performed correctly, whoever drank the potion would have the ability to go invisible for up to four hours, off and on at will. That was another tricky aspect. One had to concentrate, keep themselves invisible, while also trying to do something else. When Ora was a baby, Perdita'd practiced on the small batch she'd made. She'd taught herself how to do it, but it hadn't been easy. "I'm not exactly sure. I'll need help from anyone with Sphere magic on gathering the appropriate ingredients, and those are hard to come by. If we get those, it has to simmer for a few days. The spell is made for an individual, maybe two or three at max. I'm not sure if it can be made in large quantities. After that, other than concentrating and chanting the right words, it's pretty simple. In theory anyway."

Wade pinched the bridge of his nose. "At this point, it doesn't seem like we can use this wide scale."

Sabrina leaned on an end aisle. "Right, but if we can pull it off, it can be used for small covert missions."

"I think right now we have to work on healing the injured. You made a hard call today Ora, but it needed to be said. Meanwhile, we need to set everyone else to disassembling the guns and oiling them down. The ammo will have to be discarded. If it was underwater for that long, it won't be salvagable," Winslow said.

Steve leaned in. "Since we're going ahead with this, I agree with the strike and move tactic. I think the first place we need to hit is the Willow. Our mission should be to take as many hostages as possible. If they don't have Sphere magic, then they can't heal either, and they won't have doctors as backup."

Perdita could see the validity in the thought, but Sabrina shook her head. "The Willow is a good idea, but that's not where they'll send the injured. They'll head to the Vindeca."

"What's that?" Ora asked.

"Our equivalent of a hospital," Simeon answered.

"Isn't attacking a hospital kind of like violating the Geneva Protocols?" Ora shifted, lips pursed, clearly uncomfortable with this idea. Perdita agreed, it seemed low, even in war.

"The Geneva Protocols don't apply since we're not human," Winslow said.

"If we do this, we can't go after the injured. It's wrong." Ora paced.

"We won't be going for a few days. We'll work out the details." Aggie stood from the chair, indicating the meeting had reached its end.

"If there isn't anything else, I suggest you all go back to your teams. Do what needs to be done and get some rest. We'll meet tomorrow." Winslow rose as well.

Without another word they filed out of the Town Hall. Ora, Sabrina, and Simeon headed back to the beach to check on things there. Damien still needed blood, so Jeremiah volunteered to go with him to the hospital and help out where he could. Perdita and Wade remained behind. When everyone else had gone, Perdita jumped. Wade stood beside the Town Hall, his fist flying on the wooden post of the entryway. *Bam. Bam. Bam.*

With each blow, he screamed in fury, leaving bloody smears on the post. Perdita ran to his side, pulling him away, but she couldn't hold him. He backed away, clutching his hands to the sides of his head, and bent over halfway and screamed, voice cracking at the end.

"It's okay." Perdita patted his shoulder, her words empty, but what else could she say?

"No, it's not."

"I know. You're right." He'd be upset that so many of his friends had died.

"He's gone. He's gone."

"I know. I know." Even though she had no idea who he was talking about.

"What am I going to do?"

She rubbed his back. "We're going to make it."

"You don't understand. Finch, he's my. We're—you know."

Ohhhhhh. She never would've guessed that. Wade and Finch, a couple!

Wade straightened up, wiped his nose between his thumb and first finger with a sniff, his knuckles bloody, leaving a streak on his nose. "We have to find him. No matter what."

She understood the implication. No matter if he was dead or alive. "We will."

He said nothing else before stalking off to be alone. Perdita didn't know what to do, but she called after him, "You'd better head to the clinic. Get that hand looked at."

He didn't look behind him but lifted one bloody hand in the air in acknowledgement. Perdita shook her head in disbelief at what she had learned and walked through the town, over the boardwalk, past the bungalows, to the beach. She spotted Ora and Sabrina deep in conversation. She caught the end of their conversation as she drew closer.

Ora pulled something out of her pocket. Perdita couldn't see what she held in her hand, but at the sight of it, Sabrina and Simeon jumped back.

Sabrina yelled, "I told you that was dangerous!"

Ora nodded. "I know, but I have an idea."

8

SABRINA

Despite Ora's protests, they would forge ahead with Sabrina's simple, but morally edgy and difficult, mission. It'd taken a few days to get everything prepared and reform their ranks bringing in some more Gayden who hadn't initially wanted to fight. Sabrina agreed with her concerns, but when an ingredient they needed for the invisibility potion couldn't be found, and the only known, readily available, supply was located in the Vindeca, they had no choice. If they had to break in the hospital, they may as well steal or destroy any potions there and take as many Healers as POWs as possible.

Ora didn't agree with the ethics of the situation, but the Elders deemed the risk to be worth the greater good. A dangerous perspective with an extremely slippery slope, but Sabrina would ensure her team followed the strict rules. No harming the sick or injured, no harming children, and no unnecessary damage. Sabrina hoped there wouldn't be any children there regardless, but Ora argued that by taking away the Healers, we might as well be killing them.

Sabrina had made her peace with this mission, but she had a hard time agreeing with splitting the army in thirds and launching three simultaneous attacks. Ora would be leading the campaign to the Nook in the attempt to rescue Finch, Arameus, and the other captives that survived the attack on the Haven. Sabrina with Jeremiah would be in charge of the

Into the Fire

attack on the Vindeca. Wade and Charlie would purge Conjuragic of more Spheres for healing by overtaking the Willow.

Sabrina shuddered while readying her pack thinking of the argument between Ora and Charlie two days prior. They'd been on the beach, discussing their separate missions, when Ora gave Charlie her assignment.

Charlie screamed, "What do you mean I'm not coming with you!"

Ora held up a hand. "Look, Charlie."

"Don't you 'look Charlie' me. Arameus is there. I'm going."

Ora shook her head. "That is precisely why *you're* not going." She planted her feet, crossing her arms across her chest, leaving no room for argument. "You won't be rational. You would risk all of us if it meant rescuing him."

"No, I wouldn't. That's not fair."

"Charlie, my answer is no."

"You're not my mother or my boss. I'm going, and you can't stop me."

"I'm in charge of the mission to the Nook, and I'm commanding you to go with Wade or stay behind."

"I never joined any army. I came because you *were* my best friend," Charlie's eyes shimmered with a faint tinge of purple, "and to get revenge for *my* brother. Who you seem to have forgotten for Mr. Muscleman over there." She flicked her head toward Damien. "Honestly, Ora, he tried to sacrifice himself to save you and your mother and then when you find out he's alive, you sit here and haven't even tried to find him. You don't deserve him! When you really love someone, you'd do anything to find them. Not toss him aside for the next male to show you the slightest bit of attention."

"Enough!" Ora raised her voice, finally.

"No, it's not enough! You'd choose this guy over my brother? A Nip," Damien flinched at the racial slur, "who worked for this Mathesar person, who held Sabrina's and my Arameus's powers until they almost died, and then he says, 'Oh, I'm sorry. I was brainwashed,' so you go jumping in the sack with him."

Ora's mouth dropped open. "What? He, I, we never."

Damien held up his hands, shaking them. "Whoa. Whoa. You got the wrong idea."

"Oh, give it up, Ora. Do you think we're all stupid? We see how you two look at each other. I'm done. I'm going to rescue Arameus, and then we're going to find John and get the hell out of here. I risked my life and my family's life for you, and this is how you repay me? How you repay John?"

"Charlie, don't..." Ora's voice trembled.

"I'm done. You stay away from me. You stay away from my brother. Now get out of my way." Charlie pushed past Ora, shoving her shoulder as she passed.

Wade, Damien, and Sabrina had witnessed the argument, and they'd looked away, not knowing what to say. Ora's shoulders moved up and down as she steadied herself. She spun and narrowed her eyes. Her irises, a cool amber, which always moved, had picked up speed. Sabrina had been around her long enough to know her magic neared the surface. Ora said through gritted teeth, "You're *not* going to the Nook. Do not make me tell you again!"

Charlie swiveled fast, in an attacking stance. "Screw you!" Her Tempest magic flared, flinging an icy blast of air toward Ora.

Ora didn't flinch or even blink. A slight sparkle of rainbow in her eyes gave her away, and even then, Sabrina knew what to look for. Ora's power swatted Charlie's away. Charlie screamed and threw her arms up, not using her training to not use her hands. A tornado loosed from her hands, spinning and picking up bits of dirt. With one long scream, Charlie set the tornado at Ora. It didn't even get close before it evaporated into nothing. Charlie looked to the sky, which turned dark as she pulled the clouds together. The clouds gathered faster until a flash of lightning left the sky, launching at eye blinking speed. Ora let the blast hit her, absorbing the energy.

Sabrina had never seen anything like that. Her mouth dropped. This didn't stop Charlie; it inflamed her more. Screaming like a child in a tantrum, her spells sped and flew haphazardly, not even getting close to Ora. Her anger decreased her control. Nothing she did could hit Ora.

Ora never made a move to hit her back. She deflected and absorbed spells. When Charlie tired, she fell to her knees, sobbing. Ora made no move but watched her best friend for a long time. As Charlie's crying slowed, Ora said, "You have two choices. You can leave now or help Wade in the Willow. If you stay, you'll obey my commands and those ranked above you. You're no longer a leader of the Healing team. If Arameus is rescued, the two of you may choose to leave. But you will not receive our protection after that. When we win the war, neither you nor Arameus will be included in our negotiations with the High Council. Essentially, you will be on your own. As to your brother, you know nothing. Never speak to me about him again. You have until tomorrow to decide."

Ora didn't wait for Charlie to respond but left the beach without another word. As far as Sabrina knew, the two best friends hadn't spoken since, but Charlie hadn't left either and showed up for Wade's debriefing. Ora had been firm and fair, but Sabrina worried that Ora too would be irrational. She might jeopardize herself or the mission to get Arameus for her friend.

"Okay, everyone in positions." Ora voice rang through the comm.

Sabrina gathered her pack and threw it over her shoulder. She pulled her Glock out of the holster, checked the safety and ammunition, and then holstered her weapon. The weapon still felt foreign in her hands. She preferred her own magic, but Protectors always knew to keep a good backup. Ora marched in front of the three teams and faced away from them. In front of her, a small circle formed, surrounded by rainbow that widened, expanding larger and larger until it fit the entire group. Through the comm Ora said, "Willow team at the front."

The troops ran forward, lining up. When Ora called again, Sabrina ran with her team, taking up their position behind the Willow team. Ora gave the next command and the Nook team pulled up the rear. Ora touched the comm at her ear again and said, "Let's go."

The Willow team took off at a trot. With a roar that Sabrina echoed, hand squeezed in a fist, held high in the air, the troops ran into the Bridge, and disappeared. Pitch blackness lay beyond it. Almost like stepping into a black hole. No matter how many times Sabrina traveled through the Bridge, it still freaked her out. On and on, the troops disappeared until her turn came. She took it at a run not second guessing herself. Once inside the Bridge, she clasped hands with person next to her so they wouldn't get lost. They jogged toward their target, each step difficult. Someone once told her it felt like walking through water, but being a Naiad, she'd never had that problem. She'd had to walk on the water or push the particles away from her legs, but inside the Bridge, she had no control. That belonged to Ora and Ora alone.

The signal to stop filtered from front to back. The Willow team had reached their destination. They'd exit soon. The Elders, along with the remaining leaders, decided to go back to where they'd retreated after the raid on the Haven. No one had detected the entire army's presence, so a third shouldn't go noticed.

Weird reports chimed through the comms. Thousands of birds scattered across the sky soared above the clearing in the Willow as if flying away from something. Other than the birds, the ground remained as empty as before and Wade decided to proceed. The army moved forward almost like a collective whole instead of individuals. Sabrina joined in as a part of that whole. When the last of the Willow team stepped out, Sabrina stood of the edge of the Bridge beside Ora and looked out. The Willow team swept the perimeter of the clearing and found no immediate threats. Wade turned an about face and gave Ora a salute. She returned it, and he spun, heading out to his mission. Sabrina noted Charlie beside him, and she hadn't looked back. Ora said nothing. Going into battle wasn't the time to bring it up their fight, but Sabrina felt like they should've made up in case something happened.

Overhead, thousands of birds had taken to the sky, darkening it, stretching far off in the distance. The sight of them unnerved her. She followed their direction and decided they must be coming from the Shadow Forest, the location of the Nook.

Sabrina relayed this information to Ora. "Be careful. I don't know what would cause them to flock like that." Ora nodded, then she said through the comm, "All right, we have to move. Let's go."

The Bridge closed, and they pushed forward. Less than a minute later, they arrived at the mission's location. Sabrina led the group holding on to Ora's hand. When the Bridge opened, nothing could have prepared Sabrina for what she saw. The reports they'd gotten about the destruction of the city paled in comparison to the sight of the great city of Conjuragic destroyed. Most of the buildings stood intact, but the bricks, wood, and siding were all broken or shattered. Some buildings collapsed while others were merely crumbling ruins of what they'd once had been. The light that had always shown, even in the dead of night, left an emptiness inside Sabrina. The protecting life force that flowed through the city was gone. It took her breath away. She didn't know how many people had died that day, and even though she wasn't directly responsible, she'd still helped Ora escape and helped her still. Deep down, she knew she'd done what she had to do. Her marriage to Simeon shouldn't be illegal. Their children, if they ever had any, should be allowed to live. Germinates could learn to control their powers. They were no more dangerous than anyone else, and children like Ora, well, they would be inevitable, but it would make their whole species stronger. Just as this great city had been united by all four cores, making it much more than the sum of its parts. The more they mixed, the more their species as a whole would be united. The next step in their evolution would begin with mixing the bloodlines. While she didn't want to admit it, Gayden deserve to live too. They deserved a voice on the Council, and they should not be put to death simply for being born. When they're discovered, they would need to learn to control their powers like witches and wizards, and as Sabrina had witnessed first-hand in the last couple of months, Gayden and wizards could work together.

Ora looked at her wrist. With a slight turn of her head, she said, "We're a go in three minutes."

Sabrina's heart skipped a beat. She touched her own ear. "Vindeca Team. On my mark." Her team hooted behind her.

She checked the holster of her Glock one more time and called her magic to the surface. She felt a deep sense of betrayal carrying a human weapon, but the journey into the future had speed bumps. "You good?" Sabrina asked.

Ora nodded. "Good as I'll ever be. You?"

"Same."

"You call me as soon as you need an extraction."

"I will. I hope my dad was right about the recreators."

"Me too."

Her dad had divulged travel in Conjuragic was limited to foot, horseback, or the Transport. Materialization, the recreator, and journey dust all used versions of the Veil. It gave them a huge advantage. Sabrina had the largest group of soldiers since the most damaged needed done at the Vindeca. The Willow team would provide a distraction. The two teams should leave the Nook virtually unprotected. The birds flocking from the direction of the Nook came back to her. It was too late to turn back now. Ora glanced at her watch again. "We're a go in twenty seconds. Ten. Five. Four. Three. Two. One. Go!"

Sabrina jumped, feet smacking hard on the ground, and sprinted forward to the front of the Vindeca. Behind her, the number of Gayden in Ember red Protector's uniforms pouring out of the Bridge reminded her of a swarm of red ants erupting from a giant anthill. Those with magic huddled in the center. Those without stayed at the periphery, holding automatic rifles, marching into battle. She rounded the corner and lost sight of them.

The front of the Vindeca shimmered with crystalline glass. Her magic rolled away from her, gathering water from the air, and slammed it forward. It zoomed toward the building like a bomb. *Boom!*

The glass exploded inward. Screams followed, and bodies ran for cover. She jumped through the remains of the door, glass crunching beneath her feet, as Gayden flooded in around her. Two guards ran forward, hands raised, and she froze the water beneath their feet. She rushed past them, using the butt of her Glock against their heads. With a thud, the guards slumped to the ground. They would live.

The hospital roared with flying spells, gunfire, and screams. She spotted her first Healer, a man dressed in white healer's robes. He screamed, high-pitched, squatting and using his arms for cover. Sabrina flung a sleeping potion hitting him in the side of his face. He fell to the floor.

She rushed past, seeing the Healer pulled toward the entrance. They had to find the lavster herb needed for the invisibility spell and gather the Healers.

"Level one, clear!" A voice she didn't recognize spoke through the comm.

She touched her ear. "Second level. Now."

The Vindeca had six levels with a stairwell on each corner. She wasn't sure where the lavster would be located. A thorough search would have to be completed. Along with a full sweep to gather the Healers. They'd knock the Healers unconscious and either move them by Tempest or Sphere magic, like Fox made for her when she'd been unconscious.

The team moved up each of the stairwells, bursting onto the second floor. A blast of Ember magic singed the side of her face as the door opened. She dodged it seconds before it scorched her skin. It hit the man behind her, and he exploded with a scream. She rolled forward, out of the stairwell. An Ember wearing hospital robes leaned against the assistant's desk. A patient, but a threat. Reaching inside, into his chest, she ripped the water out of the aorta. His chest exploded in a puff of red. He died, gurgling on his own blood. Healers and patients alike emerged from their rooms, spells flying. This wasn't going as she planned. Everyone had magic. They'd been stupid to assume the patients wouldn't fight back too.

The focus of the world disappeared into a fury of spells, explosions, and screams. She had no time to think. Not using her hands gave her the advantage. She had to look, and her spells left her. Faster than she thought possible, they'd secured the second level. Flying up the stairs to the next level, she couldn't stop to think about the series of dead bodies she'd left behind. They weren't supposed to hurt anyone unless they had to, but everyone fought back.

On the third floor, she heard the chorus of screams. "Nips!"

"Nips are here!"

"Run!"

"We need help! Call the Quads!"

Sabrina twisted, back up against the door, and peeked inside the room. She wouldn't be caught unaware a second time. She soaked a communicator in an assistant's hand, using the unorthodox training, she slowed the molecules of water, turning it to ice. She didn't have time to see if it was a man, woman, or child. The spell spread, freezing the body solid. Sabrina pivoted, preparing to send a spell toward another Healer, when the woman in white collapsed, whole body flailing. One of the Gayden took her magic. Her team cleared the main areas. Throwing open every door.

Cries of "No! Please! Don't! Help!" could be heard all around, individual voices lost.

The Gayden left patients cowering in their beds unharmed.

"Stay down!"

"Shut up!"

She didn't know who spoke. The chorus of voices added to the hysteria.

"Third floor clear."

Sabrina braced herself, heading for the nearest stairwell.

The fourth floor. The children's ward.

She followed a Gayden into the main area. Several Healers slumped unconscious. Most of the patients' rooms had already been searched. The children's floor was almost empty. *Thank god.* Tears ran down the children's cheeks. They cowered in the corner with several Healers surrounding them, putting themselves between them and the children. Sabrina almost lost her nerve right then and there. The sleeping spells flew out of her hand before she knew what happened.

The Healers' eyes rolled back as they sank to the floor. The terrified screams of the children escalated. They stared at her with wide, terrified eyes. She hated herself in that moment. Her power zoomed forward, creating a cascade of water between the Healers and the children. She shoved the water forward, like a solid mass, and the Healers rolled forward to land at her feet. She left them for the Gayden to take care of.

Her cascade of water fell into a large puddle. She reached the children, and a young red-headed boy who looked to be eight raised his hands to send a spell at her.

For the first time, fear flooded her. "Don't!" Sabrina yelled, wrapping her arms behind her back. "I won't hurt you. If you get in here," her head jerked into a patient room, "we won't harm you. I promise."

The children cowered in front of her. Their palpable fear rolled off them, and her own eyes swelled with tears. "Please. We're not here for you."

The Tempest boy put his hands down and said, "Come on." The children remained motionless. The boy grabbed a little Naiad girl's hand, helping her into a back room. The rest followed his lead and ran to get inside as if their lives depended on it. As the last of them entered the room, Sabrina said, "Shut this door and don't come out no matter what you hear." She shut the door, locking it. Squeezing her eyes closed, she prayed they'd remain hidden and safe.

Out of her comm, a man said, "Team Leader, we've found the supply closet."

"Where is it?"

"Fifth floor."

"I'm on my way." Most of her team had already left the fourth floor. *Two more to go.* She took the stairs two at a time and found a few Gayden remained fighting here. A waving hand caught her attention. A Gayden, who she thought was named Alton, stood in front of a large door, waving his toward her. Sabrina sprinted to the door.

"Is this it?" he asked.

He moved aside to let her inspect the room. This had to be the place. The room was easily thirty by ten foot filled with row after row of shelves. Each shelf held pre-made potions, medicines, and herbs. She leaned her head out of the door, calling four more Gayden to her side. She left Alton in charge of look out. She sent the others searching. They had a list from Healer Roos for things they could use. "If you find the lavster herb, tell me immediately."

"Yes, Lieutenant."

Her old rank being used threw her for a second, but she shook it off. "Now move!"

She flew down the farthest aisle. She found several bottles that Healer Roos wanted. She stopped for a few seconds, tossing them into her bag. Farther down, she found the anesthesia potion, filling her bag to almost max capacity. At the end, her comm went off. "I found it. It's in the second aisle from the left, halfway down."

She touched her ear. "Everyone finish your pass. Then get to the second aisle." She panted but dashed out from the end of the aisle. Her thighs burned from the effort. Sweat poured down her back, and her chest burned needing rest and several deep breaths. At the second aisle, she rounded the corner and found the others already there. They pulled the lavster from the shelf, divided it up, and shoved into their packs. When the last of it disappeared inside her bag, she said, "Let's go."

She hoped Ora had finished the Nook mission because they'd need extraction soon. She reached her hand to her to let Ora know when someone called through it first. "Quads! The Quads are here!"

"Shit!" Sabrina flipped the channel on her comm. "Yo, Big Red. I hope you're done, because Team Vindeca needs extraction. Now!"

Static answered her. "Shit! Shit! Shit!" Sabrina evacuated the fifth floor. *How the hell were they supposed to get down now?*

"Fifth floor clear." Another voice on the comm.

Sabrina spun and gave Alton a hand signal. He nodded his understanding, reached into a side pouch, and pulled the metal rings out of three grenades. He tossed them in the supply closet. He raced out of the room, slamming the door behind him, as they took cover under the large assistant's desk. Seconds later, a loud boom rocked the building. The sound roared in her ears leaving a high-pitched twinge.

Sabrina jumped from the crouched position. They took the last set of stairs two at a time. Her mind raced, trying to think of a way to escape if Ora didn't come. She smashed through the door with her left shoulder. Her breath caught in her throat on the sixth floor.

Leigh, her best friend and former Commander, stood feet from her, fighting a Gayden.

Every Gayden had two cores of magic by now. They had no more room to take more. The fight transformed into magic on magic. The world revved down to slow motion. Leigh's head turned, and their eyes met. It took a long time for Leigh's lips to form the words. "Sabrina?"

In her hesitation, Jabez Bizard sent his go-to tornado toward her. She saw it at the last second. With a flash of her eyes, a blast of water like a giant fist hit him in the gut. He bent forward with a thud, flying backward. The window behind him crashed, and he fell out into the sky with a scream. Sabrina had time for one thought: *What the hell was he doing back on the Quad?*

Leigh recovered her shock. She glared at Sabrina, their friendship gone. Now she saw her as an enemy and nothing more. The floor beneath Sabrina's feet quivered and shook. Leigh turned it into something like quicksand. With all the Healers taken, the Gayden had plenty of Sphere magic to counteract Leigh's. A Naiad Protector attempted to sweep them off their feet. Sabrina rolled her eyes. Her replacement moves were so predictable that Sabrina wanted to laugh.

A Gayden on her left, Alton, manipulated a hanging plant to her left, extending the branch. Before the replacement even got her spell formed, the branch flicked like a snake striking its prey. Her eyes went blank as she sank to the floor. Allyn and Leigh remained fighting. Her magic ability equaled Leigh's. She hoped the new technique of handless spells would tip the scale in her favor.

Static in Sabrina's ear interrupted her concentration. It was all the time that Allyn needed. A blast of flames roared to life at her feet. Ora screamed through the comm, "I'm here! Sabrina! I'm here!"

Using the flames as cover, Sabrina squatted. "We're on the top floor, but the Quads are everywhere. We're trapped."

"Be ready," Ora said.

"For what?" Sabrina asked, but she'd gone.

"Ughhhh!" Sabrina screamed, rolling around the fire before the smoke could get to her. Leigh and Allyn fought, their movements sleek, powerful, and beautiful like a dance, reminding her why they'd made Quad One. They trained for this all the time, their entire lives, whereas the Gayden had the last couple months. They couldn't be beat with magic.

Sabrina snatched the Glock out of the holster, her movements automatic and succinct. She pointed the gun at Leigh, surprising herself. Her best friend, her commander. Leigh pivoted to face Sabrina, her face full of betrayal. Sabrina's finger squeezed the trigger. The Glock recoiled against her hand. The bullet flew straight, hitting its mark. Leigh's body launched backward. At the same time, the side of the building exploded outward. Chunks of brick, iron, and glass rained down on the street below. Sabrina ducked in response. Ora stood half in and out of the Bridge where the wall used to be.

Sabrina couldn't believe her eyes. Ora moved the Bridge as if tilting it on its side. She figured out what Ora wanted them to do. "You've got to be freaking kidding me!"

She looked around at her team, the Healers either floated or lay suspended on gurneys. Allyn sprawled face down on the ground. Sabrina hadn't seen what happened to him. Understanding flooded her team's eyes. Those controlling the unconscious healers sent them falling downwards into the Bridge.

Alton gave her a half grin and said, "Oo-rah."

They had no other choice. Sabrina rolled her eyes. "Oo-rah!" She broke out into a sprint, her feet pounding on the floor beneath her. At the edge of the building, she jumped outward, clasping hands with those behind her. Sabrina fell at astonishing speed, soaring downward, past Ora, into the Bridge, and vanished.

9

CHARLIE

The squawking of birds flying overhead covered the sound of their footsteps. Charlie didn't know why the birds were there, but it worked in their favor. She didn't bother looking back at Ora when she entered the forest. She still seethed at being shipped off like an unwanted stepchild. Ora thinking that she'd do something rash infuriated her. She should be going to the Nook to find Arameus. Charlie knew if it had been the other way around, there was no way Ora would tell Arameus that he couldn't come. She huffed, thinking what she'd do once Arameus returned. Charlie would do everything she could to find her brother and convince them both to leave with her.

Ora had let the power go to her head. The Bridge closed, and the rest of the army vanished along with it. Wade jogged ahead, getting everyone into position, and pressed his comm. "All right, team. Everybody know the mission?"

As a whole the army gave a chorus of "Yeah" and "Uh huh" that echoed through the forest. Even the birds seem to squawk in agreement.

Wade said, "If you find the Council, subdue them, but under no circumstances are you to bring them harm. If they are found, notify me immediately."

"Yes, sir!" the troops said.

Wade worked his way to the front of the group. "Gather any of the lavster herb if you find it. Healer Roos needs it. Do not harm children or anyone else who doesn't try to harm you. Anyone who looks like a Healer, take them hostage."

"Yes, sir!"

Wade looked at his watch. Charlie mimicked his movement. It was time to go. Wade touched his ear again. "From here on out, we'll be working on radio silence." His hand fell to his side as he gripped his Benelli, checking the safety. Satisfied, he took off at a run.

Charlie followed suit, as did the others. For the next few minutes, Charlie focused on their heavy breathing, the pounding of their footsteps on the forest floor, and the caws of birds of overhead. Her pack bounced on her back with a *thunk, thunk, thunk*. Her own Benelli grew heavy in her hand, and soon her arms ached from the weight. The smell of gun oil wafted through the air from the fine sweat coating her palms. She liked the running. It cleared her head and made her forget about Arameus. She watched Wade's shoulders bounce as he ran. He held up one hand, balled in a fist. She repeated him, giving the universal sign to stop. She stopped, and the action mimicked backward. Wade pivoted his body, used his first two fingers to point to his eyes then to his left. She nodded, casting her gaze to the direction he pointed. The main living quarters of the Spheres lay mere feet ahead. They'd estimated about a quarter of a mile in.

When they went in, they'd have to be fast. The Spheres lived in the trees, hundreds of feet in the air. Their army would be seen from miles away. How they hadn't been spotted already surprised her.

Charlie figured out why. It looked as if almost every Sphere had left their homes and gathered in the central clearing. They mulled around in small groups, the twinges of their conversations reached her, even that far away. Most of their heads were raised to the sky at the birds. Those birds had hidden the sounds of their approach and gotten everyone out of their houses. Charlie wasn't sure if that was a good thing or not, but she'd take it. Perhaps the strange behavior of the birds would to draw the attention of the Quads here, rather than the Vindeca, or the Nook. Another nod in their favor.

Wade motioned with his finger pointing downward and moved it in a semi-circle back and forth. She nodded and passed the signal along. The team pulling up the rear, separated into groups, each going a different direction. They would position themselves around the main area of the Willow, then the main team would advance. After the Spheres focused their attention on them, the other teams would attack from the sides. Wade looked at his watch again. He held up his hand, palm forward with three fingers held up. Glancing at her watch, she confirmed three minutes until strike time. They'd go first, Sabrina's team five minutes later. She clicked her safety off and brought her magic to the ready. Her fingertips tingled as adrenaline flood her system. The fast cadence of her heart thumped in her ears. She panted, on the verge of hyperventilating, but she couldn't calm herself down. The last time she fought, she'd lost Arameus. If she couldn't rescue him herself, she'd do everything she could to distract the Quads so he could be rescued. That focused her attention. She almost screamed and ran forward then, jumping the gun by a minute. But no, she wouldn't do anything rash. She'd prove Ora wrong.

Wade held up his fist again, all fingers outward. One at a time, his fingers bent into his fist, counting down. Five. Four. Three. Two. One. Throwing his hand forward, he screamed, "Go! Go! Go!"

Charlie screamed, her face a mask of fury. *For Arameus!* She pulled the Tempest magic within her, unleashing it in a gust of wind that took down hundreds of Spheres like they'd been hit with a giant clothesline. Their bodies flew backward, smacking into their precious trees. Most flopped to the ground, either unconscious or dead. Triumph spread through her veins like a drug.

The surprise attack threw the Spheres off their game. Confusion ran rampant, and over half of them fled. Charlie's blast had taken out another third. This left a lot fewer standing in their way, but the rest braced for a fight.

The very forest turned against them. Trees bent forward in a great crackling, sending shards of bark raining down upon them. The branches swung downward like giant arms with sharp claws. One landed a direct hit on Charlie's shoulder, slicing it, sending her sprawling to the ground. Another smaller tree came up behind her. It tried to squish her like a bug with a root.

With a scream, Charlie rolled to the side, narrowly missing being crushed. She scrambled off the ground and forgot her training. She threw her arms in front of her and sent a blast of air at the bottom of the tree. It shot upward like a rocket.

A rose bush pelted thorns like bullets. They ripped through leaves and flesh alike. To her right, a cascade of fallen leaves rose from the ground like a giant blob. It rolled toward them, too fast to be believed. It rolled over and swallowed a Gayden in a frantic scream. The blob rolled away, the Gayden silenced. Icy fear sweat broke out on Charlie's brow. Before she could calm down, another blob rolled toward her, but she sent a gust of power. The blob exploded into millions of leaves that sailed away on the winds.

With the attack from the plants in the forest, the Spheres had been able to regroup. Charlie touched her comm. "Those with Tempest magic, prepare for an aerial strike on my count. Three. Two. One. Strike!"

Charlie's eyes lifted to the sky. Her new power reached upward, joining the others with Tempest magic, swarming together like a band of angry bees. The energy sizzled, and in seconds, the sky lit up in a series of lightning strikes. The forest lit up each time. Every hit landed like a small bomb going off. *Boom. Boom. Boom.* The lightning struck trees, the ground, bushes, and Spheres. Burning smoke filled the air mingling with the sounds of terrified screams and the stench of scorched flesh.

Charlie spotted several Healers kneeling by the wounded. Once the sleeping potions hit their faces, they fell to the ground. She slid a lifting spell underneath them and their bodies hovered unconscious. She moved them toward the rendezvous point. There she spied several others already there, unconscious, and floating. Gayden surrounded the bodies to protect them.

Chaos reigned in the forest. The Spheres gained on them. This was their homeland, where their powers were the strongest, and anything and everything could be a weapon. At that moment, one third of their team, once hidden, swarmed in from the sides taking them in a second surprise attack. Screams and gunfire filled the air. Terror threatened, but Charlie fought it back, knowing she had to keep fighting or die. She listened for the call they'd all been counting on. Through her comm someone shouted, "Quads coming up the main road!"

Charlie's spun to stare at the location the Quads should be coming from. The Quads rushed in, spells flying. With a quick estimate, she figured there were about a third of the Quads there should have been. Which could mean one thing—the Quads knew about the other attacks. *Arameus!*

Giving herself a moment to feel the icy hand of fear embrace her, she braced herself for the second round of attacks. Something dark blue caught her eye. She let her gaze shift for a second, and she couldn't believe her eyes. A brown-haired figure in dark blue robes slipped through the trees, retreating from the fight. She would've recognized her brother anywhere.

Before she could consider her actions, she sprinted toward him, deserting her team to find John. She raced past falling bodies and ducked spells. Her shoulder throbbed with each movement. John was less than three hundred yards away. "John!"

He didn't pause or even act like he'd heard anyone at all. She thought perhaps he didn't hear her, so she tried again. "John! It's me, Charlie!"

He stumbled over a branch and fell forward. He sprawled flat on the ground, face in the mud. She caught up with him. "John!"

He rolled over, scrambling to his feet, staring at her, disbelief dancing in his eyes. "Charlie?"

She reached his side. They'd ran well away from the others. She bent forward, placing her hands on her knees, panting. "John, you have to come with me. We've come here to rescue you."

His face screwed up in confusion. "Who has come here to rescue me?"

Uhh, was he always this stupid? "Ora, and her mom, and me. Come on! We have to go." She grabbed his arm, pulling him up, intending on heading back toward the Willow.

He jerked his hand away from hers. "No!"

She stared at him in surprise. "What do you mean no?"

He stuttered. "I have to find my—cat."

"What the hell do you mean you have to find your cat? It's a fucking cat. I'll get you another one when we get home. Come on, we have to go!"

"No, you don't understand." He looked desperate and near tears. She hadn't seen him cry since they were kids. Something didn't seem right. He looked the same. Short brown hair, muscular body in blue robes, marking him as a human, but his eyes were those of a stranger. Charlie couldn't put her finger on it, but this wasn't her brother. He wouldn't even look at her. He spun around, looking for this stupid cat. Eyes darting around like a field mouse, cowardly came to mind.

"John McCurry, I have almost died trying to save you. Ora has started a freaking war, and you're worried about a cat. What is the hell is the matter with you?"

When she said Ora's name first, he ignored her, but this second time, he finally met her eyes. His expression changed from some lost, pathetic puppy to pure loathing. "Don't say her name. She left me here."

"She thought you were dead. We all did."

"Lies! She tried to kill me."

"What are you talking about? No, she didn't! You jumped in front of Perdita to save her." Charlie couldn't believe her ears.

John shook his head, his lips pressed into a thin line. "Yeah, she cast the spell. She was trying to kill her mother too. All she wants is power. Charlie, you should come with me. She'll probably try to kill you too."

Something clicked in her head. "John, when was the last time you saw Ora?"

"The day she left and tried to kill an entire species." John's face had never been so convulsed by hatred.

"Who's been telling you all of this?" Charlie heard the sadness in her voice. She stared at her brother, who had become a complete stranger, an imitation wearing her brother's skin. *Could they do that?*

Through her comm, Wade's voice exploded, breaking the moment, "Willow Team. Retreat to the extraction point. We're going to have to fight our way out of here. The Bridge will open ASAP."

"It doesn't matter who has been telling me this. It's the truth." John twisted his body as if he wanted to leave, eyes still skimming the forest.

"It does matter because it isn't true. I've been with Ora and Perdita. They both told me you sacrificed yourself for Perdita. After Ora thought you died, she sent out the spell that destroyed the city."

"That's enough!" a woman said, strolling from behind John. She glared at Charlie with brown eyes as if she wanted to kill her where she stood. John spun at the sound of her voice. His expression reverted back to the sappy puppy dog.

"My love, what're you doing? Someone might see you." John rushed to the woman's side and tried to put his arms around her. She lifted a hand to stop him. She pulled her jet-black hair into a tight ponytail that tumbled over her shoulder. Her lean and supple body moved with grace and lithe, reminding Charlie of a dancer.

My love?

The woman stopped and put a hand on her hip. She wore an outfit very much like a Protector's, except hers was black. "Who is this?" she asked, her voice sultry and seductive, with a hint of menace.

Before Charlie could answer, John waved a hand toward her. "That's no one. Come on. Let's go before someone sees you. We can go back to the waterfall."

His words stung. *That's no one.* After everything that she'd been through, after all the tears and sadness over losing him, and that was what he had to say about her. After she threw him in Ora's face, possibly destroying her friendship, he'd dismissed her as if she meant nothing to him.

The woman in black didn't take her eyes off Charlie, but reached one hand upward and stroked John's cheek. "My pet. She isn't no one. Tell me who she is."

Charlie lifted her head higher. "I'm his sister." Her stomach rolled seeing the woman pet her brother like a dog.

"Indeed," the woman in black said, her head tilted to one side. "How exactly did you get here?"

"That's for me to know and you to worry about." Charlie raised her power close. She'd never hated anyone more in her entire life. This vile woman did something to John.

"Oh, don't worry. I will." Her evil eyes twinkled with challenge.

Against her new training, she took her eyes from the woman. She looked to her brother, voice dropping as if speaking to a small child, reassuring, protective. "John, I don't know what you're doing with this woman, but you don't belong here. Please come with me. You'll find out the truth with people who love you."

The hatred in John's eyes returned when he looked at Charlie. "She loves me. I belong to her."

The woman in black lifted her hands with the slightest of movements, but after training with the Gayden for months, Charlie recognized the malice in the move. She sidestepped a jet of flame that burst from the woman's hands. Charlie sent a blast of air at the woman and had the satisfaction of seeing the surprise on her face when she tried to take Charlie's magic but failed. "I'm not a Tempest, you bitch. You can't take anything from me."

John screamed, "Strega!"

He ran after the woman in black, who fell after a second blast threw her backward.

"John, come on!" Charlie screamed.

Wade's voice came out far away on the comm. "The extraction is in one minute. We have to be quick. Anyone not there will be left behind."

There was no time left. Charlie had to run. "John, please! Please come!"

But John knelt beside Strega. He pulled her into a seated position on the forest floor. Blood trickled from a cut on the right side of her forehead. John gushed over her, but again, she focused all her attention on

Charlie. She wiped away the blood with the back of her hand. "It seems I have already taken something away from you."

Charlie screamed, balled her hands in fists, and ran. *How could he be so stupid? So blind? How could he not see that she didn't love him? Was using him?* She ran. She ran and ran. The comm went off in her ear. "The Bridge is closing. Anyone not here has thirty seconds before it closes."

She ran faster, panting with the effort, thighs burning. She reached the clearing as Wade stepped into the closing Bridge. "Wait!"

Through the comm, Sabrina cried, "Yo, Big Red. I hope you're done because Team Vindeca needs extraction."

Charlie sprinted forward and went through the Bridge with a jump. Ora caught her arm while Wade grabbed her hand.

Ora said, "Head straight to the clinic. Go quickly so I can get to the Vindeca."

Charlie panted. "Ora, I have to tell you something."

Ora waved her off, pulling her deeper into the Bridge, closing it behind her. "Later, I have to get to the Vindeca. Wade, get there as fast as you can."

"Copy that," Wade answered, yanking Charlie forward.

Wade pulled Charlie forward, leaving Ora behind. Her mind raced with what she'd learned. Seconds later, the Bridge lightened, and Wade jumped out of the Bridge, Charlie stumbled on numb legs. They stood outside the Harbor Hospital. Doctors and Healers alike swarmed outside, taking care of the wounded. Perdita rushed to her side, face pale. "Charlie, come with me."

Charlie shook her head even as Perdita pulled her forward, leading her inside. "No. Look, I know I hurt my shoulder, but it can wait. You won't believe what's happened."

Inside the clinic, the screams took on a life of their own. The pain from the wounded echoed off the walls, and Charlie's stomach rolled with the noise. For a second, the room darkened at the edges, and she felt close to fainting. But Perdita pulled her along and said, "I want to warn you. It's not pretty."

"My shoulder will be fine."

"It's not your shoulder."

Charlie's mind raced with thoughts of John. Ora must have known, but how? That must have been why she hadn't gone to find him. Perdita's words finally caught meaning. "What are you talking about?"

Through the double doors, leading to the back of the hospital, the screams intensified. They stopped outside of one of the rooms, and the screams inside sounded somehow familiar. Charlie's gaze flew to Perdita's, questioning.

Perdita nodded her head once, her expression grave.

"Arameus?" Charlie threw open the door. Nothing could have prepared her for what she saw. Her hand flew to her mouth, and she gasped, "Oh, God."

10

ORA

The beach stretched far in the distance, devoid of life, deserted, like a ghost town. Waves from the Severn Sea crashed on the shore. The sea looked so different from the one on Gayden Island. Here the water flowed tranquil and so clear it could be drinking water. No bits of seaweed, cracked shells, or small crabs swept upon the shore. The sand rolled through my fingers as soft as a feather, as if each grain had been polished to round perfection. Despite the beauty, I preferred the pink sands of Feròs Zile. It felt as if I could almost see the ghosts of the prisoners being ushered out of the hidden cave.

I allowed myself these brief seconds of reflection before giving the command to head forward, Mom leading the way. I tried to imagine her here at night, casting the invisibility spell, hoping to rescue me. Lailie had to be on her mind. She met the oxygenian here who helped me escape from the Kassen. She had given her life for me, but for that sacrifice, her soul had been freed.

Mom had grown close to her, but I'd met her for a moment when I'd suffocated deep underground while she'd used my body as a puppet. I'd died and risen above, seeing Mom and John waiting for me, and again while they did CPR on my lifeless body.

Possessing me cost Lailie her life, if you could even call being made of air living. In the moment of her release, I saw her in her true form, a descendent of the first Gayden. She'd been a beautiful, happy woman, and with her final death, she'd found peace. Later, I'd told mom what I'd seen, but she must still miss her.

"This way." Mom motioned with her hand, pointing up ahead.

I followed behind her, praying for no mistakes. I couldn't take many more. Damien caught up and took up my flank. We couldn't meet each other eyes since Charlie's accusations. Her words still stung, but she wasn't completely wrong. I don't know if John really kissed Strega or if I'd been dreaming. Regardless, John remained in Conjuragic because of me. If anything happened to Charlie, it would be because of me. Sometimes I wish I would've died in the Kassen.

The guilt of everything raged inside me. So many people love me, who would've suffered if I died. I know it would've broken mom's heart, devastated Charlie, and Arameus would've blamed himself. But Mom and John, posing as tourists, could've returned home and been safe. Sabrina wouldn't have betrayed her kind, and everyone who has died or been hurt would be living their lives.

A touch at my elbow caught my attention. Damien gave me his half grin, one I hadn't seen in a while. "Don't worry. We're ready. We're going to find them."

I cast a sideways glance at Jeremiah. A young innocent boy taken from his family. If I'd died in the Kassen, Damien would still be a brainwashed slave working for Mathesar, and Jeremiah would either be a prisoner or dead. The Hunter he'd been given to would've likely killed him by now, like his twin brother, Gabe.

At least two positive things had happened during all this. I tried to think of all the people that would be helped in the future if we succeed. Gayden would be protected and have a voice in the magical world where they had every right to be. They weren't human, but their own kind of wizard. I told Finch that once, and he'd scoffed and lit another cigarette. "We're human, but we've developed our own kind of sickle cell trait, and the magicians are the malaria."

The cave entrance loomed ahead, dark and foreboding. Unpleasant thoughts of bears filled my mind.

Mom said, "We have a little bit of time. This entrance is covered by water when the tide changes."

"How often is that? Like twice a day?" I asked, looking back at the sea.

"There are two moons here. This isn't the human realm." Mom removed the pistol from her holster.

Mom looked about as natural as I did with a gun, which was not at all. The stalling ended. We had to get moving.

I touched the comm. "There will be Keepers, and I know of at least two types of magical creatures inside, so we have to be ready for anything." Taking my finger off the button, I asked, "You remember the way?"

Mom didn't have the most confident expression I'd ever seen as she shrugged. "Guess we're about to find out."

Not feeling reassured in the slightest, I followed as Mom led the way. The air changed from the salty breeze of the beach to damp and musky. With each step deeper, the temperature dropped by least ten degrees. About fifty feet inside, we put on our night vision goggles. I had no idea how the Elders had gotten access to military-grade supplies, but it made our lives a lot easier.

The cave sloped upward at a steep angle. The constant drip of the stalactites echoed and made the ground slippery. I almost tripped once, but a strong hand grabbed me. It must've been Damien, and the thought brought a smile to my lips. I sent my magic toward him, and his intertwined with mine. The act comforted me, like holding hands. If I hadn't been with John first, Damien would've been a perfect match. What other couple in history had been able to truly join like the two of us? *Stupid thoughts to be having before going into battle.*

But these days, danger remained a constant shadow looming over us all, and it wasn't coming for just me, but anyone and everyone I love. Charlie could die today, and she would die mad at me. I remembered Sabrina's words before the wedding. I had to find what happiness I could, when I could, even if it meant right before a battle.

We reached the entrance to the Nook. I looked down at my watch. As always when you need time on your side, it had the nasty habit of speeding up. We had to move. Now.

I reached out and grabbed Damien by the collar. I pulled him down and found his lips in the dark. I gave him one hard kiss while our magic intertwined. The kiss exploded through me, singing my nerves, and bringing me to life in a way I'd never been before. I pulled away as Mom unlocked the door and it swung open with a long creak. The deepest dungeons of the Nook stood empty. In one absurd moment, I had the urge to call out, "Honey I'm home."

"Let's go," Mom said and inched forward, gun and magic at the ready.

I hated letting my mom lead, but what else could I do? She knew the way. We trotted after her. I wished for a spell that would dampen our footsteps, because right now we sounded like a thundering herd pounding up the steps. I lost count of the number of stairs and turns we made. The nervousness grew with each step. We should've run into someone by now. This was too easy. Like they waited to ambush us around the next corner or up the next stairwell. Before each turn, Mom paused and flicked her head around the edge. She would give out a quick, "Clear," and we'd move farther.

"It's just up here," Mom whispered.

As soon as she spoke, the smell hit me, like month-old trash, sweat-laden gym socks, and an overfilled nursing home rank with old urine. Nausea hit me like a fist. If I'd eaten breakfast, it would've made a return. A slow pounding followed the smell. *Bam. Bam. Bam.* Footsteps of something huge and stinky.

Crap. Crap. Crap.

A Styx approached. Mom slowed almost to a halt, twisted, and put a finger to her lips. Couldn't help it, but that annoyed me. Perhaps because she was my mom, but I wasn't stupid or deaf. I knew to be quiet. She glared at me as if she knew my thoughts. I weighed the options. We might be able to knock out the Styx around the corner, but as soon the thought formed, more footsteps joined in and grew closer with each step. The smell intensified, and I had to pinch my nose.

We'd have to storm them, but I couldn't tell how close they were. With the ever-changing tunnels, they could be anywhere. I touched Mom's arm, and she shimmied to the side, allowing me to get in front. I peeked, and my heart stopped. Two large Styxs headed straight for us. They stood at least seven feet tall and three feet wide. Their thick skin and round bulbous noses reminded me of a potato.

Pain hit my eyes, blinding me. Squeezing my eyes together, tears spilling out of the sides, and I twisted around the corner. I yanked the goggles off my head. A large white spot floated in front of me blocking out anything else. The afterimage of the light source the Styxs had. At the same moment a cascade of urgent and aggressive human voices joined in the barrage of noise. The Styxs grunted in some weird language.

"What is it?" Damien whispered in my ear, where no one else could hear him but me.

"Light. Someone turned on a light." Light plus night vision goggles is not a good combination.

The overall tenor of the Styxs voices came across as worried, but it was hard to tell. The Styxs changed directions toward the magicians with a guttural scream. The cave floor shook, and a shower of dust fluttered on top of us. The aerosolized dirt tickled my throat. Blind, eyes watering, and trying my hardest not to cough wasn't how I envisioned this day going. A halo floated in the center of my vision but lessened with every blink. Thank goodness the Styxs went the other way. I'd have been useless in a fight.

"That was close. Something's going on, and I don't think it has anything to do with us," Mom said.

"Me too. Those were two Styxs. Why would they run after the magicians like that? Aren't they supposed to work here?" I rubbed the tears from my face, hoping they'd stop soon.

Damien asked, "How do you know they were Styxs?"

"Saw 'em before they blinded me."

"Didn't need to see them. You could tell from the smell," Mom said. "I heard a little of the Keepers' conversation before the Styxs went after them. One of them said, 'I can smell those traitorous beasts. They must be close.'"

"What does that mean?"

"I think the Styxs and the Keepers are fighting." Mom touched my elbow, and I slipped the night vision goggles in her pack.

My vision was almost back to normal. We'd gotten closer to the cells than I'd thought. Up ahead, torches lined the walls. I didn't know how far underground the Nook went, but from my descent during my own arrest, it felt like a long, long way down. "That's good for us. Yet another distraction. Let's go before someone else comes."

"Right." Mom took the turn. She went a few feet when she pulled the night vision goggles off her head, stowing them in her bag. We reached the corridor of the High Security cells. Mom stepped out of the way. Only a key or the merging of all cores could unlock these doors. If I'd known that when I was a prisoner, I could've walked right out of my cell. I touched the comm. "We've reached the cells. Be ready to move and fast. We don't know what kind of alarms are going to go off when these cells are opened."

I nodded once at Mom and Damien before running forward, magic ripping ahead of me. The locks on the cell's door wavered, sputtered, and failed.

As the lock faltered, the door vanished with a hiss. The sound took me back to my own days trapped in the cell. But this time, I was in control.

No one waited on the other side. No alarm sounded. With careful steps, I entered the corridor and wasted no time unlocking each door as I came to it. I didn't stop and turn around to check as the troops scoured the rooms in search of the prisoners.

Seconds after the last of the doors opened, the alarm went off. A loud, piercing sound, like a woman's screaming *Here, Here, Here*!

Yet more adrenaline pulsed through me, speeding my heart, and turning my fingertips numb. I'd expected the alarm long before now. I twisted to see the progress. Our prisoners had been beaten, tortured, and left to starve. Much as I'd been. All of their hair had been removed, and they wore dark black robes. From the closest room, I heard Finch say, "About damn time y'all got here."

Despite the danger of the situation, I smiled and shouted, "Keep your panties on, Outlaw."

"Damn, Big O, is that you?"

"The one and only."

Before he could respond, a series of loud explosions occurred somewhere in the upper levels. The corridors behind the cells collapsed. Chunks of stone fell from the wall in large crumbles. Several of the Gayden died screaming. Their cries stifled as the rocks buried them alive.

As the dust cleared, Finch pushed his way past the men. When he reached me, he leaned one arm against the wall. Bald was not his look. His usual Frenchy redneck accent made worse with his bottom lip swollen to double its usual size. A large, purple knot bulged from his right temple. "Hell, don't tell me that was our way out?"

I gave him a look that said he already knew it was. Dust and debris floated in the air. I pulled a towel from out of my pack, wrapping it around my mouth as others did the same. "How are our men?" I asked Steve, a Healer who came with us on the mission.

"Most have been hurt pretty badly. The rest are starved and dehydrated. We've got one patient who needs to get out of here. Now."

"We've got to get us all out of here. Any sign of Arameus?"

Steve's face fell, and I feared the worst. "He's not here?"

Steve shook his head and said, "He's here. But he's the worst. I don't know if he was tortured or if his injuries happened during the Haven attack, but he's teetering on the edge of death right now. If we don't get him back soon… well I don't know what'll happen. He might not even survive being moved."

My heart clenched in my chest, for Charlie, and for me as well. He was the reason I'd survived. The reason I made it this far. Charlie had been foolish to think that I wouldn't do everything in my power to save him, even if she wasn't in love with him. "Then there's no time to waste. Let's move."

The wailing of the alarm continued, like a pulsating heartbeat. It grated on every nerve and I wished it would shut off. On the positive side, it did mask any sounds we'd make. Unfortunately, it would mask anyone approaching as well.

I had no idea how to get out. The depth of the Nook was like a layered, enormous maze. I'd followed between Mark and Malandra with their flaming torches. But I'd always suspected they took different ways, in case I ever escaped. The Keepers had to know shortcuts. There had to be simpler and more direct way out. *Which way to go?*

Two large wrought iron doors at the end of the corridor locked us in. My power surged out of me, blasting the doors backward. The magic inside me twisted and felt along the walls in several directions. It detected dead ends down several paths. I pressed the comm. "Anyone with Sphere come to the front." I'd explain to them what to do. With more of us scouting this way we could get out faster.

We crawled along, hindered by the injured, but made steady progress. Something huge must be going on because several more large explosions sounded above us, each time rumbling the floor, increasing the dust.

"Damn, that one was close. What the hell is going on here? Is that us?" Finch stumbled into the wall.

"No. We think the Styx are fighting the Keepers."

"Why the hell would they do that?"

"Your guess is as good as mine, but at least they're not after us."

He took a pistol from a Healer, clicking off the safety. "Seems like we're headed straight for the action and your luck is running out."

As if he'd predicted the future. The smell of more Styxs hit my nose like a baseball bat. I recoiled from the stench. One popped out from a section of solid wall. Perhaps a hidden passage. He stared down at us with large brown eyes. Greasy hair fell across his forehead. He bared his teeth and screamed in a guttural voice, "It's the Quads! Get them!"

Huge roars answered his call, rattling the walls. Thunderous footsteps galloped toward us. The Protector's outfits worked against us. We looked like a group of Protectors. I didn't have time to stop and explain that to them. I screamed, "Attack!"

Jets of spells flew toward them, doing no damage, and ricocheted off them. They must be immune to magic somehow. I had no one or time to ask. They gained on us. The one in the front raised a club high in the air. With a scream, he swung. I ducked just in time. A Gayden who'd rushed behind me wasn't so lucky. His head exploded like a watermelon. Shards of brain and bone splashed against the wall with a sickening squishing sound.

I flung my magic into the ground before he could take another swing. His large size became his disadvantage in this small space. The stone beneath him came to life like little pebbles. It crawled up his feet and around his legs. I didn't stop there. My power melded with the wall, grabbing him, pulling him backward, cementing him to the wall. Those nearest me saw what I did and followed suit. The walls melted, gathering the other Styxs like quick sand. The one in the back faltered when he figured out what was happening, but it was too late. We encased the Styxs in the wall and hardened it around them. They couldn't move. I left their faces uncovered and room enough to breathe. I walked over to the nearest one's face, the one who'd taken a swing at my head. My anger rose to the surface. The power swirled in my eyes reflecting off a metal collar around his neck. "What the hell is going on here?"

He spat in my face. "You think I'd tell you anything?" His spit ran down my cheeks in thick, warm, and slimy rivulets. It carried the stench of him. My disgust rose so palpable that I almost encased him inside the stone like a tomb. Instead, I yanked the scarf from around my mouth and used it to clean my face. I threw it on the ground. "Why don't you open your big stupid eyes and pay attention! We're all wearing red except for me or black prisoner's robes. We're not the Quads."

The Styx inspected the group. He finally spotted a few of our prisoners in the black robes. The one who spat in my face expression changed and comprehension dawned in his eyes. "You're the Nips?" he said in more of a question than a statement.

Not bothering to correct him about the racial slur, I said, "You bet your ass we are. Now what the hell is going on here?"

His gaze faltered for a moment as if deciding whether or not to tell me. But the one on the end, the one that showed fear, shouted, "We're raiding the Nook."

The one in the middle attempted to turn toward the one in the back. "Shut your trap!"

I moved to the one in the end. He licked his lips, a nervous gesture.

"If you tell me what's going on, I promise I'm not going to hurt anybody. I'll let you go."

The third one's eyes shifted, but he couldn't see his companions. His eyes met mine again. "Like I said, we're raiding the Nook. The wizards are losing this war, so we're not going to stand by on the losing side."

I wasn't sure why, but this aggravated me, and I put my hand on my hip. "As long as they were winning, you'd stand by their side, but now you're leaving them because they're losing?"

"We've stood by them for decades, but our alliance with the wizards has always been shaky. Every time we strive for a position of power, we're denied. Instead, we're forced into lowly jobs of servitude. Guarding their prisoners, serving their food, or doing the heavy lifting."

This made me wonder how many other magical creatures had been oppressed by the magicians. Had we, inadvertently, not even considered another set of allies? "Would you show us the way out?"

The third Styx nodded once as much as he could. I moved to look at his companions and asked, "Would you two help as well if we let you out?"

The first one appeared to be the leader. He replied with his own question, "If we show you the way out, will you help us fight?"

I looked at my watch. The clock ticked forward. We didn't have much time. The other teams would have to be extracted and soon. "We'll do what we can. We're on a tight time schedule, and we have many injured that need a Healer."

The leader's eyed me as if wanting to know more, but I couldn't tell him. If something happened and I got captured, he could let others know our plans. The leader sighed and said, "We will lead you out if you will give us whatever help you can."

"You won't try and hurt us when we let you out?"

"No."

"Deal."

The magic surrounding the Styxs fell away and they ripped free from the wall. The wall also encased their smell. It almost knocked me over.

Finch waved a hand by his face. "Jesus! Ever heard of soap?"

The leader glanced behind him with a weird look on his face. Crap! Did Finch renege our deal by offending him? But he sniffed the air through his large bulbous nostrils, lifted his arm, and smelled his pits. Then he shrugged and led the way. I let out a breath I wasn't aware of holding. Mom elbowed Finch in the ribs, a reprimand, and he cringed, but waved her off. "What? You were thinking it too."

Once the Styx showed them the secret passage ways, the way out was simple. At the top of a long narrowing staircase, a chorus of screams, flashes of light, and ear splitting cracks greeted us. The floor rumbled. The battle that I'd been expecting the whole time was moments away.

"Go up the tubes," the lead Styx said.

"What the hell does that mean?" Finch yelled at the Styx back.

The tubes could mean only one thing. They'd led us to the processing room. Unlike the calm, cavernous place where I'd been taken right after being arrested, the hall exploded with activity. Bodies of both Keepers and Styxs clashed in battle. The blue lights from the cylindrical tubes shined brighter, giving the battle an incandescent glow. Before we threw ourselves into the processing room and the upcoming fight, I reached forward and grabbed the leader's arm, "Why exactly are you guys raiding the Nook? What could you possibly want?"

"They're holding one of our most important leaders. He's been rotting in this prison for many, many years. Those of us that are guards here are viewed as the lowest of the low in our home. Since there's been talk of rebelling, we decided to start it."

I thought it ironic that two rescue missions were going on at the same time. "Okay what's the plan?"

The leader bounced from one foot to the other, grinding his teeth, eyes bright with battle lust. "We're going to run to the left. Do you see there?" He pointed with a finger as thick as a two by four. "There are six transport pods grouped together." At that exact moment, through the fighting, one of those transport pods exploded into a thousand shards of glass. The Styx cocked his head to the side. "Okay, five transfer pods over there. We're going to fight our way to them and then up you go. Easy as that."

Damien pushed his way forward. "What's at the top?"

A valid question that I didn't want to ask. The Styx snarled as a female Styx hit the ground with a heavy thud. "There's a few guards at the top, but nothing you shouldn't be able to handle."

Mom, Damien, and I formed a little huddle. I said, "Okay, once we get there, we're going to send a small team up the tubes to secure the area. Once it's clear, we're going to send up the injured while the rest of us remain at the bottom to keep guard. Once they're all up there, then the rest of us go. Agreed?"

Damien and Mom nodded. I touched my ear, relaying a message to the troops. "How are our men?"

Healer Steve tipped his outstretched hand back and forth. "Some are circling the drain. We've got to get them somewhere where we can treat them."

I nodded to the Styx. "Let's move."

The three Styxs ran out of the cave. They formed a semi-circle, and as much as possible, they sheltered our injured soldiers behind them, using their own magical repellent as extra protection. We swarmed around them like one huge collection of angry bees.

The huge, football field-sized room hadn't changed much since my arrest, other than the battle ground reaching every corner of the place. The ceiling stretched hundreds of feet high, with hundreds of blue tubes extending from the floor to the ceiling, glowing with an iridescent blue light. The fighting raged all around us. The Styxs and Keepers fought each other. No one gave us more than a glance. The Styxs' roars echoed off the walls. Most of the Styxs carried great clubs, and others pummeled the Keepers with their fists. The Keepers screamed, either in pain, dying, or in rage, sending as many spells as possible flying in every direction. It ricocheted off their skins and reverberated around the walls.

I couldn't believe my eyes. Mark, the Keeper who broke my jaw, fought near one of the transport pods. The bastard had been content to let me starve. Now he was one of the last Keepers standing his ground against the Styxs. Spells bounced off him as if he were part Styx himself. Malandra sprawled at an odd angle a few feet from him. Her face pale with lifeless eyes staring. Her chest crushed as if she'd been trampled. Life was so unfair. It should've been Mark dead and not her.

A Styx finally spotted us. Like the others, she assumed we were Quads coming to stop them. She ran forward, club flying. With a scream, she jumped, swinging the club downward, racing straight for Damien. The leader of our group flung his club up to block her. The two clubs smashed together. The force splintered the other's club. The leader of our group growled something at her in their own tongue. It took a moment for comprehension to reach her eyes. With one long inspecting look, she rejoined the battle.

Mark tracked the female Styx. With a smile, he charged after her. "No!" I screamed and flung my magic into the ground. The stones rippled as my power burrowed underneath. As Mark raised his hands to attack, the ground exploded around him. In seconds, the ground encased him, dragging his flaying body into the stone, solidifying him in a tomb, still alive, but not for long. His own magic fought against mine, but I pushed harder, crushing him deep underground. His days of hurting people had reached an end.

Inching along, we reached the transport pods. I didn't know how they worked. "What do we do?"

"Who's going first?" the Styx asked.

The recon team made it to the front. He shoved the closest one through the glass tube. I may have failed to mention to the team that the tubes weren't solid, but more like a liquid mist you could walk right through. The pods could fit about three people a piece. We filled up the pods with about fifteen people. Once inside, one of the groups tried to talk, but we couldn't hear him. I shook my head, pointing to my ears. He lifted his hands I finally understood. I looked at the Styx. "How do they make it go?"

I'd remembered being inside them. There were no buttons or knobs or anything else. I stepped in and then exploded from the ground like a rocket.

"There are stones at the bottom. You step on them."

Of course! It worked like the stones I'd pushed inside my cell to get water and a bathroom. Something no one had bothered to tell me for three days while I almost starved to death. "Which button is the way out?"

The Styx looked at me as if I was stupid and said, "The one that says exit."

I touched my comm, hoping it would work through the tube. "Press the EXIT button on the floor." The man inside looked down, nodded in comprehension, and then pressed the button. With a whoosh, they soared into the air. The others stepped on the stone, shooting up. I touched the comm. "Did you make it up?"

A few seconds later, I received a jumbled static-filled signal.

We'd finally been spotted. The Keepers split. Some of them ran toward us, attacking, while the others stayed engaged in combat with the Styxs. "Defensive positions!" I screamed.

As always in battle, everything came down to the simplest of movements. A spell flew at my face. I dodged it, rolled to the side, coming up to fling my own counter spell. My target flew backward, eliminated. Next obstacle, a ball of flame zoomed at my feet. Seconds before it connected, I pulled the water from the air. The flame sizzled into extinction by a water shield. An explosion rattled the ground. A loud ringing dimmed the chorus of fighting. Shards of shrapnel whizzed through the air. Several pieces made contact with my arms and face. Adrenaline blocked the pain. My magic pulled inward healing me before expanding again. Out of my peripheral vision, another Keeper rose her hands to send a spell. I twisted, throwing a shard of ice underneath my arm. It struck her sending her flying backward, eyes wide in death. It's odd the things that stick out in battle—a small trickle of blood ran from the left side of her mouth.

Someone shouted through the comm, "Clear...," static, "... Ready... Clear..." I weaved through the soldiers fighting and touched Healer Steve on the shoulder. He squatted, healing the wounded as they fought.

I gave him the signal, and we formed a protective a circle around our injured soldiers. Over and over again, they went up in the tubes. The rest of us at the bottom did all we could to keep them safe. A stray spell went past us, and a woman in black robes screamed and died. The battle grew fiercer. We had to get out of there and fast.

The time came for the rest of us to move. We went in three by three while four or five Keepers still fought. The rest had either run or focused their attention back on the Styxs. Many of which had taken to protecting us.

I got in my tube with Mom and Damien and looked down. The little stone had the smallest print that read Exit. Three more soldiers to my left zoomed up the tube. The Styxs from the hallway each entered the last three tubes. I pressed the exit button and felt the familiar air blowing underneath my feet. My braid swirled upward, and my stomach went out from under me as we zoomed toward the ceiling. From the ground, a great ball of light flew toward us. I watched in horror, helpless, as the spell hit the tube to my right. The leader of the Styxs, the one who had done so much to help us, was blasted out of the transport tube. It collapsed in tiny pieces of glass as he fell the hundreds of feet back to the ground. We disappeared through the ceiling before he landed. I never even knew his name.

We emerged in what must be the entrance to the Nook. A large lobby area with a front desk made of solid black wood. Behind it, several Keepers littered the floor, either dead or unconscious. Gayden huddled by the twenty-foot-high wooden entrance doors helping the injured.

Damien, looking pale, bent in half, placing his hands on his knees, panting. "How do we get out? We can't go outside; the gas is out there."

The first time I'd seen the Nook, it'd looked on fire like Lucifer's personal getaway. I'd later learned in the Shadow Forest thousands and thousands of mushrooms grew. They released spores that caused fear-laden hallucinations. The Styxs live in the Shadow Forest and are immune to the spores. Unfortunately, we weren't.

I thought I might be able to open the Bridge large enough to get us all out here if everyone could fit in the lobby. Through my comm, Wade said, "Willow team ready for extraction."

Time's up. We had to go, but we promised the Styxs we'd help them. All we'd done was escape.

My magic extended, searching, but the Bridge wouldn't budge. "It won't open. Something's blocking my power!"

Finch hobbled to my side. "We're going to have to go outside. You go first and open the Bridge as wide as you can. We'll take it as a run and hope the fumes aren't too thick today."

Guilt pressed in on me. "We said we'd help them fight, but we haven't done anything." I waved a hand toward the two Styxs crouched in a corner.

Finch nodded. "You're right. Did you guys bring any gas masks?"

"A few."

"Fine. I'll stay along with anyone who is willing to fight. We'll stay here and give as much help to them as we can." He leaned toward me, whispering, "Perhaps they can take us to their leaders and we can make an official alliance."

I crossed my arms like an x. "You can't be the one to stay. We rescued you. I can't leave you behind again. You need medical attention."

Healer Steve left the wounded, waved a hand over Finch, going down his body. "I've done what I can, but overall, he isn't too bad."

Finch smirked, rolling his shoulders. "Thanks, doc." He turned away from the Healer whose lips pressed into a thin line at being called doc. "Come on, Big O, who do you think is the most troll-like of all of us?"

Wade chimed again through my comm. At the sound of his voice, Finch's face contorted. "You've got to go."

"I know." I threw myself forward, hugging him, pulled in so many different directions.

"Now don't go getting all weepy-eyed on me," Finch said, trying unsuccessfully to hide his own emotions.

I pulled back from him, still holding his shoulders. "I'll be back for you as soon as I can."

He gave me one curt nod. Damien tossed me a gas mask, and I pulled it over my face. Voice muffled, I said, "Give me a minute. I'm going to open it up right outside the doors."

Damien slipped on his own mask.

"What're you doing?" I asked.

"I got a Tempest Keeper. I'm going to blow the spores away from the door. Cut back on the risk."

We trotted over to the doors as Wade called again for extraction. I touched my comm and said, "Be there in three minutes." *I hope.*

I spun, pulled the mask off for a second. "Healer Steve, you take the lead. Head straight for the clinic."

He gave me a thumbs up. I yanked down the mask and opened the doors a crack. We slipped out, and I yelled, "Crap." The forest outside rumbled with no less than a hundred Styxs running toward the doors, clubs held high. I estimated we had less than a minute before they reached us. I opened the Bridge, wide, threw open the doors, and waved at the soldiers. "No time. Move now! Now! Now!"

The soldiers led by Healer Steve ran through the doors, the injured either immobilized by spells or carried. They disappeared one by one as the pounding of the Styxs' stampede grew closer. The birds abandoned the forest by the thousands, scattering from the onslaught. I had a feeling that pretty soon the castle really would be on fire. No spore induced hallucination required. When the last of us stepped through the Bridge, I ripped off my mask, threw it back inside for the others. Damien went first, and I clasped his hand. My last thought before closing the Bridge was hoping Finch was as troll-like as he appeared.

11

PERDITA

The hospital came to life as soon as the Bridge opened. Perdita wasted no time in helping the wounded. She assisted them onto gurneys and wheeled them inside, giving them over to the care of the doctors and Healers.

One doctor wore a long white lab coat, a stethoscope around his neck, with gray hair and lines around his light blue eyes. He asked, "Why are the women bald?"

Perdita answered, "Hair length is a mark of stature in Conjuragic."

The doctor nodded and disappeared behind the double doors. Once everyone made it out, Perdita searched for Ora. She found her at the edge of the Bridge, about to step inside. She shouted her name and ran to Ora's side before she could leave. Perdita threw her arms around her, not able to let her go without holding her, for one moment. There had been so much loss, and with every mission each time she returned unharmed, Perdita consider it a miracle.

"I'm okay, Mom."

"I know you are, baby girl. But I'm not."

Ora pulled back, face blanching, looking her up and down.

Perdita shook her head. "No. No, I'm not injured. This is so...overwhelming."

Relief filled Ora's expression, and her shoulders relaxed. "I know what you mean. I got to go. The other teams need to get out of there."

Perdita reluctantly let go. "Be careful."

"I will."

Ora stepped into the black void. Something shimmered around Ora that left a wavering scent of cinnamon and butter. Perdita saw the figure of a man for one brief second. The sight of him shocked her to her very core. He had the same red hair, the same amber eyes. But it couldn't be. With that thought, the Bridge closed, taking her Ora with it.

These days the hospital screaming, injured people filled every room. She entered the building seeking one face in particular. She ran from room to room, patient to patient. *Where was Arameus?* During the mission, Perdita hadn't seen him, but the doctor's question came back to her about the hair length. No wonder she couldn't find him. His flaming red hair would be grown long. Instead, she searched her memory of the injured. Had she seen him? Her hand flew to her mouth. He'd been in the first room, but that couldn't possibly be him. Something was very, very wrong. She backtracked her steps and found him.

Dirt and grime covered him from head to toe. The long hair tangled in a ratty mess with splatters of mud. He wore black robes stained with blood and dirt, sleeveless on the left side, marking him as a prisoner. The number of cuts and bruises left his face barely recognizable. His nose bent at an odd angle, and one eye was swollen shut.

The sight of the infected, mangled remains of his left leg brought bile to the back of her throat. An angry red and black wound extended the length of his foot to just above the knee. A mixture of smells resembling rotting meat and soured eggs poured off the wound. Sweat glistened over his face, chest, and arms, and heat radiated off him. Perdita sensed it even from the doorway.

"Here! Here! This man needs medical attention and now." Perdita stepped from the doorway, waving her arms around, but no one came as if the world had gone deaf. All the patients needed medical attention. Ora's commands came back to her from before. Those prisoners that could be saved easily would go first. Those who had worse injuries, like Arameus, would have to wait. If they survived, then they would be attended to. They left him there because he may not survive.

Perdita couldn't let him die. He'd always done anything and everything he could to help her daughter. He saved Perdita's life. They owed him this. She ran, grabbing each doctor she saw, and they rushed away from her. Each waving her off and dashing away to attend other patients. The

Healers did much the same. Healer Roos emerged from a room, calling out orders to her attendants.

Perdita grabbed her elbow. "It's Arameus. He has to be helped. Please, you have to try to save him."

Healer Roos stared at her with pity in her eyes, as if she wasn't going to help. That look put a spark in Perdita. She would have none of her pity. "Ora wouldn't stand for this."

The Healer sighed. "Fine. Let's go."

The Healer waved two hands motioning for three attendants to come with her. The Healer assessed Arameus, the expression on her face grave, shaking her head. Perdita feared the worst. Healer Roos stared at her again with pity. Perdita lowered her eyes, shaking her head, refusing to believe it. "You have to try."

The Healer looked around at her assistants as if asking if they had any ideas. The doctor who spoke to Perdita when they first emerged from the Bridge walked past the room. Something drew his attention, and he walked in. "Can I be of some assistance?"

Healer Roos filled him in. Perdita didn't really know how a Healer and a doctor could communicate as their approaches to treating patients were vastly different, but somehow, they understood each other. "I'm a surgeon. A trauma surgeon. I might be able to help. Perhaps with the two of us working together, we can save him."

"The infection is very advanced. I can spare a little potion." She didn't have to say that she didn't want to waste it on a lost cause.

The doctor shook his head. "We can put him on antibiotics. See what happens. Once we get him to the OR, I can go in and debride the wound, and you do your best to heal any salvageable tissue behind me."

The Healer looked at Arameus, calculating. "I don't know if he'll survive the move again to get him to the operating room."

Perdita glanced at the doctor's name tag, it read Stanley Jones, MD. Dr. Jones eyes flicked back and forth as he thought through the problem. "He's pretty much out of it. We can do the procedure here, but it won't be pretty. But it's his only chance."

Healer Roos stared at Arameus, assessing the situation as well. She looked at Perdita and asked, "Are you sure this one is worth the resources?"

"Absolutely."

Healer Roos fixed Dr. Jones with a grim stare and said, "Okay, let's do this."

Dr. Jones left the room with his coattails flying. He emerged a few minutes later with a group of nurses. Within seconds, they started an IV in both arms, running fluids at full speed, added the IV bags of antibiotics. Another team stripped Arameus of his robes, cutting them off him, covering him with the blue sheet, exposing the ragged remains of his left leg. Being completely uncovered, the sight was even worse than what she'd originally thought. The bottom half of his leg hung on by a thread of bone at the shin. The flesh was torn away at different angles, and the smell intensified. Arameus moaned in pain but never opened his eyes. The doctor covered his leg with an orange liquid, iodine Perdita guessed, then tied a tourniquet around the upper part of his leg.

Healer Roos said, "My Healers can decrease the blood flow to a minimum. You won't need that."

Dr. Jones looked at his work, nodded, and removed the tourniquet. They brought in two boards that attached to the bed. The nurses tied Arameus's arms down at the wrist then strapped another band around his chest and waist.

Perdita asked, "What's that for?"

Dr. Jones said, "I doubt he'll feel anything, but at least this way he won't move."

Healer Roos gathered her own team. She placed herself at the head at the bed. She instructed a Tempest to help maintain his air supply, the Naiad to keep the blood flow to a minimum, and an Ember to do cauterization if needed.

Dr. Jones stepped away to scrub. The IVs hummed as fluid trickled through the clear tubing. Dr. Jones already wearing a mask over his mouth, eye shield, medical gown and boots, put on two pairs of sterile gloves.

In the meantime, another group whose name tags labeled them as surgical techs, prepared medical instruments. They brought in trays and trays of various metal pliers and pincers and scissors and knives. The sight overwhelmed Perdita and she felt a wave of lightheadedness. Another woman dressed in the same gown as the doctor stood opposite him. They faced each other over the bed. Healer Roos moved to the bottom to control the tissue regeneration using Sphere magic. Dr. Jones looked at her and asked, "Are we ready?"

She nodded, and Dr. Jones picked up a scalpel. Shouts erupted from the hallway and Perdita leaned her head out to find out what was going on. The Willow team had returned. Charlie must be here. Perdita excused herself and went looking for her.

She knew she had to get Charlie and let her know what was going on before the child found out on her own, and Perdita didn't mind having an excuse to step away from the surgery. Blood and guts weren't her forte.

Ora stood at the edge of the open Bridge, urging people out and fast. Perdita did a quick assessment and couldn't detect any injuries to Ora, but every gesture and movement she made screamed agitation and impatience. Something must be wrong.

Perdita ran to the edge of the Bridge and extended her hand. Soldier after soldier jumped out. Ora looked at her watch. She must need to get back to get Sabrina's team, and time was running out. It took forever as one by one they emerged. She caught sight of Wade and wanted to let him know about Finch, but there wasn't time. Charlie stumbled out last. Instead of jumping, she stopped, grabbing onto Ora. Her mouth moved, but the words were lost inside the Bridge.

Ora pushed Charlie with a gentle shove. "Tell me later. I've got to get back to Sabrina."

For one brief moment, Perdita saw the man again. This time their eyes connected, and he smiled and disappeared with Ora. She'd seen him twice. It couldn't be a coincidence.

Perdita wrapped an arm around Charlie. "You have to come with me."

Charlie resisted, trying to tell her something, but it didn't matter right now. Whatever she had to say could wait. She needed to be by Arameus's side. As they drew closer, the screams coming from the room were some of the most horrible sounds that Perdita had ever heard. He must've woken up.

Dr. Jones shouted, "More morphine!"

Comprehension darkened Charlie's face. "Who's in the room?" By the look on her face, Perdita guessed she already knew.

They took the last steps and stood in the doorway of Arameus's room. Charlie let go of Perdita's hand, her own flying to her mouth. "Oh, God."

Perdita completely agreed. Arameus had indeed awoken and now screamed in agony. He fought, spittle flying, wild to get free from the restraints. Healer Roos and Dr. Jones ignored him and kept going. The pain wouldn't end if they halted, so they plowed ahead, hurrying to get the ghastly deed done.

Arameus's leg had a fresh cut, encircling his leg just below his knee, trickling a slow amount of blood. Dr. Jones held up a saw and turned it on. With a great screeching sound, he drew the saw closer to the exposed bone of Arameus's leg. Arameus screamed and struggled, eyes wide. Perdita didn't think he could scream any louder, but when the saw passed through his flesh, he did. A nurse rushed by, bumping them out of her way. She ran to the IV pole and injected medicine. Perdita had never been more thankful for pain medicine in her entire life. Arameus's screams faded into quiet. His movements stopped and eyes fluttered closed. Perdita said a silent prayer. He fell unconscious. Healer Roos shook her head and said, "Your pain medicines really need some work."

"Agreed."

Perdita could barely hear them over the sound of the saw. The saw clicked off, and the room quieted. Dr. Jones picked up what remained of Arameus's leg and dropped it into a metal bucket on the side of the bed. With the squish and rumble of the leg hitting the bucket, Charlie swayed, nearly fainting. Her skin paled with a greenish hue. Perdita reached out and grabbed Charlie around the waist before she hit the ground. She eased her into a seat and tilted her head down, putting it between her knees. By the time Perdita looked up, Dr. Jones had stepped back, and Healer Roos had taken over. The tissue of the stump gathered around itself. The nerves curled inward, and the skin wrapped around like a living blanket and sealed at the edges. There would be no gross flap left of what remained.

The doctor and the Healer stepped back from Arameus, examining their work. The doctor said, "Looks good. Great job, Doctor."

"I'm not a doctor."

The doctor pulled his mask down and smiled, "My apologies. Great job, Healer."

Healer Roos pulled off the blue gloves, tossing them to the floor amidst the enormous pile of collected bloody trash. "Not bad yourself."

The surgical techs gathered the medical instruments while the nurses took down and threw away all the blue sheets. The doctor stripped out of his medical gown, leaving the boots.

"Now what?" Perdita asked.

Healer Roos shrugged. "Now we wait and see if the human antibiotics work."

"Will he get a fake leg, or need physical therapy, or what?" Charlie asked

"We should see if he makes it first," Healer Roos said, before leaving. "I'll be back in a few minutes."

Dr. Jones shook their hands. "Thank you."

Perdita dipped her head, grateful. "No, thank you. I don't know if we would've convinced her to help him without you."

The doctor smiled. "I was in the right place at the right time. I hope it was enough. Please excuse me, I'm going to see if I can attend to some of the other patients."

Perdita nodded and moved to the side so he could leave.

Nurses swarmed Arameus, like busy bees attending to various flowers. They cleaned him from head to toe. Afterward, they put him in a fresh gown with clean, warm blankets. Healer Roos returned and lifted her hands over his body running it up and down. One of the attendants trimmed his hair to the previous length.

"What're you doing?" Perdita asked, curious.

The Healer smiled. "I'm assessing for any internal damage or other injuries we might've missed." She lifted her hands again and ran them over him one more time. This time, the bruising and swelling on his face retreated. "Now he has to fight the infection. Since we had to use the human antibiotics, I'm not sure what the effects will be. Hopefully the Vindeca team will bring back some of our own medicines."

The Healer lifted a hand over Charlie, and the cut on her shoulder pulled together. Afterward there wasn't even a mark on Charlie, as if it had never been. Roos smiled at her work and left once more. Perdita checked on Charlie. She'd sat up, no longer looking close to fainting, but remained pale. Tiny spots of blood remained on her arm from her injuries, and dirt covered her like a fine blanket. Perdita touched Charlie's elbow, easing her into a standing position. "Come on, child. There's nothing more you can do for him. We have to give the antibiotics time to work, and after all the pain medicine, he'll be asleep for a while. We need to make sure you get something to eat and some sleep. We can get you cleaned up."

Charlie stared at Arameus, shaking her head as a tear trickled out of her left eye. "I can't. I can't leave him."

"You won't do him any good unless you take care of yourself."

"But what if he wakes up and I'm not here?"

"You can go take a shower and eat. He knows you love him. Arameus is a good man. He would want you to make sure you're taken care of. He wouldn't be angry at that. He would understand."

"But what if I can't live with myself? What if he wakes up one more time and I'm not there?" Her bottom lip quivered as another two tears spilled down and she wiped them away with the back of her hand.

Perdita sighed. This was too much to deal with. She never would've wished this for Charlie or Ora or even Sabrina, yet she couldn't do anything about it except be there for them. "Okay, there's a bathroom right through that door. You can go in there and take your shower. I'll have an assistant come in here with him, and in the meantime, I'll go get you some clean clothes and some food. That way if he wakes up, they can get you, but you're still taking care of yourself. You can sleep here. We'll get you a cot." That satisfied her because she took a few shuffling steps toward the bathroom on shaky feet. Perdita pressed the call button asking for an attendant and also some clean towels. She helped Charlie into the bathroom and turned on the water for her.

Charlie needed directing, like a small child, lost and unsure of what to do. Perdita helped her get out of the Protector's leathers and into the shower. The attendant, a young pretty brunette looking as overwhelmed as Perdita felt, stood inside the room. She handed Perdita the clean towels.

"Thank you." Perdita left the towels in the bathroom for Charlie.

To the attendant, Perdita said, "He should be fine, but sit with him until Charlie's done or I get back. Okay?"

The girl nodded and took Charlie's vacated seat. Perdita left in search of new clothes and a hot meal.

Perdita found some clean scrubs, but it didn't look as if any of them would be getting a hot meal anytime soon. The best she could come up with was a cold turkey sandwich wrapped up in cellophane, along with a bag of chips and a soft drink. She carried everything back to Arameus's room. His condition remained unchanged, sleeping and breathing heavy. Perdita said to the attendant, "You may go."

She hurried out the door, eager to get to the next task. Perdita went to the bathroom door and knocked with three quick taps. She opened the door at the same time Charlie turned off the water. She laid the clothes on the back of the commode for her and went back to the room, laying out four brown paper bags holding the sandwiches. A few minutes later, Charlie opened the bathroom door. Her hair dripped in a small steady stream off her shoulders. Large dark circles remained under eyes, and she had a haunted look about her. Charlie flopped down in the chair, staring straight ahead.

"Eat, child."

Charlie's head dipped. She leaned forward, picked up one of the brown paper bags, opened it, and pulled out her sandwich. The cellophane creaked as she unwrapped it. She put it to her mouth, bit, and chewed. Her movements were robotic, eating because she had to, taking no enjoyment. Perdita would've felt the same way. It didn't help that the sandwich looked as dry as sand.

For the third time that day, another commotion occurred outside the hospital. The Vindeca team must've returned. Perdita poked her head out of the door but couldn't see anything. "I'll be right back. Will you be okay?" she asked.

Charlie nodded, not looking at her, her sole focus on Arameus. Perdita grabbed the brown bags and left her, going in search of Ora. She hugged the brown paper bags close to her body, intending to make Ora eat before she did anything else. The Bridge closed as Perdita stepped out of the hospital, not giving Perdita the chance to look at the man again. She couldn't wait to tell Ora.

Ora chatted with Sabrina and Wade. Guilt wiggled in her belly. She'd brought three sandwiches instead of four. She'd give hers to Wade. She extended a bag to him first, but he waved her off. "You need to eat," Perdita said, feeling very much like a mother.

Ignoring her, Sabrina punched Ora in the arm, the movement playful. "I can't believe you made me jump out of a building!"

Ora smiled, the first Perdita had seen all day. "What's the problem? You had to jump like twenty feet into the Bridge. There's no way you could've missed it."

"You could have gotten us closer so we could have stepped in the Bridge."

"I could have, but what fun would that have been?"

Wade cleared his throat. "Did you find Finch?" The concern laced the very timber of his voice. Perdita touched his arm. "I'm sorry. I should've found you sooner. He's okay. He stayed back at the Nook with a small group to help the Styxs. They're raiding the Nook."

Relief ran across his face before he furrowed his brow. "The sticks?"

Ora leaned her head to the side. "Trolls."

Wade's eyebrows lifted into his hairline. The sight was almost comical.

Ora gaze moved between the three of them. "I want to leave in a few minutes. Half hour at most. We need to gather as many people as we can who are still willing to fight and get back to the Nook to help them."

Sabrina nodded, touching her ear. "Calling any and all available troops to the Harbor Hospital for another mission."

"Absolutely not." Perdita waved the brown bags around. They all stared at her in disbelief, but she would hear none of it. "Now look, I know Ora has to open the Bridge and help someone get across, but why does it have to be you all that goes? You're going in, picking them up, and coming back." Even with her own ears the arguments sounded stupid. Nothing was ever as simple as going to Conjuragic, having the troops stroll right in, and return home. Plus, Finch stayed to fulfill the deal they made with the Styxs and to form an alliance. If he was successful, Ora needed to be there, as well as the heads of the different units. But, dang it, Ora had already risked herself so much, and she hadn't eaten or slept in hours. Dark circles rimmed her daughter's eyes, and she looked as if she might fall over at any minute. The Bridge zapped her of so much energy. The mother in her raged at letting her go, but war didn't stop because the leaders needed to eat and sleep. There was a reason why mothers weren't allowed to go into battle with their children.

Ora opened her mouth to argue, but Perdita held up her hand. "Just don't. I know you have to go. All of you do and so do I."

Ora shook her head. "You should stay here."

"No. If you get a change to meet with the Styxs, you need representatives from each of your groups and a geminate." Perdita bent her head upward, stretching her neck and rubbing it. *There is no rest for the wary.*

"She's right you know," Sabrina cocked one hip, "but it's a good idea not to take all of the leaders in case it is a trap, and you'll need bodyguards."

Wade said, "Definitely."

"Why?"

"Because, O, if something happens to you, the Bridge doesn't work. We'd be trapped there and handed over to the Quads."

"We wouldn't even have the ability to continue the fight if the Bridge is sealed and the Veil closed." Wade shifted the MK47 on his shoulder.

The comms chattered in the background, muffled by the sounds of waves crashing in the distance. A siren wailed from an approaching ambulance. The four of them moved out of the way to give it room. *What now?* Perdita wondered.

The back doors of the ambulance opened. One of the medics jumped out of the rig. The young man in his early twenties with short brown hair in a blue shirt and black pants ignored them. Various IDs and badges on his shirt reflected off the afternoon sun. A team of doctors and nurses raced out of the hospital, pulling on gloves. The medic said, "Seventy-eight-year-old man with history of hypertension, hyperlipidemia, diabetes, and gout. He reported having chest pains this morning radiating to his jaw and diaphoresis. His wife called 911. His BP is 180/110, pulse 98, O2 sats 98%, and EKG shows ST elevation in the lateral leads."

The doctor nodded as the EMTs wheeled an old man off the rig. The nurses and doctors swarmed around him and rolled him inside. Perdita heard the doctor shout, "Right! We have an acute STEMI. Page the cardio and the cath lab. We need to get him in there *stat*." The group disappeared into the hospital.

Perdita didn't know exactly what all those big words meant, but she guessed a heart attack. The rest all stopped to watch the surreal scene unfold. Surreal because someone was in trouble from normal life, and Perdita had the strangest thought. She hoped Ora would grow old enough to even have a heart attack. She decided she definitely needed a good rest, and soon, but it'd have to wait.

Ora shook her head, as if clearing her thoughts. "Okay fine, but I think we have to talk with the Elders first."

Wade made a small noise of protest.

"A quick talk because we have to get back, but we have to include them on this." Ora waved an arm toward Wade.

He nodded, clearly unhappy about having to wait longer to go get Finch. A swell of pride filled Perdita's heart. She hadn't even thought to include the Elders. *Crap!* Arameus. Ora had to know about Arameus.

Sabrina pivoted as soldiers began appearing, getting their gear ready. "All right, you all go ahead and meet with Elders, I'll get a team ready here and debrief them on the situation. Let's meet back here in say fifteen and head out."

Ora tucked an escaped strand of hair out of her eye and said, "Agreed."

Perdita held up her hands. "Better make it thirty. Ora, come on. You've got to see Arameus first."

12

ORA

Retreating to a bathroom, I leaned over the toilet, hacking but brought up nothing. Not surprising since I hadn't eaten since last night. The faucet squealed as I turned the handle, gathering a handful of cool water and rinsed my mouth out. I stared at my pale face with little red splotches where blood vessels had burst with the violence of the dry heaves. Tiny strands of hair escaped my braid and dried blood splattered over my face, hair, and left ear. Waving at the automated towel dispenser, I ripped off three sheets in quick succession, and dipped it into the now warm water. I scrubbed at the dried blood as if I'd been contaminated. The sight of Arameus's stump felt as if would forever be stamped upon my retina. His leg was gone. Just gone.

Arameus, my vital friend, full of life, was now lying unconscious, eyes sunken, sweat upon his brow with a stump in place of a leg. First Damien stole his magic and he almost died, and now this. He still might not survive, but Healer Roos said now that she'd gotten more ingredients she and the other Healers would make what potions they could for infections. He wouldn't be in any pain since Sabrina's team had been smart enough to gather loads of anesthesia potion. If he survives, he'll be crippled. Never able to live his life the way he used to.

The mere thought of it sent me running back to the toilet for round two. A soft tap at sounded while I rinsed again. It had to be Mom. I took down my hair and with my fingers, brushed through my hair and redid my braid. It wasn't perfect, but at least it was presentable for the Elders. I could've cleaned the blood and fixed my hair with magic, but it felt better not to. A pounding headache rampaged behind my right eye. Using magic over and over again always drained me and there had been no breaks today.

I pulled the lamè amulet from underneath the purple leathers. I rubbed the shiny, smooth metal, still warm from contact with my skin, between my fingertips. This simple act comforted me, reminding me of my old necklace. The one infused with spells blocking my magic. If that chain hadn't broken, how my life would be so different now. It was early March. I would've been studying for my mid-terms and looking for a summer job. Or maybe I would've gotten into a summer research position. Perhaps I would've taken the summer to study for the MCATs, an exam to get into medical school. Or spent long, lazy afternoons with John at the river again. I pushed that bittersweet thought away, tucked the charm back into the shirt, where it couldn't be grabbed during a fight.

Mom waited for me outside the door. She took me in her arms, and I laid my head against her shoulder and wrapped my arms around her. She smelled like I remembered, minus the weird Ben-Gay menthol smell that she so often had been infused with. Mostly I remembered being a little kid, curling up beside her while she stroked my hair while we watched a movie. My life had always been hard, growing up in Raleigh where everyone, except for Charlie and her family, thought of us as weirdos. Now I would give anything to be back in my old town and be left alone to snuggle on the couch and watch a movie. I'd take being a weirdo to this any day.

No matter how I wished for a normal life, I didn't have one. I never had, and it wouldn't do anyone any good if I continued this wishful thinking. I had to meet Sabrina back in twenty minutes and I'd already wasted ten. I slipped out of my mother's arms, and she fell in beside me. Outside the hospital, I nodded toward Sabrina, and she flung both arms outward in a "hurry the hell up' kind of way, but she hadn't seen Arameus. Wade had a car waiting for us out front.

I slipped into the front seat of the white Honda Accord, marveling at the weirdness of traveling by car. I hadn't been in a vehicle since we left the lake town in North Carolina and taken the bus to Tennessee to find Fox, Leigh's uncle who trained me in Sphere magic. "Whose car is this?"

"Finch's," Wade said, turning the wheel with expertise.

I couldn't imagine Finch driving around the island in a white Honda Accord. It didn't fit. "Huh. He seems more like a beat-up pickup truck with tobacco stains down the driver's side kind of guy."

"A beat-up truck." Wade chuckled. "He'd have himself a right ole hissy fit if he heard you say that."

"Can't you see it? Ya know, the kind that scares the crap out of you because the piece of junk backfires at every stop."

Wade burst out laughing. His laughter affected all of us. Within moments, Mom and I belly laughed along with him. That good laughter, the kind that hurts the stomach, and when Mom yelled, "Stop! Stop! I'm going to pee my pants," we laughed even harder.

I don't know how Wade managed to be able to drive, but we pulled in front of the Town Hall, and as the guards stepped off of the porch, our laughter died away. Back to business. Wade placed the car in park and killed the engine. The door opened with a click and a small dinging sound before Wade pulled out the keys. I slammed the door behind me and met up with the ever-changing guards. These two were older, fifty-ish with salt and pepper hair and a gruffness that had to come from working hard. Wade knew them. He extended his hand and shook the one on the right. "James."

"Wade."

He let go and held out his hand to the other, who shook it in one quick up and down movement. "Andrew."

Andrew put his right hand on his hip, close to the holstered pistol hanging on a vest. A movement to keep his weapon within easy reach. "Glad to see you made it. You get *our* men back?"

I noted Andrew focused on Wade and wouldn't cast a gaze in my direction. The way he said "our men" gave me the impression he was one of the few who still didn't think the Gayden should be helping me. I didn't have time nor the patience to deal with ignorance and prejudice. There was enough of that in the world. Both worlds for that matter.

I stepped in front of Wade. "We did pretty good, but right now we need to talk with the Elders because a few of *our* men still need us." I stressed the word *our* to emphasize I considered his people my people.

Andrew glared at me, but James answered, "Right this way."

"Thank you," I said to James and resisted the urge to bump Andrew with my shoulder as I pushed past him and decided to save that anger for any magicians still fighting back at the Nook. Once James opened the door, I walked right in, strolling to the double doors leading to the Elders' meeting chambers.

I think they made their headquarters in an old church on purpose. It always made me feel like I addressed someone holy whenever I met with them. But like outside with Andrew, I wasn't in the mood for games.

Maggie and Winslow sat in the front pulpit area when we walked in. The rest of the Elders absent.

Maggie said, "The rest will be here shortly."

"I'm very sorry, Madam Elder," I stumbled over the title, unsure what to call her as I had never used her name, "but I'm afraid we're in a bit of a hurry. You can fill in the others later."

Briefly, Wade updated them on the success in the Willow drawing the Quads from our two main missions. I debriefed them on the Vindeca and Nook missions. There were pleased with the success of discovering the missing ingredient for the invisibility potions as well as other potions for healing our wounded and how we'd obtained about two hundred Healers in the process. I went on to explain the deal we'd struck with the Styxs and how Finch agreed to stay behind. "What I need to know and quickly is what terms would you agree if their leaders agree to an alliance?"

Maggie and Winslow looked at each other, unsure of what to say. A third Elder had come in during my debriefing, this one's name I didn't know. he answered, "We agree with the magicians that the Styxs, as you call them, should remain beyond the Veil. Humanity isn't ready for their kind, as it isn't ready for Gayden or the magicians. We will not grant them passage to this realm. Other than that, we don't have much of an input. If what you say is true and they don't have a say, then they should be given one, whether that is a seat on the Council or something equivalent. We could back them on that. Also, we need to find out more why their own former leaders were imprisoned to begin with."

Maggie nodded, sounding for the first time like a scared little old lady, guess trolls would do that. "I agree. An alliance with their knowledge and strength would be beneficial; however, we don't know enough about them to warrant if it is a positive or negative having them on our side."

The Elders nodded between them, and I could tell they were starting to think we should get our people out and leave the Styxs to their own fate. I cursed myself for not thinking to bring Sabrina. She was the only one who had lived in Conjuragic that the Elders would listen to and would've been able to answer any of these questions. "I understand your concerns. However, Sabrina will be present, and she discussed this with us. She lived in Conjuragic. I'm sure if she had any concerns, she would've voiced them."

I looked at my watch, hoping they would get the drift that we needed to go. My comment about Sabrina gave them pause. They looked between each other, uncertain. "I really hate to be pushy, but we really need an answer so I can go get our people."

"Pardon me," Wade said, bowing, much more formal than I'd been treating them today, "Finch is there. He's been one of your advisors for nearly fifteen years. Before any final negotiations are agreed upon, Sabrina and Finch can speak. She can give him the political history, and he can assess it. I think we can trust him to make the best decision possible for our people." He bowed again.

Winslow squeezed his eyebrows together, and with the amount of hair, it looked like a small rodent rested on his forehead. "You're very wise, Wade. Perhaps you'll finally agree to be an advisor yourself."

"I appreciate it, but as always, not at this time."

I rolled my eyes. This was not the time to be kissing ass. It was time to make a decision and move. "We're agreed then. We go get our people, have Sabrina and Finch talk, and then Finch will make the negotiations with your voice, with one stipulation. The Styxs stay in Conjuragic. Right?"

"Uh, well. Yes, I guess so." Winslow's hand shook.

"Great. Let's roll." I tipped my head and jogged out of the Town Hall.

Mom glowered at me when we stepped out of the old sanctuary. "That wasn't very respectful."

"I know, but these are old people used to debating on topics for days or weeks at a time. We needed an answer and now."

"I know that, but they are the leaders of the Gayden. You can't piss them off."

I narrowed my eyes at Andrew as we stormed out of the door and jumped off the steps of the porch. Andrew and James lunged atop two motorcycles chained to the side of the building. Something about the sight gave me an idea. I opened the passenger side, slid in, and closed it behind me. I glanced at my watch, listening as Wade and Mom got in the car, their own doors closing and the rev of the engine. We were eight minutes late. "Uhhh, Wade how long will the drive to the hospital take?"

"Five or six minutes. Why?"

"Scoot over, let me drive. I have an idea."

Wade shrugged, opened his door, and slid out. I climbed over the middle console to the driver's seat as Wade got in. I slipped on my seatbelt and told them to do the same. Before they could stop me, I opened the Bridge, floored the gas pedal, and disappeared into the blackness to the sounds of their screams.

13

ORA

Curiosity killed the cat, or so I'd been told. Perhaps today the cat would live. That is if its mother didn't kill it first. I'd always wondered if I could travel through the Bridge in a vehicle. Why I decided in that moment to find out, I'll never know.

In what would've taken us five to six minutes to get to the hospital took us two seconds through the Bridge. I slammed on the breaks the moment we broke through, but it was totally worth it by the look on Sabrina's face when Finch's little Honda Accord popped out. I about lost it when she waved back with a look of pure shock on her face.

Mom leaned forward, pelting the back of the seat with each syllable. "Ora Arlena Stone, what in the world were you thinking? You could've been killed. You could've killed us. You could've killed someone on the other side. What if they walked right in front of the Bridge when you came out?"

I turned off the car, tossing the keys back at Wade. "Relax, Mom. Those things could've happened, but they didn't, so chill out."

"Chill out? Chill out? I know you didn't tell me to chill out." She fussed away at me in typical mom fashion.

I rolled my eyes and waved her off. She was about to start again, but she stopped when she saw the devilish smile on my face. "Sabrina, I have such an idea."

Mom pursed her lips. "What now?"

About fifteen men and women gathered for the voluntary mission. When I explained my idea, they went into overdrive hurrying to get the rest of the equipment we needed.

Sabrina shook her head with a smile. "I think you're losing your mind."

I considered that because every other time before going into a hostile situation I was nervous and wishing I didn't have to. But this time, I was excited. "Talk about the element of surprise."

It'd taken double the time to get ready. Mom emerged from the hospital, wearing her blue leathers.

"Charlie still sleeping?"

She nodded. "Healer Roos gave her a sleeping potion."

"That's good, and Arameus, he's the same?"

"Yes."

Guilt squirmed in my stomach like a writhing snake.

Sabrina tossed me a gas mask. "You sure about this?"

"Absolutely." I straddled the motorcycle. Another thought pushed to the forefront of my mind. Was I going in, guns blazing, as it were, because I was avoiding having to think about everything that happened today? How many people had died or were injured? My stomach rumbled at the thought…or because of hunger. I kept going on pure adrenaline, but I couldn't stop moving. If I did, I might collapse, and the guilt rolled through me again. How could I be hungry or thinking of sleep after today? I shoved the worry deep, way, way deep, where I wouldn't have to deal with it until later. Maybe never. Finch was counting on me.

A hooting holler brought me out of my speculations, just in time. Damien grinned in his brown leathers and climbed on top of another motorcycle. "This should be interesting." Jeremiah jumped on behind him, grinning from ear to ear. Mom and Wade straddled the next bike in line.

I grabbed the chain and tossed it to the bike behind me. I slipped the gas mask over my head, and Sabrina did the same, throwing one long leg over the bike. Was there nothing she did that didn't ooze sexiness? She kick-started the engine, and it roared to life underneath my legs giving off diesel smoke. The vibrations traveled between my legs and up my back making my teeth chatter. The engines behind me turned over in a deafening sound like a pack of wolves growling. Exhilaration rippled through my limbs in time with the humming of the bike. I touched the comm. "Everyone ready?"

A string of "we're a go" followed over the comm.

The Bridge came to life. I secured the chain around my wrist. Instead of holding hands inside the Bridge, we would be connected by a series of chains. I wrapped my arms around Sabrina's waist, awkwardly due to the chain, but I managed. With a tilt of the head and shrug of the shoulder, I managed to hit the comm. "We're a go in five, four, three, two, one."

Sabrina sped into the Bridge with a roar, tires squealing, smoke wafting behind us. The chain pulled tight against my hand, almost jerking me off the bike, but I held on. Sabrina slowed her speed so the chain wasn't pulled as taut. I wondered if Jiminy was nearby and what he would think of our little motorcycle gang. I doubted I'd be able to hear him. Sabrina led the way, and when she slowed on the gas pedal, I gave a tug on the chain one time, the signal to slow down. The chain pulled straighter then relaxed again. We reached the edge of the Shadow Forest. As I predicted, the Nook was aflame and parts of it in crumbles. Other than a sea of dead bodies, the place was deserted. The bodies of Keepers, prisoners, along with a handful of Protectors and three Styx lay scattered like bits of trash over the crumbled remains of the Nook. Otherwise, the place held no sign of anyone still alive. Dread rolled through my veins. *Finch!*

Sabrina pulled forward out of the Bridge. Dark clouds covered the sky as far as the eye could see. I'd never seen it rain in Conjuragic, which gave me the willies. Sabrina looked at the sky as well, her shoulders tensing.

"Something up?" I asked through the comm.

"Tempests must be upset. That's never a good sign," Sabrina answered.

"Why?" I asked, while checking the last motorcycle exited the Bridge before I closed it.

"They control the weather. When they get all in a tizzy, bad things happen. Hurricanes, tornados, blizzards, tsunamis, lightning storms, you name it. They can get very passionate, so it's not good if they can't calm down."

Finch spoke over the comm. "Ladies, are you going to continue with the history lesson or did you come to take my ass home?"

"Finch!" Wade called, nearly crashing into us.

"It's me," Finch said, sounding different from his usual gruff self. "I'm okay. The Styxs succeeded. Between their attack and ours at the other two sites, the majority of the Quads are out of the equation. I'm walking with them now to their home. We don't think the Quads will show up there. No one escaped. To anyone who investigates, we'll be blamed. Not them."

Good thinking, Finch, I thought. By taking the blame, we had an upper hand regarding an alliance. The Styxs' attack wasn't sanctioned by their leaders and started by a bunch of renegades. Their uprising and alliance could be hidden from the Council until the right time. *If this goes well.*

Sabrina gave Finch the lowdown on the Styxs. "The Elders gave you the approval to be their spokesman. Their one concession was they can't cross the Veil," Sabrina said.

"Their spokesman, eh? Well, aren't I all important."

Sabrina switched to a secure channel for the leaders.

Sabrina's shoulder stiffened in front of me at Finch's attitude. "Cool it, Outlaw. Don't be such a jerk. Here's the deal. We have a peace with all magical creatures who live here, but there are some, not the Styxs, that can be somewhat untrustworthy, mainly the mermaids and some of the tree sprites. To avoid a political mess, we have a peace, but no magical creatures are allowed a say in the Council or any major decisions. They obey our laws within our cities, but in their own lands, like the Styxs in the Shadow Forest, they rule as they see fit."

Static through the comm, then Finch said, "Yeah, by the way, it was a mermaid who ousted us to the Council about the Haven."

I felt more than heard Sabrina curse. I recalled seeing one right before her wedding.

"The Styxs got their prisoners out of the Nook. I thought you'd be happy to hear that," Finch said.

I understood. He couldn't ask questions outright but wanted to know why they had political prisoners.

Overhead, the last of the birds left the Shadow Forest. The fog slowed our progress and was thicker here than even in front of the Nook. The weird mushrooms grew in a wild overabundance puffing out bucketful after bucketful of hallucinogenic spores. The deeper we went into the forest, the bumpier the ride became.

Sabrina said, "The prisoners were a few of their Elders who disagreed with the sanction against them. They felt that as a loyal species they should be given a say and a separate committee be formed made up of representatives from each of the magical creatures, much like the High Council of today. When they were denied, the leaders revolted and launched an attack on the Guidance Hall. They didn't get very far."

The static on the line stretched as Finch processed what she'd said. The brush and twigs intertwined around every tree limb and bush, littering the ground, making the bikes crawl across the forest floor as if the Shadow Forest were angry we weren't lost to the madness. Could we possibly have made a wrong turn? Styxs are huge. There was no way they could get through all this foliage without breaking down some trees.

"Copy that," Finch said. "We're almost here."

"We're coming in the back way," Sabrina informed both of us through the comm. That would explain the thick brush. This wasn't a well-traveled path. I wondered why we were sneaking up the back way. Didn't seem like a very good way to start out our alliance.

Sabrina slowed even further, basically using her feet and minimal gas to get over a large tree root exposed in the ground.

The comm chimed in my ear. "Do you all hear that roaring sound? We have almost reached their homeland. They're starting to panic, and there's lots of activity up ahead."

"Tell them that is us and not to be worried. Styxs are fine unless they get upset." Sabrina rolled past the worst of the branches. A few feet ahead, the forest cleared as if stamped out with trees uprooted, knocked to the ground, or broken in half as if a Styx had pushed it away with an elbow. We must be very close to their home. The bushes looked as if they'd been crushed under the weight of their huge feet, making the terrain uneven and hazardous. Tree limbs and roots littered the ground, as if begging for a foot to get caught and twist an ankle.

"How is that you?" Finch asked, but as the bike engines shut off, the silence that followed stretched as thick as the fog.

"Are we ready?" Sabrina asked, and I nodded, seeing my masked face reflected in hers. My breath echoed inside the small space. I couldn't help it. The thought, *No, I am your father*, floated in my mind, and hysterical giggles threatened to escape. Starwars quotes were totally inappropriate. I managed to let a few hiccups of sound leave me, and I'd been smart enough not to hit the button on my comm. I had to rest soon and eat, not in that order, or else I'd be doomed to delirium.

Sabrina turned, giving the hand signal for the men to follow her. As I trotted behind her, a terrifying thought filled me. How were we going to talk with the Styxs wearing masks? Sabrina called out, "Finch let them know we're coming in the back."

"Will do, sugar lips."

We ran around the left side of the destroyed forest, closer to the smoke that drifted from what once was the Nook. Following an unnatural and irregular circle of trees, we came across what had to be the opening to the Styx's home. Two large trees flanked a central clearing with a hand-carved wooden banner extending between the two trees. The ornate carving displayed with exquisite beauty every magical creature I'd ever seen or imagined. We stopped beneath the sculpture. My heart dropped as I got my first glimpse inside.

14

SABRINA

A swarm of Styx stood beyond the gates, all in an uproar. Sabrina had never seen so many all at once. Even for her, this was daunting. Hundreds and hundreds of half-giants roamed the empty clearing. She couldn't decipher their emotions. They stomped from one to another waving their elongated arms and shouting, more like a grumble than actual speech.

Farther in the Styx's home, the air cleared, not showing the mushroom spores. Other creatures weaved in between the feet of the Styxs. The unmistakable ripples of shimmering light reflecting off fairy wings as they flitted to and fro in a haphazard dance. She spotted a few elves, dwarf-like with childish faces and short, stubby legs. Tyke, an elf who worked at the Nook, sat cross-legged at the base of an enormous tree. His blond hair appeared more ginger from blood not his own.

Still more supernatural beings than elves and Styxs emerged from different parts of the forest beyond. Water nymphs strolled around the clearing as well. A tall, graceful species that moved more cat-like than human with a faint bluish tinge to their skin and vertical slits for pupils. One closest to the opening raised her webbed hands in a wave before tucking a stray strand of vibrant white hair behind her pointed ear. She'd closed the gills on the side of her neck and instead breathed with the lungs the change brought when on land. Sabrina assumed they would represent themselves as well as the mermaids. Unlike the fables in the human world, mermaids couldn't form legs and walk on land, no more than a fish could. The stories came from the water nymphs, who unlike the mermaids, couldn't swim into great depths since they had lungs as well as gills. They had two legs with fins around the calves that would fan out while they swam. Those same fins would shed when it dried out and regrow once back in the water.

Sabrina wasn't sure how she felt about the water nymphs being here. She understood why some elves would be there. They worked at the Nook along with the Keepers and Styx. Then she remembered a few nymphs worked in the few underwater cells. Most of the time mermaids governed themselves, as did all magical creatures, but occasionally they asked the Council to imprison one of their own. They never disclosed the reason behind the imprisonment. Still, like the mermaids, the nymphs weren't always trustworthy. They would betray you in an instant, if it meant getting a leg up. Or fin up, whichever the case may be.

Sabrina, with the group on her heels, walked farther into the clearing of the Styxs' homeland. She had no idea why there are so many different magical creatures present. Their little group had finally been spotted. A Styx closest to them raised a hand and pointed in their direction, grunting in his natural language, one that Sabrina had never mastered, and the ongoing conversations faded away into nothing. All eyes turned, focusing on them. Sabrina had been in some pretty tight situations, but there was nothing like a hundred Styx staring at you to get the nerves teetering on edge.

One Styx, bigger than anything Sabrina had ever seen, sauntered forward, weaving in and out of his brethren to stand in front of the group, looking down on them. Turning her neck up and up and up, she peered into the Styx's face. Ones like these is what made it hard to differentiate between Styxs and Giants. These larger ones were usually the leaders and the oldest and barely left their forest. This one was no less than fifteen feet tall with fine gray hair sprinkled over his whole body with more coming out of his ears and eyebrows than anywhere else. He kind of reminded her of Winslow, and she had to choke down a laugh. His potato-like nose looked more like three or four potatoes combined into one. His face shown the lines of his age, and several teeth were missing. Whether from decay or fighting was anyone's guess. Unlike the others in the Nook, this one appeared to have bathed within the last month.

Sabrina recognized this particular Styx as the new leader from a flyer.

He'd been appointed after the others had been imprisoned. The ones imprisoned, and presumably rescued today, were nowhere to be seen. As that realization hit, the unease coursing through her veins spiked. The leader's focus turned to Sabrina first. "You must be the traitor." He said it more as a statement than a question. Despite his size, the irritation swam up in Sabrina like a nasty tidal wave. He must have read her thoughts by her expression because he laughed, with real amusement. "We're all traitors here today, so welcome. I am called Carth, son of Howe. Leader of the Styx."

Ora's head tilted a fraction in Sabrina's direction. If Sabrina didn't know her so well, she would have missed it. Taking the hint, Sabrina took the lead. "I am Sabrina Sun, daughter of Robert Sun. Former Protector of Naiad. I come to you in peace." Carth nodded his approval and turned his eyes to Ora.

To Ora's credit, she did not stutter and had the tiniest of shaking in her voice when she said, "I am Ora Stone, daughter of Philo Stone." Ora paused, searching for the right words. "A witch possessing all cores of magic and I come to you in peace."

Carth cocked his head to the side, considering her words a moment, before he said, "You are a Forbidden."

The word was foreign, even to Sabrina. Ora took it in stride. "I'm not sure. I wasn't aware there was a name for what I am." Sabrina's own words, thrown out in anger, came back to her. *You're an abomination.* Guilt tickled along her spine.

Carth realizing the strain on their necks, sank to one knee, an enormous sign of respect. Perhaps things would turn out well after all. "It's not a formal name. It's what we have come to call what you are. We have never agreed with the Council, but their prejudice amongst their own kind isn't our place."

Ora tilted her head. "I beg your pardon, great Carth, but I don't understand. What have you not agreed with?"

"We've never thought they shouldn't mix the bloodlines. It's a natural progression. Yes, there are those that would not survive, but those that do are stronger than all others. Look at yourself. Can you be overtaken by a Nip?"

Ora's head shook. "No. They can take a fraction of it, and they cannot hold it for long."

Carth lifted one hand, palm upward, the size of a small car. "You see. You're proof of natural selection. You possess the protection they need. If they would've allowed the bloodlines to mix, then this Nip war they're facing now wouldn't even be an issue. They would be immune." Carth rose to his full height and stretched, bones popping like gunshots. He hacked a cough that made the ground rumble. "Besides, if they were like you, then you wouldn't have been arrested. Nips could do them no harm, so other than breeching the Concealment Code, there was no harm done, especially with their powers over memory, and when you destroyed the Unity Statue and sealed the Veil, they could've fixed it. Your power would've been theirs."

Such an idea had never occurred to Sabrina before. She knew what she'd been taught. The bloodlines were pure and couldn't be mixed.

Carth shrugged. "We better get this shindig on the road. We have matters to discuss. I've heard you wish to discuss an alliance. Come. It's through here." Carth led the way through the back of the clearing into yet another set of trees. He walked through the opening barely wide enough to allow him to make it through. The branches of the trees brushed against his massive shoulders, splintering and raining down twigs and branches upon them. Ora deflected the onslaught to the sides, and Carth laughed, low and deep, shaking the ground. Ora led them while Sabrina followed. Perdita and Wade came next. Finch joined them as they passed through the opening, taking a place beside Wade. Sabrina caught the slight hand touch between them but didn't have time to figure out that mystery. Damien and Jeremiah picked up the rear, followed by the rest of the team. She'd kept that old habit of paying attention to everyone's location—one that she wouldn't break.

She'd never been inside the inner circle of the Styxs' homeland and never could have imagined what she saw. She had been here a few times for a raid or to break up a feud but had never been allowed into the inner sanctum. The honor of being allowed here spoke volumes about their current position. The area stretched larger than two football stadiums with entrances to underground caves, where Sabrina supposed the Styx slept. At the edge, trees had been cut to stumps and sanded into large chairs or benches forming half circles. The area in front of the chairs held the remnants of fire, as if the Styx hung out here by the campfire, sitting and talking. Despite the normal appearance, unease arose in Sabrina.

Styx and other magical creatures surrounded them. A quick escape would be near impossible with the bikes so far away. That wasn't all that bothered her. Creatures of every sort that lived in Conjuragic gathered together. Centaurs and satyrs separated the vampires from the weres.

Bright dots of light that Sabrina recognized as wisps floated near the trees. Movement caught her eye, drawing her attention to large boulders, but upon closer inspection their chests rose and fell—golems. A coldness like death breathed outward from the darkest of shadows to the edges of the Styx homeland. That could mean either shades or the black-eyed ones, or both. This felt like a trap, and adrenaline poured through her veins, ready to run.

As if sensing her unease, Carth turned. "Calm yourself, little Protector. They're here to talk."

"But how did they know? They couldn't have gotten here so fast." Ora picked up on the conversation, as did the rest of them. The group moved into defensive positions, and Sabrina knew Ora readied herself to throw open the Bridge if they needed an escape. With the number of creatures present, Sabrina doubted they could all make it out without a straggler or two. The human world didn't need any of these creatures prowling around.

Carth scoffed. "Little Protector, we magical creatures, as you call us, have ways of moving that you know nothing of. This is our world as much as the witches and wizards. So far, your little war has not reached us, but not for long. They all have a right to hear what you say and must decide for themselves. If this is not agreeable, then we have a problem." The threat hung in the air, like an axe ready to fall. Sabrina had no doubt they wouldn't be able to walk out without a fight if they rejected the others without first speaking to them.

As always, Ora surprised Sabrina. "We came to you in peace and with a measure of secrecy, or so we had thought. You're right. This war affects us and the magicians. If you trust those here, then we trust them."

Carth stared at Ora, considering, what exactly Sabrina couldn't tell. "This is a parley of sort, an agreed upon peace where no one will be harmed and can speak freely. Our agreement is anything said during these meetings is strictly confidential. There will be no fighting here, but to leave before all is settled would be a sign of great disrespect, and the protection granted to you would be forfeit."

"As long as we come in, say our peace, allow others to say theirs, then at the conclusion we can leave, free from harm, and this meeting will stay within these—this clearing?" Ora asked.

Carth nodded once.

"Even if an alliance cannot be reached, we will still be allowed to leave? Unharmed? What has been said here today remains secret?"

A single nod again.

"Very well. Please lead the way." Ora extended a hand, almost as if handing Carth his fate. Sabrina didn't like this, not one little bit. Their eyes met, sharing their misgivings, but they couldn't turn back now. Farther into the clearing, Sabrina's stomach gave a large grumble as the smells of food reached her nose. Around a bend in the forest, hidden behind some trees, several female Styxs laid large trays upon makeshift tables. A large whole roasted boar, mounds of wild birds plucked and roasted, fish, and what looked like steak, a human dish Sabrina loved. Another table sank under the weight of mashed potatoes, turnips, carrots, sweet potatoes, squash, and beets. A third table held more types of fresh fruit than Sabrina could name, along with cakes, pies, and cookies. She met Ora's eyes again, they shared a look that said they must not have bad intentions if they intended on feeding them. Hopefully they wouldn't end up on the menu.

One of the Styxs from the Nook marched over and extended a huge hand and practically shook Finch's whole arm. "I want to thank you for sticking around and helping. I know you could've left, but you all kept your promise, and if you hadn't, several of us wouldn't have made it back. That makes you all right in my book." He was hard to understand, teeth protruding from his bottom lip. Sabrina held her breath, attempting to ward off the rotting fish reek of his breath.

"You all are some damn good fighters. It was my honor."

Carth patted the Styx on the back causing clouds of dirt to rise in the air. "Ladies and gentlemen, let me introduce Asher. The other who was with them was Gunther."

Asher smiled, huge green crooked teeth looming at them. "Gunther is off getting his wounds tended to, along with those we rescued."

Sabrina's tension eased a fraction.

Ora asked, "What about your leader? The one who didn't make it?"

Asher's smile vanished, a forlorn expression on his face. "Lyons. Gunther's brother."

"Please pass on our respect," Finch said with a nod from the rest of them.

Asher nodded then looked to Carth. "They got my vote."

One down, so many more to go, Sabrina thought.

Carth grunted. "I'll keep that in mind. Come this way." Carth offered them seats, but they stood, waiting. In a loud voice, Carth said, "My fellow creatures, come join in this monumental occasion."

Each creature, both big and small, moved from around the perimeter and formed a circle taking places to either side of their small group.

Carth spoke again. "May I introduce Ora Stone, daughter of Philo, a Forbidden; Sabrina Sun, daughter of Robert, former Naiad Protector; and Finch Outlaw, a Nip."

Ora cleared her throat.

Carth paused, looking down at her.

"My apologies. The word Nip is considered in poor taste. They prefer the term Gayden."

Carth's eyebrows rose. "Excuse me. Finch Outlaw, a Gayden. They're here today representing the rebels and have brought us together to ask for our aid in their war. I've called the Magical Brethren here today in the honor of peace, for which we, the magical creatures in this kingdom of Conjuragic, will listen, unbiased, but also in secrecy, to hear their words, and as a people decide, and make your own opinion on whether or not to join them. What is said here today is to remain in confidence to those present. If it's discovered that this has leaked out beyond these forest walls, the brethren of magical creatures will hereby and forevermore banish your species, and those responsible will be put to the sword. Is everyone under agreement?"

Murmurs of agreements spread throughout the crowd. Sabrina couldn't tell whether Carth's proclamation of Ora being a Forbidden and Sabrina a former Protector raised more murmurs than the agreement, and what were these magical brethren? Sabrina had never heard of such things, but this wasn't the time to be asking those questions.

"Then let us begin. Ora, you have the floor."

Carth sat, his movement indicating for others to do the same. The creatures gathered around the perimeter, found their places, and sat, leaving their group standing. Ora gave Sabrina a nod. Sabrina inclined her head and found an open seat as the others did the same.

Quiet settled through the expansive clearing. Ora's shoulders moved with a deep breath. "Thank you all for coming today. I want to thank Carth for allowing us to be in your presence. As he said, I am a Forbidden, but I was brought to Conjuragic and accused of being a Nip, a hateful word used by the magicians to describe a Gayden. While that is not what I am, I have met many Gayden on my journey. We have come together to fight against the leaders of Conjuragic. We're seeking justice and equality. It has come to my attention that, like the Gayden, you as well, have been treated unfairly. Even though you've been allowed to live and not destroyed at birth, they still leave you with no voice in Conjuragic. You're seen and treated as lesser beings, but I say they're wrong. I say the High Council should have more than witches and wizards, but representatives from each of you, working together to better this land."

At the last words, cries and whispers broke out.

In the back someone, no, something stood, part man part insect, large black wings, but a man's chest, arms, and legs. His large insect-like head bobbed while two round red eyes stared at them. He opened the pinchers covering his mouth and his voice came out as a series of clicks. Chill bumps spread along Sabrina's arms. Ora's eyes flashed wide. She turned her head and mouthed the words where no one else could see, "Mothman?"

Sabrina nodded. No surprise Ora had heard of their kind since one of them had escaped, traveling across the Veil to West Virginia. The humans had called him Mothman. Growing up in West Virginia, she would've heard of him. They even made a movie about it several years ago.

The creature, an Om Gandac, clicked away, waving his clawed hands about, red eyes gleaming. Carth listened and nodded. Sabrina had never mastered their language, Tempest were usually better skilled at such things.

When the Om Gandac quieted, Carth translated, "Lanear, son of Miglena, speaks. He wants to know why you aren't going to destroy the wizards. They have oppressed and sought genocide for the race you fight with. They have dominated this land for too long. You seek to join them, but what you should be doing is crushing them. Make them the bottom of races. Force them to work for us."

Roars of agreement rose from the crowd. Thankfully, all the creatures didn't agree.

Ora waited, letting the commotion die down, until Carth held up one hand, silencing them. Ora bowed her head as if considering. "While that does sound tempting, it wouldn't be right. We're here today because they've done that to all of us. We have felt their bite of oppression, known its pain. Why would we choose to do that to others? Why would we belittle ourselves to be like them? You say I'm seeking to join them, but what we're doing is striving to be better than them. If we win against them and put them in chains, sometime, maybe not today, maybe not in any of our lifetimes, but sometime, they will fight back. It will become a vicious circle, a wheel spinning round and round with hate. I want to tip over that wheel. That is what I seek to destroy."

At her words, the Om Gandacs shook their heads. Lanear clicked a response before bowing, and the members of his race stood and disappeared through the back trees. Not far behind them, the black-eyed ones followed. The unnatural chill in the air lessened at their departure, but not completely as the shades hadn't gone too. The shadows of the dead hovered at the edges, out of sight. The vamps and weres had stuck around as well, which didn't match their legendary blood lust. Perhaps they stayed to spill any blood at all.

Ora didn't seem fazed at all with the Om Gandac or the black-eyed ones leaving. "We respect their decision, but it's clear they had different goals in mind than we do."

Carth nodded as the last of them departed. "What is it that you want from us?"

The question hung in the air, floating, daunting, heavy. What exactly did they want from the magical creatures? It had never been discussed, was never part of the original plan. In fact, they should be back on the island, healing the wounded, working on the invisibility potion, a thousand other things, but yet when the raid began at the Nook, an opportunity presented itself. Sabrina had no idea what Ora would say.

Ora bowed her head, clasping her hands in front of her, as if she too hadn't thought this far. *Stupid. Stupid. Stupid.*

"Originally, we overtook the Haven. Someone," Ora's head inclined to the nearest water nymph, "ratted us out to the Council." A thousand eyes from every size, shape, and hue of the rainbow turned on the nymphs. If the mermaids had ratted them out, the nymphs delivered the message. "For that reason, despite your reassurances, Carth, I'm hesitant to reveal our plans until those who choose to join us have agreed, and those who haven't are gone."

The tension in the clearing skyrocketed. Several creatures roared, vamps exposed their fangs, hiding in the shadows to avoid the sun, fur rippled along the weres' skin, and the nymphs shook their heads, denying they had anything to do with the Gayden discovery.

Carth stood, waving his arms. "Everyone, calm down. It's not unreasonable to withhold key elements of their battle plans." Shouts and roars answered him. He stomped one large foot, leaving a huge indent in the ground as a rumble rippled along the ground. Ora stumbled, but righted herself before she fell. The arguing settled. He returned his attention to Ora. "However, you should, at least, give us an idea of what you want us to do."

Ora, head held high, looked around the clearing, at each of the magical creatures then said, "We want, when the time is right, for you to fight with us. We have two enemies."

A water nymph stood, putting a hand on her hips and said in her singsong voice, "We all know that. The Council and the Quads."

"No, we consider them to be one of the same. The Quads are simply an extension of the Council. We're talking about another. He goes by many names—Master, the Experimenter. We're not sure if the Council is aware of him or not, but he has been collecting Gayden for many decades and has been creating Geminates."

Whatever Sabrina thought would happen, the dead silence that followed wasn't it. A few of the satyrs flinched uncomfortably at the mention of Master, but the rest remained still.

Ora threw her braid over her shoulder. "He keeps them prisoner, trying to fulfill a prophecy."

Carth held up an enormous hand to stop her. "What prophecy? The age of seers and prophecy has long since passed."

Ora tilted her head to peer in his face before looking away and taking slow steps around the clearing. Sabrina jumped to her feet to follow Ora, not letting her go unprotected. The atmosphere, already brimming with tension, rose a notch, but Ora walked as if oblivious to it all. "Despite my powers, I don't know much about this world. I cannot speak about the age of seers or other prophecies, but I've met the seer herself, and she told me she'd set the Experimenter on his current path from her prophecy. He wishes to use Geminates to create a rock that controls all cores of magic. Our other objective is to find this man, where his secret lair is, and take him down. We anticipate he has his own followers we'll have to fight, but we intend to set his prisoners free and destroy those who stand with him. He will not come easy. Those of you who desire bloodshed will get your wish."

Weres, Vamps, and a few Styxs clapped at her words. Sabrina didn't know why she acted like they needed help finding out where Mathesar had hidden the Gayden. They already knew. Perdita had grown up there. At her thought, she met Perdita's eyes. They shared a heavy look as Ora finished her round of the clearing. "There you have it. We need to overthrow the Council and find the Experimenter and free his prisoners. We want you to feed us information, be our eyes and ears, and when the time comes, stand and fight with us."

"Anything else?" Carth asked.

"Yes. Not only will we fight for our equality and yours, we will also forbid any further slaughter of Geminate babies, but the blood on their hands will never be clean. They will never be forgiven for their celebration of innocent death."

Shock reverberated through Sabrina at Ora's words. *Did she really know so little of Conjuragic?* Then it hit her. It couldn't have been more obvious! She didn't know anything. How could she? She'd spent all her time in Conjuragic as a prisoner with everyone hating her on sight. It was no wonder she thought them all monsters.

She couldn't let her continue thinking this. "Excuse me. I think now would be a good time for a break. Let everyone think on it."

Carth nodded, getting to his large feet. "Agreed. Let's take thirty minutes, during such time each of the magical brethren are to convene, and when we return, a decision will be made." Carth towered over every creature. The others followed suit. "I believe some of the others have brought food from the Human Eatery. They set up tables over there." He pointed with a long, fat finger that looked more like a tree branch.

Finch's stomach growled in response, getting a few laughs. Asher thumped him on the back, almost sending him tumbling, and pulled him along toward the food. Despite Finch's gruff demeanor, people always liked him.

As the crowd dispersed, heading toward the food tables, Ora shot Sabrina a questioning glare. Sabrina tilted her head, opposite the crowd, and set off in that direction, knowing Ora would follow.

They stepped beyond the clearing into a patch hidden from prying eyes and ears. Ora crossed her arms over her chest. "What are you thinking? We were finally getting somewhere!"

Sabrina chewed her bottom lip, wanting to phrase her words gently. "If you're going to win them to our side, you have to know who you're fighting against, what the odds are."

Ora's expression contorted in both confusion and anger. "You know I know who we're fighting and the odds if we lose!"

Ora's condescending tone quickened Sabrina's own anger. Her own memories were like fuel to the fire. "Do you really? What do you think you know? This is my home. Mine. You spit out that we're monsters because of what we do to Geminate children. But do you have any idea what actually happens?"

Ora floundered for words, but Sabrina didn't give her a chance to say anything. "What exactly is it that you think we do?" Sabrina asked, crossing her arms over her chest. "You think we go hunt down innocent baby Geminates in huge mobs with large pick forks? Drag them out of their cribs screaming, with their mothers and fathers begging us to stop? March them through the street, crying out in victory? Lay them on the steps of the Guidance Hall? Rip them to shreds while everyone rejoices that we've killed the evil spawn?"

Ora looked appalled, whether from the picture that exact scenario created or at her tone, Sabrina couldn't tell. The fire left Sabrina almost as quickly as it'd come. "That's not how it is at all." Images of the newborn boy swaddled in a blanket flashed before her eyes. As always, the same heartache arose whenever the memories returned. Keeping her arms across her body, as if protecting herself, Sabrina pivoted, looking out over the horizon as she prepared to tell this story.

She felt more than heard Ora come by her side. She said, "You're right. I don't know. Tell me. If you want to."

Sabrina's chest tightened, the ache a real thing caused by what she'd done. At what she felt she had to do. She had never told this story—not to anyone. It wasn't something that anyone in Conjuragic would've ever asked her to talk about, but she knew she'd have to in order for Ora to understand they weren't all monsters. To let her know that it wasn't the horror that she imagined.

"The Quads are called whenever a Geminate is born. It has happened to me only one time. Thankfully. In every report I read, the parents have always left the child and went in hiding. The one I went to, the mother stayed. She waited for us, alone with the babe." Tears swam in her eyes, and one dropped, and she brushed it away with the back of her hand. She never used to cry, but after that call, she balled for days, and ever since being on the run with Ora, the tears came so much easier now. "Okay, you've been told that most Geminates die before they're born. They're stillborn. Mainly when the Quads are called we collect the…body of the infant and then go in search of the parents. We hate it, and even dodge the call if we can, because no one wants to go retrieve a child who died. But the call I went on, that wasn't what happened. Like I said, the mother was there, sleeping when we got there, but woke as soon as we entered. As if she was waiting for us. She was pretty with long dark hair but haunted eyes. In her arms, she stared at her beautiful, perfect baby boy." Sabrina paused for a moment until the emotions settled. "What you need to understand is we've been taught Geminates don't survive, and those who do grow up normal until they get their powers at five or six years old.

Then they go mad. The pain of the conflicting magic rages through them. They're dangerous. They can't control the power. It leaks out of them, hitting people, and things at random. To give you an idea, there were some who tried to escape into the human world to protect their children. Many of the natural disasters in your world are due to Geminates."

Gooseflesh rose on Ora's arms. Sabrina hoped she was starting to understand how dangerous Geminates could be or at least what she'd been taught. "That's not the worst part. Like I said, the two cores don't mix. They're like oil and water. The children scream in agony. All the time. Some have clawed their own eyes out, chewed off their fingers. Even killed themselves."

As a Protector, she had to look through pictures and the videos of memories from those near the children. It wasn't anything she'd ever recommend watching. Protectors had to know the consequences so they would do their duty. "When my Quad came in, the mother rolled to her feet, not waking her son, and handed him to me. There was no fight, no pleading. She never stopped looking at her son, as if memorizing every moment, every feature of his face. Leigh asked her who the father was. She shook her head and said, 'I loved his father, I still do. I'll never tell you his name. I erased the memory of him, leaving the love I have for him, but all other details are gone.' Her eyes finally left her boy and found mine. 'I know what you think you have to do, but you're wrong.' She kissed her son and whispered goodbye. The other Quad arrested her and mine took the child to the Vindeca."

Sabrina quivered from head to toe. She didn't want to go on. Didn't want to say it. Ora touched her shoulder. "It's okay."

Sabrina's head shook fast, and she brushed Ora's arm away. She rounded on her and tried her best not to scream. "No, it's not! It's not okay. I took that baby boy to the Healers, and they gave him medicine so he wouldn't feel anything, then some more to make him fall asleep and not wake up. We went in the back. There was no rejoicing. It broke my heart! Everyone was sad. No one wanted to do what we did. What I did." Snot dripped down her nose and her vision blurred from tears. She hated everything about herself in that moment. "How do you think I feel? Especially now after meeting your mom and you? That boy could've survived, but we thought that he didn't have a chance. I thought I was protecting him. Saving him from growing up and dying a horrible death. I thought I was doing the right thing. I didn't know." Sabrina lost it. She sank to the ground, gathering her legs to her chest and wrapping her arms around them. She buried her head in her knees, hiding her face as the tears flowed. Ora's arm gathered around her and she whispered, but nothing she said made a difference. The guilt of what she'd done ate away at her soul.

After long, long moments of crying, the tears finally slowed. She felt dead inside. The toll of everything left her spent, feeling raw and hollow. Sabrina's head turned to the right, still resting on her knees, and looked at Ora. "I shouldn't have married Simeon. After what I've done, if we survive, I don't deserve to have a child, a Geminate. I don't deserve it."

Ora's face was red and blotchy herself. Her forehead wrinkled as she fought to keep from crying. "You didn't know. We have to teach them," she waved a hand toward the Styx and other magical creatures, "all of them that this is wrong. If we win, and Geminates are allowed to live, then you honor that little boy. You have risked your life so many times already. It won't bring him back, but if we win, he too will be avenged. This war will mean they didn't die for nothing."

Ora's words rang true, but at this moment, with the memory being so fresh and raw, nothing could make her feel better. Yet Sabrina could tell that the words were like a seed, a tiny glimmer of hope and may be forgiveness, and it would grow. She sent out a silent apology to the mother of the boy. The mother's young face swam in her eyes. "You're wrong," she'd said and even at the time, deep down, Sabrina knew the truth. *I was wrong.*

15

PERDITA

Perdita slipped away to give Ora and Sabrina some privacy and also to take attention away from them. She sent a tendril of magic to gust the air around them, dampening the sounds of their conversation. It wouldn't be good to let the magical creatures see them in such a vulnerable state. Being seen as weak wouldn't do them any favors. Sabrina's reaction surprised Perdita. The Protector, once so cold and unapproachable, had become sensitive especially since returning to Conjuragic and her reunion with Simeon. But Ora should know better than to cry like this. Perdita thought it should make her happy, knowing her daughter still had enough hope and love inside her to feel such sorrow, but this wasn't the time or the place. Carth ushered everyone away, and the groups separated and immersed themselves in deep conversation.

What a strange and unexpected turn of events. This meeting was a gamble, in more ways than one. This could still be a trap, but even the best actors didn't bring food to a con. At least Perdita didn't think so. If Perdita hadn't seen the comical food tables with her own eyes, she never would've believed it. Three tables sat one on top of each other, but with varying heights. The Styx gathered food from the highest, those with wings fluttered about the middle table gathering food, leaving the bottom for everyone else. The sight of everyone lined up reminded Perdita of their hometown festivals, feeling more like a large family reunion, rather than a community of strangers and exotic magical creatures. Though this festival couldn't have been more different than the family reunions the McCurry's invited them to in Raleigh—every color of skin, from blue to pink to transparent reflected back at her. She had seen a few of these creatures during her days at the Pyre, feeling like Master…no Mathesar, must have spies everywhere. Carth's proclamation of punishing the entire race of creatures eased some of that worry. Some, but not all. How they'd go about finding out exactly who betrayed them, Perdita didn't know. With the bureaucracy of the Council, such spies couldn't hide long, but with the Experimenter who knew.

Ora and Sabrina joined Perdita. Both their faces blotchy, further showing evidence of their crying. Perdita sent a jolt of air toward them, cooling them, hoping it would cause the remnants of crying to vanish.

"Thanks," Sabrina said, pulling her composure around her like a well-worn glove. At least she realized her mistake. Perdita could tell from her hardened expression.

Underneath her breath, Ora asked, "What do you think?"

Perdita picked up a plate and loaded it with food. Eating was the furthest thing from her mind, but she guessed the creatures would be insulted if they refused their hospitality. Plus, none of them had really eaten all day. Even the pitiful hospital turkey sandwiches had gone to waste. It would also give them time to talk. "Get some food. Then we'll talk."

Ora opened her mouth and by instinct, Perdita knew the next words out of her mouth would be, "But Moooooom," carrying out the middle syllable.

"Eat. Both of you."

Sabrina's nose curled. "I haven't really had much of an appetite lately. The smells are getting to me."

Her skin, always fair, paled until her skin resembled the faint blue of the water nymphs. *Yet another reason for her to eat.* She stared at them, not backing down until they both reached for a plate and started scooping up various dishes. They walked together, away from the others, and sat down. Finch sat beside Asher, stuffing his face, laughing loudly along with the rest of them, but when he caught sight of them, a dark look passed over his face. He stood, excused himself, and headed their way. Perdita sat at a small, sturdy table. She picked up a plastic fork, wondering where in the world they got them from, before putting a bite of roasted red potatoes in her mouth. The food might have been the best she'd ever had, but she couldn't taste a single thing. Finch joined them at their table, the other Gayden sat close by, like them picking at their food and eying everyone with suspicion. Perdita chewed as Wade, Damien, and Jeremiah joined them. Sabrina chewed on a cracker, leaving her hand hovering over her mouth, blocking anyone from seeing her mouth moving. "What did you find out?" Sabrina gave Finch the briefest of glances.

He popped the last of what looked like a BBQ sandwich in his mouth, chewed, and swallowed. "Styxs seem okay. I think they'll join up. Carth was real grateful when we returned and he found out we helped. Their rebellion was coming, but the guards at the Nook pushed up their timeline. When I explained before the others got here that our presence gave them cover, he'd been pleased. Said this would allow them to work behind the scenes until they decided if they are going to come out against the Council in force. Which made Asher happy because it got him out of the hot seat. Now he's my number one fan."

Ora leaned in, elbows on the table. "How'd the others get here?"

Finch shook his head, waving a hand around the clearing. "Man, I couldn't tell ya. One minute it was just us, the next Carth said we've got to call a gathering, and within minutes, magical creatures started popping up every damn where. Creepy like something out of the movies."

"I thought all transportation was down? Isn't it linked with the Veil?" Ora asked, facing Sabrina.

Sabrina rolled her shoulders. "Beats me. There have always been rumors that magical creatures had separate ways of traveling, but no one ever bothered to look into it."

Finch wiped the leftover BBQ sauce from his chin. "Guess you know now."

Ora met eyes with Finch, Sabrina, and finally Perdita. "We're almost positive the Styx are in. Who else?"

"No way to tell," Sabrina said, before nibbling on a cracker. "But I don't trust the water nymphs and the satyrs. Did you all pick that up?"

"Yeah, I noticed." Ora moved the food around on her plate. "Guess the better question is who don't we want on our side? Who would you not trust, besides water nymphs and satyrs?"

Sabrina considered her words, chewing on them like another cracker. "I'm surprised there are as many creatures here now. From what I knew, most of them were happy or impartial. Sure, the weres and vamps will come sniffing around if there is a chance to spill blood, and I don't know much about the black-eyed ones and shades. We avoided dealing with them."

"For good reason." Perdita swallowed a bit of mashed potatoes.

Sabrina agreed, raising her eyebrows. "True, but like I said, most appeared content. I'd never have thought they would even consider turning on the Council."

Finch burped, the sound ripping through the air like a rotten rocket launcher. "Now, sister, they wouldn't have come to you, a Protector, complaining about the government, would they? I'd say we take anyone's help who offers it, give enough information so they can help us, but major plans we keep to ourselves. It's what they're going to do to us, and we have to be ready for a back stabbing at any moment. Until this shindig is wrapped up and put to bed like a sleeping babe, we trust no one but us."

His words rang true. Despite his roughened ways, the Elders respected him. He had a good head on his shoulders for strategy and reading people. He had a mind for battle and, surprisingly, for politics. As if Ora had the same thoughts as Perdita, she said, "You're the speaker for the Elders. We'll follow your lead."

He answered with another enormous burp, sounding more like a demon being released from Hell, followed by slurping of his tongue across his teeth. Perdita shook her head as she saw Wade's hand move subtly under the table, reprimanding Finch.

Ora rolled her eyes, then leaned in closer to Damien. "What about you? You know of any alliances with your former friend with any magical creatures?"

Damien took a moment to gaze around at the creatures gathered before shrugging. "Can't say as a pawn I was privy to the inner workings. He sent me away from here to be a henchman to one of his bigger fish. I heard things about the human side of things, and there aren't many magical creatures running around over there. You know what I mean? Sorry, babe, but I was the muscle."

Ora's forehead constricted in thought. "We'll have to chat more about the human side of things."

A horn blew in the distance. Perdita's heart rate sped, expecting the worst, but apparently it signaled the end of the break. Creatures both big and small stood and cleared the tables. Their group did the same and then made their way back to the seating area. The creatures moved without hesitation or confusion, as if this sort of meeting took place regularly.

Back in position, Carth cleared his throat. "Now that we are all fed and watered, have we all come to a decision?"

Nerves took over Perdita, sweat beaded on her brow and making her hands clammy. The food she'd ate churned deep in her belly, threatening to return. Nods of agreement spread like the wave at a football game. Ora paled, but she kept a composed expression.

"Very well then. I'll start. Again, I must remind all of you that whatever is discussed in this meeting is to remain here. If you chose not to join, you're forbidden from warning the wizards. I'm sure all will be revealed in due time. Your loyalty is to the magical brethren. If you out us, then many will die, and it'll be on your hands. We will retaliate. Understood?"

Murmurs of agreement flitted around the clearing from many mouths.

"Very well." Carth stood, waving his massive tree trunk arms outward. "The Styxs have decided to join with the Gayden."

Perdita expected some sort of reaction to the formal decree, but all creatures reacted with no more pizazz than if he announced the sky was blue. Relief swept through the Gayden.

"In return for our aid, we wish that when we overthrow the Council, a new one be formed, adding in representatives from each of the magical species. We would like to trade from the human world as well, and no discrimination to any position within Conjuragic due to our race. It goes without saying, standard qualifications for any position must be met."

Finch tilted his head. "Define 'trade from the human world'?"

Carth bellowed a laugh that Perdita felt as a rumbling beneath her feet. "Why, we would like to buy things and sell our goods, but we would need a representative. Magical creatures agreed to leave the human world so we could live in safety and without dealing with human nonsense. We have no wish to return, but the financial benefits are lost to us. Since we're establishing a relationship with the Gayden, who are profoundly more capable of living in the human world than the wizards, we would suggest that one of you be our middle man in the endeavor. You sell our goods, keeping a small profit for yourselves, a finder's fee if you will, and the rest will come to us. Same goes for the things we would like to buy."

Finch and Ora exchanged a look. Finch nodded once. "I believe that can be arranged. Specific details about exactly which goods your great people are wishing to buy and sell can be settled at a later date. I would like to further add the stipulation that nothing with any magical properties will be sold to humans. After all, I think keeping our existence a secret is the one thing that every Gayden, Magician, and magical being can agree on.

Perdita sensed Wade's wave of relief at the speculation to leave which goods would be eligible for trade open. Perdita hoped weapons would be placed on the banned list. She thought each item would have to be reviewed in close detail and anything with potential harm would be banned, but most everyday items shouldn't be an issue.

Carth returned to his seat, swiveling his large head to the Centaur to his left. The centaur stood, human body elongated, ears pointed, and said, "The centaurs will join. We ask the same as the Styxs."

Ora nodded. A satyr leapt from his seat, quivering. "We are undecided. We will hold the secrets here today, but for now, we will stay neutral." His eyes flitted back and forth, nervous with a bead of sweat dripping down his face, despite the cool day.

The rest answered one at a time. At the end the Styx, centaurs, elves, weres, vamps, and golems joined them. The satyrs and mermaids via the water nymphs stayed neutral. The shades and wisps refused. Carth stood. "Magical brethren, I put it to a vote. To those who refuse to join or remain neutral will not have representatives on the Council. Those who agree, raise your hands." Hands sprouted. "The ayes have it. If any choose to change their minds either way, you have one day. Meeting adjourned."

16

ORA

With the meeting adjourned, I bid Carth and the other Styxs farewell. The troops had reached the end of their endurance, myself included. We couldn't wait to get back to the island for a long overdue rest. Although I doubted rest would come for a long, long time.

My leg swung over the back of the motorcycle when a swarm of angry air encircled us like a tornado. Off the bike in a second, magic at the ready, I searched for the source, but I couldn't find anyone. Through the comm, I yelled, "Where are they?"

A voice answered through the comm. "It's not a Tempest."

"A magical creature?" I asked, forming a protective circle with Damien, Sabrina, Mom, and Jeremiah. The rest of the troops paired up in a similar pattern, covering each of our backs and allowing the broadest range of defense. Finch and Wade protected a group behind us.

"Not that I can tell," another voice answered.

"It can't be," Mom said, stepping away from us with an outstretched hand.

"Mom! What're you doing?" Automatically, we closed our ranks, moving as one unit to grab her arm and pull her back inside. My fingertips missed her by inches. She slipped closer to the swirling whirlwind.

"An oxygenian," she murmured through the comm, her voice full of wonder.

The vortex fell away, leaving dust and mushroom spores raining down in a slow dance toward the ground. Like with Lailie, a voice spoke inside my head, *We've been listening.*

The voice had to be in all our heads because when it spoke, everyone jumped.

"And?" Mom asked, face serene.

I wasn't as trusting. The oxygenians were the Experimenter's creations. Just because Lailie had turned against him didn't mean they all had. Besides, I thought they were rare, and this thing had said *we*.

We would like to join with you as well. My brothers and I, the airy voice spoke again. *We can be your eyes and ears. We saw what you did for our sister. You named her Lailie.*

"Why would you help us?" I asked, testing a theory, and as I guessed, the oxygenian heard me without the comm even through the mask.

You saved our sister. You released her.

"She sacrificed herself helping my daughter. It was she who helped us," Mom said, using her comm. "We should be helping you."

Yesssss, it said, stretching the s like a hiss. *We cannot die. We can be released from this form if we enter another. If we do that without a higher purpose, we cease to exist.*

The ground rumbled a few feet to my left. Rising from the earth in a billowing mound of dirt and mud, a human-like shape appeared. My first instinct roared at me to send Sphere at it and destroy it where it stood, but something held me back. After a moment, it spoke. Its voice was ragged and hoarse as if it took great energy to speak, "The noroins will help."

What the hell is a noroin?

"A being made of earth," Sabrina said through the comm, more to herself, than at anyone. Before we could answer, lava pooled from beneath the noroin who moved away with sloshing wet footsteps to a safer location. The lava also pulled itself together forming a human-esque shape. With a voice like the sound of crackling wood, it said, "The feirians are at your service."

"As are the hydrenians." Yet another human form stood before us. This one looking as if someone used naiad magic and water sucked out of the ground. With all of them together, I understood. The oxygenians weren't the only new species to be formed by experimenting on Gayden and magicians.

"You're all creations of the Experimenter?" I asked. All except the oxygenian nodded.

"Why do you take these shapes?"

The feirian answered, "We miss our former selves."

The oxygenian swirled itself in the floating mushroom spores, giving it a human form too. *We wish to help you. If some of us truly die, then it will not be in vain and we can move on.*

The noroin spit mud with each word. "We would not see any more of our kind created. We heard you're searching for the Experimenter. We know where he is."

"What would you ask of us?" Sabrina asked, using her comm on an open channel.

The oxygenian blew through us, I felt as if it tasted each of us. *We want justice for what was done to us. You're the first to ever stand against him.*

"You didn't answer my question."

We have no purpose. We exist. We have escaped the Experimenter, but we cannot live real lives. By helping you we have purpose, and when all is over, if you can help us regain our true forms or release us, that will be enough.

My mom's face told me everything. She was sold.

Doubt still raged inside me. More alliances showing up out of nowhere to help us. It was too easy, too convenient, and where had they been all this time? "Then as a show of good faith, give us something now. Something given freely so we know what you say is true." For the rest of my life, I would regret speaking those words, but I couldn't have known what was to come.

The noroin's head turned my way. Its faceless form sent chills of unease running down my spine. Perhaps a sign I shouldn't have ignored, but I did, shrugging it off as nerves. "The Willow is deserted, but deeper into the forest lies something that you lost."

"What did I lose?"

"A human boy."

I felt more than heard the sharp intake of Damien's breath at this news. Mom spun, meeting my eyes, searching for my reaction. My resolved hardened like steel. I could put it off no longer. After seeing Arameus, I couldn't not go after John. I owed Charlie that.

"Where exactly?"

The hydrenian gave us directions.

"Very well. Thank you. How can we get in touch with you?" The words left my mouth, sounding far, far away, as if someone else had spoken them.

We're always watching, the oxygenian said, voice disappearing as a gust of wind soared upward, the hydrenian splashed soared upward, followed by the feirian and noroin descending back into the soil.

"I don't like that they can do that," Finch said, voicing exactly what I felt.

"Are you sure we should be doing this?" Sabrina asked. "I know it's Charlie's brother and your," she stopped with an awkward glance at Damien, "friend, but this could be a trap."

"Sabrina's right. We need to get back. Talk with the Elders. We'll come back for this dude, but on our terms," Finch said.

I met Mom's eyes. She smiled. "You're in charge, sweetie. I'll do whatever you think is best."

"Let's go back to the island," I said, climbing on the back of the bike for the second time, and without waiting for anyone else, I tore the Bridge open. Mom gasped, but I didn't bother looking to see why.

Finch whooped. "I tell you what, Big O. You've got some balls to take these through the Bridge."

Back on the island, the troops dispatched to get some food and rest. For one peaceful moment, we didn't have to do anything. The wounded were being tended to while someone prepared those who died to be laid to rest. Healer Roos had the invisibility potion brewing. I stood alone on the beach, staring out at the waves, thinking about that morning at the Severn Sea. My mind made up, I opened the Bridge. Before I could step through, Sabrina spoke at my back, "Where do you think you are going alone?"

"Nowhere," I lied, unconvincingly.

Mom put her hands on her hips. "Did you think we were stupid? We know you're going to get John. You think we would let you go alone?" She radiated beauty standing there as the day faded into night. She'd changed from the Protector's outfit into tan corduroy pants flowing around her ankles with tennis shoes along with a peach button-up blouse. She saw me eyeing her clothes, and she shrugged. "I figured he'd respond better if I looked like myself."

"It doesn't give you much protection." Sabrina inspected her outfit, walking around her in a slow circle. She pulled her blond hair up in a bun just like I'd always remembered her, but so many years younger.

Wade appeared from behind a dune, wearing his red leather, gun holstered at his side. "I agree. You need more than that."

"What're you doing here?" I demanded. I could understand why Mom and Sabrina were here, but why Wade?

"You need someone impartial. You two are too emotionally involved." His eyes moved from Mom to me before moving on to Sabrina. "You, while impressive, aren't enough. Go change Perdita." He finished by giving a backward nod toward the island.

Mom held up a hand. "I'll be fine, but I do think we ought to wait. Get some rest so we're in top form when we find him."

My mom saw the agony in my eyes. I couldn't wait. If I didn't go now, I would hate myself.

Mom patted Wade on the shoulder then waved a hand forward. "Shall we?"

I clasped their hands and stepped into the Bridge. Someone called my name, the fear and urgency in that sound chilled my blood. Looking over my shoulder, I caught a glimpse of Charlie racing toward us as if her life depended on it. I couldn't handle her right now. She'd still been asleep when we got back. I couldn't bring back her Arameus whole, but I could get John. Maybe then she wouldn't hate me. Instead of waiting, I closed the Bridge behind me with her scream of, "No!" echoing through the vast emptiness.

17

ORA

The Willow, the beautiful home of the Spheres, lay in shattered pieces all over the forest floor. A dirty ripped teddy bear sat on his side, forgotten, alone, destroyed. We had done that. I imagined the child the little bear belonged to. Where was he or she? Did the child get hurt? Or die? I stumbled, and Sabrina grabbed my arm, holding me up when I couldn't.

Moving as swift and silent, we followed the directions the hydrenian gave to us. All the while, I ran through a thousand scenarios of what the reunion with John would look like.

The sky overhead gave an angry flash of lightning followed by the crash of thunder. The wind snuck through the trees with a whipping howl before the clouds burst open. Fat, cold, hard rain fell. Unlike any storm I'd ever seen in the human world. This one didn't start with a small drizzle building up to a downpour. As soon as the first drops fell, a thousand more followed. Using Naiad, we kept ourselves dry, otherwise we'd have been soaked in seconds as if we stepped right into an icy shower.

Deeper into the forest, the storm grew worse as if somewhere the Tempests knew what horrors would soon befall. The trees grew thicker making what little light remained of twilight disappear. I drew a fire hovering above my palm to cast some light over the grounds. At the same moment the attack came.

A blow I hadn't seen coming sent me flying backward. My back slammed up against a tree, knocking the wind from me, and I crumpled to the ground. I sucked in a ragged breath. A ringing sound buzzed in my ears dampening grunts nearby.

A tree burst into a thousand splinters to my left. I ducked, covering my head. The wood poured down, mingling with the rain. As predicted, without blocking the rain, water covered me in seconds. My hair hung in a wet blob over the side of my face. Using the tree as support, I pulled to my feet, the ground moving underneath me. It took several seconds to realize the ground hadn't been turned to quicksand. The blow screwed with my vision, confusing up with down. Nausea swirled deep in my belly, and I had to choke it down. The sense of urgency came from far away. A warm trickle winded its way down my right forehead, mingling with the cold raindrops.

Up ahead, I tried to make sense of what the images flashing through the lightning strikes. Someone had set a few trees on fire. Shadows danced and screamed. Realization seeped slowly back to me. Someone attacked us. I staggered forward holding on trees so I wouldn't fall.

John towered over a collapsed Sabrina. Her body convulsed in an image that was way too familiar. A Gayden attack, stealing her magic. Over and over his foot came down on her back. His face contorted into an animalistic rage I'd seen one other time. When he fought the three attackers who tried to assault me the night of our first kiss.

Sensing my presence, John stopped, looked up, our eyes locked. A thousand emotions flashed through his eyes before settling on one—hate. I opened my mouth to speak. He couldn't hate me. I wasn't the enemy, but Aryiana's words returned to me. "The boy you loved is dead." She was right. Whoever John had been before had died. This stranger stood before me now. A wolf in his skin, but I couldn't look away. Over and over, images of him jumping in front of Mom to save her.

I wanted him back. I wanted the old John. The one who held my hand, who kissed the top of my head. The John who loved me and wanted to marry me. The John who risked his life to come to Conjuragic to save me.

A spell flew past me, missing me by inches. Indecision rattled through me. I tore my eyes from John and Sabrina. Mom battled Strega, a Gayden experiment half her age. She had little chance of winning. Mom ducked and sent spells flying. Her left shoulder had a deep gash and her right thigh singed. I couldn't see Wade anywhere. I should move, but paralysis clung to my limbs.

Strega fought like second nature. Her body moved and twisted, dodging spells at an inhuman speed. Agile as a feline, she hurdled and dodged everything Mom threw at her. Without thought, my power snaked through the earth penetrating a tree branch. It swept out, grabbing Strega's ankle. Rage renewed my power's focus. This one nothing to the rage I'd possessed when I thought she'd killed John. A hazy whiteness blossomed over my vision as my eyes blazed with in-human brightness.

I wanted her dead. She was trying to hurt my mom! She killed my John. His body might be here, but he wasn't, and she'd done it. I knew it. With everything in me, I knew it. She would pay for taking him from me. She turned her attention from Mom to me. She smiled. The bitch smiled like she laughed when she sent the boulder. But this time, Mom had a clear shot. I saw it a second before it happened. Nothing stood between her and Strega. The magic sizzled in the air around her. I sensed it like static electricity in the air. Before she could release it, a haunted scream broke out of the forest, "No!"

As if stuck in quicksand, I watched, horrified, as John ran forward, slinging his arm forward, at an impossible speed. The metal reflected in his hand as lightning flashed overhead. Mom's scream drowned out by the proceeding thunder. The knife protruded from her soaked back. Blood pooled underneath the blade, staining her peach blouse. She fell to her knees, leaning forward, one hand supporting her weight.

Coming back to life, I flung a spell at John. I didn't know which one. It didn't matter. It struck true, and he flew backward, far away, and out of my sight.

Strega freed herself from the branch. She sneered, turning her nose up at Mom. I reached mom as she slumped to the side unable to hold herself up.

From the corner of my eye, Wade stumbled from the forest. A forest fire illuminated his features in shadow. His eyes swept the scene finding me crouched, holding Mom, before turning his focus on Strega. She lifted her hands, gathering Sabrina's magic to use against me. If Wade hadn't been there, this might've been it. With her attention elsewhere, Wade snuck up to her side and gripped her shoulder. Her mouth opened in a silent scream, eyes rolling in the back of her head. Her torso convulsed, and in seconds, she slumped to the ground.

Wade released a breath, long and slow, and to my left Sabrina stopped shaking and regained consciousness. "What did you do?" I asked.

"Took her stolen magic. I gave it back."

Wade's energy had been zapped. I had no idea Gayden could do that.

He swayed on his feet. My ears still buzzed, and the forest swayed, and Mom... We had to get out of here and now.

With my eyes squeezed shut, I prayed the last ten minutes hadn't happened. I wished we were back on the island and we'd never come here.

A shaking hand touched my face. The rain, as suddenly as it appeared, disappeared. The smell of burning wood and blood filled the air. My eyes stung. "Ora, baby. Look at me."

With eyes still closed, I shook my head side to side.

"You can do it. You're so strong." Mom's voice was so low, almost a whisper, and full of pain.

I reluctantly opened my eyes, looking down at her face. Her head nestled in my arms, like she was the child, and I the mother. Her normal fair skin faded to a bluish white. Her lips quivered, and she cringed with a moan with the slightest movement. "Mom, you're going to be okay. We'll get you back to the Healers. You're going to be fine."

Her hand stroked my face with a smile. "I'm so sorry, honey. I'm sorry."

"Don't. Don't you dare."

"I'm so proud of you." A spasm rippled through her. She took deep gasping breaths with a gurgling sound.

"We've got to get her back. Now," Wade said, standing over us.

"How're we going to move her?" Sabrina asked, voice thick, almost breaking.

"We could make a stretcher, use Sphere," I suggested, desperate now to get her back to the island. I craned my head to look for something to use. My knee bumped the knife, and Mom screamed. "Oh, God. I'm sorry. I'm sorry."

"I don't know if it'll work in the Bridge," Sabrina said, tears running down her cheeks.

"The Bridge," Mom whispered, "take me into the Bridge."

"We've got to figure out how to move you," I told her, leaning down, careful with the knife. I kissed her forehead as she had done to mine a thousand times.

Her eyes closed, face strained in pain, but then it relaxed as if all the pain faded. God that wasn't good. "Take me to the Bridge."

"Okay."

"Now."

Now? I had nothing to put her on. I couldn't carry her.

"Wait." Her eyes opened finding me in the darkness, "I love you. I've always loved you. You have to go on. You can't give up."

"Mom, don't. You're going to be fine."

"Shhh. It's okay now. Promise me. You'll keep going. You fight so no one else has to go through what we have. Okay?"

"Okay, I promise." My voice broke, eyes stinging, blurring my beautiful mom's face. "Okay, Mommy. I love you. I love you so much."

"I love you too." She gasped between each word.

"Stop!" A dark, cold, commanding voice rang out in the darkness. I jerked my head toward the sound, a blond man, older, with crow's feet, and long blue robes slithered from the shadows. My stomach recoiled as if I had drunk something poisoned. I recognized him immediately, not needing to hear Sabrina's words.

"Mathesar Enochs."

His hands rose, not in a spell, but as if to summon others. With his movement, I sensed a shifting in the forest, subtle, then the tell-tale crackling of leaves almost masked by the burning trees.

"How?" Wade whispered, moving to my right.

Sabrina rounded to stand by my left. "Monster!"

"Such judgment from a traitor. Tell me, did you get the privilege of seeing your father die?"

"Bastard!" Sabrina moved as if to attack, but held her position.

Mathesar turned his attention from Sabrina to Mom. "My pet. You see what happens when you leave me? I have Healers with me. They can help you."

"Stay away from her!" I pulled her closer to me, rage filling me, but I pushed down the urge to let it rise to my eyes.

"What do you care?" Mathesar asked, looking from her face to mine. "It can't be." He spoke as if bored, but his expression told a different story. Anger rumbled below the surface, like an asp, ready to strike. "You gave my love to another."

Mom, who until this moment refused to open her eyes, now glared at him, her power rising, stinging my skin. "You don't know the meaning of the word."

Those in the forest drew closer. I didn't know how many he brought, but we weren't safe. We had to go and now. Willing them to listen, I sent a silent message to Sabrina and Wade. I'll never know if they heard or if they sensed the danger as well. They touched my shoulder with a fast jerking motion. I opened the Bridge, underneath us, sinking inside like quick sand. Gone in a flash with Mathesar's scream of rage following behind.

Inside the blackness of the Bridge, my mother glowed. Her body quivered in my arms, seeming to grow smaller. She looked out into the darkness and whispered to me, "It's okay. Let me go."

"I can't. If I do, you'll get lost in here."

"Let go, baby. I love you. Forever. Now let me go." She focused on me for the last time. I did as she asked, finding myself standing, holding her like an infant. I kissed her forehead once again, tears spilling onto her face. I let my arms drift to my sides and she didn't fall, instead, her body broke apart into a million pieces. "No."

In that moment, I felt Jiminy. I hadn't noticed him before, but I felt him as soon as we entered the Bridge. For the smallest of seconds, Mom vanished into nothing, leaving us in blackness. The next she stood before me, a shadow of her former self, but younger, my age. Beside her a young man flanked her, who I guessed was Jiminy. Their arms wrapped around each other and they smiled back at me. My mom didn't say a word, as always, she didn't have to. She told me goodbye with her eyes. She turned her attention to the man beside her. The same red hair and amber eyes as mine. In that instant, I knew.

They faded back into the darkness and beyond.

18

CHARLIE

Arameus moaned, the stark white bed sheet covering his form, lumpy underneath, with one distinct piece missing. His skin remained a sickly greenish shade. Even his freckles had faded with this latest in a series of injuries he sustained when they ambushed the Haven, then again, and not long after those healed, he'd been captured and tortured. Teetering on the edge of death, he'd managed to survive the injury, but his leg hadn't been so lucky. Charlie sat in a chair beside his bed, leaned over, elbows on her jean-clad thighs. He hadn't regained consciousness. Roos said that he should've been awake by now.

The last of her fingernails had been nibbled off hours ago. Her leg shook in a continuous rhythm as if subconsciously trying to comfort herself. She had no idea if he'd ever wake up or if he'd live. Ora, Perdita, and Sabrina had disappeared through the Bridge without telling anyone. Her grandparents remained in hiding, and her brother was... She didn't even know how to describe his condition—worse than dead. She'd never felt more lost or alone. Or more angry at her best friend, she could've asked her to go along or at least given her the time of day before disappearing again. Charlie didn't want to leave Arameus, but waiting without being able to do anything grated on her nerves. The distraction would've been welcome. No matter what it was Ora went off to do.

More importantly, she needed to talk to Ora. Even though Charlie had been, well, a bitch. A big fat one. She could see that now. Ora had been right. She couldn't have gone to rescue Arameus. She would've been useless when they found him. The condition of his leg alone would've undone her. She couldn't have helped and would've been another liability. But her grandma always said hindsight was twenty-twenty. Whatever that meant. If she hadn't been in the Willow, she wouldn't have seen John.

Arameus moaned again, and Charlie stood, treading close to the bed, looking for any signs that his condition grew worse. Another Healer had come in earlier, an assistant, and given him more anesthesia potion. He shouldn't be in any pain, and unlike human pain meds, those made using magic didn't leave you feeling groggy, or have ill side effects. He moaned again, turned his head to the side, eyes fluttering underneath paper-thin lids. With tremendous effort, Arameus opened his eyes.

Charlie gasped, hands flying to her mouth, tears springing to her eyes. He was awake. "Arameus, I'm here. I'm right here. You're safe."

He turned his head, searching her face, forehead crinkled. He took a long time for his forehead to smooth. "Hey, baby. Is Sabrina ready?"

Jealousy rose in a flash. "Ready for what?"

"For me to walk her down the aisle. I'm so honored she asked me."

Charlie, taking great care, sat beside Arameus. He reached out, taking her hand, not noticing the shakiness with which it moved.

"Sweetie, you already walked Sabrina down the aisle."

Arameus blinked. "No, I haven't. That's today."

"No. Sabrina already got married. You walked her down the aisle. The ceremony was beautiful. You did an amazing job."

"I did?" Fear etched itself in his face and his hand turned clammy in hers.

She kept her voice light and soft, reassuring. "You did."

"What happened? Why don't I remember?"

"Retrograde amnesia," a voice said from the door. Charlie turned to see Healer Roos in the doorway. "It has been a number of days since the wedding. You were injured."

It really was the Healer's job to tell him, but injured didn't adequately describe being tortured, getting an infection, almost dying, and losing a leg. She turned away from the woman. "At the reception, the Quads showed up and captured you along with others. Ora and a team rescued you. You were hurt pretty bad."

Roos stepped up to the foot of the bed while Arameus looked from Charlie to Roos and back again. "How many did we lose?"

"Don't concern yourself with those things right now. You're back on the island. You need to focus on you and getting better." She moved up the side of the bed and lifted a hand over his chest. The air over Arameus's chest shimmered as her power flowed over him. "You're healing nicely. The infection is receding. It seems the human meds aren't as useless as I thought. They tell me you'll need another week or so of the antibiotics. Are you in any pain?"

"My head's a bit foggy. Are we about ready to get started? I bet Sabrina is nervous. Pre-wedding jitters," Arameus said, face blank once again.

"No, honey," Charlie began, but a Roos interrupted her.

"Don't bother. You'll waste your breath if you try explaining things to him now. No, it's best if I get him another sleeping draft."

"No. Let him be. He's slept enough. I'll call if he gets worked up," Charlie said, but Arameus's eyes were already drooping. She doubted he'd remember this conversation.

Roos nodded once and disappeared through the door, pulling it shut behind her. The door clicked, and Arameus lifted his head off the bed, then looked back at Charlie. "Now tell me what really happened."

Her jaw fell open. He'd been pretending. "Don't give me that look. Roos wasn't going to tell me anything, so I wanted to get rid of her. Now she's gone. What happened?"

"What do you remember?"

"Before the wedding. You said the Quads showed up."

Charlie filled him in and through her story, his complexion blanched. He'd been so pale already if he went any whiter he'd be invisible. She stood and pulled the sheet aside, showing him his leg. A look of complete horror filled his face, his bottom lip trembled, and his left hand kept opening and clenching closed. She covered his leg, and he didn't say a word.

Neither of them spoke for quite a long time. "It doesn't look real. Does it?"

Charlie didn't know how to answer, so she remained quiet while Arameus stared at the ceiling. Only his unsteady breathing filled the room as he fought to control his emotions. Lightning flashed outside followed by a thunderous boom. Charlie could've sworn there wasn't a cloud in the night sky when she followed Ora out on the beach. As if the heavens broke open, rain pelted the hospital, sounding more like a monsoon.

With never a dull moment in this hospital, voices sounded outside the corridor. Charlie didn't want to leave Arameus, but one never knew what could possibly be going on. She patted his hand. "I'll be right back."

He gripped her hand until his knuckles turned white, as if he didn't want to be alone either, but then let go. He gave a quick jerk of his head, eyes squeezed shut, a tear sneaking out of his left eye. "I won't go if you don't want me to."

As if he couldn't speak, he turned away from her, waving toward the door.

Charlie cringed, unsure what he wanted her to do. "Do you want me to stay?" He shook his head no again. "Okay. I'll be right back."

She slipped out of the doorway, hating to leave him, but for all she knew, he could be in more danger. A general air of confusion swirled around the nurses' station. The small, brick, three-floored hospital, which hardly ever saw any action, remained packed to the gills these days. Magical healing certainly sped things up a bit, but couldn't do everything, despite what television and movies would lead you to believe. Arameus had been moved from the trauma/ER unit on the bottom floor to another room in the ICU on the third floor. Glass enclosed the room, with the bathroom open, no shower, and one large bed with many hook ups for various IV lines and monitors. Roos and the other Healers scoffed at the idea of the monitors, but as Dr. Jones pointed out, even with their magic, they couldn't monitor everyone all the time.

Charlie gathered the doctors had reached the end of their understanding. They constantly had to remind the Healers they weren't in Conjuragic and they did things differently. Despite all the help the Healers provided, they weren't totally trusted, even Roos. They Gayden doctors never forgot this was war and the magicians were fighting against their own. Charlie didn't overall agree with this theory, but she could be wrong. She didn't trust her own judgment these days. She'd been too emotional, too raw, too overwhelmed to decide much of anything.

Stepping up to the nurses' station, Charlie placed her elbows and leaned over to talk to the heavy-set black woman in front of the desk, staring at the screen, as if reading something. She cleared her throat. "Excuse me. Do you know what's going on?"

The black woman, whose name tag identified her as Deborah, rolled her eyes at the disturbance. "Nope." The one word came across as both offensive and dismissive at the same time. How amazing that one simple word could come across so perfectly as "screw you." Much more effective than giving someone the bird. Charlie bit her tongue, thinking the foul woman wasn't worth it, but she let a bit of her new power slip from her fingers and blew nearby papers right into the woman's face. Sure, it'd been childish and petty, but damn it felt good.

Charlie went to the elevators and pressed down. Rain and thunder boomed outside, pelting the hospital with fat heavy raindrops. The lights flickered as the elevator door opened. Inside, she pressed the down button and waited. When the doors swung open, she knew something had gone terribly wrong.

A group of people ran past the elevator opening toward the entrance. Charlie recognized Damien in the lead, followed by Jeremiah, and Finch hobbling in the rear. A number of Healers weaved in between, and Charlie trailed after, catching up with Finch. "What's going on?" she shouted, above the pounding of their feet on the white-tiled floor.

Nurses, Healers, and visitors all pushed themselves to the edge of the tan walls to get out of their way. "Ora's back. Something bad has happened."

Charlie felt as if she'd been kicked in the stomach. *What had happened? Was Ora hurt? Had she been killed?* No, surely not. Finch would've told her. If she died, they couldn't have made it back. *Right? But what if she died in the Veil? Would people get stuck in there or would it remain open until they could bring her back?* Her worry and imagination flared hot and eyes burned. Nothing could happen to Ora. Charlie couldn't bear it. She was her friend. Her best friend, more like a sister. She'd been so stupid to fight with her.

Charlie's heart stuttered when the double doors opened onto the emergency room entrance. Wade held a limp Ora in his arms. She appeared so small his arms, child-like, eyes closed, covered in blood. Sabrina stood to the side, face grim, blond hair unkempt with large pieces escaping from the braid. "Back up." Wade jogged, parting the crowd as he carried her.

Charlie hadn't been aware of stopping, placing her hands over her mouth, as if trying to suppress a scream.

Damien didn't back up, as he pressed forward, and reached out a shaking hand, looking like he wanted nothing more than for Wade to hand Ora to him like a precious gem. "Is she?" Damien paused.

"She's in shock," Wade said.

"But the blood?" Jeremiah's throat bobbed.

"It isn't hers." Wade pushed past, stone faced, into a triage area, and placed Ora down on an empty bed. A Healer shooed most of them away, but Charlie refused to leave. Sabrina and Wade stayed.

"Tell me what happened?" the Healer asked.
"We went to find John," Wade began.
Charlie gasped. "Oh no! I tried to tell her."

19

ORA

Voices talked around me, but the words floated, without meaning, empty, like my heart. The moment her last breath left her, Wade uttered the final words, "She's gone."

A nothingness descended over me, heavy, as if some vital part of myself had suddenly disappeared. Instead of making me lighter, the hole filled me with a heavy weight like lead, throwing me off balance. I couldn't stand. I couldn't breathe. The world had changed forever. Surreal and strange, like an unpleasant dream, leaving an uneasy queasy feeling deep in the pit of my stomach.

I'd had dreams like that before, where something awful had happened, and a similar feeling would overcome me. This wasn't right. This couldn't be happening. I would wake up, shake my head, then fall asleep again, earlier in the dream, and start over, fixing the bad part.

I kept waiting to fall back asleep, so I could rewind it, to fix it, but I stayed awake. Awake in this terrible, terrible reality, which I couldn't accept.

Any slight movement of my hand revealed stickiness, reminding me of the truth. Her blood on my hands, spilled because of me. How many roads and choices had I made that had led to this?

Hands touched me, gentle, but everything hurt. How could I still be alive when she wasn't? My mom was gone. I couldn't breathe. No pain had ever felt like this before. I thought I could never feel the agony of loss as potent as when I'd thought John died. Rage had overtaken me that fateful day. The magic inside me demanded retribution, and I destroyed the Unity Statue. That rage and pain could never compare to this. This time the magic turned back against me, and now instead of a city, my entire world had been destroyed.

A light flickered, and visions of the flashing knife rippled up from my mind's eye. John killed my mother. The same John who'd started this whole thing. The betrayal of it zapped through my veins like lightning. How could it have been him? Images flashed in my head—fast. John as a boy running in my yard. Mom pouring him lemonade. John sitting at our table eating dinner. John hugging Mom when he graduated high school. John smiling at Mom after he'd asked me to marry him. John jumping in front of that boulder to save her. Then John's face, full of rage, as the knife flashed in his hand, hurtling toward her back. She'd stood in front of him, protecting him, and he'd betrayed her. Betrayed me. He would pay for this. He was supposed to keep her safe, be on our side, and he'd went over to Strega—to Mathesar.

Mathesar's face replaced John's, white blond hair, aqua robes, teal blue eyes, evil lurking in their depths. Mathesar killing my grandma, my true one, enslaving my parents, and having Strega as his little minion. He would pay too.

The hands around me vanished, followed by a scream of pain—not from me this time. My vision blared white hot. I jerked upward, magic at the ready, recognizing a hospital bed. The monitor screen wavered and flickered. A young Sphere held a blistered angry red hand in front of him. I reached toward him as if trying to take it back. "I'm sorry."

He looked from his hand to me then back to his blistered covered hand. Before my eyes the blisters faded from purplish pustules back to pale, smooth skin. "No worries. I should've known not to touch you right now."

"What do you mean?" My voice came out thick and frog-like, as if it hadn't been used in a thousand years.

"During times of great stress, some witches wall themselves in their power. Like a cocoon of sorts. It's a form of protection."

Magical cocoon? Other than lying on the hospital bed, still wearing the mud-covered lavender protector's leathers, nothing looked any different. My vision blurred as the realization of what that dried blood mingled with the mud meant.

The Sphere said, "It broke when you sat up."

"Oh." The reply sounded lame even to my own ears. He smiled, trying to pull me the rest of the way out of the mental shell.

The smile faded transforming into a look of cautious concern. "How're you feeling?"

"Okay." This was the furthest from the truth, but nothing else came to mind, except that I felt in a fog, numb to anything else, but even that didn't quite cover it. "How long have I been in the cocoon thing?"

"A few hours."

A few hours. She'd been gone a few hours already. Did this Healer know?

"Would you like to get cleaned up?" He spoke to me as if I might fall apart, which who was I kidding—I might. The cocoon hadn't protected me from anything. The enemy wasn't outside, it was in my own head, replaying the scene over and over again. Her choked sobs, the fear and pain etched on her once smooth face, drowning in her own blood. The blood still on my hands and forever staining my soul. He'd asked if I wanted to get cleaned up. Wash the last of her away from me. It would flow down the drain, into the sewer, like trash, as if she didn't matter. The monitor beside me burst outward, showering the place in a storm of broken glass.

The Sphere ducked. When the pieces settled, he straightened, brushing down his brown robes. "Clearly not. Is there anything I can get you? Would you like to sleep some more?"

The Sphere hadn't been fazed at all by the sudden outburst. Guilt of a different sort swirled inside me. Where the guilt of Mom's death swarmed through me like a thick inky blackness, this guilt slid around more orange and smelled like overripe bananas. "Sorry." I nodded toward the now shattered monitor.

"It's okay. I'm Healer Bishop." He maintained the gentile smile that lit up kind, brown eyes. "Kris," he offered with the smallest shrug, as if this wasn't a name he often gave. I let my gaze fall away. The sudden intimacy in my raw state grated on my fragile nerves. He wore tennis shoes, orange and purple underneath the brown robes. Although I couldn't confirm it, his broad shoulders underneath the robes made me think he worked out. Although I couldn't imagine a gym in Conjuragic. He had longer brown hair than the others I'd seen, meaning he must be a new Healer. He pulled it back at his neck. He didn't shy from my survey of him, but his awareness of it brought the faintest of redness to my cheeks. Under other circumstances, I would've told Charlie all about the guy I met who reminded me of Jacob from that sparkling vampire movie.

It occurred to me I hadn't told him my name. "I'm Ora. Ora Stone."

Kris gave a half laugh. "I know who you are." He said this as if I were someone famous. I felt nothing like that. My earlier thoughts returned. I stared down at my hands, tears welling in my eyes, blurring the darkened stain on me. Squeezing my eyes shut, my balled-up fists clutched at my chest, as close to my heart as I could get, and the sobs broke. I wailed like a small child. I knew, knew without a shadow of doubt that I couldn't keep this part of her. That I would have to remove it, but I couldn't. I wanted her with me—in any way that I could. I cried and cried, letting the tears spill down my cheeks. My voice cracked as if my body was incapable of holding the pain, but my small mouth wasn't large enough to allow the rage and pain inside to escape. I shielded my hands, not letting the tears touch her blood, and sobbed. I don't know how long I stayed this way, but then, little by little, the weight of it eased. In no way did it become lighter, but it's almost like when I'd moved into my dorm and tried to carry the biggest, heaviest box myself, but then Charlie's granddad grabbed the other side. The weight remained, distributed between the two of us. I opened my eyes, and Kris stood silent beside me, a hand on my shoulder, silent tears rolling down his face as well.

The shock of it silenced me. He opened his eyes, and my grief stared back at me through another. He shuttered a breath that flowed through me as well. Then he released me, wiping his eyes. I didn't ask, but he didn't need me to. "I'm a special kind of Healer. I help with emotional problems."

This revelation left me half pissed, half interested. "You're like a shrink?" I asked with too much bite to my tone.

He chuckled. "Perhaps. I'm more of what humans would call an empath. Healer Roos asked me to see you when you cocooned yourself. It's my area of specialty. Emotionally labile witches can be dangerous." He made a point of glancing at the monitor. A flash of my magic tearing out of me, set out to destroy Conjuragic came back to me.

"I can imagine."

His smile, never wavered, but grew wider with each moment. He radiated calmness—like a warm fire on a cold winter's day. "Do you feel better?"

Doing a mental evaluation of myself, I found that I did. The numbness lingered, but the wall of grief had subsided. I knew it wasn't gone, and it would rise up again and again in the coming hours and days, hell, perhaps the next coming months and years, but the tidal wave had gone back to sea. Kris helped me withstand it, hold it up, and ease it into something manageable.

His smile faded like the setting sun, replaced by a somber expression. "Tell me what is the one thing that is playing through your mind. Even if you feel it is stupid and illogical. Tell me. I won't laugh or judge you."

I couldn't face looking at them again. "Her blood on my hands." My voice quivered, the pain washing ashore like a wave. "I don't want to throw it away."

He nodded, then took my hands in his. "Trust me?"

I nodded and watched as her blood peeled from my skin, rising into the air in small fragments. From a pocket inside his robes, he pulled out a small glass stopper, no bigger than half an inch, and removed the lid. The pieces entered the bottle, and he replaced the cap. "Now you don't have to."

Gratefulness filled me as I took the bottle from him and wrapped my clean fingers around it, around this small kindness that I could have forever. Words I didn't have struggled in my mind, but his hands squeezed mine, pressing the small bottle closer. "It's okay. I can feel what you feel."

My body quivered as I inhaled his calm, sensing, or perhaps imaging it absorbing into my blood and running through my veins. My job wasn't finished. If I didn't keep going, then it would be for nothing. Grief would have to wait. So many people counted on me. Would there be a funeral? I didn't know. The countless others who died hadn't gotten one. Why should my mom be any different?

After several long minutes of letting Kris siphon his eternal calmness into me, I swung my feet off the hospital bed. Every movement felt foreign, like driving a new car. The movements remained the same, but the amount of control on the steering wheel and gas and brake pedals varied. Kris led me to a shower and turned it on as if he had been doing this his whole life.

Without a word, Kris left. He certainly was good at his job. I needed quiet, not to fill the silence with senseless talking, not to say the generic statement "I'm sorry for your loss." Those inevitable words would come. I'd heard them before. Uttered them myself, never quite understand how lame and inadequate they were. I looked at the ceiling to avoid the sight of the bloodstained leathers. Concentrating on the dust-covered drop ceiling, I waited for the water to warm. The cool air mingled with the scent of pungent sterilization chemicals. Steam filled the room, dampening my skin, mingling with tear-soaked cheeks. Touching the skin with my cleaned hands, I pulled off my boots one at a time. My fingers fumbled with the straps at my sides and then slid the leathers off and struggling with the pants finishing with bra and panties. Everything I wore I simultaneously wanted to burn and keep forever. I kept the tiny vial and amulet that embraced me as if we belonged together.

A long while later, there came a soft knock at the door—tentative, questioning, but imposing none the less. "I'm coming." With a slow twist of the knob, the water died save for a tiny *drip, drip, drip*. The soiled clothes had disappeared, and fresh clothes waited for me. It had to have been Kris. No anger in me rose; instead, gratefulness flowed through me. I dressed quickly in a plain white cotton bra and panties, soft worn jeans, white socks, and an old T-shirt supporting some metal band. The odd T-shirt brought a smile to my lips although I wasn't quite sure if it was a joke or an oversight, but Mom would've found it funny.

The knock didn't come again. Outside the room a pair of sneakers perched in the door in front of me. Perhaps Kris had brought the clothes, forgot shoes, and didn't want to risk walking in on me stepping out of the shower so he knocked instead.

I slipped on the shoes, tying one then the other. I swallowed as I stood, knowing I'd ran out of time. I couldn't stall anymore. I'd have to face people. Right now, a part of me could still pretend this was all a bad dream, but when I witnessed my grief reflected in another, when the words came, it would be real. No turning back. Her voice spoke in my head then, not as I would've wished, a real voice, like an oxygenian or even a ghost, but an imagined one. *Come on. Time's awaiting*, a phrase I grew up hearing her speak a thousand times. I nodded. "Time's awaiting."

The memory of my mom and I stepped out of the room, toward the others, toward the future—the one where she no longer existed, toward a sadder destiny.

20

ORA

The Town Hall loomed before me. Judgment radiated off it like heat in the mid-day sun. Everyone important waited inside. I stepped out of a cab, and the tiny olive-skinned man waved as he pulled away. The Hospital voucher paid for my ride. I'd refused Healer Kris's offer to call someone to come get me, and I couldn't face the Bridge. Not yet. The oddity of something so ordinary as taking a cab threw off my already unstable equilibrium. Two guards stepped off the porch of the old church, packing a ton of heat, but not bothering to draw their weapons. I hadn't seen them before, but they acted like they recognized me.

A tall one, dark hair, hint of a five o'clock shadow, and a slight limp to his step bowed his head to me. "I'm sorry for your loss."

"Yeah, me too," the second one added, this one short and about thirty pounds overweight. He took off his baseball cap and did a kind of awkward bow.

So it begins, I thought. "Thank you. Are the others inside?"

The tall one nodded. "The Elders are there along with the head honchos of your people." *Still us and them, I see. Some things never change.*

The door opened as I approached. Finch emerged from the door, head down, pulling a cigarette from his pack. He popped one in-between his lips, lit the lighter, and paused, hand wrapped around his mouth in a circle, and stared at me. The surprise in his expression melted away into grief, sadness, and unmistakable pity. He lifted his arms coming toward me. "Come here, darling." His big bear arms wrapped around me. The scent of his stale cigarettes and cologne mingling into a comforting smell. The warmth of his embrace steadied me, helped me, instead of what I'd expected—alienation. "I'm sorry, kid. She was a damn fine lady."

The past tense of her rippled through me, but the emotions settled behind a wall. "Thank you." My voice sounded drone-like. Finch rubbed my back, giving me one final squeeze, before releasing me.

I stepped back, eying the open doorway, not wanting to go in. Finch lit his cigarette and inhaled. The sound seemed so relaxing that it tempted me to ask for a hit. On cue, Mom's voice spoke to me. *Are you kidding me? Smoking is a nasty habit. You'll stink and have bad breath and yellow teeth.*

Moving toward the doorway, Finch squeezed my shoulder before I entered the building. Voices carried from the closed door of the inner sanctum. Raised voices—not what I'd expected. I hesitated before using my shoulder to push the door open. The arguing sputtered into nothing as one by one the group turned to look at me. Charlie's red, swollen eyes met mine first. Her cheeks blanched with streaks of red and white surrounding a pink-tinged nose and sorrow etched into her forehead. Sabrina kept her expression guarded, not displaying emotion, and after knowing her for this long, I recognized her inner battle. Wade stood out of respect and touched my elbow as Finch had. I hadn't even been aware of walking farther in. Damien wouldn't face me, and Jeremiah buried his hands in his face, fighting his own tears. The Elders shifted as if uncomfortable, and I could guess as to what the argument had been.

Arameus twisted in his seat from the front pew to face me. The sight of him alive, awake, and out of the hospital stalled my progress. His missing left leg jarred me as his fingers grazed the cut-off pants, sewed together to hide his stump. His presence almost broke through my wall. It took conscience effort to hold it in. Once controlled, I faced the Elders. "What were the raised voices for?"

As I suspected, a guilty flush passed through them, save for Steve, the lone Elder who never hid his contempt. The smugness radiated from him as he waved a hand toward me. "The Elders have expressed concern about your judgement."

Arameus's voice cut through the tension building inside me. "Those loyal still stand with you."

Steve scoffed. "After the battle on this island, she meditated for hours without anyone being able to wake her. Now after the death of her mother, she walled herself in this cocoon. We have every right to be concerned that at a critical moment, she'll be unable to handle it and lose her sanity placing our men at risk."

"May I remind you that during her rumination, not meditation, she fixed the island, and afterward received your thanks and you agreed to help her." Arameus flung an arm out.

Winslow, eyebrows flapping like overgrown caterpillars, waved a hand. "Perhaps, but the Veil is sealed. No other has come to our island, and if they do, we're safe. Too many lives have been lost. We think this war has cost us too much with no gain."

Aggie nodded. "With the Veil sealed, we're safe. There is no need to further this war. It was folly to begin with."

I could take no more. "You think that the Veil will remain sealed forever? You think you will be safe then? What if Mathesar succeeds in creating this gem that can control all four cores? You think he won't enslave your race?"

Steve stood, voice trembling, "There is no guarantee, you stupid, silly child, that any of this will happen. You're trying to scare us, to use the Gayden for your own personal agenda. What do we care of Geminates? We have given enough to your cause." He made to leave the hall.

"What do you suggest we do with the prisoners?" Finch crossed his arms, glaring at his leaders, tone laced with malice.

Winslow and Aggie paused on the edge of their seats. Steve stopped before leaving through the side door. "Kill them."

Healer Roos flung out a hand, sealing the door, rising to her feet. Sabrina sprung to her feet. The tension rose in seconds. Steve bared his teeth. "You're outnumbered, magician."

"Enough!" My voice couldn't rise to full volume. "As leaders you have every right to pull out of this engagement. I don't intend to stop because if I do, then all the lives lost will have been for nothing. Anyone who wants to walk away may do so, but I hope many will choose to keep fighting. I'll ask nothing else of you, including resources, but if we're successful, none of your demands will be asked for. You'll not be under our protection."

"Is that a threat?" Steve crossed his arms over his chest.

"No. It's a fact. Shall we win, none of your demands will be asked for. Including immunity for crimes committed. Our negotiations will include those who stand with us until the end. You've openly violated your treaty with Conjuragic and will pay. It's no wonder the magicians fear you. You don't keep your word. Not with them or with me."

Aggie shrugged. "As if that wouldn't happen if you lose your little war."

"We'll all die if we lose, but if you take the coward's way out, you'll lose either way."

Winslow and Aggie shared a look. Steve's expression remained vacant, unmoved. I didn't feel like dealing with this now. I wanted my friends, my family, those loyal to me, and to grieve for my mother. "Before you make a mistake, take the night to consider."

"What if we decide to continue fighting—under one condition?" Winslow asked Finch.

Finch in his gruff voice, sounding more pissed off than usual. "Which is?"

"You lead the army. Remove her from the equation." Winslow wouldn't look at me and instead jerked his head in my direction.

Finch cursed under his breath. Finch met Wade's eyes, and they had a silent conversation before Finch answered, "In case you," he paused, and I imagined the words "fucking idiots" ran through his head, "forgot she's the only one able to open the Bridge. The men are loyal to her. I fight with her or not at all."

Wade nodded. "Me too."

Aggie stood, taking her time, face cringing in pain from arthritis in her knees. "We shall discuss the matter further. Until tomorrow. If you please." She gestured toward the door and a stony-faced Roos flicked her hand, and the door slammed open. As the Elders retreated, the others surrounded me. Charlie grasped my shoulders in a desperate hug. "God, O. I don't. I can't. Tell me it's not true." Like me she couldn't put it into words how she felt. We leaned into each other, holding on to what felt like the only thing we had left. Which in so many ways was true. She couldn't be with her grandparents. John—I shoved the thought of him away—hard. Now my mom was gone. All hurtful words between us— vanished as if they'd never been, disappearing like smoke in the wind.

She stepped back, wiping her eyes. "It was really," she paused, closing her eyes building up the courage to say it, "John."

I nodded, and her tears welled up. "I saw him in the Willow. I tried to tell your mom, but then I saw Arameus. I thought I had time." Her voice cracked against the torment on her face. Shock rolled over me. She'd known he'd become a danger. I wanted to be angry, but a small voice in the back of my mind reminded me that Charlie had ran after us. She tried to stop us. To stop me.

"Strega."

That name jerked me back to attention. "What about her?"

"I saw him with her in the Willow during the mission, something was wrong with him. She called him her pet."

We were surrounded, everyone listening in, Damien, Jeremiah, Finch, Wade, Simeon, and even Arameus hobbled over on a prosthetic leg and cane. Sabrina inched her way toward us. "There is no magic that can do that."

Damien ran a hand through his hair. "Torture can." He shuddered, and I guessed a buried memory floated close to the surface.

"Regardless, he killed Perdita. He deserves to die." Sabrina told no one in particular.

Charlie's mouth dropped open. "What? He's my brother."

"He killed her mother!"

"But he isn't himself. He would never. I believe that with all my heart. Tell them, O."

Charlie and Sabrina were inches apart, the air tingling with unreleased power. At the mention of my name, they turned toward me in unison. "I don't know what I believe."

"O?" The betrayal slid off Charlie's tongue.

"All I know is he's with *her*." I packed as much venom in the last word as I could. "Whether by choice or some other reason. But he's dangerous. We should try to capture him, alive, and later decide what to do."

No one objected, whether because I was the so-called leader, or because my mother died, I couldn't say. Their repetitious hugs followed, along with the "I'm sorry for your loss" speeches. They talked about how much they loved her and how they would miss her. Only Charlie's pain could match my own. Mom had been like another parent to Charlie.

During the onslaught of sympathy, we left the Town Hall, making our way toward the bungalows that had become a temporary home on the island. Wade fetched drinks and food. I ate fried chicken and a roll but couldn't tell you what it tasted like. The stories faded into happy memories of Mom. My whole body ached, and after a while, I wished nothing more than for everyone to leave me alone. Sleep called to me, though I fear insomnia would take her place as soon as my head hit the pillow.

A knock sounded at the door. Sabrina rose to answer it, and Roos stood at the door. No one had noticed that she'd slipped away earlier. In her usual stiff manner, she entered the bungalow meeting no one's eyes but mine. "I'm sorry to intrude."

"It's okay. What is it?" Weariness carried on every sound I made. Whatever she wanted I didn't want to hear it. I'd lost Mom, dealt with the Elders lack of confidence, and endured the forced socialization of the last few hours. My brain was mush.

"I informed the Elders that the invisibility potion is complete."

Whispers broke out as everyone stared at her.

Roos nodded. "Yes, complete. The troops want to know what you're going to do now."

"First, we need a way to subdue the High Council. I don't want to kill anyone." I didn't add the word else.

Simeon stood. "I have an idea, but it would mean we have to go to a transport gate."

I nodded. "Then to the Meadow." This meant relying on the oxygenian's information given after the meeting with the Magical Brethren, but what choice did we have?

I so wanted to walk away now. No one else would die because of me. The Veil could stay sealed until long after I'd grown old and died. If I did that, everyone that had already died would've died for nothing. My head rose a little higher. "Tomorrow, we leave at dawn. The High Council is waiting."

I stood in front of my bungalow, my heart in ribbons, as a great weight clenched inside my stomach. I couldn't go inside. Charlie had slipped away with Arameus. Sabrina and Simeon had their own place, and Damien and Jeremiah shared a bungalow. Mom and I had shared this one, and I couldn't make myself open the dang door.

Footsteps approached, inching along the boardwalk, still I couldn't move. The door loomed before me, mocking and cruel. The footsteps halted, and Damien leaned against the wooden siding. "Hey."

"Hey."

"I would like your help," he said.

Help? I couldn't help anyone. "With what?"

He reached out and slid me to the side. "Be right back, gorgeous." He winked and opened the door to my bungalow, stepped inside, and slammed the door in my face.

I shoved the door open, following him inside. The sound of the water running from the shower greeting me. "What the hell are you doing?"

"Oh good. You're here."

I placed my hands on my hips. "Seriously, what are you doing?"

He pulled a dripping hand out from behind the shower curtain. "You see, I have a problem. Jeremiah. My God, that guy reeks of garlic all the time, and he snores like all night." Damien pulled his gray T-shirt off, wadded it up, and tossed it to the corner hamper.

"Your point is?"

"Well, I'm exhausted." He unbuttoned the front of his jeans. "I've got to get some sleep, so I'm staying here tonight." He pulled down his jeans, showing off maroon boxers and long, muscular legs.

I closed my eyes and turned around. "Are you kidding me?"

"Nope." Maroon boxers flew past my head. The shower curtain clinked as it opened and rippled closed.

"Who do you think you are? You can't just come in here and get naked." I felt my cheeks flush.

"Wow, this shampoo smells great!"

"What are you even going to wear?"

Faster than I thought possible, the shower turned off. "Hmm, I didn't think about that. Guess nothing."

"Oh, no you don't." I stormed into the bedroom, out the door, and charged down to Jeremiah and Damien's bungalow. I knocked hard three times. A minute later, Jeremiah opened the door. Without waiting, I pushed past him into their bedroom. Piles and piles of old food containers, dirty clothes, various weapons, and leathers littered every surface.

"What's going on? Is everything okay?" Jeremiah asked.

"Nothing. Everything is fine. Where are Damien's clothes?"

Jeremiah's eyebrows lifted, and he pointed to a chest of drawers. I yanked open drawers, pulling out clothes.

"Want to tell me what's going on?"

I jerked my chin back toward my place. "Damien. He just barged in and helped himself to my shower. Said he's staying the night."

"Oh." Jeremiah's eyes bulged wide and looked away.

"It's not even like that."

He held up his hands in mock surrender. "No judgement."

I huffed and stormed toward him. Jeremiah opened the door for me. "So, should I expect to be alone tonight?"

"No!" I screamed over my shoulder, ignoring Jeremiah's laughter.

Back in my own place, I found Damien sitting on my bed, wearing a towel and nothing else. Water dripped from his dusty blond hair, gray eyes twinkling. I threw his clothes toward him. Instead of a satisfying smack, the clothes flew in all directions, landing haphazard around the room. "Prick."

He laughed, leaning farther onto my bed, and patted beside him.

Magic rose in me, but his power arched out fast then retreated, like he poked me. My mouth popped open, shocked at the playful action. He tilted his head back and laughed, then his power zapped again, skimming mine in a kind of tickle. I pushed my magic back toward him, but he jumped from the bed. The towel slipped lower on his hips, but he ignored it. He jogged the two steps toward me and picked me up.

He tossed me onto the bed, letting his fingers tickle where his magic trailed. I screamed, while a laugh pulled from me. "Ahhh! No!" I pushed back against the bed, grabbing underneath his arms, tickling him back. He laughed, and the towel slipped more.

I closed my eyes. "The towel! The towel!"

He lifted my shirt and put his mouth on my belly. He blew a raspberry, and laughter tore through me. He did it again and again. I forced my eyes to remain closed as I tried to get away while laughing. As the last of my breath waned, Damien stepped back from me. I peeked and caught him bent over, pulling a pair of sweatpants up his legs.

He flashed me a grin and fell on the bed beside me. "You totally looked."

"I did not."

"Mmmm, hmmm." He rolled over, propping his head on his hand, while the other reached out and pushed the hair from my face. He wiggled his eyebrows. "Like what you saw?"

"I didn't see anything." I swatted his hand away as he snickered at me. He sat up and pulled me to sit in front of him. "What are you doing now?"

"Quiet."

I cringed, waiting for another round of tickling, when he gathered my hair and began running a brush through the long, red, tangled mess. He brushed and brushed without saying a word. While he worked at the tangles, my eyes roamed, picking out Mom's things lying around, just waiting for her to come back, and she never would. It hit me then what Damien had done. He'd distracted me so I didn't have to face that first time alone. When all the tangles were done, he squeezed at my shoulders, rubbing my neck, soothing the sore, tight muscles. I moaned as he found one particular spot.

Damien pulled me against him, his warmth soothing the ache in my heart. "Do you want me to go?"

I shook my head and faced him. He leaned forward and kissed me light and sweet before kissing my nose. "Go get changed."

I tried not to rush changing into my sleeping shorts and a ratty old T-shirt. I emerged from the bathroom, and he'd pulled the covers down. I slid in and curled beside him. He kissed me again, and it raced through me, igniting my blood. Our kiss deepened, but he pulled back and stroked my cheek. "Not like this."

I snuggled next to him, grateful he wouldn't push.

"Ora?"

"Hmm."

"I've been thinking." He tensed beside me and I held my breath. "We need someone on the inside. A spy."

"Who could we even send?"

"Me."

My pulse spiked. I didn't want him in harm's way. "I can't ask you to do that."

He pulled me tighter to him. "You aren't. I'm volunteering."

I sighed. "Can we not talk about any of that tonight?"

"Okay."

He turned out the light and rubbed my back, easing out soreness after soreness, and worry after worry. While he rubbed, we talked late into the night about everything and nothing. He held me as I cried until sleep finally claimed me.

21

SABRINA

Simeon had a great idea. The transport gates had been abandoned. Why would there be anyone around when the Veil was sealed? They hadn't even locked up the supplies. Sabrina, Ora, and Damien made up the skeleton crew of this mission. Ora didn't want to risk anyone else. She'd stayed inside the Bridge while Sabrina made a break for it, grabbed the package, and hightailed it back while Damien provided cover.

Back on the island, the others waited for phase two of the mission. Once they got back, they wasted no time distributing the potion. If Sabrina knew nothing else, she knew for certain she hated being invisible. The potion, while tedious to make, was the vilest substance she'd ever had the displeasure to taste—thick and slimy, reminding her of putrid mud. It hit her stomach and spread with a tingling sensation like a million spiders scattering over her entire body. Afterward she watched as her hand—a steadfast certainty of existence—faded away from solid to hazy, growing ever lighter, until it vanished. She sighed in relief when she discovered her clothes faded along with her. She hated the idea of going on this mission naked. A supply bag hung over her shoulder and onto her back. Luckily, it and the contents inside vanished as well.

An interesting revelation came when the group realized that each person experienced something different when they drank the potion.

Simeon's face turned red as he drank his potion. He said it reminded him of red hots, a spicy cinnamon candy from the human world. Charlie's potion tasted citrusy with a hint of fresh-cut grass. Instead of feeling spiders, a warmth spread through her, leaving her calm and relaxed. Damien tasted fruit, a mixture of grapes and strawberries. Jeremiah said it reminded him of sea water. Finch said it was like warm, sweet chocolate, thicker than chocolate milk but thinning as it went down his throat. Ora had the strangest of them all. To her, the potion was thick like honey, but odorless and flavorless at first, with hints at the end of a mingling of smog, wet asphalt on a hot day, and finally crisp winter air after a snowfall. Sabrina decided that the potion must reflect your personality, whether or not you want to become invisible. Sabrina clearly did not, and Ora appeared undecided.

The second revelation happened shortly after the first. None of them realized how heavily they relied on sight. Sabrina lost count how many times they bumped into one another. Screams of "Ouch! That's my foot." "Who's that?" and "Where did everyone go?" were repeated over and over.

Training sessions should've been planned, but how could they have simulated being invisible? Even if they had done something with blindfolds, that still wouldn't have been adequate because they couldn't have seen anything. Being invisible also meant having no eyelids. The blinding sun of the island bounced off the sea. Sabrina dropped her head, noticing their footsteps in the sand. "Everyone, look down. We should be able to see by the depressions in the sand. Once we're through the Veil, the Meadow is a grassland. That should at least give us an idea of where everyone is standing."

"Let's hope the Tempests don't notice as well." Finch's voice rang out from somewhere to Sabrina's back right.

"Those with Sphere, wipe our footsteps behind us," Ora said. "It's time to go." Without another word, she opened the Bridge. The potion wouldn't last forever, and this mission was of utmost importance. They'd planned to kidnap the High Council with a skeleton crew in one of the most highly guarded areas of Conjuragic, and with the loss of Perdita so fresh in everyone's mind, the margin for error was huge. Way more than Sabrina was comfortable with, but without Perdita or her books, they couldn't know how long the potion remained stable. Besides, without this, their plans had ground to a halt.

Ora asked, "You all sure about this? We're going without the sanction of the Elders."

Quiet followed with the shifting of footprints on the sand as an answer. Everyone knew she'd directed the question at Finch and Wade. Jeremiah, Damien, Simeon, and Sabrina weren't a part of this island. It wouldn't make a difference what they thought. But for Finch and Wade, this was their home, their family, their tribe.

"Fuck um," Wade answered, surprising them all. "My great granddaddy, granddaddy, and daddy grew up on this island, all afraid of the magicians. I'm tired of living in fear. No more generations should have to face this. Either it ends, or we all do."

Finch made a sound of assent. Only the sounds of hands clasping and their footsteps disappearing inside the Bridge followed his proclamation. Sabrina welcomed the blackness after the overpowering sun.

Simeon's voice quivered behind Sabrina, "Oh I don't like this." Simeon had passed through the Bridge only a few times.

Sabrina noted an immediate difference. Before Perdita died, traveling through the Bridge felt almost fluid, as if walking, not through water, but with the slightest resistance. Now each step pulled as if ripping your foot out of tar to take the next foot forward. Ora wasn't focused. Her mother had died less than twenty-four hours before.

Ora stopped. "I don't know where I'm going." Her voice was weak, far away, which made no sense since Damien separated them. She shouldn't have had any trouble hearing her.

Red flags rippled in the wind of Sabrina's mind. An entire wing of the Vindeca was dedicated to those sustaining accidents in the Veil, everything from losing parts of their limbs, to those who claimed to have lived full lives, and the worst were the ones who disappeared and returned years later. The Veil was dangerous, something that some witches would never cross no matter what, and right now, in this moment, Ora could get them all stuck here forever. She pulled her two hands together, making them form the connection, while she held on and moved forward to Ora. She knew from her slight frame and slumped shoulders that sorrow radiated off her. She leaned in close. "Let me lead. Concentrate on keeping the Bridge open. We need you. Okay? Stick with me."

"Okay," came the weak reply, but Ora made the shift to let Sabrina take the lead. She concentrated with all her will to the Meadow. Protectors were required during training to cross alone through the Veil and to have a strong strength of will. Sabrina pulled on that training, yanking them forward, praying that Ora could maintain the connection, and with each step, the tar feeling slacked off. Their destination neared closer. Only a few more steps.

Sabrina emerged into Conjuragic with the feeling of someone who had come close to drowning. She pulled air deep into her lungs and didn't even mind the sting of the pouring cold rain as she yanked the others out. "Everyone out?"

Choruses of agreement came from everyone. Sabrina added missing unspoken communication to the growing list of dislikes of invisibility, how much could be understood with head tilts and eye movements. Sabrina would have liked to signal to the others to watch Ora, but she had no way of doing so without her hearing.

"Jesus Christ, it's like a monsoon out here," Finch said.

Covering her eyes, not wanting to get rain in her face, Sabrina looked to the sky. Darkness with gray clouds stretched in every direction. Ahead the grass had been trampled, lying flat, taking a pounding from the unforgiving rain.

Simeon clasped her hand, giving her reassurance, even if she couldn't see him. She called out as loud as she dared to the others. "I told you. When Tempests are upset or scared, the weather turns nasty." To prove the point, lightning rippled across the sky hitting five places at once. Ora screamed.

"We'll use this to our advantage. They'll be inside, hiding from the storm. If they look outside, they won't be able to tell the difference between our walking through the grass and the movement from the rain and wind."

"Yeah, if we don't get electrocuted first," Jeremiah muttered.

He had a point. "Okay. Their homes are up ahead in between the rolling hills." She realized she was pointing uselessly. "To the left of that tree."

"They live in holes in the ground? Like hobbits?"

Sabrina did a double take. "Like what?"

Damien chuckled, an odd sound in the tense situation. "Don't worry about it. Yeah, man, it's like hobbit holes."

"When did you watch the movie?" Jeremiah asked.

Simeon asked, "What's a hobbit hole?"

Damien, ignoring Simeon, answered Jeremiah, "After I came to the human world as the dragon's henchman. We got to watch movies in our downtime."

"Focus," Sabrina said, wishing she could show off the glare on her face.

"The deepest tunnel is the middle on the left. You remember the layout?" Arameus had extensively went over his home. As a Defender, he had intimate access to all areas of the land. If the Council had indeed made this their hiding place, that tunnel would be where they were. Sabrina paid no mind to their murmurs. "We have to get in and get to the Council. Let's go."

Sabrina burst into life, not looking behind to see if ghost-like footprints followed her. In seconds, she had crossed through the flattest part of the land. The rain pelted down even harder. Against her nature, she let the water drench her. A moving invisible umbrella wouldn't go unnoticed. Except the place appeared deserted. The longer she didn't see any people, the more unnerved she became. Could this be a trap? But how could it? No one knew they were coming.

She passed into the layers of hills where the doors of the Tempest homes peeked outward. Lights blazed inside, so it wasn't empty after all. She counted the little round doors, and at the right one, she pressed her comm and made a single click. She stopped and either no one followed or else the message went through and they'd stopped. She put her hand flat against the door and with the other, touched the comm and clicked twice. Then she opened the door, and chaos ensued.

As soon as the door swung open an alarm buzzed—loud, piercing, accusing. *No turning back now.* Sabrina raced inside, staying to the side. Silk-like tiles covered the inside of the walls while molded stones formed the stairs. She took in these details in a heartbeat. Keeping as far to the left as possible, she took the steps two at a time, trusting the alarm to hide her approaching footsteps. At the bottom, three paths opened up. Guards raced down each of them. *Crap!* They would run right into them! As the guards burst into the small foyer at the bottom of the stairs, the unmistakable sound of a rock teetered down the left hallway. All of the guards turned at once and raced toward it. With a quick sigh of relief, Sabrina turned down the right hallway, sprinting to the end, then turning right again into a long hallway of red brick lighted with lanterns hanging beside dozens of doorways on either side.

Simeon whispered through the comm, "They'll be in the last room."

A single closed door stood at the end of the hallway, accusing and suspicious. Shadows danced along the bottom and sides, silhouettes from the lights inside. Someone pacing. A guard. Simeon's guess work had been spot on. The Council was in that room. For one brief second, doubt flooded her senses. This was her government, the people she'd been trained to defend, and she was going to attack them. Simeon's hand grasped her shoulder. She knew it was him. Offering encouragement. How well he knew her. If those people at the end were left in charge, they would kill him for loving her. In the second that it took for those thoughts to form, the doubt vanished. She raced down the empty hallway fully expecting for someone to die in the next few minutes.

22

SABRINA

The gray door was all that stood between the turn in the war. The war that so many died for—Sabrina's father, Ora's mother, and so many others. All because of hate, and today it might finally end. Sabrina reached with an invisible hand and knocked three times upon the door. The door jerked open with Corporal Allyn staring at her, no, through her. She shouldn't have been surprised to recognize the guards, but she hadn't expected a member of her old Quad.

The sleeping bag flew out of her hand without her even realizing it. Time slowed down. Confusion shown in Allyn's eyes as he opened his mouth and said, "There's no one." His words cut short as the bag hit him in the face. His eyes rolled in the back of his head as he slumped to the ground. Sabrina tucked and rolled into the room as she felt spells fly over her head. In seconds, screams filled the room. An invisible hand flung the door closed, locking it. Sabrina slid into a crouched position. Leigh, healed from the gunshot wound, put herself between the Councilmen. Sabrina did a quick estimate concluding two Quads guarded the High Council—three on the floor already, including Allyn.

The Councilors cowered in the corner. Cilla Souse, Sabrina's grandmother's friend, covered her pale face with a trembling hand. "What's going on?"

Another sleeping bag knocked out a Tempest Protector nearest her. At the same time, three other sleeping spells appeared out of nowhere, hitting two of the targets, but missing the third. Leigh ducked at the last second, sending a blast of water toward the bag. An invisible scream followed that Sabrina recognized as Simeon's. Only three remained. A Naiad flung a spell, and he collapsed, writhing in pain, as a Gayden captured him.

Amidst the chaos, a hysterical laugh cut through the shrieks.

Leigh and Sabrina screamed at the same time, "No!"

Everyone froze.

Jabez Bizard stood behind Mira Drecoll, Sphere's Councilwoman, a bloody knife at her throat. Dharr, her husband, lay on the ground, blood oozing out of a wound over his heart. Jabez's cold eyes met Leigh's, and a slow smile spread over his face. Nothing had scared Sabrina as much as that did. "I told all of you I would get you all back for everything."

"Jabez, you're a traitor." Leigh lifted her hands while steel settled in her eyes. The rest of the Councilors watched in silent horror.

Gripping Mira's long hair in a tight fist, he jerked her head back, drawing a small trickle of blood from her neck. "When are you going to realize that their time is done? They couldn't even handle one little Nip. My master is ripe to take over."

"Your master? What're you talking about?" Leigh's cool composure shook. Sabrina had never seen her like this.

"Nothing you need to worry about. You won't live that long, you disgusting dyke."

Leigh flinched.

"Yeah. Ever since your little Naiad bitch girlfriend sold us all out, you've been weak. Then she shot you." He laughed, cruel, bitter. "Guess she's done with fish." He flicked his tongue at Leigh. "Next time I see her, I'll give her some of this." He rubbed his pelvis up against Mira, who had been silent with round horror-filled eyes, but shuddered in response. "Oh, you like it too? I can give it to you before you die." He licked her face.

Leigh's composure snapped into place like a mask. "This was your doing?"

"My master's plan." He moved forward, dragging Mira along.

Mathesar must be on his way to kill the Council. Jabez thought they were here to help him. Confirming Sabrina's suspicions, Jabez jerked his head. "Go on, guys. Take care of the dykadelic Commander so we can take out the rest of the trash." He pushed the knife along Mira's throat more, drawing a thin line of blood as she whimpered. Sabrina couldn't believe the Council, witches and wizards themselves, had done nothing—like lambs being led to the slaughter. Leigh pulled herself up straight. The room sizzled with her magic. She wasn't planning on going out without taking a few of them with her.

Sabrina had no idea how many of her team had made it inside. She knew someone pinned Simeon against the wall. She had no idea if he'd wiggled free or not. She had to take Jabez out, but she needed to get Leigh out of harm's way first.

For what felt like a long moment, no one moved. At the same time, Sabrina and a Gayden sent Naiad spells screaming toward Leigh. She deflected one with the flinch of her hand. The stone floor rose from the ground as if made of liquid, solidifying, blocking one of the waves. Leigh'd missed the other. It hit her in the side, sending her slipping and sliding backward—out of harm's way. Moving like lightning, Sabrina raced behind Jabez, grabbing the knife from his hand.

He bucked, but the knife slipped free of his hand. "What the…?"

Without warning, a blast of air, swirling like a death spiral, shot straight through the room. The spell drilled through the middle of Jabez's face. In the blink of an eye, his face disappeared into a spray of blood and brains. As he fell to the floor, Charlie laughed. "Payback's a bitch."

Mira screamed as Jabez fell backward. His blood sprayed all over the side of her face and brown hair. She dropped to her knees throwing herself over Dharr.

"Now," Sabrina ordered anyone on her side. She tossed bag after bag of sleeping bags. The Council still did nothing to counteract them.

Leigh lay on the ground, blood oozing from her temple. Sabrina ran to her side, feeling her neck. Her friend's pulse beat hard and steady against her finger. She would be fine. For all of a second, quiet settled over everything.

Banging rattled the doors.

A deep voice demanded, "Open the door or we'll blast it apart!"

Ora asked from the corner of the room, behind the Council, "Who's here?"

Voices of Charlie, Damien, Sabrina, and Finch called out. Damien said, "Jeremiah was hit with a spell. I can feel his body."

Sabrina ran to the wall where she'd heard Simeon scream. Her heart hammering in her chest. He had to be okay. She touched where his face would be. Her finger tips traced something warm and soft, but an area of the wall covered his mouth. She heard soft muffles and hard breathing through his nose. "Simeon is here. Someone needs to move this."

The wall rolled to life. It jerked outward like a snake, grabbing Sabrina, pinning her to the wall. Leigh had awoken, crouching, eyes alive with purpose.

"Leigh, please. It's me. It's Sabrina. Let me explain."

"Ha. Explain how you betrayed our entire race, our friendship, how you tried to kill me?"

"I didn't. I shot you in the shoulder. It wasn't a killing shot."

The banging on the door grew louder. Time was running out. Ora flung her last sleeping bag, striking Leigh in the side of the head. She blasted the wall away from Sabrina and Simeon. As Sabrina hit her knees, she noticed a shadow of her hands. She looked around at the others. The invisibility spell faded with every breath.

A split formed in the door as what sounded like a battering ram slammed into the other side. They were trapped. They had failed.

The invisibility spell slid off Ora—amber eyes glowing with a strange warping rainbow. The amulet at her throat cast a sinister glow around her face. Her long red hair, escaped from her typical braid, whipped behind her by an unseen wind. Raw power radiated off her, driving the temperature up. Her purple leathers rippled, growing darker, singed black and orange-red, as if she walked into the fire.

She squatted to the ground, holding onto two members of the Council. "Come close together and make sure everyone is touching someone else." Her voice warbled sounding like one and many, resonating, pulling a primal fear from Sabrina. Her hair stood on end, goosebumps rising. Never had she felt raw power such as this.

In a scramble of motion, the unconscious bodies of the Council, Leigh, and Jeremiah were piled in the center of the floor. The others squatted on the ground around them. A large piece of wood ripped through the door as Ora screamed, "Hold on!"

The world fell from under Sabrina as Ora opened the Bridge yet again in the nick of time.

23

CHARLIE

The Bridge, an in-between of reality, a dimension beyond time and space, still on every other occasion had felt horizontal, as if walking through a straight line. When Ora opened it this last time, the floor dropped from under Charlie's feet. Like a pitch-black water slide, the group thrashed and rolled, gripping onto each other. They had no time to prepare before plunging. Charlie could pray they didn't lose anyone along the way. Hers scream joined others in filling the emptiness. Her scream became a mere droplet in a sea of such incredible vastness that the Veil swallowed the sounds. Her heart plummeted while her stomach jumped to her throat. At one point, up became down, and down became up. The unexpected ride went on and on, tumbling and falling, like Alice down the rabbit hole. An eternity later the group fell at least four feet out of the Bridge onto the white sands of Gayden Island.

As she landed the wind rushed out of her chest and she lay gasping as air refilled her lungs. The Bridge loomed above her head like the mouth of a great monster about to devour them whole. Other pains became more prominent in her awareness—the sting of what she guessed was a cut on her leg and throbbing of various bruises. Her back protested at landing on something sharp and uneven. She reached underneath herself, arms stiff, and removed her pistol, thankful that it hadn't gone off when she'd landed, shooting another hole in her butt—*the one God made was good enough for her, thank you very much*. Perhaps she should invest in one of those thigh holsters. Her weapon had gotten dislodged during their very unorthodox departure. She sat up, wondering when traveling through the Bridge hadn't been unorthodox.

The invisibility spells had worn off them all. Finch managed to land on his feet while everyone else fell on their ass. The rest maneuvered to their feet. The Council and the woman called Leigh lay unconscious on the ground. Sabrina had an arm around Simeon's waist. His arm hung at an odd angle, and his face had turned white and clammy. Sabrina slipped the supply bag off her shoulder, bypassing Damien, whom she'd never quite trusted since he almost killed her and Arameus by stealing their magic, and handed Charlie the bag. "You remember how to use these?"

Charlie nodded, taking the bag—surprised. It wasn't like Sabrina to not follow through with a mission, but her new husband usually didn't tag along. Without another word, Sabrina escorted Simeon off the beach, toward the boardwalk leading back to the Harbor Hospital. In Charlie's opinion all of them had spent way too much time at the little hospital.

Charlie passed out one of the two elongated silver injectors to Damien along with an ice-cold black sparkling jewel. They loaded the small, vile jewels into the injectors. They approached each of the Councilors, pushing the end of the injector, and clicked a button at the end. The silver stick clicked as the jewel pushed through the skin. At each site, a bruise-like line spread over the arm. Ora shivered, watching the unconscious Mira, the line solidifying, looking like a tattoo. Branding had been one of the first things Ora experienced when she had been arrested. These marked the person as a prisoner and blocked them from using their magic. From what Charlie had been told later by Perdita, Ora had been branded fully conscious without anything to numb the pain.

"Looks like we got a spare," Finch said, rolling a young man, red hair waving in the breeze.

"Anyone know who he is?" Damien asked.

Finch rolled his eyes. "How the hell would anyone here know who he is? The only ones who actually lived in Conjuragic left to go to the hospital."

Ora tore her gaze from the branded Mira. "It doesn't matter who he is. Inject him and bring him along. I'd like to get them to the barracks before they wake up."

Finch raised a hand, pointing down the beach. They all turned to see Wade on a golf cart driving along the sands toward them. Behind him, an empty trailer rocked on the sand. He pulled up, parking alongside the group. He stepped down. "I've been watching from the roof of the defense tower. Figured you all would need a hand, and..." his gaze moved through the group, "a special prison has been set up for them."

"Where?" Ora's eyes flickered and glowed, a sure sign of danger. Her emotions had been on high alert ever since Perdita. Charlie's heart stung whenever she thought about her. She'd been like another mother to her, and guilt weighed on her as well. Her brother, her own brother, had killed her. She knew beyond a doubt that he'd been bewitched or brainwashed, but that did nothing for the sting, and if he could be brought back, how could he live with himself? How could she look at him the same? How could Ora? Yet Charlie still loved him—he was her brother. She wouldn't let anyone hurt him. Plus, Ora could forgive Damien, but he hadn't killed her mom.

"It's in the basement of the Town Hall. Beneath the Defense Tower. The Elders have decided to rejoin the war."

Damien kicked the sand, swearing. "Of course they have. Now we've returned with the Council."

"They decided before you left. I didn't get back in time to inform you." Wade shrugged, no apology noted in his tone.

Ora rubbed her forehead. "Let's get this done."

They loaded the bodies on the trailer, one at a time, with more swearing and a lot of grunting. They could've used magic, but they all needed a lot of rest. Magic used more energy than manual labor. With two bodies left to load, Jeremiah groaned and rolled over. "Uhh. What happened?"

Damien went to his side, helping him to his feet. "Come on, man. Let's get you to the hospital. You all got this?" He nodded his head toward the last two. Leigh and another woman, hair down to her ankles, tangled, and covered in sand.

"Yeah. Get out of here." Finch strained as he picked up Leigh, dropping her with a *thunk* onto the trailer, bodies piled on one another. He jerked his head toward Wade. "You couldn't have gotten a bigger trailer?"

As soon as the last body tumbled onto the trailer, Charlie, Ora, Finch, and Wade piled into the golf cart and set out toward the Town Hall, no one speaking, everyone bone tired. Charlie wondered what the High Council of Conjuragic would think about being transported in such a manner.

The humor died away, replaced with worry for Arameus as it always did when she got tired. He'd received a prosthetic yesterday. Physical therapy drained him, but he'd made progress, and he'd started way beyond what any of the Healers or doctors thought he would. The Healers had never heard of such things as a prosthetic. Despite everything that had happened, his spirits were up and he was ready to get back in the fray. Her exhaustion pressed upon her like a weight, making her movement ten times harder. As soon as they completed this last part of the mission, Charlie would find Arameus, lay in his arms, and fall sleep for a few precious hours without drama, but she had a sinking feeling that was a luxury neither she nor anyone else would likely get for a long time.

The cart bumped and jostled until they got off the sand. As they passed through the streets, eyes watched them, but no one said a thing. If anyone ever thought their enemy's leaders would be passed out, on their island, and under their mercy, no one would dare speak it. At the Town Hall, unloading the prisoners went considerably smoother with the small arsenal of guards to help. They placed each of the Councilors in a separate cell, Leigh and the spare Tempest sharing one since they had one extra after Bizard killed one of them.

Ora stared at their prisoners in the concrete cells fitted with metal bars that swung closed with a squeaky slam. The silver of the metal had long since faded and now was chipping and rusted. These cells had been here for a very long time. Manacles hung at the backs of the cells drilled into the concrete with thick dark stains that could only mean blood. She shivered, grateful someone had added commodes and sinks. "They'll be asleep for a while. We should take a break. Get our strength back. I imagine the Elders would like to talk to them when they wake up."

Finch nodded, his usual smart-ass jovial expression turned stern. "Yes, I imagine they would. Let them stew. We'll be back for them later."

Stew they did. They left the Councilors alone the rest of the day, overnight, and into the next morning save for food and water.

Charlie walked with Arameus, holding his arm, as he maneuvered them into an elevator leading them to the dungeon. The three main Elders stood in front—Winslow, Aggie, and Steve—followed by Ora and Finch. Behind them, Sabrina walked beside Charlie, and Damien brought up the rear. The rest overnight had done them all some good, except for Ora. Dark circles rimmed her eyes, and grief hung around her like a veil. Charlie watched her best friend grieve after they thought John died, but losing her mother had stolen something from her—a vitality, a tie to this world. At this point, Ora no longer cared about anything but went through the motions, carrying on because she had nothing else.

The Council scrambled to their feet, staring out at their little ensemble as if they faced a firing squad. Charlie couldn't blame them. The Elders sat on chairs brought down here, set up in front of the prison doors, facing the Council like equals, but the power equality was a political move in and of itself. Everyone knew the Elders held all the cards.

Winslow cleared his raspy throat. "Morning."

All at once, the Councilors started talking, their voices mingling, echoing off the stone walls. Only Leigh and the strange young Tempest remained quiet. Winslow held up a hand, but it wasn't until Ora took a step, eyes sparkling, that they fell quiet.

Winslow rested his hand on his lap. "We've brought you here to discuss the conditions of your surrender."

Another round of outburst and Steve shouted, "Enough." The shouting dwindled over a minute or two. "You're here with your magic blocked in our world and the Veil to yours closed to you. If we wanted you dead, you would be already. Instead, we would like to end this war. You have lost."

This time, instead of shouting, the group all turned their heads toward Mira. Their shared decision making altered since Dharr's death, as if now her authority had doubled and she'd absorbed his power. "You might kill us," she said, voice as hollow as her eyes, "but we haven't lost the war. You lost your hold on the Haven. There isn't enough of you to completely overtake Conjuragic. We have our advisors. They will carry on in our place."

Sabrina laughed. "Have you forgotten what Bizard said? You have more than one enemy. I'm sure we're the lesser of the two evils."

The blond Naiad Councilman scoffed. "Oh, it's *we* now. You have truly become a traitor to your people, Sabrina Sun. What would your father think of you now?"

Her spine stiffened, but Arameus answered. "Her father, in fact, converted to our side before he died, Talon."

He turned away in disgust. "Another traitor."

Damien stepped forward. "You have had an even bigger traitor in your midst for years. Working right under your nose. Stealing your prisoners marked for death, kidnapping Gayden children like myself, and working against you."

"Who are you?" the Tempest Council woman asked.

Arameus leaned down to whisper in Charlie's ear, "That is Nissa Kefira. Her husband is Fath."

"My name is Damien Snider. One of your tribunals voted to have me sent to the Kassen at four years old."

She paled, having the decency to look horrified.

His lips curved up, but no warmth reached his eyes. "Yes, but instead of dying, one of your own smuggled me out. He enslaved me, turned me into a weapon, and he has hundreds more, hidden in the human world and in Conjuragic."

"Impossible."

"We would've known."

"Lies."

The Council's cries mingled. Aggie raised a hand. "It's true. We know who he is and where he is hidden, and you have also broken our treaty."

Talon slammed his fist on the bars. "Us? You sent one of your spies to us." He flicked a head in Ora's direction. "To seal our Veil, destroy our Unity Statue, and then invade our land. It is you who has violated the treaty."

"Oh really? When this Gayden and the falsely accused," Aggie lifted a withered, age spotted hand, gesturing to Damien, and then to Ora, "were brought to Conjuragic and tried, convicted, and sentenced to death without informing us, without giving us a chance to intervene, especially since that boy had been no more than four years old. *That* wasn't a violation of the treaty. Without bringing him to us, let us raise him, teach him our ways. That violation happened long before she sealed your Veil."

"For the record," Steve wrinkled his nose at Ora, "she is no Gayden. She is one of you or sort of."

All eyes turned to Ora, back stiffened, head raised, a faint smile traced on her mouth, making her look sinister, nothing of my best friend shining from her eyes. "My parents were Geminates. Your true enemy has been amassing his own personal army of Gayden and Geminates, primed to take you out, and you've had no clue for decades."

The Council stared at her, mouths agape, until finally Leigh stepped forward. "Get to the point. What do you want?" Charlie noted how both Sabrina and Leigh avoided looking at each other.

Winslow sighed, the gesture both bored and calculated, the face of politics. "We're here to discuss a new treaty, and in return, we will remove your enemy for you."

Mira tossed her hair back, spun around, and with a flourish of golden robes, sat upon the squeaking metal-framed bed in her cell. Despite the long tattoo showing underneath her robes on her neck and the noise of the bed, she remained a Councilwoman, the power behind Conjuragic. The others looked upon her and mimicked the behavior. Mira bowed her head with utmost poise. "Very well. What are your terms?"

A palpable wave of relief flooded through the underground dungeon. A small glimmer of hope for the fighting to end.

Finch handed Aggie a binder. She placed it on her lap, skeletal fingers running over the leather cover. Before she opened it, she slipped on a pair of reading glasses hanging on a chain around her wrinkled neck. "Our first condition is the Council will add two positions. One for a male and female Gayden of our choosing."

Mira recoiled, opened her mouth to speak.

Aggie raised a hand without even looking up. "You will hear our demands and then you can counter. No interruptions." Her hand floated back to the paper, and she continued reading. "Condition two. Gayden shall henceforth no longer be banned from Conjuragic. Travel to and from our world shall be allowed and regulated by the same standards. Three. Trade between our worlds will be arranged. Four. A bank for conversions between human and magician money will be created for exchange. Five. Any illegal activity done in the other realm shall be handled according to the world's decisions. However, in the cases of Gayden trails, the tribunal must be half Gayden. Punishment is no longer death unless agreed by the Council unanimously. Six." Aggie paused, taking a sip of water. Though her timing was questionable. "Geminates shall no longer be illegal."

Mira stood. "That is none of your concern, Gayden. Your demands thus far have made sense. This is our law, based on purity, and for the safety of everyone in our realm. Geminates are dangerous."

Ora's eyes flashed, lighting up the small space, making Charlie's hair stand on edge. "Don't forget you have an entire army of full-grown Geminates living in Conjuragic, and it hasn't blown up. My mother was a geminate and could control her power and even to have me."

"You're a disgrace to everything we are. An impurity." Fath Kefira's green eyes blazed in fury.

"I disagree," said the stranger in the cell with Leigh.

"Who are you?" Fath wrinkled his nose.

"William Thatcher. I work for the Human Protection Department, and I'm the Knowledge Keeper."

Arms crossed, expression dripping with sarcasm. "That makes you an authority on this matter how?"

"It doesn't."

"Why are you here, anyway?" Fath glared at Thatcher. The arrogance of the man got under Charlie's skin like fingernails on a chalkboard.

"The Council summoned me to your quarters to give testimony on the Gayden attacks, and since I'm an expert in humans, you all asked for my opinion. I have long since stated the Unity Statue was formed for us to embrace the races, not still divide us. Geminates surviving and making other Geminate children is testimony to that." While he spoke, he kept his gaze on Ora instead of the Council. At his words, the strangest expression crossed over William's face—one of affection and longing.

"She isn't a Geminate." Damien stepped in front of Ora, blocking Will's view of her. "She has all four cores. Not two."

Ora locked eyes with Charlie, a spark of curiosity rested there, the first sign of life she'd seen in her best friend's eyes, but Charlie had no idea what that was about and gave her friend the smallest of shrugs.

"Like Aggie said, no interruptions. We will finish our conditions, and then you can deliberate." Winslow lifted a hand, not bothering to turn toward them.

Aggie resumed reading the list as if nothing had happened. "Six. Geminates shall no longer be illegal and have full rights and protection as every other magician and Gayden. Seven. Once their numbers are high enough, a place shall be made for them on the Council. Eight. A list of magical creatures, henceforth called MCs, will be provided, and they will also have representation on the Council. Nine. Trade between the human world via the Gayden people shall also be permitted with MCs, but at this time they shall not be permitted to travel to the human realm. Ten. MCs shall have equal rights to acquire jobs and fair wages in Conjuragic based on knowledge and experiences. Eleven. We agree to uphold Conjuragic law. No hate crimes shall be permitted. Twelve. We agree to not violate the Concealment Code. Thirteen. Upon agreement of the treaty and the announcement to all of Conjuragic of our new peace, we shall unseal the Veil."

Aggie slipped the glasses from her face and closed the binder. She got to her feet, shuffling toward the closest cell. Mira rose, strolling toward Aggie, who slid the binder between the bars.

Steve ushered Aggie back toward the elevators, but called over his shoulder, "You shall have a day to discuss. If you have made a decision sooner, you may call for us. The guards will bring you food and drink."

The dungeon remained oddly quiet but hummed with tension. Breaking the silence, the man called William called out, not bothering to hide his smile. "Laurie. It's me, Will."

Ora paused, turning to stare at him, bewilderment on her face. "Excuse me?"

"Laurie, don't you remember me? We were friends as kids."

Ora shook her head. "No, I didn't have any friends until I was eight, and my name is Ora, not Laurie."

"Then you must have been using a fake name, but I would bet my life it's you."

Damien pulled Ora toward the door. "She said you were mistaken."

"I haven't seen you since your eighth birthday. When you caught everything on fire like an Ember, but I'd assumed you were a Sphere."

Ora's face looked as if she'd swallowed a bucket full of ice water. She squeezed her eyes shut, forehead crinkling, then opened her eyes, and said, "Will? The Dodgers?"

"Yes! It's me."

Ora shuddered, swaying on her feet. "Oh, my God. I remember."

24

ORA

The dungeon spun, or felt as if it did. One second I felt like a fog covered me, half listening to the conversation, except when they mentioned Geminates, then the next Will's face unlocked something deep inside me. Locked away underneath years of suppression and magic. The lights and sounds around me faded and wavered drawing out other sounds and sights from long ago—a cold icy morning, the snow melting as flowers grew impossibly in winter, a red-headed boy, an injured dog. As foreign and disorienting as that made me, I recognized they were memories. Memories from my childhood. Memories of performing magic. Now that the door had opened, memories flooded out, like water pouring into a busted ship, flipping and rolling, coming in no particular order, leaving my mind staggering, and having to regroup the pieces later.

When the amulet blocking my magic broke, a few memories returned, unclear, the details lost, like oil smeared over them, but these came at me sharp and crystal. Smells and tastes returned. Mom's scent lingered on the air. Images of her young, alive and vital. Images of me calling out for mommy. Will in a forest, a mere boy, using his Tempest magic while I laughed. I didn't recall tilting and losing my balance, but I blinked, and Damien held my arm, holding me up.

"What's wrong?" His forehead screwed up.

"Nothing. I'm dizzy." The here and now blinked in and out of existence. The past flashing as more and more memories returned. Each one breaking my heart. At last I saw Mom, older, wearing her own amulet. *Ora, you must never take it off. If you do, you will be in grave danger. Promise me. Promise me you won't ever take it off.*

The onslaught trickled to a halt. The images jostled around my head, trying to make sense, to be put in order. So much of it snapped into place as easy as breathing. The memories I'd already had sharpened in detail, but the ones with Will were the most powerful. The ones where I'd used my magic fully, the ones that represented the closest version of my true self, and I'd shared it with Will. Been the true me for the first and last time. Even my memories with Charlie couldn't compare to these. The two of us had used our powers for good.

My mom's face, the youngest I'd ever seen it, loomed in my mind's eye. Mom, not pretending to be my grandmother to protect me, the memory bittersweet. Because of my friendship with Will, that continued use of magic caused my powers to grow, lingering close to the surface, and was why I'd lost control at my birthday party. The Ember inside me ignited the gazebo where all the presents had been. Why I'd had to lose my memory and Mom's youth. Why I stood in this very dungeon. Yet, I held no hate in my heart for him. For besides Mom, Will had been the only other one to understand me for who I truly am and love me for it anyway. He'd thought I was a Sphere, but that didn't matter. He knew I was a witch from the moment he'd met me, and he'd never been afraid of me, even when the gazebo ignited around me at my eighth birthday party. His expression held sadness without a hint of distrust as Mom and I pulled away.

As the fire blazed and children ran for cover, he'd caught my eye as Mom dragged me away. In that moment, he knew I had Ember magic as well—knew I hadn't been totally honest with him as he'd been with me. Yet here it was, eleven years later, and at his first sight of me, his expression held nothing but acceptance. This was too much. Too much with everything that had been going on.

It took all of my strength of will to walk into the elevator and not run like the hounds of Hell were chasing me as I left the Town Hall. The others stopped to discuss the encounter and to schedule another meeting. Always, meeting after meeting. Talking. Talking. Never ending. I had to be alone. Had to let this process. They called my name, but I didn't stop.

The ocean called to me. The cores of magic sang in my blood for release. I stopped, briefly, driven by instinct, or the sway of the lamé amulet, thumping against my skin, into the bungalows to grab my go bag. I had no intention of leaving. No intentions to do anything except to get to the sea. My newly blackened boots sank into the sand, growing hot in the early morning sun. Seagulls called as they circled looking for a meal. The newly created black and red leathers changed by my magic to suit me pushed against me and every thick breath pulled into my lungs heavy and suffocating. I stripped, throwing the outfit on the white sand. I rushed past them, lying black as death on the sand. Dropping the go bag, I stepped into the sea, wearing nothing but bra and panties. The cool water washed over my toes, rising fast up to my knees, before retreating backward. The magic squirmed upward, seeking release, like a plant pulling toward the sun. The sea rose again caressing my legs. This time pulled by Naiad magic rather than the waves. Sea weed slithered to wrap around my waist like a slimy wet green snake. An unnatural salty breeze blew my hair behind as fire blossomed from my palms. The cores energized me, taking away the pain, allowing the memories to settle. The hole in my heart from mom's death didn't disappear, but muffled somehow, offering protection so I could go on.

A voice carried on the wind, *It's time, my child.*

The sea crashed down, the wind ceased, the sea weed withered, and slid away. "Mom?"

It wasn't her. As soon as I voiced the question, my answer was obvious. "Aryiana?"

Yes, came her reply, the sound airy and far away.

Recalling her beautiful dark skin and calming brown eyes, I hadn't realized that I had missed her. "Mom died." My voice cracking on the words—blunt and final.

I know.

I supposed she did. She would have, being a seer, but I had to ask. "You knew before, didn't you?"

A pause. I thought she had gone until she said, *Yes. I'm sorry.*

"Could I have stopped it?"

No.

I had that at least.

Again Aryiana said, *It's time, my child.*

"Time for what?" I was so done with games and riddles, with this never-ending drama that had become my life.

Look in your bag. The answers you seek are there. With that, Aryiana had gone. Not that she'd ever really been there, broadcasting her thoughts across the thousands of miles between us, a psychic link. How powerful was she? The thought terrified me.

The sun had moved far in the sky. While I thought my little foray into the sea had been mere seconds, hours had passed, yet again. A new form of rumination I guessed. Sighing, I wished I could do that faster or without looking like a coward. Losing hours wasn't pleasant. I'd ventured to the deserted beach on the far side of the island. The majority of the Gayden stayed mainly on the other side where most of the town shops and restaurants were located. That place felt like a million miles away. Even the hospital, located in the heart of the small town, felt separate, haunted, as this small part of this hidden world.

I left the sea, pushing the water from my skin, and instead of putting on black and red battle leathers, I removed jean shorts and a T-shirt, wanting at that moment to feel like a normal nineteen-year-old girl instead of a witch in the middle of a rebellion.

The clothes weren't what Aryiana pointed me to, but I avoided looking for a few more minutes. At last I gave in to temptation, searching through the bits of clothes, discarded hair ties, an old brush, and a single unmatched sock with a large hole in it, to find a wrinkled paper that had settled to the very bottom.

Pulling it out, I unfolded it, taking my time, caressing the pages, because I knew how important this would be. Inside, written in a tiny neat handwriting, the note read:

By the hands of two Geminates, a jewel of light—fierce and fiery—will be formed. When unification shatters, when the sanctuary sinks, when the parents fall, the master of the four cores will rise up, and the leader of Gayden shall battle good against evil. Only the one with true power shall prevail.

I read the paper over and over again, understanding coming in slow waves. But no matter how long I sat there, my fate had always been this. Hiding from it wouldn't change it. It had been predestined before I'd even been born. But who did it mean? The leader of Gayden. Did that mean me or Mathesar with his? Was I the evil one in this prophecy? But how could I be if Aryiana had helped my family? But she had given the prophecy to Mathesar right in front of my dad. She had set everything in motion. But had she been pushing all this time so we would be defeated or for Mathesar to be?

Someone had to read this prophecy, but who? Charlie was my first thought, but she had no way of knowing what this meant any more than I did. Sabrina perhaps, but she enforced the law, and for that matter, so did Arameus. But Will, the Human Protection Department and Knowledge Keeper. That sounded promising.

But how to get him alone?

25

SABRINA

Sabrina returned to the dungeons. Raised voices greeted her as she descended the stairs, avoiding the elevator, not trusting the human mechanics. The arguing ground to a halt as she approached. She didn't even look at the Council as she held up a hand. "I'm not here for you." She turned her attention to the guards. "I ask that you release this woman into my custody."

Leigh hadn't looked up, not even when Sabrina stopped in front of her cell. Her long hair, silky black, encased in a braid, tumbled over her shoulder to her stomach. The little end she caressed between her fingers. One of her very few tells of anxiety. The guard cleared his throat. "This is very unorthodox. First Miss Stone takes the Tempest prisoner and now you wish for the Sphere Protector."

Only then Sabrina noted Leigh was in her cell alone. Ora had taken the wizard William away somewhere. It wasn't surprising given that he'd said they'd known each other as children, but Sabrina made a mental note to find out more about this, but not wanting to be caught unaware, she raised her head higher. "It isn't your place to question those in charge. She has her mission. I have mine." Sabrina dared not take a breath. If they checked, she hadn't discussed this plan with anyone.

The guard didn't hide the roll of his eyes as he nodded to the other guard. The second hesitated.

Sabrina placed her hands on her hips. "I can handle her. Besides the pellucid black jewel is in her." She ran a hand down her left arm drawing attention to the mark on Leigh. "Her magic is blocked. Open the door. Now." She let her voice fill with steel.

The door swung open, but Leigh remained in her seat, legs crossed, indifferent to the conversation.

"Come on, Commander."

At this, Leigh's head snapped in attention, anger laced in every line of her face. "Commander? You're no lieutenant of mine. Traitor." Venom oozed from every syllable. Her words stung, but she'd deserved them.

"Very well, Leigh Stewart. You are my prisoner and you will come with me." Leigh stared, unblinking, challenging. "One way or the other."

Without looking away, Leigh rose, head held high, and stepped out of the cell, past Sabrina, exposing her back. Letting her know she didn't view her as a threat, magic blocked or not. She sucked in a breath as she allowed the insult to slide off her and followed Leigh to the stairs, gripping her arm as they ascended.

Not wanting to be overheard Sabrina led her not to the old church section, but to the back where the offices were held. She found an empty one, save for a desk and two chairs, flipped on the light, and directed Leigh to sit. She closed the door behind them and took her place across the desk, facing her best friend.

Leigh stared, face blank, and eyes empty. This was going to be much harder than she thought.

"I want to explain."

"If you've brought me here to listen to your petty excuses, then you can save your breath and take me back to my cell."

"I deserved that, but regardless, you're going to hear me out. What you decide to do after that is up to you."

Dark eyes rolled as Leigh slumped in her seat, bored and indifferent.

Now that she had her here, she wasn't exactly sure what to say. "I didn't intend to betray our kind or our friendship." A deep pause followed, allowing her guilt to settle and shift. "The morning they notified us of Ora's escape from the Kassen, we all went hunting her. I found her." The image of looking down a side street, seeing that bald head, face white in fear, staring back at her. "We both knew she wasn't a Nip." Sabrina shook her head. "A Gayden. We knew we had almost executed an innocent young girl. I don't know how you spent that night, but I struggled to know how I could ever forgive myself. How I could keep doing this job?

But when I saw her, I knew I'd been given a second chance. I intended to free her."

The small room with tan walls and a wooden desk melted away and Sabrina ran through the streets of Conjuragic leading Ora to safety in her mind's eye. "All I had to do was get her to the gate, but a shapeshifter stopped us."

This got Leigh's attention. Her chin snapped up. Shapeshifters had died out long ago. They had never been natural, a totally different being than a were, instead a creation made by the darkest of magic. "The shifter attacked, and we thought one of the humans was killed. The man you all know as Jack Hamilton." Sabrina paused, recalling the horror of watching Ora as the rubble smashed him backward. "Ora's eyes glowed white, while pure magic ripped out of her. I'd never seen anything like it. None of us had. I'm ashamed to admit the sight of it petrified me, and when Ora demanded that all of us escape through the Veil, I blindly obeyed."

Leigh watched her as she spoke, listening, which was more than Sabrina could've hoped for. "Afterward, I couldn't leave. At first because she sealed the Veil. I had no way home, and I figured if I stayed with them, then I could eventually find a way back. Ora had almost drained herself. She still doesn't fully understand there are limits to our magic."

"She thinks what, it's an endless well?"

"She understands that if she uses too much, she gets tired. Eventually has to ruminate. She can't comprehend that rumination allows her magic to rebuild." Sabrina shook her head. She tried to get Ora and her mother to understand, but Ora kept pushing and pushing. "After we crossed Ora collapsed for days. With the Veil sealed, I had to get her to safety. I didn't know if the Veil could ever be reopened if she died. Our Protectors and Hunters in the human world were after them. I fought them to rescue her friend."

Leigh's brows came together. "What friend?"

"Charlie. The one Bizard tortured during Ora's arrest."

"Ahh yes." Leigh nodded. "Then what?"

Hope trickled through Sabrina. Perhaps her friendship hadn't died. "They thought her collapse was due to her grief, but..."

"She drained herself right to the edge of her own death."

Sabrina closed her eyes, remembering trying to hide that from Perdita, hoping Ora would survive so she could get home. "She lived, and I helped her learn magic so she could lead me home, and during our travels, a Gayden attacked me."

Leigh gasped. "Now you fight alongside them?"

Resisting the urge to shudder, she continued, "It wasn't the same ones. This one belonged to the man who calls himself master or the experimenter." A half truth, half lie. Damien had done it, but he had been a pawn of Mathesar's, a slave since childhood, but saved by Ora and her belief in him, in her mercy, but now wasn't the time to tell Leigh this. "She risked herself, her mother, her best friend. She wouldn't leave me or Arameus behind." She watched her friend as she spoke and didn't miss the slight change in her expression. Leigh was impressed, and dare she hope grateful, that Sabrina had been spared. "After that, everything changed. I knew her for what she was and accepted her, and her mother, a Geminate. I met your uncle Fox. He's quite a character."

Sabrina's back stiffened at the mention of her uncle's name. "Why were you near my family?"

"Your uncle helped save me, and he taught Ora how to wield her Sphere magic."

Leigh sucked in a breath, not bothering to hide her shock anymore. "How? Why?"

"She won him over like she did me, and then we found the Gayden people and they led us back to their home. She won them over too. Like she won us over during her trial."

Leigh jerked to her feet. "What? I never."

Deliberately rising slowly, Sabrina smiled. "Don't lie. To yourself or to me. We both knew she wasn't a Gayden when we took her to be executed. You grieved that day, as I did."

Her mouth opened and closed several times before she put her arms behind her back and paced. Sabrina smirked as she sat remembering all the times she saw her best friend and Commander do this very same thing in their office. "Then what? None of this explains why you shot me."

The small bud of hope shriveled. "The Gayden joined her, and we began training with magic and human weapons. I'm now as deadly with them as I am with Naiad."

Her pacing ceased in an instant. She shot a sideways glance at Sabrina, understanding filling her mind. But Sabrina said it out loud anyway, "We raided the Haven and over took it. My dad began to accept us, but then the Quads attacked." With a pointed look, she let Leigh know she wasn't innocent either. The loss of her dad and his dying words still ate away at her. "He was killed in that battle, and when we raided the Vindeca, I had to get you out of harm's way. I couldn't think of anything else."

"Shooting me? That was what you thought of to get me out of harm's way!" Her arms crossed not needing to say, *Are you freaking kidding me?*

"Better a non-fatal shot to the shoulder than a fatal one dealt by another."

Leigh strutted to her chair and sat, arms on the table, leaning in close. "Fine. But what about everything else. Like how the hell did you get here if the Veil is closed? What does she and these Gayden want? This master person, he truly exists?"

That bud of happiness bloomed. The tide had turned. Leigh wasn't totally convinced to jump sides, but she at least believed her. The hate had receded, but she still couldn't tell her everything. Not yet. "Ora can manipulate the Veil. As she sealed it, which I don't pretend to understand, she can also open small portals. What she wants is exactly what you heard during the demands. In short, equality, and as far as Master, he does exist. I saw him with my own eyes, with the shapeshifter and the human male who we thought died when she sealed the Veil. We know who he is."

"Is that who Bizard was working with?"

"Yes."

"The human, Jack, was captured. Deemed to be an innocent hostage along with his mother. What was the real connection?"

"The boy is her best friend's brother and was her boyfriend. His real name is John McCurry."

Leigh rolled her eyes. "The mother?"

"She was Ora's mother. Perdita Stone."

"Was?"

Sabrina hesitated, hurt still wringing her heart. "Something's happened with John. He's with the shapeshifter, a woman name Strega. She transforms into a tailless black cat. She's brainwashed him or something. We went to rescue him in the Meadow." She sighed. "Strega and John ambushed us. John stabbed Perdita, Ora's mother."

Leigh covered her mouth, turning pale. "Gods." Her eyes flickered back and forth, thinking fast, putting things together. "I thought her mother died and her grandmother raised her."

"Perdita made a deception to keep Ora hidden from us about ten years ago. She aged herself and blocked their magic. Again, what we said to the Council was true."

Her former Commander got to her feet, absentmindedly scratching at the black mark running along her left arm. Sabrina knew better than to speak. Leigh needed time to process all of this, to let it sink in, to piece everything together.

Surprising her, Leigh leaned over the table. "What do you want from me? Why tell me all of this?"

Sabrina's heart constricted as her eyes stung. "I want you to understand. To forgive me if you can, and," she dropped the final bomb that could end her friendship forever, "bless my marriage."

Leigh pulled up straight. "Marriage?"

Of all the things she'd said of in the last thirty minutes, this was what she'd been most afraid her best friend wouldn't be able to forgive. "Simeon," Sabrina whispered his name.

Leigh spun and punched the wall, leaving a bloody streak. "We aren't supposed to mix the bloodlines. If we could, then I would've." Leigh's eyes met hers, full of longing, as her voice trailed off, and Bizard's cruel words returned to her. She'd always been curious if her friend's feelings went deeper than mere friendship. Not that same sex relationships even in the same houses were allowed, but they should be. The humans and Gayden were definitely more civilized about such things.

"This is one of the reasons why I'm fighting. We were wrong. Geminates can survive and thrive. That Master has who knows how many Geminate slaves. I've seen what Ora can do. How much stronger we can be if the blood lines mix."

"Don't you see? She's too powerful. No one should have that much power. We're not gods."

Her words didn't sit well, but part of what she said rang true, but Ora wasn't all powerful. She could be stopped. She could be overpowered, and to say Geminates couldn't be together would start another cycle of prejudice. Instead she said, "If we win, then tolerance can spread. I know they're other ways of life that need addressed." A world in which Leigh could fall in love with whoever she chose, male or female.

Leigh studied the table for longer than necessary, taking long deep breaths. She stared at her hand as the skin on her bloody knuckles knitted back together. "Congratulations on your marriage. I hope you two will be very happy together."

"Thank you."

"Who is this Master?"

"Mathesar Enochs. Naiad advisor." Sabrina waited for the shocked look, then denial.

Leigh's back stiffened. "I knew it."

26

CHARLIE

Arameus and Charlie walked hand in hand down the white sandy beach. The wind unnaturally blew around them, adding an extra support, powered by the two of them to keep Arameus upright. Both the doctors and the Healers were amazed by his recovery, already planning how to merge the two modalities of the prosthesis and his magic, but Charlie suspected his recovery spawned from how he'd reacted back at Fox's place. As if Perdita still pushed him. The first thing he'd done when he'd heard the news of her death he got out of the hospital bed. She couldn't help but admire him, and she'd tried to do her best not to coddle him like she'd done before.

His hair shone like molten gold, green eyes intelligent and kind, always crinkled in halfhearted amusement. Yet he would do anything if he thought it was the right thing to do. He'd been the first wizard she'd ever known to not fear Gayden at first sight. Even though an uncle of his had been captured and died at the hands of a Gayden, he chose not to hate, not to let prejudice in his heart, to truly see and value people for their true selves. Despite one of them taking his power and almost dying. Why else would he have decided to defend Ora in the first place? The best part of all was how much he loved her, the insignificant human friend of the omega, Charlie's private name for her bestie.

Charlie had always felt inferior to Ora. Growing up, Ora always perceived how other people treated her as distant, like they didn't like her. She said they must've known something about her was different, but Ora could never comprehend that she outshined all of them, and that had nothing to do with magic.

Everything about Ora screamed unearthly, from the fire in her hair, the swirling color of her eyes, the almond shape of her face, flawless perfect skin, the intelligence, sense of humor, and the grace with which she moved. All of this set her apart. Made others distance themselves because they weren't worthy to stand beside her—this angel made flesh. Despite that irresistible charm, Arameus had picked Charlie instead. She hadn't had the courage to ask him why.

"Penny for your thoughts," he said, shifting his weight, balancing against the uneven sand.

"Nothing. Just thinking."

He stopped, and with an easy shift that surprised her, he kissed the top of her head. "You know I've been questioning prisoners for a long, long time. I know when someone is lying to me."

She stuck her tongue out at him.

He laughed, loud and joyous, full of life, "My, my, what a mature woman I have."

She giggled, looking to the sea. "Fine. I was wondering why you would pick me instead of her."

His arm around her waist pulled her closer. "I love Ora, but like a sister."

"But she looks like a Tempest. Like the girl you're supposed to be with, and she can..."

He turned her, interrupting her words, and with a gentle nudge raised her head to meet his eyes. "None of that matters. I don't feel that way about her, and one of the reasons we've been fighting is so I wouldn't have to choose a Tempest. You're everything I've ever wanted." His lips touched hers, and the worry slipped away as her blood heated.

They resumed walking, taking in the beautiful skyline, the stillness of the moment. They'd had so few moments like these recently. Today felt like a calm in the storm. At the end of the stretch, the island turned, and voices reached them, carried on the wind.

Charlie spotted Finch and Wade tucked against a rock, close together, but not quite touching. In the moments before they saw them, Charlie glimpsed another moment of stillness. They smiled at each other, faces relaxed, for once not etched in worry or covered in dirt or blood. Even when they spotted Charlie and Arameus, Finch raised an easy hand, holding a beer can. "Why hello there, young lovers. Come join us."

A blush rose in her cheeks and the casual toss of the word lovers.

Arameus, unfazed, nodded his head, and eased into a curve in the rock, leaning his back up against it. "Thanks. I could use a little rest."

"You're getting around on that pretty well." Wade gestured to the prosthetic leg and cane. His short dark hair gleamed with dried gel, his cologne wafted in the air, a husky scent. Charlie liked Wade. She hadn't at first, but she'd come to see him as the quiet calm one, the stone and foundation to them all, to balance Finch's passion and fire. Ying and yang. Two sides of the same coin. Something clicked in Charlie's head. Something she hadn't seen before now. Finch guzzled down his beer, a cooler by his side, opened with several more inside, but Wade watched, quiet and guarded, waiting for her reaction. She hadn't expected this, but nothing about it disturbed her. She gave him her most accepting smile, and his shoulders relaxed.

Arameus crossed his arms, that peaceful expression vanishing. "Any news?"

Finch burped an answer, and Wade rolled his eyes and said, "No. The Elders have given the Council until the morning. That's why," Wade searched for the right word which Finch supplied, "I decided to take the night off and get shit faced."

Charlie snorted.

"I figured it was a good idea. Letting him unwind. No matter what happens, nothing will be happening tonight. Besides, we'll need to plan." Wade gathered up the crushed beer can Finch tossed on the ground, placing it in a plastic bag sounding as if it had joined several others. Finch bent over, reaching into the cooler, jeans sliding down his ass showing his butt crack.

"Shouldn't that be what we're doing now? Planning?" Arameus chose to ignore the plumber strip tease.

Another beer can snapped open as Finch straightened, hiked up his pants, and took another long swig. "I'm sure someone is. Another meeting. Tonight, I say hell with it. Those fucking magicians, no offense," Finch waved his free hand toward them, "can't get through the Veil. I can afford to relax, remember what the hell I'm fighting for." He reached behind him and squeezed Wade's butt. Wade avoided looking at them.

"And if the attack happens in the morning?" Arameus asked.

Finch barked a laugh. "Won't be the first battle I've done hung over."

That wasn't the least bit reassuring. Charlie couldn't blame him for needing to unwind, heck, their little romantic walk had been the same thing under the ruse of physical therapy. Still, she didn't want a man fighting beside her to not be a hundred percent.

Wade patted Finch on the shoulder, and the masculinity softened. "I wouldn't suggest going into the battle hung over, but he does have a point. If the Council agrees to our terms, we're not in any hurry. They have no prisoners. There is no deadline, save for our own. We should be smart about it."

Arameus leaned forward, elbows on his knees. "Yes, but right now I, a mere magician..."

"He didn't mean that." Wade placed a hand on his shoulder, and Charlie half expected him to shrug it off.

"It doesn't matter, but I have to think about both sides." He straightened, facing both men. "We might not have a deadline, but we have left Conjuragic in the hands of Mathesar. They are without rulers, and who knows what their fate may be. There are innocent people there. People in danger and no one else can protect them except us."

"What about their Protectors? The advisors to the Council? Won't they take over?" Wade's body tensed.

"Nothing like this has ever happened. Typically, when one of the Council dies, the living spouse retires, and the advisors meet with their homelands, and two new ones are chosen. This is unprecedented. The Council has never vanished. The homelands will be in an uproar. In a time like this, it wouldn't surprise me if Mathesar, the great manipulator, would try to change our ways. Suggest a temporary shift in power to a single person. Blaming us. If we're defeated, he'll find a way to never relinquish control."

"He might have had the other advisors assassinated as well," Charlie thought out loud.

Arameus's spine stiffened, meeting her gaze, the color fading from his. "You're right. I'm sure that's what has happened. He would've planned to take them all out at once. Make it look as if he was the last surviving member of the government. No one would stand in his way. Come on." He reached out a hand for her to help him up. "We've got to get back. Warn the Council about what's at stake."

Finch and Wade followed them, Finch growling the whole time about everyone needing a night off. At the foyer in the Town Hall, Ora stood with William, his black jewel blocking his magic removed and in her hand. As they entered, William looked their way, and his face lit in delight. "Arameus, I thought that was you in the back."

"Will." Arameus limped forward and reached out an arm.

It shouldn't have surprised her that Arameus knew Will, but he should've mentioned it before now.

Everyone stared as the two Tempests hugged, smacking each other on the back with one arm before retreating. Ora asked the obvious question, "How do you two know each other?"

Will grinned, looking like a little boy. "He's my cousin."

Arameus tilted his head. "Like distantly related. If you look back far enough into everyone's family tree, everyone is related to someone else with the Houses."

"Uh, a bunch of in-breeders," Finch slurred.

The good-natured man she knew vanished under an icy murderous stare. Wade blocked Finch from Arameus's view. "Sorry. He's not usually such an unpleasant drunk."

"Where were you headed, cuz?" Will asked, ignoring the tension in the air. Ora cocked her head, interested as well.

"We believe Mathesar has had the rest of the Council's advisors murdered. Like he sent spies to murder the Council. He is in Conjuragic, in control and unchecked."

"What the hell is going on?" Sabrina's voice rang through the hall, suspicion dripping from every word. Leigh Stewart trailed behind her, her black markings still in place.

Ora cocked her head. "I could ask the same of you?" The question wasn't an accusation, not really, but something like it coated the question, testing.

Instead of answering, Sabrina jerked her head toward Will. "Why is his jewel removed?"

"Because I removed it, and I trust him. That should be enough for you."

The two stared each other down, two strong women, talking with their eyes, their expressions.

"Leigh has been my friend since forever." She flicked her gaze between Ora and Charlie. "I had to explain myself."

"And?"

Leigh stepped forward, holding her hands up as everyone moved into defensive positions. "I'm not your enemy. I will not say that I'm on your side, as my loyalty is to my home."

Finch wobbled, glassy-eyed. "Makes it a little hard to trust you, buttercup."

Leigh's face remained calm, but Charlie suspected he would've been harmed if she'd had her powers. The sight of Leigh unnerved Charlie. The fear and power she'd had the day they'd taken Ora scared her even now, plagued her nightmares. They had lessened after she'd killed Bizard. *Served the cocky bastard right!* That was one kill she'd never be ashamed of.

Leigh let her eyes travel to each of them. "If I said anything but that you'd be fools to trust me. However, I don't plan to stop you. I think some of our ways need to change, but I will always support my own people first. I cannot fight alongside you. I could never fight against the people I have sworn to protect."

"How about those who stand with Mathesar? Will you fight them? The Gayden and Geminates he's collected like a puppet master. What about those of your world that have joined him? Plotted to kill your Council?" Ora faced the woman down. Such a stark contrast to their first meeting.

Leigh made eye contact with Sabrina, the first sign of weakness she'd shown so far, and Sabrina raised an eyebrow. "I see what you mean," Leigh said.

"Told you."

Leigh nodded. "She told me you'd changed much since I'd last seen you."

"What of it?"

"You passed my test."

Ora's eyebrows raised. "Which was?"

"You've shown yourself not to be bloodthirsty. To want to fight against wrong. I admire that. I can fight against traitors, but I'm afraid I'll only be able to assist if my Council deems it appropriate."

Ora watched her, assessing. "Very well. I can accept that."

Ora and Sabrina caught each other's eyes, and something passed between them. A twinge of jealousy ran through Charlie. Sabrina would never take her place, but the two of them shared something that Charlie couldn't compete with. Arameus squeeze her hand and she realized she could share.

With an almost imperceptible nod, Ora broke eye contact. Sabrina walked around Leigh, placing a hand over the darkest part of the blackness on her arm, and closed her eyes. Within moments and a sharp intake of breath from Leigh, the black jewel pulled out of Leigh's arm.

A new tentative alliance formed. Ora stared into a corner, seeing nothing, but a deep weight had been placed on her shoulders. Her best friend had been pushed and pushed, beyond the point where most people could withstand, yet she still fought. She loved Ora as a sister, much more than a friend, and she wished she could take this burden from her.

Some new sorrow had befallen Ora since Will reappeared. Charlie felt her magic simmer to the surface, an icy breeze tingling at her fingertips, wanting to lash out, to hurt this unseen enemy. Nostrils flaring, Ora noticed Charlie's fingers and held up a hand. "I've discovered something."

Arameus limped forward. "You heard what I said. We have to go to the Elders and the Council. If we wait any longer, there won't be a Conjuragic left."

Ora reached toward him without looking up. Her touch, so full of tenderness, settled on his chest, above his heart. "I know you're afraid for your home and your people, but there are things we have to discuss."

He opened his mouth to argue, but Ora kept talking. "The news I've been given," she paused, considering her words, "changes nothing, but it's been a day already. Mathesar doesn't want to destroy Conjuragic. He wants to rule it. I agree the advisors are already dead. With the Council missing and no bodies to prove their deaths may delay his plans. We have time."

"Time for what?" They all jumped as a voice echoed from behind and Winslow shuffled out of the shadows.

Finch barked a laugh. "Damn stealthy for an old man."

Without bothering to smile, Winslow said, "It has its uses."

Ora crossed the distance between them. "I want our people to see their families, bury their loved ones, make those phone calls in case this is their last chance. Because this time..." She sighed. "This time decides it all. Mathesar will have gathered his forces. He'll know we're coming. This will be the final battle that decides the war."

"How much time do you want? A week, two?"

"Two days. Two days and then we march on the Pyre."

Wade stepped to them. "This is all well and good, but what of the Council?"

Winslow face wrinkled further in a quirky grin. "Negotiations have already been finalized. We signed the new treaty moments ago."

Shocked rippled through Charlie and the rest stood stunned as well.

They'd made an agreement without telling any of them? Wade's back stiffened.

Finch eyebrows lifted to his hairline. "Why the hell weren't we notified?"

Winslow shrugged. "The Council requested for the Elders to be present since we're the rulers here. Lest you all forget."

The sting of that blow didn't go unnoticed. The Elders didn't mind them being the muscle, but now the battle had moved to the realm of diplomacy, they enacted their dominance.

"May we ask if they agreed to the terms?" Wade reigned in the anger that flowed through the group and braved the question.

Winslow stared at him, as if considering if he should divulge the information. "They agreed to everything with a few concessions. They denied allowing each magical creature a spot on the high Council, but did concede to allowing the Magical Brethren, I believe they call themselves, a diplomat to represent them."

Wade nodded. "That's it?"

"The appointment of two Gayden on the High Council shall, like the magicians, be male and female, married and reside in Conjuragic. Plus, they must study and learn Conjuragic law, and we, the Elders, I mean, will have to come up with a set of laws regarding Gayden. They decline a new bank stating theirs is already capable of making the financial exchange and another branch shall be located here."

Finch barked a laugh. "That's it? Suckers."

Indeed, it did seem as if they had gotten everything they'd asked for. That's when Winslow dropped the other shoe, while nodding. "Mmmm. And Wade?"

"Yes?"

"You shall be the male representative in Conjuragic. The Elders would like you to give us suggestions on which female," Winslow stressed the word while shooting a glance at Finch, "you would consider as your wife. Now get ready. You leave in two days' time."

At Winslow's words, Finch sucked in a breath, and Wade blanched. The Elders had played a cunning move. A way to hurt them all and put them in their place. Winslow turned to head back to the others.

"You'll want to be careful," Ora said so low that Charlie had to strain to hear her. Winslow paused, turning to face her. Head held high, steel in her eyes, she added, "The Elders should not forget how they won this victory."

Winslow flushed purple. "You threaten us girl?"

Ora smiled a predator's smile, a white flame of her intertwined magic flicking at her fingertips. "Of course not, Elder, but a promise." Her eyes shifted looking below to where the Council was held captive. "Governments rise, and governments fall. Best watch your step."

27

ORA

My magic swirled deep inside, rising to the surface as the Elders' betrayal washed over me, flickers of it danced along my fingers. It longed to lash out and destroy this new threat. Since Mom died, my power went on the defense, like a dog protecting its master. It took every ounce of control I had to push that power down. Winslow was a Gayden after all, he could take at least two cores of my power, but never hold it. I wasn't afraid of what he would do to me, but what the repercussions would be.

Clinching a fist and snuffing out my magic, I marched out of the Town Hall sensing the others following me with Winslow at a loss for words. He didn't follow, but he knew better than to push me. Their treaty was contingent upon the capture of Mathesar and the Council's return to Conjuragic. They still needed us—needed me. I didn't have it in me to go against yet another leadership. Those in power are conniving, bordering on dishonesty, and manipulation. None could be truly trusted, because most of them would throw others to the wolves if they posed a threat to their position. How typical in this critical time to remind us that they were the face of Gayden and we'd been doing their dirty work.

The beach, always my sanctuary, loomed in the distance, black clouds streaming in from the west, lightning sparking in the distance. I felt the single drop of water first, landing on my cheek, and hissing into steam the moment it hit me. The surprise brought me back to myself.

My magic rippled along my skin blocking the rain from touching me again. The touch of Ember magic roared to be let loose. Needing to calm down, my eyes closed, and I inhaled, held it, and let the air slip from my lips slow and long. The shield around me relaxed as the Ember settled downward, deep inside. A cool kiss of rain touched my forehead.

The others gathered around me, a group of equals, friends, family even with Finch swaying. The tension each of them felt presented itself in different ways—a stiffening of shoulders, lips set in a grim thin line, furrowed brows, arms crossed over a chest.

Not caring what any of them thought, I said, "Before we leave, the Elders and the Council will sign a document guaranteeing all of us immunity from any punishments."

"Damn right!" Finch said from behind, words less slurred.

"I want memorials for those who died, for," I swallowed a lump in my throat, "Mom. There will be more memorials needed before we're done, but I can't go on until I know her memory will be honored."

Sabrina stiffened. "My dad too." Leigh moved closer, their shoulders touching.

"Then what?" Arameus, always able to read me, asked.

"Aryiana gave me a prophecy. *The* prophecy. What Mathesar has been basing all of his actions on. Will has helped me try to figure out its meaning."

With a silent gesture from me, Will cleared his throat. "Prophecy is very tricky. It can say one thing and the meaning would still hold true for many outcomes. This one is even more convoluted." He relayed the prophecy. Hearing it from his mouth didn't bring any illuminating thoughts.

When he finished, no one spoke, and the thunder rolling in the distance with the gushing of the salty wind filled the heavy moment. The rain now flowed in a heavy sheet, and we should retreat into dryer places, but I wanted this said, and then I wanted to start planning for Mom's memorial. The pain of her loss pulled at me, trying to get my attention, but I couldn't heed to it. Not until we'd finished the war. Damien had helped me see that last night after everyone else retreated to their own bungalows.

"What does that mean?" Wade shouted above the roaring sea.

Lightning struck seconds after the air thrummed with the electricity, exciting my magic, making it want to rise, and meet it. "It means that our prime objective when we go up against Mathesar is to steal his fiery jewel."

"Because only the one with the true power, the one who possesses this jewel, will win?" Charlie shuffled closer to Arameus as if she needed his reassurance.

Leigh pushed her wet hair back from her forehead. "Prophecy is stupid. What if we lose because we're trying to get this jewel? I say the true power is taking down our enemies. Prophecies and a fictional jewel that may or may not even exist isn't the way to proceed."

Sabrina extended her power to cover us, protecting everyone from the onslaught of the storm. "I'm sorry, O, but she's right. We have to keep focused. Not going on some wild goose chase."

The words rattled in my brain. I knew they were right. Knew it, but I couldn't help but wonder if I didn't follow this path would we fail? "We send in Damien and Jeremiah across enemy lines. They'll be our insiders. Blend in. They can go after the jewel." Everything in me hated the idea. Damien and I had argued about it all morning. Right after I figured out he loved me and I loved him and he wanted to serve himself to the enemy.

Sabrina's mouth dropped open. "Are you kidding me? They'll be killed instantly. They're both supposed to be here in the human realm. I'm sure they've been spotted."

I wouldn't give up, even as the storm raged harder, making us all have to scream to hear each other. "The Gayden slaves don't know each other." Damien's words crushed my heart. "Not unless they had to work together. They weren't allowed to have friends. If Mathesar has gathered his forces, and we can all guess that he has, then there will be hundreds of them."

"You're throwing them to the wolves!"

"They agreed to this. I talked to both of them this morning. They know what they're getting into." Guilt rippled along my nerves, numbing my fingertips.

"Damien, fine! It's his choice, but Jeremiah's a kid. He's barely sixteen. You can't ask him to do this!" Sabrina sent shards of rain pelting toward me. With half a flicker of thought, my power halted them. Sabrina swallowed, calming herself.

"If we lose this war, he'll die. His brother already did. He has the right to fight if he wants to, but they've always had a choice, like all of you. If they decline, I won't force them."

With a swift nod of assent, our little group disbanded, heading in our own directions. I opened the Bridge, exiting at the hospital.

The following day, the storm had swept back out to sea leaving the island cleansed but had done nothing for the mood inside the Town Hall. Aggie stood at the top of the podium, the seats filled to capacity, with the leaders of each division seated behind the Elders at the platform. I'd never seen the place so full. Picture after picture of our fallen soldiers lined the walls, from floor to ceiling. Most of those in attendance wore black, me included. I couldn't recall what Aggie said. Only the feeling of sadness and the sniffles and quiet crying from the families of those lost. I didn't want to meet any of their eyes. I had asked this of them and doubted the guilt of their loss would ever leave me. Mom's picture on the wall comforted me. She understood the guilt I bare and wouldn't have thought less of me.

Afterward, the procession parted to go to some banquet hall, to feast and mingle, but it wasn't a place for me. My little family left the others for our own private funeral.

Sabrina and I needed a special memorial for our parents. Healer and empath Kris Bishop met us on the top of the highest dune, where I'd asked him to meet us last night. The others paused staring between the two of us. "Thank you for coming."

Kris nodded, and his magic caressed me, searching for my mood. I guessed he'd done the same to all of us.

Charlie wrapped her arm through mine. "Why is he here?" She blushed when he turned his attention to her. "No offense."

"None taken."

"I asked him here because he's a special kind of Healer. I wanted him to help us with our mood—my mood. To help keep me calm."

"You're an *amore mossar*?" Leigh circled him, breathing deeply as if taking in his scent.

"I am."

"Is that a bad thing?" Unease rose in my gut. I hadn't thought this through, maybe his own kind feared him.

She jerked her head once, a silent no, but still eyed him. "It's very rare. I hadn't heard of one in a long time."

"They hide us." Kris answered my unspoken question. "Our services are highly coveted."

"Shall we begin?" I gestured for everyone to sit down. Kris took a spot to my right, Damien hurried to my left, beating out Will. Sabrina, Simeon, Leigh, Finch, Wade, Jeremiah, Charlie, and Arameus formed a circle.

Kris smiled, his power flowing outward, a sweet breeze on my cheek, and picked up a handful of sand. "Place your hand over mine." I did as he asked, and his magic questioned mine. Mine answered, flowing into his hands, glowing. Memories of Mom raced through my mind, all her love, her kindness. Thousands and thousands of images left me as if copied and transferred into his mind. He moved once, and the connection fizzled out.

"What the hell was that?" Finch demanded. No one else spoke, but their faces turned white.

"If anyone would like to step out of the circle, you should do so now. I will ask each of you who stay to join hands. Bring any memories you have of Perdita Stone into your mind. The love or admiration. Anything. Then going from left to right, I would like you to share a memory of her."

Only Will, Simeon and Leigh moved out of the circle. Understandable since they hadn't really known her.

As our hands joined and a current ran through us, I should've been scared, but I wasn't. Sabrina closed her eyes and the rest followed her lead. "Perdita opened my eyes. She showed me a different way of looking at the world, showed me true friendship, and love. I hope I might be half the mother she was one day." Her voice cracked on the last few words.

Tears burned on my cheeks.

Finch, voice somber, said, "What can I say except she was the best mother I've ever seen. The sacrifice and love she showed for her daughter and anyone she loved amazed me. She was the kind of person we should all hope to be."

Next Wade said, "I didn't get to know her long enough. She left us all too soon. In the short time I knew her, she accepted me for who I am with no judgment or hatred. I will miss her and wish I could've known her better."

The waves crashed and rolled mingling with the calls of seagulls to create a sweet melody carried on the salty sea breeze. The sounds and smells to me became a thousand times more beautiful and precious than any in the Town Hall. Jeremiah sniffled. "I was taken away from my mother. Before I got to see her again, Perdita cared for me. She always made sure people ate and slept. That we were kind to each other, and to love and to hope. She gave me that. Hope that I would see my mom again. Hope that this wasn't it. Hope for a better future. I'll gladly fight or put myself at risk for what she believed in." At this my eyes opened, and Jeremiah watched me, expression fierce, and I knew Damien or one of the others had told him of my plan. I nodded, putting as much gratitude in the motion as I could.

A soft sob broke from Charlie. Tears streamed down her eyes. "Oh, Grandma Perdita. I know you weren't a grandma, but that's who you will always be to me. Family. You were and always will be my family. You were always there for me. I'll miss your pancakes." I snorted a laugh, tears slipping out of my eyes. Remembering all the sleepovers and how Charlie loved Mom's pancakes. "I'm sorry. I'm so sorry. I don't know why he did it, but it wasn't him. He'd have never hurt you. He loved you. I loved you. Love you." Not breaking the connection, she leaned into Arameus and sobbed.

I'd shoved thoughts of John and what he'd done deep down, but at her words, rage rose up. My magic uncoiling, ready to strike, to hunt him down, but Kris's power intertwined with mine, like holding my hand, and calm flowed into me. I understood how his powers could be coveted.

"There are no words to give Perdita Stone justice. Beautiful outside as well as in. She was everything we should aspire to be. Willing to sacrifice for what she believed in. Family. Love. Friendship. I was honored to have known her, and the world is a better placed because she was in it. I will keep the memory of her as a strong woman capable to look past her sorrowful beginnings and still find peace and hope. She will be greatly missed by her friends and her daughter. I pray to the gods to take up her soul and join her with her ancestors." Trust Arameus to speak with such grace. With each word spoken, my time to speak grew closer. What could I say that hadn't been said? How could I sum her up and say goodbye?

Clearing his throat, Damien squeezed my hand. "I didn't get to meet Perdita under the best of circumstances. Ora, her daughter, saw the good in me. Chose to give me a second chance. After getting to know Perdita better, I know Ora got that from her. So much of her still lives on in Ora. She was so proud at the woman her daughter has grown up to be and accepted me as well. Like the rest of you, I wish I could've gotten to know her better. To honor her, I pledge to spend my life protecting her daughter. Come what may."

My palm grew sweaty in his hand. He'd practically declared himself for me. In front of everyone. Peeking at him, he met my gaze and I read the unspoken words there. He was mine if I wanted him and when I wanted him. He would wait. With the slightest dip of my head, I acknowledged him. Our magics mingled, love intertwining, as a promise.

Silence pressed in all around me. My heart pumped hard as my mouth turned to ash. The time had come. Voice cracking, I said, "Mom." Tears rolled over my cheeks, nose trickled, as my eyes stung. "I wish your life could've been different. You had no childhood." Memories of my own playing with Charlie, climbing trees, playing with toys, celebrating holidays, and she'd never had that. "As soon as you got your freedom, you came to a strange world where you knew no one. You'd lost dad and were completely alone, and then you had me. The rest of your life you devoted to keeping me safe." Only deep breathing settled the sobs, preventing them from breaking free. "I wanted to give you a better life. A life of peace and happiness. A life not having to always watch our backs, and now you're gone. It doesn't seem real." My eyes burned and vision blurred. Each breath seared my chest, and once again Kris calmed the rising sorrow, enough so I could speak. "I'm going to keep going. Keep fighting so no one else has to go through what you did. What we did. I love you, and I miss you." My words trailed away replaced by quiet sobs shaking my shoulders.

Kris's arm shook and grew hot as love and loss and happiness and hope flowed from each of us, and as he broke the connection, his hands parted revealing the ball of sand transformed into a crystal rose shimmering with a golden liquid. He handed it to me, warm and quivering, as the scent of roses, Mom's favorite flower, drifted toward me. When I squeezed it, those feelings of my mom from all of us drifted through me.

"For as long as you live, this will work as it does now."

Gratefulness unlike any I'd ever known came over me. "Thank you."

I slipped away with most of the others as Kris started the same process for Sabrina's dad. Holding the crystal in my hand, cherishing it, mind working. Afterward Kris appeared at my side, face gaunt and hollow. This ceremony had taken a lot out of him. I didn't want to ask this of him, not after the gift he'd given me, and what it would cost him, but I would for Mom, for all of us. "Healer Kris."

"Yes?"

"Are your abilities limited to calmness and peace?"

His eyes darkened, a look of agony as well as anticipation shown in them. "No."

Ask I did.

28

ORA

The hour had come. From the moment the pen held suspended in the air, so long ago in biology class, it had all led to this. A fleeting wondering thought occurred to me, did Aryiana know it all along? Then I realized it didn't really matter, in the end, did it?

The oxygenian swarmed around my head, whispering, more into my thoughts than in my ears. We were ready, but Mathesar had been warned as well, his troops were ready according to Damien and Jeremiah, who had infiltrated enemy lines yesterday. Before they'd gone, Damien wrapped his warm, strong arms around my waist. I stretched to put my arms around his neck, drawing him closer, enjoying the brief moment of safety, even his smell comforted me. A dangerous thing with what we had to face.

Jeremiah hugged me after. He had filled out since I'd first met him. No longer that scared little boy, but then again, I wasn't that helpless little girl that I'd been when the Quad first appeared.

I closed my eyes, focusing on the whispering words, letting them form a map inside my head. The oxygenians' intel helped, but we needed the advantage from the sky. Our aerial team would need to be swift to win the sky. Mathesar had assumed he would've enough advantage from the tops of the Pyre, but I knew better than to underestimate him. His cunning had been going on for decades, unbeknownst to most everyone in Conjuragic, save for those few he'd recruited.

My eyes opened and cascaded across the preparation line. Every fighting Gayden stood by, some looking nervous, but most held steel in their eyes as well as their hands. My roaming gaze stopped at Sabrina. A swell of gratitude rose in me. Words could never describe how grateful I was to have her by my side at that moment. Her expression held the same feeling. Charlie approached, face grave, and bumped her shoulder against mine. It wasn't a mere gesture, but held a multitude of meaning. A goodbye to all that we'd been, all that we might become, because beyond this moment nothing was certain. She stepped back and moved to Sabrina who stood beside Simeon, shoulder to shoulder. Finch and Wade stood side by side and lifted their heads toward me in unison, which I returned.

I didn't want it to happen, but my heart ached, wishing my mom stood there with us. No, not with us, with me. A physical pain pierced my chest, squeezing as if I couldn't breathe, ripping tears from my eyes. Turning away, feeling like a coward, but I couldn't, wouldn't let the Gayden or my friends see me this way. The smell of roses flitted through my memory, and I felt the now-familiar pull of Kris's magic. I pushed the last images of her away—hard. The pain lingered inside me, palpable, but that pain would get me killed, tear away my focus, and then it would've all been for nothing. She would understand. I knew she would. The pain settled, like a pebble, joining the thousands of others I had pushed away, deep in the ocean of my soul. I faced my men, ready. Hitting the comm by my ear, I said, "Good morning."

Murmurs of greeting blurred as if they were one collective being instead of individuals. I recalled my speech before we'd cross the Bridge. "It's humbling knowing that today will be one of those momentous occasions in history. A day that will be remembered forever, but how and what we are remembered for remains in question. I cannot stand before you and tell you we will be victorious. I cannot tell you that you will be alive when the sun sets tonight, but that isn't the point."

I'd moved through the crowd, considering each face I passed, letting my words carry. "It doesn't matter if we live or die. It doesn't matter whether we win or lose. What matters is that we fight. We stand together, united, for what we believe in, and I believe in the goodness of people—humans, Gayden, Geminates, and Magicians alike. We have sent a message here in Conjuragic, ripped a crack in their belief system. We planted a seed of doubt in how things have been and what they should be. That seed will grow in the hearts of those in Conjuragic, and it will spread. It may take many, many years, but their way of thinking will change. Someday, they will fight for what we fight for today. You see, my friends, my family, we have already won."

I paused, and Finch raised a silent arm upward, not wanting to interrupt me, but still needing to acknowledge me, honor me, honor us. Others joined in until I stared at a sea of faces with an arm raised. I held up a hand honoring them in return. "I wish my mother was with us today. She started this all. She was brave enough to escape and bring me into this world. One person can make a difference. One person can change the world. She never envisioned this when she raced across the Veil with me growing inside her. Our actions and our lives may not be what we've planned, and we may never fully see the difference we make. But we are all important. Our lives matter. Our deaths matter. We all have a choice. There is still time. If anyone here wants to walk away, now is your chance. Leave freely, with no judgment or hate. I want those beside me today who know exactly that this is where they're supposed to be. If you have any doubt, you will be in our way."

Only a few heads moved, searching what the others would do, most held their heads high. An old Gayden with light brown skin and graying hair clasped my shoulder. "There is no walking away. We're with you to the end. Isn't that right, men?" He'd shouted the last line.

Men and women hollered. Ready to fight. I let them scream, building them up, while I stared on, face emotionless. I had become a machine, devoid of emotion. I had a job to do. I nodded once, making my way back to the front of the crowd. The time to face Mathesar had come.

The oxygenian introduced herself as Akshae. She volunteered to be the spokesman. She circled near my ear, stretching her essence over the great distance, rising higher and higher.

Mistress, Akshae spoke, stretching the word out like a hiss, *the Experimenter's forces are gathered, but disorganized.*

They wouldn't have the advantage of a surprise attack, but that wasn't unexpected. I hadn't expected to storm the place and capture Mathesar without a fight.

Shall I tell the others?

"Yes."

Sabrina's voice chimed in my ear, "I don't like this."

I half smiled at the thousandth time I'd heard the comment. "We've discussed it. It's now or never." I flipped the switch on the comm to the open channel. "Troops, you know why we are here. You know what is at stake. You know you fight for yourselves, your children, and all the unborn generations to follow. On my mark. Go!"

The aerial team, hundreds, shot into the air like bullets. Without warning, dark clouds swarmed, throwing the sunlit valley in semi-darkness. Lightning exploded downward in quick succession. The ground shook with each hit. The peace of the valley moments before vanished. The singing of birds halted in terrified shrieks. Screams competed with thunder. A symphony of destruction carried on the wind.

Lightning flashed in great arcs. Dirt, debris, flung into the air carrying bits of singed bone and sinew. To the west fog rolled in, succumbing the enemy, thick and heavy, blinding them. The battle had begun.

I met eyes with Kris and nodded. His expression grave, he focused ahead, over the hill, and a dark forced rippled past me. In seconds, the terrified screaming of the enemy rose as his power swept through them. Traveling with his magic, those with Tempest yanked the wind from behind. The force of it pushed me forward two steps before it rode up the embankment. Like a caged monster set free, it spun around on itself gathering speed. Faster and faster until *wham*! It struck the ground, swirling toward the base of the Pyre, further engulfing the place in a nightmare.

Through it all Akshae spoke, relaying the scene. The surprise only lasted moments. The top of the Pyre opened, glowing red hot. It spat blasts of hot lava. The molten rocks flew into the air, whistling as steam jetted behind them. The aerial team switched gears, focusing on blowing them backward. The tornados died away. Fog lifted, revealing craters lined with bodies. Hundreds, if not thousands, more emerged from the Pyre's base.

The first of many lava rockets made it through our defenses. One member of the aerial team received a direct hit. They exploded in mid-air, screams mingling with the steam. *Charlie*! my mind screamed, but violently I shoved the thought away. This wasn't the time. We might all die today, but if I lost my head, I might as well surrender now.

Through the comm, I said, "Medical team, get to the top of the hill. Take control. Hit them back."

Hundreds of Gayden and Spheres who fought with us raced up the hill. The fire bombs halted in mid-air, wavering under the competing forces. "Hold them steady. The rest of you, hit them from below."

The ground exploded underneath the Pyre. The noroins erupted from the ground. Solidified mud and rock come to life. They roared an ethereal unnatural call that turned my blood cold. Animated by the spirits within.

Ironic how the Experimenter's own experiments fought against him. They swung great arms catching the others. Bodies flew backward like rag dolls. Those on the hill sent other jets of small pebbles zooming like bullets. When they hit, blood ripped from the wounds.

Like before, their retaliation didn't take long. They hit us first with Naiad magic. Through Akshae, I saw several of our soldiers wilt. The fluids pulled from their bodies in the blink of a heartbeat. Our aquatics team went on full defense pushing the powers of those away.

"Pyro-kinetics team hit them back."

Running to the top, another hundred Gayden heated the air, sweeping it toward the enemy. Any surprises we had left vanished. Almost as soon as we executed an attack, Mathesar's forces countered them. The elementals gave us a slight advantage. The feirians, like walking demons, sprung from the depths of the Pyre, behind the enemy. The earth beneath their feet singed and sizzled with each step. One wrapped great arms around a blond woman. Her body engulfed in flames, only to be stifled by a hydrenian and burned again by the feirian.

"Stop," I whispered to Akshae. I didn't want to get that close again. Seeing, hearing, but not fighting. Her whispering slowed, and instead, she showed me the horde of wizards broken away from the base of the Pyre. They ran full force toward us.

"Here they come," I said through the comm. "Let's go."

Without running, I proceeded with slow deliberate steps toward my fate. Every step and action from losing that necklace on my first day of college had led me to this. Deep down, I'd always known it. It's time for Mathesar or me to end.

In answer, all the power in me sped to the surface, humming with need, a hunger to be unleashed. "Akshae, tell them it's time."

"Yes, mistress."

She left me as I rounded over the top of the hill. As Akshae described, magic battled for supremacy in the valley below. Mathesar was nowhere to be found nor his bitch, Strega. *How typical. The coward would be hiding.*

The rumbling of the ground, a minute ago deafening, now shook with such ferocity making us halt our progress for fear of falling. From the sides, the Styxs roared a battle cry as they thundered toward the foray of bloodied bodies. The sight of their impossible size and speed unnerved me. I spared one thankful thought that I wasn't in their path.

Bones crunched, snapping through the valley, as Styx crushed men and women underneath their massive feet. Spells bounced off them.

Those in their path fled from them. The golems—living, breathing, walking statues—followed right on the Styxs' heels. Three with the wingspan of four men swooped down, picking up someone, rising high in the air, before dropping them.

Not to be outdone, vampires sticking to the shadows snatched people. Not bothering to bite and drain their victims. Instead, powerful arms gripped them before pulling them into pieces. Werewolves howled, weaving in between the fighters taking down any stragglers. From behind the Pyre, the centaurs shot arrows into the crowd.

The Gayden on Mathesar's side without magic ran for the Pyre. They found their way blocked. He'd locked them out. Not expecting non-magical attacks, they had been solely unprepared. Not like our side. Those Gayden without magic held automatic weapons taking aim and firing round after round into the crowd, the sputtering noise of gunfire almost lost among the sounds of the battle. I stood my ground, not proceeding, letting the magic build. As easy as exhaling, it left me. A ball of white light, pure magical energy, flew into the crowd. I followed its progress. It hit a man, an older Gayden that belonged to Mathesar, and he disappeared. One moment he existed, and the next he'd vanished. Gone. Turned to nothing as if he had never been. Every part of his being dispersing back into separate molecules.

With small sure steps, I resumed the slow walk into the crowd. Again and again, I released this power. At the mouth of the valley, a werewolf paused to stare at me. His large brown eyes reflected the unnatural spectrum of light resonating from mine.

They hadn't been prepared for the likes of us. The Gayden slaves and those on Mathesar's side attempted to run. A wave of thirty of them almost to the tree line in the east. With a thought, the Sight zoomed inward. The enemy's racing forms became a swarm of ethereal bees. With a giant mental hand, I swatted at them. They dispersed into a million pieces, scattering like ash in the wind.

Those left fighting diminished by the second. Many fell to their knees. Bodies piled everywhere. In death, it became impossible to tell which side they'd fought on. More lost lives to lie at Mathesar's feet. Where was he? Hiding behind others as always. Operating in shadow. No longer.

A spell whizzed by my left ear, missing me by inches. A familiar scream came from behind me. Turning, I spotted Finch clutching a bleeding side. His face pale. My distraction cost me. Another spell hit me. It sent me flying. Air ripped from my lungs. Terror filled my veins as I sucked desperate for air. The warm wet feeling of unmistakable blood trickled from my nostrils. The monster who'd hit me smiled like an asp. He sent wind at impossible speeds further sucking the oxygen from the air. I couldn't breathe, couldn't think. In the blink of an eye, long enough for my brain to process what he planned, he raised his hands for the killing attack. Before either of us could react, Wade slammed into the earth between us. Bits of dirt and debris flew around him as he landed from the sky. Both the Gayden and I jumped in surprise. Air rushed into my lungs. I coughed and sputtered. Wade faced my would-be killer, whose expression turned dumbfounded before broadening that hateful smile. Wade wasted no time on pleasantries. Jets flew at the man in quick succession. *Bam. Bam. Bam.* They kept coming faster and faster.

The man buckled, then screamed a battle cry, bloodlust interwoven in the sound. Neither Wade nor I knew exactly what happened. Until the air finally stilled.

Slow trickles of blood spread outward. One from each arm at Wade's shoulders. More blood splotches appeared at his knees, ankles, and wrists. Three more appeared from his lower back. He fell sideways, unable to break his fall. He landed hard on his side. Bewilderment sang in his eyes, wondering what had happened to him. Finch screamed, "Wade!"

His anguish matched my own. The monster smiled in triumph at Finch. Wade wouldn't die for quite a while, but the pain would linger. Wade wouldn't be allowed a quick death.

I held no pity.

Surprise replaced the brute's expression. His mouth opened to scream. With a thought, the skin around his lips sealed. I wouldn't even give him the gift of screaming. Blood spilled from his nostrils and ears. His eyes liquefied as his internal organs burned from inside out. The air filled with the stench of burning blood, cooking organs, and the remnants of his intestines as the filth escaped in his pants. He sunk to the floor writhing in pain. A killing calm settled over me.

I stepped over the dead man. Finch fell behind me, holding on to his love, murmuring in Wade's ear. Perhaps he could get him to a Healer. I turned, heading toward them, but Finch shook his head, motioning me to go on. I couldn't do anything to save him. With a grim nod, I turned away.

The chaos of the battle fell away. Nothing else mattered but where I headed next. Innumerable nameless faces crossed my path. Their spells bounced off me like gnats. Annoyances blocking my path. I dissolved into movement. Dodge. Attack. Roll. Attack. Attack. I had no idea how of many I killed. At some point Sabrina, Charlie, and Damien reached my side. The barricaded Pyre stood before me with Mathesar beyond. My eyes burned bright white. A thunderous boom rumbled the ground, felt in every inch of Conjuragic, as my magic tore through his wards. Nothing stood now between me and my great enemy. He was mine.

29

ORA

The way inside the Pyre stretched open before me, devoid of life. Nothing stirred, nor did any light show. Fear forgotten, still being driven by calm rage, I stepped inside flanked by Charlie and Sabrina. Damien watched my back. Leigh sprung up two steps in the Pyre behind Sabrina. A few feet inside, the passageway veered to the left. We stepped through something that zinged all over my body. The sensation lasted a second. I managed a sharp intake of breath at the uncomfortable feeling before it disappeared, carrying the symphony of the dying outside the mountain with it.

"What the hell was that?" I asked.

Leigh shivered beside me as if shaking off whatever that had been. "Security ward, no doubt. He'll know we're coming."

Damien grabbed my elbow. "Before we go any farther, Jeremiah and I overheard Mathesar's Geminates finally succeeded. He has a core that allows him to control all cores of magic."

The prophecy floated from my memory. It didn't surprise me, not in the least. "Good. That means he'll be overconfident. He thinks he's already won. Let's move."

Our breathing mixed with the crunching of our footsteps on the gravel bottom of the mountain floor. The sound ricocheted around the walls more like shotgun blasts. Torches lined the walls as we traveled deeper and deeper inside. The ground sloped leading down, down, down. The uneven ground kept us off kilter especially as the pathway varied in width. Sometimes the walls skimmed along my red cloak. At other places, the space spanned large enough to fit several Styxs. The temperature inside the Pyre rose with every step. Sweat trickled down my back, making my skin itch. At times, an icy gust of air zipped through the caverns. The sudden drop in temperature had everyone's teeth chattering.

Passages sprung up around darkened corners, but I led us straight, following the path of lit torches. "How do you know where you are going?" Charlie asked, her voice a whisper, but felt like a scream in the silence.

"He's waiting for us." The lack of people hadn't been a mistake, nor the torches. This was an invitation.

"It could be a trap," Sabrina voiced what I'd been thinking.

"I'm sure it is."

Their eyes followed me as I kept going while they paused. They didn't understand why I would willingly walk into a trap, but I couldn't turn back now. He might think he'd tricked me. Screams pierced the darkness far below us. We halted, listening, fearing who those screams belonged to.

"It's coming from down there." Leigh pointed a finger to a tiny gap in the wall.

Through the darkness Sabrina paled, swaying on her feet. "Those sound like children."

"I'll go." Leigh squeezed her friend's shoulder and headed for the gap.

"Wait, you can't see anything. Take one of the torches." Sabrina grabbed Leigh's arm.

Leigh waved her away. "I can't. I'm sure the torches have a charm upon them. They will know exactly where we are."

"I'll go with you. I have some Ember." Damien stepped toward Leigh, meeting my eyes, the unspoken question hanging between us. Leigh was right. The torches had a wave of power around them, a spell I'd never seen. This could be another trap, but if Mathesar was slaughtering his slaves, destroying any evidence of their existence, we couldn't pass by and do nothing. This could be a twist in Mathesar's plan, to separate us, but one look at Sabrina convinced me. I knew images of that Geminate child plagued her. "Go and be careful." Damien squeezed my hand, conveying how much he didn't want to leave me. I squeezed back, hoping he'd notice the tendril of magic caressing his. He shivered, let go of my hand, and ignited a ball of flame hovering above an open palm.

Damien and Leigh disappeared, and for a long while we listened to their footsteps retreating as the ball of light in Damien's hand faded away. Only three of us remained, and I had no way of knowing how many would be waiting for us at the end. "Let's go."

The urge to run, to get to Mathesar, to fight overwhelmed me, but that was his plan, to fuel my bloodlust, to make me run into a fight, and then this to unnerve me, get me off balance. I refused to play along with his game and kept up a steady, even pace, even when a light in the distance grew brighter and brighter. The mouth of a huge cavern grew larger with each step. I didn't pause when I stepped through the opening and into the heart of the Pyre.

Mathesar smiled like an adder sitting upon his makeshift throne in the center of the stadium-sized out cove. Stalagmites and stalagmites touched, writhing together to form his throne. The blond hair shined like a golden crown on his head. He held a staff in his right hand. A thousand tiny branches wound together, opening at the top, like an outstretched hand holding a white shimmering stone alight with firelight. This had to be the jewel the prophecy spoke of. I hoped Sabrina and Charlie saw it too.

Lava flowed down the cavern walls, making torches unnecessary. In the very back, an archway led to a separate area. Lava flowed around the archway to cascade on either side. The heat, instead of being overwhelming, remained the tiniest bit uncomfortable, but manageable. I imagine some Ember spell held the heat at bay. "I knew you'd come," Mathesar's voice came out loud, clearly pronouncing every word, like a politician. He should sound high pitched and evil.

I raised my chin higher. "Mathesar Enoch, I have come here in the name of the High Council. Evidence of your treason has been brought before them. Give yourself up without a fight and no one else will get hurt."

He laughed, no humor reaching his eyes, the true monster showing underneath. "Come now, my child. You and I both know that we are above such petty laws."

"I'm *not* your child." I shouldn't have spoken, but he had said the word with such a patronizing tone.

He leaned forward, and my magic reared back in a defensive position. "Oh, but you are. The only reason you exist is because I had your grandmother bred like a bitch. Then your mother went and had you."

"You're wrong." I hated the weakness in my voice and how easily he manipulated me into playing his game. A game to get inside my head. I should end him now. Then I could take his precious jewel of light and this would all be over.

"Am I? I knew your mother as soon as I saw her in that clearing with that bloody blade protruding from her back." I flinched, and an expression of delicious delight rippled over his face. "Was as in past tense. Since she didn't survive her injuries in the Willow."

"Shut up!" Charlie shouted.

His malicious gaze fell on Charlie. "You must be Charlie. I've heard so much about you. You see, your brother, John," he paused beaming at her reaction of hearing her brother's name, "has fallen in love with one of my most loyal servants. Isn't that right, Strega?" Mathesar inclined his head. Despite the warning bells in my head, I turned where he'd gestured.

Charlie whimpered, and I watched, helpless, as John strolled out of the darkness emerging from the archway in the back, a tailless black cat nestled in his arms, purring. Mud and congealed blood matted John's brown hair. His navy-blue robes had been ripped to shreds, and dirt lined his hands and nails, but they did the worst damage to his face. His right eye was swollen shut, bottom lip split down the center, and bruises spread across the left side of his face. The cat reached out and scratched his face, leaving a new trickle of blood running over his cheek. He halted mere feet from Mathesar and placed the cat on the floor. With the sounds of a long screeching meow and the crunching and snapping of bones, Strega stood before them in black leather, dark hair falling in wavy curls down her face. "Did you lose something, Ora?"

Strega reached behind her and stroked John's face. He looked at no one but Strega, and he crooned when she touched him. "I have to thank you for telling me exactly how to break him." The rattlesnake smile she gave me leeched pure poison.

Charlie angled toward me, and without looking, I knew she had accusing eyes on me. Strega's evil smile grew even wider as her focus shifted to Charlie. "Oh yes, Charlie, the clueless best friend and sister." I could have sworn John stiffened a fraction of a second, but I couldn't be sure. "Your conniving friend told me all the juicy details of their relationship while she wasted away in the Nook awaiting her trial. Details that I used to gain his trust. Such a naïve, stupid girl. Now he is mine." She snapped her fingers and pointed down. John dropped to the ground as if yanked by an invisible whip. With a twist of her fingers, John rolled over on his back, and she placed the wicked sharp tip of her stiletto on his throat.

Bile threatened. What had happened to him? "Please." Charlie reached a hand out, the plea breaking my heart.

Mathesar's laughter cut in. Charlie never looked away from her brother, but that had been part of their plan, except it'd been for me. I shoved the horror down deep, as hard as I could, locking it into some hidden corner of my mind. I used the image of the knife flashing through the air toward my mother's back to turn the key. Calm settled back over me as I let my eyes roam, searching for any hidden traps, anything to be used as a weapon.

"Strega, keep your pet alive for now. He has been so helpful." Mathesar swept to his feet and took the stone steps down from his throne. My magic sensed his mingled with the stone inside the staff. My magic recoiled from the wrongness of it, sensing the pain and suffering that came from its unnatural making. This was the true abomination. Something that should never have existed. The power inside fought itself, begging to be set free, pleading for sanctuary.

Mathesar strolled toward me, not a hint of fear, and he looked at me with a crazed desire bordering on insanity, as if I were a new toy to be claimed. It took all of my self-control not to step back. He stopped a foot from me and leaned forward, sniffing. Everything about him revolted me. To some, he may have looked handsome, but the insanity inside him had been set free.

"John told me all about you. I've been waiting for this moment for so long." He reached out a hand toward me, coming mere inches from my cheek, and moved as if to stroke it, but not daring to get too close. "What an incredible creature you are. A Geminate mated with a human. What sort of powers do you possess? I've seen your handiwork, and I wouldn't have believed it." *Mated with a human? He must not know about my dad.*

"You aren't afraid of me? You know what I can do." My voice never wavered and came out calmer than I would've guessed.

He smiled, craziness peeking out behind his expression. "I might've been except now that the stone of light has finally been created, no one can stop me." He wore the same longing expression he'd given me while looking at the stone on top of the staff. Something inside my head clicked. Did he say stone of light, not jewel of light?

While he was distracted, I signaled to Sabrina with a tiny gesture of my hand. She'd been quiet this whole time, but I knew she'd caught everything. Charlie shook beside me, tears rolling down her cheeks, staring at her brother.

By the hands of two Geminates, a jewel of light—fierce and fiery—will be formed. When unification shatters, when the sanctuary sinks, when the parents fall, the master of the four cores will rise, and the leader of Gayden shall battle good against evil. Only the one with true power shall prevail.

Sabrina opened her mouth to distract him while I could think. "Mathesar Enoch, by the order of the High Council and the Magical Detection Agency, I, Lieutenant Sabrina Sun, a Protector of the House of Naiad, arrest you for crimes of high treason. In addition, you have been charged with violation of the peace treaty with the Elders of the Gayden. You shall be escorted to the Nook where you will wait until your trial begins."

His lunacy faded, replaced by a mask of rage. "I am Mathesar Enoch, ruler of the stone of light, and appointed by the people of Conjuragic as supreme leader. The High Council has been assassinated by the Nips. The Magical Detection Agency has been placed under martial law. You, Sabrina Sun, are a traitor to Conjuragic, and will be punished for your crimes. You are stripped of all manner of authority; all of your property and assets have been frozen. You have no authority here."

"The High Council still lives. They have made a pact with the Gayden. Your play for dictatorship is finished, Enoch!"

"You have no power here!" Mathesar screamed, and with the wave of the staff, he blasted Sabrina off her feet, flying back, and slamming into the far wall. Blood ran down the side of her face mingling with murky gray debris from the shattered rocks.

I stepped in front of him, blocking Sabrina from his line of sight, and smiled, matching his venom. "But I do, and you have made a grave mistake, Mathesar."

We began a slow circle, walking around each other. My magic bubbled underneath the surface, churning, building, freed by fear or mercy.

"You shall call me Master."

"Never."

"Strega."

"No!" Charlie screamed, and I saw the flash of her brown hair before the sizzle of her magic flew forward.

A cacophony of noise erupted from where Charlie, John, and Strega stood, but I couldn't look away from Mathesar. Couldn't give him any kind of upper hand.

"You're out of allies. It's just you and me."

"As it was meant to be."

Mathesar tossed his staff from one hand to the other, taunting me. "Don't you know that it's already been prophesied I am the winner."

"I did hear from Aryiana that you'd think that." For the first time his eyes wavered, unsure of himself. "Oh you didn't know that I knew Aryiana? She helped train me. Helped my mother escape."

"It's of no matter. I summoned her to me long ago. To see how I could finish my plans."

It was my turn for my face to falter. Our circling continued as the power inside me flowed through my veins, desperate to show itself, to gleam bright as the sun, showing through my eyes.

"What was the point in any of this?" I hadn't meant to ask, but I had to know. He could have been power hungry, but he'd been breeding Geminates before Aryiana had come to him with the prophecy.

"The point? You stupid girl, Nips are the point. The High Council went against everything we have fought against for centuries. Ever since we discovered Nips and the harm they could bring to us. You proved that by bringing them here. Look at the devastation done by them. I couldn't let it happen. Nips can't be trusted."

"If they can't be trusted, why do you surround yourself with them?"

He swung the staff in a great arc, striking at nothing, but a wave of his magic slithered down the staff from his palm to the moonstone. The jewel glowed bright white contrasting with the red-hot light of the lava. "Keep your enemies closer, my child. Besides, they have been here since they were children. I broke their will long ago."

The scuffling behind me changed, the difference almost imperceptible. Mathesar noticed it too. His gaze shifted from me. In the split second, I saw my chance. The magic inside me answered my unspoken call. The ground rose upward, grabbing at his ankles, ensnaring him. My power flowed like a living thing—seeking to destroy, but he didn't deserve an easy death.

The trap couldn't hold him long. That moonstone pulsated, and the rock shattered. The waves of energy it gave off shrieked like fingernails running down a chalkboard.

"Stupid girl." He lifted the staff and a wave of light shot toward me, similar yet so different from my own. Inches from me, that foreign power halted. The beam of light wavered. Inside me, the magic took control. It reached out from me blocking its opposite. The ying to my yang.

"No!" Mathesar screamed, fury and disbelief in the sound. Nothing should've stood against his legendary stone of prophecy, but he knew nothing.

Somehow, I found my voice. "I told you were wrong, Mathesar."

He rose the staff higher, his own magic powering the stone, taking more and more from him. His screams changed from frustration to pain. My magic stayed strong, pushing back against his unnatural one. The staff's light cracked and vibrated. The ground shook beneath my feet. The battle between those two forces sent waves of energy all around. Cracks rippled in the ground, along the walls, and ceiling.

"It isn't possible!" Mathesar screamed. His blond hair lost what little color it had, turning stark white. The color faded from his face taking on the hue of bluish veins underneath. His eyes sank into his face and cheeks thinned transforming him into a living skeleton.

In the attempt to stand against me, against my power, the Geminate stone, tied to his magic, drained and depleted his life force. Despite the tremendous power of the Geminate moonstone, it had nothing to compare to the vast chasm of magic inside me.

"You're wrong. You've always been wrong. The prophecy was never about the abomination in your staff."

His hand shook as if he tried to let go, but the staff had taken over, extended beyond his control. The foreign magic continued to fight me, but the fierceness in his eyes vanished. Instead, he watched me with fear etched in his face. "How?"

The ground rumbled, and even I stumbled with the force of it. The volcano itself awakened with the raw power coursing inside it. The staff's magic gained on me, then zoomed forward. I side-stepped in time for it to graze my side. Hot blood squirted from the wound, pouring down my leg. As it hit the ground, it evaporated into a cloud of charred smoke.

Another blow came right after. I rolled, but it found its mark. The bone of my right arm snapped. The pain rippled through me. A new wave of cold sweat prickled on my forehead. The walls closed in as nausea rumbled deep in my stomach.

From behind me, Charlie screamed, "Ora, help!"

I couldn't do anything for her. I ran for cover, finding a huge stalagmite to hide behind. Blasts of pure power zoomed past me, accompanied by the crazed screams of Mathesar. Directing my power inward, the bone in my arm snapped together. Doubling over, I sucked in a breath of air to calm the rising tide of nausea. I prayed the helpless pains of my body would pass before he reached me.

Aryiana's voice spoke in my head when the waves stopped. *You aren't wrong. Tell him.*

Her words wrapped around me like a warm hug, giving me the courage to go on. "Give up." I scaled the top of the stalagmite, looking down at Mathesar, now barely more than skin, bones, and hate. A slave to the power he'd created. A fitting end. "My mother never married a human."

Mathesar raised the staff, but I sent a blast of magic. It deflected his shot. He sent spell after spell. Each blasted away, ricocheting in every direction. "You know my mother was Perdita. But my father was Philo Stone."

Finally, something clicked in his eyes, a horror of realization.

"That's right, Mathesar. By the hands of two Geminates, a jewel of light—fierce and fiery—will be formed. You called it the stone of light. My name is Ora. Ora means light. I *am* the stone of light. I shattered unification when the Unity Statue fell. I fought in the Haven, the sanctuary, when it sank. When my mother died, both of my parents fell. I'm the master of the four cores, and I have risen against you with my army of Gayden at my side, and only the one with true power shall prevail."

His lips mouthed, "No."

In answer, my power surged forward. Blasted open wide, the chasm exploding from deep, deep inside me, flowing forward with cold purpose.

The power flowed, and flowed, and flowed. On and on, my power raged and pushed against the enemy power of the Gayden stone.

My body shook. I closed my eyes to the scene before me, opening my arms wide, giving everything, as my head lulled back.

The last dregs of power rose. I'd give this. I'd give all of me to save those I love. Pain, pain, pain spread through me.

In an instant, the connection snapped. The tiniest fragment of my power ricocheted back into me. I stumbled backward, falling hard on my butt.

Mathesar's staff shattered into a million pieces, sending his limp body sailing backward, landing in a heap, unmoving, back on his makeshift throne. The moonstone rolled away, stopping at the base of his throne. I jumped down from the stalagmite and ran to Mathesar. He breathed slow, but even. I forced my power to relax. Forced it not to send the killing blow. Forced it to be satisfied he'd been knocked unconscious and hadn't died.

With another spell, taking the last of my energy, his own throne wrapped around him, turning his throne into a cage. My magic, a powerful thing, had been pushed to the breaking point.

"Charlie, go!" John's voice cut through the cavern.

I spun to the sound and screamed, "Charlie! No!"

30

CHARLIE

"You shall call me Master."

"Never," Ora said. Charlie focused on her brother and that bitch standing above him. Strega sneered at her, ignoring Ora and her master, enjoying her power over John.

Mathesar's voice cut through Charlie like a blade. "Strega."

The devil woman's viper smile widened at the subtle command. Her body pivoted, and Charlie knew. Strega planned to step down, pressing the heel of her stiletto into his throat.

"No!" Charlie screamed and released her power. The supernatural wind blasted into Strega's leg, blowing her backward. Far, far away from John. She fell to her knees beside him, yanking him to a seated position. His swollen eye stared forward, seeing nothing, once again in a stupor. "John. Get up. Please. Get up. We have to go."

From the corner of her eye, she caught movement and pushed herself and John forward. An icicle missed her by inches. It she hadn't moved, it'd have impaled her. With all her strength, she yanked John. He got to his feet, swaying. Charlie put herself between John and Strega.

Gray dust sprinkled the wench's black hair from the destroyed mountain rocks, and a trickle of blood grazed her cheeks. "You're one lucky bitch, aren't you? But don't worry, it won't last."

Charlie screamed a slurry of obscenities, reaching toward the pistol strapped to her side.

Strega clicked her tongue. "Now. Now. What would Grandma Evelyn think?"

Charlie's back stiffened. How did she know her grandma's name? John had to have told her. *What all had he told this woman?*

"I'm going to enjoy killing her and your granddad. Perhaps I'll make John do it. You'd do that for me, wouldn't you, my pet?" Strega crooned, not even bothering to look at John.

"Yes, my love," John said, voice cracking as if he'd screamed more than spoken in the last few days.

"Then start now. Kill her."

Faster than she'd have believed, John grabbed her throat. She managed to get the pistol out of the holster, but she wasn't fast enough. He pinned her arms to her sides, close to his body. The metal clanged as the gun hit the ground.

Charlie struggled, but she couldn't break free. Something cold and hard pressed against her throat. She froze. John pressed the knife he held down, and a bee sting of pain sprang up at the tip of the blade. The blood that bubbled upward stung more from the betrayal than the actual wound. She felt the muscle in his arm contract, preparing to push harder, to slice across her throat. *No! Not like this!* She couldn't die like this!

"Wait, my pet." At her slightest command, his hand halted. "While ending your pathetic sister with the same blade that killed the Geminate bitch would be so poetic, I think death by the knife is too quick. I want it to be personal. I want her to see that you're mine when she dies. Strangle her."

In a swift movement, John whirled Charlie around, the knife crashing to the ground, and his hands wrapped around her throat. He squeezed.

Pain and panic mingled.

Her hands clawed at his arms, hands, smacking. She fought as he pressed harder. She sank to her knees. John followed her, shoving her to the floor, not lessening his grip a fraction. Her head felt as if it would explode as her lungs screamed for air. She looked into his eyes. Knowing in some part of her that this was exactly what Strega wanted. John's empty eyes stared back at her.

A stranger.

She quit fighting, reaching up to touch his face. She still loved him. No matter what, he was her brother. Her vision faded at the edges. She'd die soon.

Her hand drifted away, and recognition flashed in John's eyes. His hands decreased their grip, and in the moment of hesitation, her magic woke with a vengeance. A whirlwind sprang to life, surrounding her. Bits of dirt and small rocks flew into the air. John inhaled the debris, sucking in the particles into his lungs. He released her, falling back, coughing, rubbing at his eyes.

"No!" Strega screamed, running toward them.

Charlie rolled over, dragging in deep mouthfuls of air. Her eyes watered, and her throat screamed in protest. A tornado swirled around her forming a shield of her power. Strega sent spell after spell at it, but nothing got through.

Charlie pushed herself to her knees and then to her feet, leaning forward, steadying herself with hands on her knees. Strega wouldn't stop. John had backed away. Numb and as impassive as a statue. Whatever had been in his eyes had vanished.

Charlie risked a glance toward Ora. Mathesar's staff pointed toward her, a white light of energy shot out from the top. Ora's eyes blazed from rainbow to pure white.

"No!" Mathesar screamed.

"I told you were wrong, Mathesar," Ora said, her voice reverberating as if a thousand voices spoke with one mouth. Chill bumps ran along Charlie's arms at the sound as spiders danced along her spine.

The tornado around Charlie wavered. She couldn't maintain this expenditure of energy forever. The magic faltered already. She turned her attention back to Strega. Perhaps she could part the tornado enough to slip in and get John. Then she could get them both out. Strega swore, throwing one final spell. She turned, stomping toward John. She reached his side. She bent and straightened. The glint of steel against his throat shimmered with Mathesar's white light.

The world slowed to a stop. As if all the other noises faded away, Charlie heard the click of her semi-automatic Beretta sliding into place as Strega placed the gun at his temple.

The tornado vanished, and she screamed, "Ora, help!" She took two steps toward John. Strega lifted the gun, pointing it straight at Charlie. Her finger shifted, pulling the trigger. The pistol jumped. Charlie squeezed her eyes, bracing for the pain. Her brain couldn't process what happened. She'd stopped mid-stride, looking down at a small hole punctured through her leathers above her belly button. A searing tendril of pain swirled around it as sticky warmth pooled around it.

Strega had shot her.

Strega's finger remained on the trigger. She adjusted the aim higher, for her head. Charlie couldn't move. Frozen in place, not by any sort of magic, but by shock and fear.

A stalactite fell from the ceiling at the same time a gush of water slammed into Strega's arm. She lost her grip on the gun. It clattered to the ground. Charlie followed her gaze.

Sabrina and Leigh glowered at Strega. Together they stood as cold and impersonal as ice, the faces of Conjuragic's Protectors. They wore the same expressions when they'd arrested Ora.

The three women paused, staring at each other for a moment. Then all hell broke loose. Spells flew on both sides. Charlie and John were forgotten.

As the women fought, nothing came close to touching him. Charlie realized her magic encircled him. Even unconsciously she'd protected him. As the fighting moved away, farther to the back, she inched toward him. Once again, she pulled him to his feet. The gunshot wound protesting. Sweat prickled on her brow and nausea rumbled in her stomach. The thought of the pain from vomiting halted the feeling. "John!" she shouted. He still focused on nothing.

"John!"

He blinked a few times, looking around as if noticing where he was. His eyes found her, confused and glazed. "Where is my mistress?"

"John, who am I?"

He tilted his head, then pivoted, as if he would start looking for Strega. Charlie grabbed his chin, forcing him to look into her eyes.

"John, I'm Charlie. Your sister. Do you remember me?"

He looked in her eyes, unfocused.

His face blurred as tears swam in her eyes. "John, please. Please. It's me. It's Charlie. Remember who you are." She took his hand, making him touch her face.

His vision cleared, and recognition filled his eyes. "Charlie?"

A relieved sob left her lips. "Yes. It's me."

His eyes roamed over her as if he couldn't believe she was real. He paused when he got to her stomach. He reached out, touching, pulling his hand away as if he'd been bitten. He stared open-mouthed at the sticky blood on his hands. "You're hurt. Who did this?"

Charlie feared to say the woman's name. "It doesn't matter. We have to get you out of here. Let's go, okay?"

He nodded, putting an arm around her.

"I don't think so!" came an icy voice from behind. A rope of water wrapped around Charlie's waist. It squeezed. The pain in her stomach tripled. She screamed as the rope yanked her backward. The cave melded into a sea of gray rocks and red lava.

31

JOHN

John stumbled and saw two strange women. A blond one stared at Charlie. Her brows stitched in concentration as a second body of water fought the first that held Charlie. The other woman touched the ground as if listening to it, trying to find his mistress, who was hidden somewhere in the back. He could still feel her.

The blond's power won out. The water rope around Charlie splashed to the ground, but not before Charlie's body crashed into the archway in the back and fell to the center.

The archway cracked. Lava inched its way through. At first nothing more than a trickle, but the crack widened. Charlie wriggled on the ground beneath, the lava heading right for her. He bolted toward her, but his mistress crooned from his right. "My pet."

Black spiderwebs wriggled in his mind, trying to blind him again, but he fought this time. Unleashing the memories of when he'd fought before. Unleashing how the webs had formed. One by one, the webs weaved through his mind.

At first, he'd been at a nice waterfall where his mistress had taken him away from the prison. The memory so like one he had with Ora that it hurt. His mistress's words, *She left you behind. She told me all about how pathetic she thought you were. Untalented. A stupid redneck hick. How she was glad the two of you had broken up.* He'd let her kiss him, and he'd kissed her back.

Another web emerged of pushing her away during that kiss and the beating she had given him after. That beating and the next and the next. Each time he wouldn't say he hated Ora. Each time he refused to say he wanted her dead. Each time he refused his mistress anything.

The memories snapped away, revealing his mistress healing his broken ribs, crushed fingers when he cursed Ora's name the first time. The pain she took away when he did what she wanted. It didn't matter anymore that she'd been the one who'd hurt him. She loved him. Who else would make him feel better? Who else would take away the pain? Ora had never loved him. He knew that. Didn't he?

More spiderwebs weaved through his mind as he did anything and everything his mistress asked. Images of himself removing her clothes before his. How his mistress had pleased him the more he'd obeyed her. His body shuddered at the memory. At how his body betrayed him when she straddled him. Anything she wanted. He was hers.

Each step toward Charlie snapped more and more of those spiderwebs. His head cleared. Images of Charlie as he grabbed her, pressed a knife to her throat. Charlie's face, horrified as his hands slipped around her neck. Images of a darkened forest. Images of Perdita and a knife in his hand. Images of blood. Ora's face staring at him with shock and betrayal. The pain in his head ruptured as if tearing him apart. The web vanished into oblivion as he remembered Ora's lips on his. Her smile at the lake, and Charlie. The way she'd touched his cheek. That was love. That was loyalty.

His mistress's smile faltered as she said once again, "My pet?"

Rage spread over his face. He sprinted toward his tormenter. Shock replaced the confused expression on her face. She didn't even block him as he swung. His fist connected with her cheek. Her head whipped around. Before she could react, he grabbed her by the shoulders and threw her over his shoulder. With all the strength he had, he ran toward Charlie, his sister. She wouldn't die because of him.

John passed the dark-haired woman, letting the bitch slip off his shoulders, and fall to the ground. The dark-haired woman smiled and stomped her foot. The ground shook, flinging his tormentor up, up, up into the air, before another boulder of rocks pummeled her stomach. She flew sideways, screaming. The screams ended as her back slammed into the wall. The stone pinned her in place before liquefying. The mountain sucked the devil woman inside a wall of lava. The faint linger scent of burnt meat was all that remained.

The archway above Charlie groaned. A single drip slipped through as John reached it. He flung his arms upward, holding the archway in place. The single drip landed on his neck, burning through his soft flesh. He screamed, "Charlie, go!"

32

CHARLIE

The archway snapped. Charlie rolled over, staring upward. John shifted his legs. One on either side of her.

The stranger's eyes had vanished. Her brother watched her. His face scrunched up with the effort of holding the doorway. There is no physical way he should've been able to hold it. The archway cracked a little more, and Ora screamed through the hall, "Charlie! No!"

John screamed as the archway sank deeper. Droplets of lava fell off him, singing his skin. The smell of burnt flesh surrounded her.

The very cave rumbled. Ora, Sabrina, and Leigh stood at Charlie's head at the mouth of the archway.

Ora bent down, pulling Charlie to safety. Charlie screamed, reaching for her brother. "No! John! Come with us!"

"He can't. The spell holding this place cracked," Leigh said, "if he lets go, this entire place is going to be flooded with lava in seconds."

"Hold it up. Stabilize it. You're a Sphere. It's rock."

Leigh shook her head. "The lava is spelled with Ember. I can't manipulate it."

Charlie screamed, tears streaming down her face, finding Sabrina. "Then cool the lava with Naiad."

Sabrina wouldn't meet her eyes. "There's too much lava. I'd have to solidify the entire volcano."

Ora pulled on Charlie's arm. "We have to go."

Charlie shook her head. "No! No! No! We can't leave him! You have all the cores. You can save him."

Ora's eyes constricted in pain, before shaking her head. Tears spilling down her face. "I used too much fighting Mathesar. I can't. I don't have any magic left."

John spoke, face gritted, "Go. I'll hold this as long as I can."

Ora faced John. Pain etched on both of their faces. Their expressions a mimicry of the others. An expression of pain, loss, regret, and a life together that was forever gone.

John said, "I'm sorry. For Gran." The weight of his words almost took his strength. "Grandma Perdita. I'm sorry."

Ora tilted her chin, an almost imperceptible movement, fighting back the sorrow.

"I love you, Ora Stone"

"I love you, John," Ora mouthed, unable to make a sound.

John turned his attention to Charlie. "I love you, baby sister. Tell Grandma and Granddad I love them, and I'll miss them."

Charlie shook her head. "No. Come with us. You tell them."

"Go!" John shouted as the archway groaned further, more lava dripping on him, burning him alive.

Ora yanked on Charlie, using the last ounce of her remaining strength and willpower to pull her friend away, and to pull herself from John. Charlie screamed, reaching back. "No! I won't leave you! No!"

Sabrina and Ora hooked their arms around Charlie, yanking her back.

As they passed the still unconscious Mathesar at a run, Ora shot Leigh a look. She nodded and sent her power to the throne.

Stalactites crashed from the ceiling. The volcano moaned its displeasure but held. Ora and Sabrina yanked the still screaming Charlie from the cave. Leigh let the gurney race out ahead, taking their prisoner with it, and stepped out of the cave. If Ora had looked back, even once, she couldn't have been able to stop herself from going back after John.

They ran out of the cavern and Leigh sealed the room behind them. Ora asked, voice cracking, "Where's Damien?"

Leigh said, "Outside with the Geminate children we rescued."

Sabrina and Leigh ran as the rumbling continued, raining debris down upon them. Ora and Charlie followed, hearts breaking as the horrifying crash of the archway and the screams of flooding lava followed them out of the Pyre.

33

ORA

"To the citizens of Conjuragic," Mira Drecoll, head high, spoke into one of a million strange devices in this magical land. "There are many things which I have to convey. The first is to quench the rumor of the Council's demise. Only my husband, Sphere's High Councilman, Dharr Drecoll perished." She paused as if she truly did have a connection to the man. "His death was not due to the army of Nips we've been warring against." I could almost hear the unified gasps from across Conjuragic. "The Nip army invaded our lands for a number of reasons. The main one was to bring to light a traitor in our midst. The Naiad advisor, Mathesar Enochs, has been plotting against this Council for a very long time. I will let Naiad Councilman Talon Souse explain further."

The magical camera, for lack of a better word, pivoted to Talon. Expression grave, he spoke, "Good day citizens of Conjuragic. I'm afraid I must tell you that this Council entered into a secret peace treaty with the Nips long ago. We bridged our differences and learned they call themselves Gayden. Due to the actions of Mr. Enochs, that treaty was violated, and the Gayden had every right to retaliate. It will be hard for many of us to accept, but we wanted peace between our races. Mr. Enoch's has been stealing Gayden children from the human realm. He has also kidnapped witches and wizards and created an army of Geminates." He paused letting his words sink in. "This Council was ignorant to his actions. Perhaps we would've remained ignorant if it hadn't been for the arrest and trial of Ora Stone. To remind you all, she was tried and convicted of being a Gayden and sentenced to death. She escaped and destroyed our Unity Statue and sealed the Veil. We were wrong. Ora Stone is not a Gayden. She is, in fact, the daughter of two Geminates who escaped from Mr. Enoch. We are happy to announce that Mr. Enoch has been captured, and with the supporting evidence, he faced a swift trial. He has been found guilty. His punishment shall be public execution."

My heart pounded in my chest listening to the Council's speech and airing everything about me and the fate of Mathesar to all of Conjuragic. Damien reached down and squeezed my hand, interlocking his power with mine.

"Ora found the real Gayden, and they agreed to aid her to bring the traitor to our attention. We agreed to meet with them to discuss new terms. They agreed to help us locate Mr. Enoch and bring him to justice since he had lured many allies to his cause. In return, we agreed to make a new treaty and this time it would be public. No longer can we fear each other. We are two sides of the same coin. Therefore, from this day forward, Gayden shall have a voice on this Council. Two members shall join us and live here as ambassadors. Gayden shall also be allowed to travel and live here if they wish, and in no way shall hate crimes or prejudice be tolerated. Also," he took a deep breath, "Geminates are no longer illegal. As Mr. Enoch demonstrated, unethically, they can control their power and survive. We still encourage the purity of our houses, but unions will no longer be illegal, and Geminates shall be offered full protection under magical law."

A slow smile spread over my face. This finally made it real. We'd done it. A tightness grew in my chest as thoughts of Mom came to me. Mathesar had been captured, and the Geminates were free. It's what she always wanted, but as if she spoke into my mind, I corrected myself. No, she wanted me to be free, and we'd done it, but also freed the others. It wouldn't be perfect and would take a while for everyone to adjust, but the foundation for true change was in place.

I let the details of the rest of the speeches slip away until the Elders were introduced to the magical world and they pronounced Finch as the male Gayden representative on the Council and let everyone know a search for his female counterpart remained underway.

Leaving the Guidance Hall, a new peace treaty officially signed, I stopped at the top of the marble stairs looking out over the horizon of the once beautiful city. Its white buildings still gleamed in the sunlight, but the unearthly pulsating white light was nowhere to be found. Beyond the line of the city, I imagined the homelands of the magicians. I couldn't guess how long the peace would last. After hundreds of years of prejudice and mistrust piled against the treaty, it would be shaky for a long while, but I had hope. Sabrina stood next to the enormous cracked statue a few levels above me. Joining her, I beheld the figures of four women, holding hands, heads thrown back, staring into the great beyond. The foundation held one long divide with smudges of burn marks on each of their beautiful faces.

"Those are the four great mothers." Sabrina broke the silence, entwining her arm with mine, looking stunning in blue robes, her customary leathers absent.

"Who were they?" Over this last year, I'd heard much about the Unity Statue, but never the full details.

"This realm was created hundreds of years ago. Wizards wanted to be separate from the humans and so for the first time in our history worked together to rip our homelands out of the human realm, creating a ripple that became the Veil. We left to live here together, and at first, we lived together in harmony, but soon the fighting began, escalating over the centuries, and so the four houses engaged in the House Wars. The fighting went on for decades, and it felt as if peace would never return. This was the battleground where the armies fought for dominance. Only wizards ruled in those times, and the women were left as second class, but one night the wives of the four generals met here in secret. They copied our ancestors, when the Houses worked together to remove ourselves from the humans, and created the Guidance Hall, merging their magic, fortifying this building with peace and unity, and to seal the deal, they let their magic flow out of themselves, merge into one, and it began flowing through the Guidance Hall. After that, the House Wars ended, and the High Council was formed. Later, as new buildings were made, the light from the great mothers flowed into the new buildings ensuring our peace and their light flowed until..."

"Until I destroyed it?" The guilt weighed heavy on my heart. These women sacrificed their lives to bring peace and I'd destroyed it in a fit of rage.

"Yes, it could only be destroyed using all cores of magic. Only someone like you could have destroyed it." Her arm squeezed mine, and I knew she didn't blame me. After a moment she asked, "Tell me about your fight with Mathesar."

I sighed, hoping I wouldn't have to relive it. "Mathesar wanted the 'jewel of light' to destroy the Unity Statue, then to murder the High Council, to make himself dictator, using his Gayden as further ammunition. Little did he know that prophecy actually meant my last name. Stone."

Sabrina laughed without mirth, nodding as comprehension dawned. "And Ora means light."

"Why didn't you take the Council's offer to continue being a Protector?"

"Protectors generally take a leave of absence when they're pregnant." Her cheeks flushed red.

"Pregnant! Oh my! Congratulations!"

She shook her head, waving me away. "Yes well. It's still very early, and you know Naiad and Tempest. Lots of Geminates don't make it."

I couldn't help but smile. "But at least he or she has a chance."

She rubbed her belly. "At least it has a chance."

"Yo, Stone!" Finch appeared out of the doorway. As soon as he stepped out in the sunlight, he reached up and lit his customary cigarette.

"High Councilman."

With a roll of his eyes and an exhalation of smoke, he said, "Yeah, yeah."

I covered my face to hide the smirk. "Are you going to get you some shiny golden robes and a headdress?"

"Shut up, Stone."

Sabrina cocked her head to the side. "He will look so good bald."

"Absolutely not. Bald my ass!"

Sabrina held my arm as laughter erupted from our lips.

"What did we miss?" Arameus asked, walking hand in hand with a healed Charlie. If I didn't know, I wouldn't have picked up on his subtle limp. The prosthetic now hidden underneath his lavender robes. Sabrina filled them in. Charlie's laugh couldn't hide her sadness. She wouldn't quite meet my eyes. I'd pulled her away from John. I'd truly let him sacrifice himself for us and I didn't know if she'd ever forgive me, if ever we'd be as close as we once were. As if reading my mind, she met my questioning stare.

For once, I couldn't read her expression. She looked away having a silent conversation with Arameus. "Charlie and I are heading to get her grandparents out of hiding. They'll need to be updated." Updated, such a delicate way to say their grandson had truly died. I wondered if they would also tell them how he killed Mom. It was good I wasn't going, but I didn't fail to notice their lack of invitation. "We also wanted to tell them of our engagement."

"Engagement?" Sabrina and I asked in unison.

Charlie beamed. "We're hoping in about a year." Her eyes flicked between Sabrina and me. "You'll be my maid and matron of honor?"

A trickle of happiness awoke at her words. *Yes, we would be okay. Eventually.* "Absolutely. Oh, Congratulations." I hugged both of them, one at a time, happy they'd found each other.

"Where will you live?" Sabrina pulled back from Arameus.

"We'd like to stay here with frequent visits to her grandparents. We're not sure where they'll want to end up."

"Oh, I forgot to tell you all," Finch slapped Arameus on the shoulder. "Jeremiah's family is going to move to the island. He has a few younger sisters who have shown the Gayden trait."

"That's wonderful." Sabrina practically glowed, but that could've been due to the pregnancy.

"Sabrina has something to tell you all."

She glared at me before announcing her pregnancy. "Simeon and I are so excited. We're nervous as well, but it'll be good. We're going back to the Haven. Rebuilding it and going to move back in. My sister and nieces are going to help out with the baby."

As the others took turns hugging her, Damien stepped from the hall. His brown hair reflecting golden streaks from the sun, gray eyes penetrating mine, wearing a white T-shirt and jeans that did nothing to hide the bulging muscles underneath. My heart did a little flip flop and his mouth curved in a wicked smile as if he knew what thoughts ran through my head. "The Council and Elders pulled a few of us behind. Since we have discovered that Gayden and Wizard power can be used symbiotically, I'm going to be joining a Quad as a pilot project to see if a Gayden can be added as a fifth member."

"You wouldn't really be a Quad then would you? A Cinco?"

Charlie shook her head at Arameus. "Really? You couldn't let it go? Always the Defender being specific."

"That'll take some getting used to. What did Leigh say?" Sabrina asked.

Damien snorted. "She said if I hurt any of her team she would remove my manhood, Gayden or not. Although she didn't put it quite as nicely."

"After you saved the roomful of Gayden and Geminate beneath the Pyre, she has to trust you a little."

Damien shrugged, giving me that crooked smile that made my toes curl.

"It'll be strange after today. We won't be all together anymore," I said as their smiles faded as everyone realized the truth.

"We might not be together every day, but we're a family now. I won't let any of you disappear for too long." Arameus pulled me in for another hug and I breathed in the smell of him, mint and fresh lumber, remembering the first time, when he saved me from the cell.

"Thank you," I whispered where only he could hear me, and he answered with a larger squeeze. I owed my life to everyone here.

"My first assignment was to take you to unseal the Veil," Damien's voice broke the connection.

"Right."

Damien and I left the others with plans to meet for dinner. None of us would head out until tomorrow, so tonight we'd spend our last night together. The two of us were quiet as we walked through the still broken city. The people we ran across, thankfully, ignored us. Wizards opened their shops. Whispered conversations commenced in the shops, undoubtedly discussing the new treaty announced by the Council, but never did I hear cries of outrage or fear. Passing one store several women sat outside eating lunch with a playground nearby.

"I want things to go back to normal. My boys need to get back to school." Others murmured their ascent. Their children's laughter carried on the wind.

"I know. Arthur is driving me crazy. His cousin lives in South Carolina and we used to visit him every few months. He's an artist and what he can do with human paint is magic. He can't wait until the Veil is unsealed."

The woman reached out and patted an older woman on the hand. "And I know you'll be glad to see your son."

The older woman sniffled and wiped her eyes. "I can't wait for David to come home. He wasn't even supposed to go into work that day."

"The Transport is opening soon too, I heard."

Their conversation faded away the farther away Damien and I got. The war had affected everyone. The guilt pressed upon me that I'd hurt the people here. They had their own hopes and dreams and lives, all affected, as ours had been.

"Something wrong?" Damien nudged me.

The words and feelings struggled in my brain, trying to voice how I felt. "You remember how beautiful all the buildings were?"

He nodded. "I saw it a few times. He kept me hidden, but a few times when I was smuggled in and out of the Veil, I got to see the shimmering light flowing through the buildings. Why?"

"I broke that light. That symbol of peace and unity. Most of the people here are good. I took that away from them. It was selfish." Remembering why I did it and the look on John's face hurt deep in my heart.

We turned the last corner, following the signs to the Transport gates, and went the rest of the way in silence, each of us lost in our own thoughts. The gate had one attendant, a white-haired Ember with frayed red robes. The man forced a smile as we approached. "Welcome to Gate 617."

I stumbled, and Damien snatched my elbow, righting me. "What's wrong?"

"This is the same gate I came through when I was arrested. How ironic this would be the gate where the Veil is unsealed."

"So it began, so shall it end."

"I guess so."

The Ember stepped aside, allowing me to pass, and with an exhale the Bridge opened before me. I stepped inside the black tunnel once more. Damien on my heels, touching the small of my back.

The same vast emptiness as always loomed before me inside the Bridge. The silence wrapping around my soul, but where it used to suffocating, now felt lighter and free. Except Mom disappeared here and what would happen when I released the Veil?

Through the darkness a shimmering light like a million diamonds floated toward me. The light grew brighter and brighter, yet no pain stung my eyes, because my eyes didn't exist in this place. The light drew nearer and nearer, and I wasn't afraid. The mysterious light wasn't part of the Veil, which still trickled like tar.

The light coalesced forming two distinct forms. Mom's face shown from the center of one side and Jiminy's from the other—no, not Jiminy. Philo Stone. My father.

Without using words, Mom conveyed that she was okay and ready to move on. She directed my attention to my dad and his face grew clearer. He had the same shape of my eyes, the same red shade of my hair, the same nose, and slight tilt of his lips when he smiled.

The memory of Lailie reemerged. Her disappearance into the light beyond, and I knew this parting from my parents wasn't a forever goodbye, but temporary until I crossed to the other side. There was so much I wanted to say, wanted to ask. I so wished I could hug her one more time. Wished I'd have known my dad guided me through the Bridge. I would've cherished every moment more.

Mom pointed behind me. The Unity Statue wavered through the rainbow echoes of the Veil. *Why was she showing me this?*

Her hand appeared before me, holding the moonstone, Mathesar's abomination, that vanished into the pits of the Pyre. *How had it gotten here?* The feeling of John's warm arms settled over me before moving to the small of my back. John's presence touched the place where Damien had his hand on my back and warmed, as if in approval. He shifted again. This time I sensed him in front of me. I lifted my arm to touch him, but instead he backed away, the weight of the moonstone dropped into my palm. I knew what I had to do.

With all my heart I whispered goodbye. John's presence faded along with my parents. Faded not into the shadows of the Bridge, but to the beyond. I wasn't sad. I'd felt it down deep. They were happy, safe, and free.

Damien still touched the small of my back. I reached behind me, grabbing his hand, and stepped toward the Unity Statue. With a sound like a whirlwind combined with a sensation of being squeezed through a tight tube, our feet hit the ground. The Bridge opened behind me, blackness fading, replaced by the rainbow shimmering liquid light. The same I'd seen in the classroom when the Quad pulled me into this world of magic. A lifetime ago, and with one final thought, it vanished. The Veil was open once more.

"What are we doing back here?"

The Guidance Hall steps were empty. "I have one final mission, and I need your help."

"Always."

Grasping the moonstone, I stepped onto the broken platform, dipped underneath the clasped hands of two of the great mothers. The power and lives that had been lost to forge this stone wouldn't be wasted or abused. Pulling my magic upward, it reached out toward the stone, curious, feeling a power like its own. The wrongness of the moonstone wavered as if calling to me and to the statue, begging for what I planned.

Fear rippled through me. The danger of what I was about to do pressed in on me, but I ignored it, trusting in the wisdom of my mom and in Damien to protect me.

Reaching down in myself, falling farther and farther than I'd ever had, into the deepest trenches of my magic, until I found the bottom. Not even when fighting Mathesar had I been so deep.

Damien's magic called out to me, keeping me tethered to this world, reminding me who I was, instead of getting lost in the magic. Pushing off from the bottom, my magic ignited out of me without restraints, boiling outward in a great wave, large enough to destroy the world. With an atomic rush of energy, my magic reached out, crashing into the moonstone, splitting it wide open, the force of it ricocheting to every corner of Conjuragic.

From the great beyond, the figures in the Unity Statue inhaled a sharp intake of breath, the great mother's magic reawakening, gaining strength from me, and the stone.

Damien's power intertwined with mine, fighting against the pull to give it all, tethering me to life. The statue had enough. My life didn't need to be forfeit like the great mothers. The connection broke. I stumbled but before I hit the ground. Damien reached through the arms of the great mother and yanked me out.

The white light burned bright from the Unity Statue shot into the air like a beacon before slamming back into the platform of the statue, sealing it, and spreading outward to touch every building in the city, healing every crack, every hurt.

Every inch of my body ached. The moonstone lay in crumbled pieces in the center of the statue before disintegrating further into dust. My breath came out in pants matched by Damien's. Once again, I'd released all but the last dredges of my power. Each beat of my heart an effort, but a trickle remained, and it would refill. It would take longer than when I'd fought Mathesar, but my magic wasn't gone. Damien's power siphoned some to me, giving me strength.

Damien groaned as he pulled me into his arms. "I thought I almost lost you."

"You almost did, but your power holding mine saved me." I didn't recognize my voice, a tiny scruffy whisper.

His eyes flicked to the statue and back to me. "You fixed it. You gave it the moonstone's power and almost all of your magic."

I managed a nod.

"If I hadn't been here, it would have taken all of you, like it did those women? You would have become a fifth part of it?"

I shrugged. "Yeah well. I figured after all this, it would be a horrible time to die."

He laughed, the most beautiful sound I'd ever heard. "But how did you get the moonstone?"

I guessed he hadn't seen my parents or felt John and his approval. "It's a long story. I'll tell you later."

He raised his eyebrows. "Now what?"

I pulled him toward me, bringing his warm lips to mine. The kiss lasted mere seconds but communicated the promise of forever, of hope, in each heartbeat. "Whatever we want."

THE END

ACKNOWLEDGMENTS

The world of Conjuragic would never been what it is without my amazing editor and friend, Melissa Gilbert. I can never thank you enough.

A special thanks to my hubby, Dallas Hughes, for understanding and being my cheerleader.

To my babies, Nicholas, Katie, and Nathan, I love you all so very much.

To Cheri and Makayla Prince, for being Ora's fan through all versions.

James Christopher Hill who illustrated the awesome covers. You're truly amazing. More of his work can be found at www.jameshillstudios.com

No matter how many stories I write, Ora will always hold a special place in my heart since she is named after my grandma, a truly outstanding woman who I will always strive to mirror.

Thank you to all the readers for following along with Ora and me. We have had quite an adventure, haven't we?

I'll see you in the next world!

ABOUT THE AUTHOR

Leann M. Rettell was born and raised in West Virginia but now lives in North Carolina with her husband, three children, three crazy dogs, and two aloof cats.

She is the author of the Conjuragic Series and the upcoming Dream Thief Series published by Falstaff Books.

She has dreamed of being a writer since she was a little girl. Never give up. Dare to dream and believe in magic.

ALSO BY LEANN M. RETTELL

Across the Veil

Over the Bridge

Out of the Shadows - A Conjuragic Short Story

Made in the USA
Columbia, SC
21 December 2018